BANE OF ALL THINGS

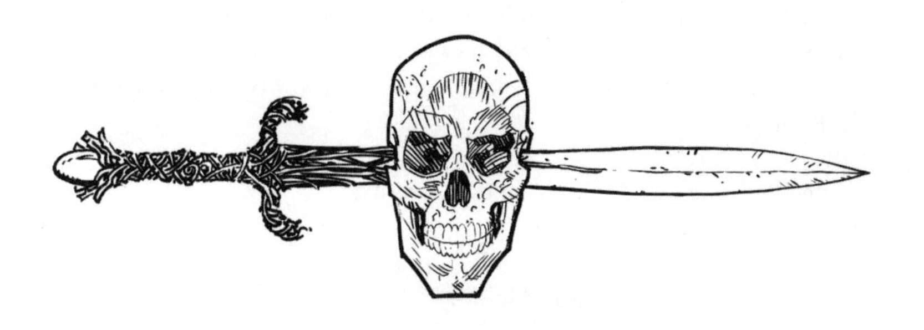

LEO VALIQUETTE

This is a work of fiction. Names, characters, organizations, places, events, and incidents are either products of the author's imagination or are used fictitiously.

Published by Inkshares, Inc., Oakland, California
www.inkshares.com

Edited by Sarah Nivala and Pam McElroy
Cover design by Tim Barber
Interior design by Kevin G. Summers
Sword and Skull image by Dominic Bercier of Mirror Comics Studios

ISBN: 9781950301270
e-ISBN: 9781950301287
LCCN: 2021935613

First edition

Printed in the United States of America

To my mother, who first fed this addiction to words and weirdness with a book club purchase when I was seven that included *Star Wars: A New Hope* and *Charlotte's Web*.

To my father, who proved by example the virtues of moderation, diligence, and hard work, even if our chosen tools don't fit the same belt.

And most of all, to Natalie—my partner, wellspring, and sanity check. She still puts up with this moody-loner-writer vibe and I couldn't love her more for it.

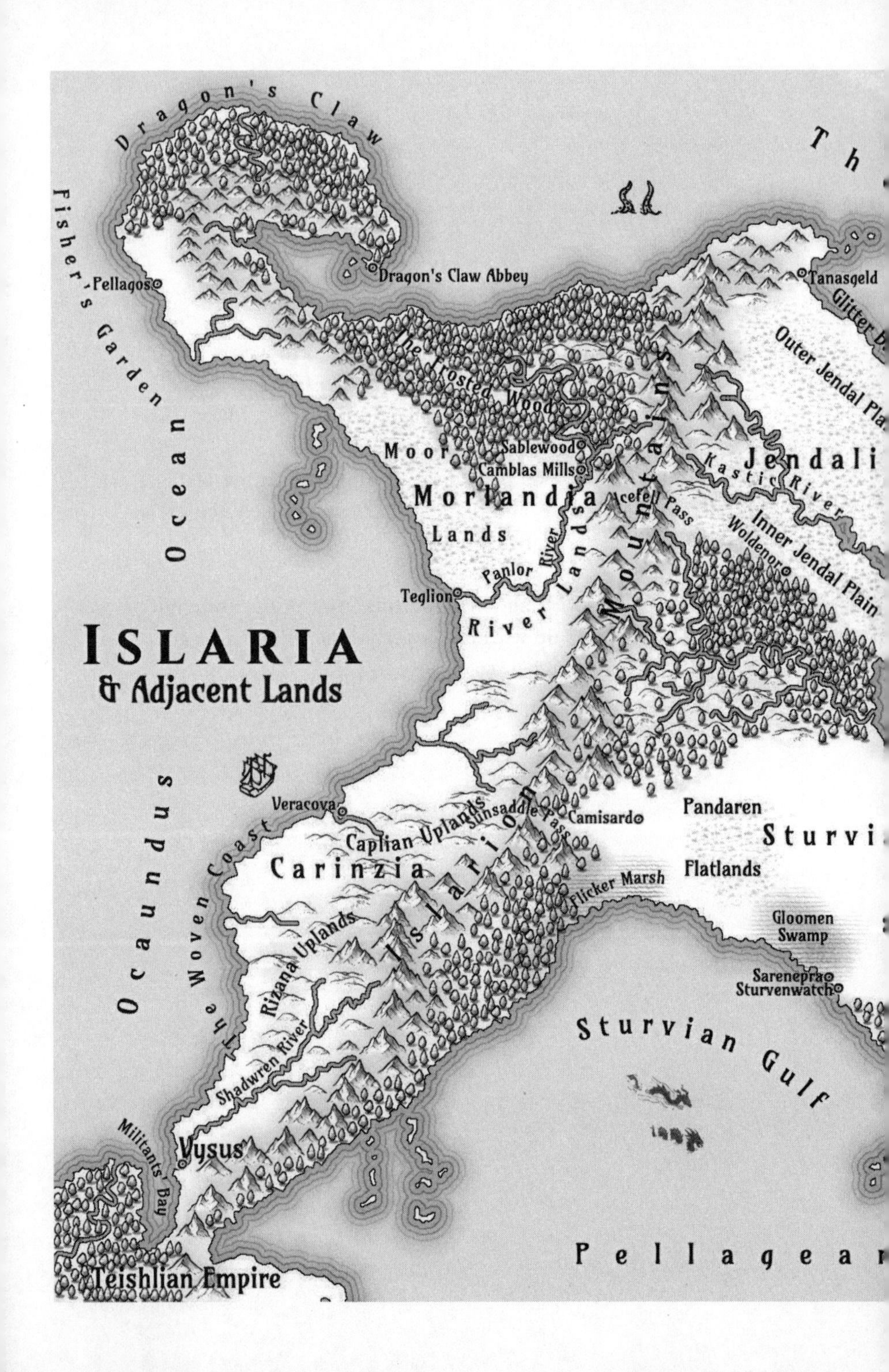
ISLARIA
& Adjacent Lands
Dragon's Claw
Dragon's Claw Abbey
Fisher's Garden
Pellagos
Ocean
The Frosted Wood
Moor
Sablewood
Camblas Mills
Morlandia
Lands
Acefell Pass
Panlor River
River Lands
Teglion
River
Mountains
Tanasgeld
Outer Jendal Plain
Jendali
Kastic River
Inner Jendal Plain
Woldenor
Veracova
Caplian Uplands
Sunsaddle Pass
Camisardo
Pandaren
Flatlands
Sturvi
Carinzia
Islarion
Flicker Marsh
Gloomen Swamp
Sarenepra
Sturvenwatch
The Woven Coast
Ocaundus
Rizana Uplands
Shadwren River
Sturvian Gulf
Militants' Bay
Vysus
Teishlian Empire
Pellagea

The Great Glacier

Iceberg Sea

N

Pincer Gap

Austacian Sea

Mountains

The Great Steppe Plateau

Sevrenia

Jaegen

esla

Penance Pass

ner Reach

Viglias

Stormcrest Hills

Beris River

gliad

Jade Lake

Gostemere

Impalas

Crescent of Fire

The Boiling Sea

Keshauk Dominion

of Ash

Sea

Scale (miles):

0 30 60 90 120 150

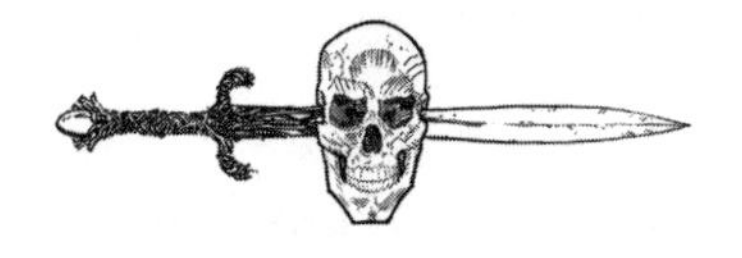

ISLARIA AND ADJACENT LANDS

Our story takes place in the Four Kingdoms, which includes Morlandia, Jendalia, Carinzia, and Sturvia. These Kingdoms are bound by a church called the Holy Clerisy, which tolerates no rival.

The ancient name of the Four Kingdoms is Islaria, and some still refer to it as such. Many nation-states and petty kingdoms have come and gone in Islaria over the roll of centuries, the most prominent and infamous being the empire of Pandaris. The modern Four Kingdoms were born from its ashes, and its demon-enchanted relics still pose a threat to the unwary.

To the south of the Four Kingdoms lies the Teishlian Empire. The Teishlians are shamanists and ancestor worshippers who give allegiance to no god, governed by a strict caste system that spurns outsiders.

Seven hundred years ago, the Kingdoms claimed victory in their war with the Teishlians and took the Empire's northern provinces as Protectorates with Vysus as their capital. After the Teishlians reclaimed their territory, new peace accords made Vysus an independent buffer state. In the centuries since, Vysus has grown fat and decadent with the flow of trade on the Pilgrim Road between the Kingdoms and the Empire.

Together, the Four Kingdoms, Vysus, and the Teishlian Empire constitute what is known as the West.

To the east, the Distant East, lies the Keshauk Dominion. This vast stretch is occupied by many peoples and many nations, all in some measure subject to the oppression of the Keshauk's All-Father Priesthood.

Betwixt East and West lies Sevrenia—the battleground of a war about two centuries ago between the Four Kingdoms and the Keshauk. It was here that a group of heretics, the Sevrendine, who'd been persecuted in the Kingdoms, were left to meet their end. Sevrenia is widely believed in the Kingdoms to be a place of ghosts, forsaken by all.

But of course, the wise soul knows to take what is "widely believed" with a dash of salt.

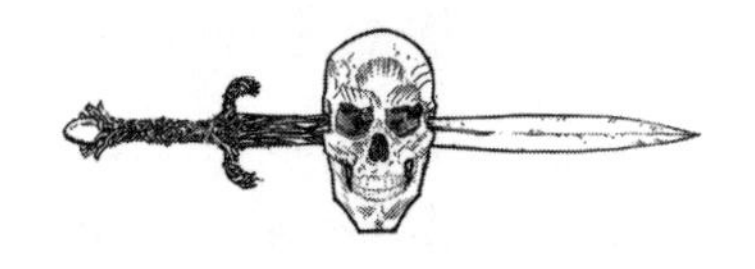

THE CHILD AND THE FORTUNE-TELLER

The gods and their servants

o, my little angel, I see you trying to read the tea leaves by your nosy little self, to puzzle from their shape and color the fate of the man Ryn and the woman Josalind. But you must understand, there is no grand destiny. Nothing is preordained. It is ever the way of mortals to rise up and manage the impossible—and just as surely stumble and fall when all seems certain in their favor.

All we can do is work to understand what things might help or hinder Ryn and Josalind. I see a day when one of them will arrive on our doorstep. What meaning we take from the leaves on that day will sway the fates of us all.

The gods . . . it all flows from the gods, doesn't it? Let's start your education there.

First, the Great Deceiver, who afflicts a score of nations in the Distant East. The peoples of the Keshauk Dominion call him All-Father and show their devotion with blood and human sacrifice. The church of the Four Kingdoms, the Holy Clerisy, clings to the idea that the Deceiver exists only to corrupt and to conquer—be assured, pet, the truth is something far more terrible and sublime.

Then there is Fraia—the goddess who's kept the whole world from falling into the Great Deceiver's grasp. She is the shepherdess who holds that mad boar by the tusks. Her mortal servants are the Sevrendine. The Clerisy, bound as it is by old superstition and baseless fear, won't acknowledge her and condemned the Sevrendine as heretics.

And then we have Fraia and the Deceiver's children—the Four: Sovaris, Mygalor, Koglar, and last but not least, Kyvros.

I should also give mention to the Earthborn. They are long-lived but not immortal. Nor are they ethereal beings like angels and demons. Some call them the Elder Races, for they gained reason and craft before humanity and passed it on. The Earthborn were not created by the Four, but nonetheless had great affection for them and often served them. The Clerisy considers the Earthborn extinct.

Now, how did Fraia and the Deceiver, such enemies and opposites, come to sire and conceive the Four? We will get to the story of why that odd conception came to be—patience.

What is important for now is that these gods, these Four, were struck down and lost. The Clerisy honors the Four but will suffer no prayer or supplication to be made to them. It believes prayer to dead gods is a needful weakness that only invites corruption by the Great Deceiver and his demons. The only hope to join the Four's souls in Paradise and avoid the Hells is to die pure after a long and upright life. Meditation on the Nine Virtues, Confession, and Absolution—these are the only rituals that the Clerisy believes can bring salvation.

It's an attractive notion, so far as quaint notions go. The Clerisy's inquisitars persecute anyone in the Four Kingdoms who claims different.

Now, how were the Four struck down? By a sword, a living sword—Mordyth Ral, the Gods Bane. This very blade also crippled the Great Deceiver many thousand years past.

And that brings us to Xangtemias.

Xang is the Deceiver's mortal-born son. A demigod bred of a human mother to be strong where his crippled father is weak. His father's Keshauk priests raised Xang to be some dark savior who might undo the West and bring it under their Dominion.

Seven hundred years ago, pet, the Four Kingdoms invaded the Teishlian Empire for purposes of greed. This gave Xang the perfect opportunity. The Kingdoms forced the Teishlians into a corner and left them so desperate that Xang could gain the trust of their Emperor with promises of victory.

And Xang delivered. He summoned a legion of demons to fight on the battlefield. He tore babes from their wailing mothers' teats and gutted them on black altars. Thousands sacrificed until the sea of blood could have floated a fleet of ships. Little did the Teishlians know that these sacrifices only nourished the Great Deceiver and did nothing to aid in the defense of their homeland. Xang was the worst kind of monster—the sort driven by true belief and conviction. He lived only to honor and restore his father at any cost.

Yes, pet, a young prince named Aegias did ride among those invaders from the Kingdoms. A noble and humble soul who had the potential to be more than just another vainglorious tyrant. To prevent Xang's victory, the Mother Goddess Fraia saw that the Sword, Mordyth Ral, came to Aegias.

Another time, I will tell you why the Sword is such a terrible burden, driven by a purpose and a will all its own. Aegias made the choice to bind himself to Mordyth Ral till death, knowing that it might damn his very soul. If he hadn't used the Sword and given his own life to stop Xang, all the West would have fallen.

But Aegias is revered for so much more than that. The Clerisy venerates him as the Prince Messiah, though he would have rolled his eyes at the thought. He gave us the Virtues. He freed the Four Kingdoms from centuries of false belief. What the Clerisy doesn't mention, of course, is Fraia's hand in all of it. Aegias would never have become the man he did without the guidance of Fraia's angels.

But the tea leaves tell me this story is far from over. Xang isn't content to stay dead so long as his bloody work remains unfinished. The Sword, too, is still out there, somewhere, eager to achieve its once and final end—waiting to turn a mere mortal into the Earth-Breaker, the Soul-Taker, the Bane of All Things.

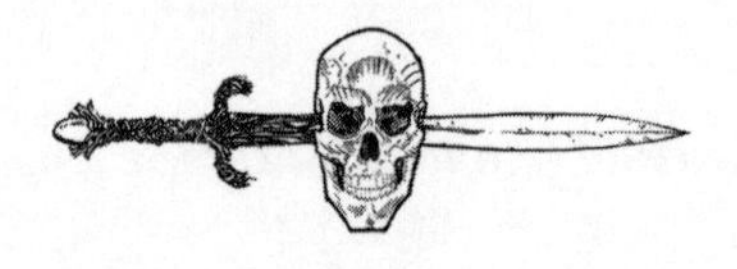

ONE

he *Fool's Fortune* rode the swells of a mellow sea kissed by a late-spring sun. Ryn perched on a coil of rope in the ship's forecastle and eyed the weapons store. The bosun's mate had been doing counts, but he left it unlocked when called away. Ryn could see enough for a count of his own: eight doglock muskets; sixteen pistols; twenty cutlasses; twenty-four paper cartridges for each firearm, wrapped in oilskin to keep the powder dry.

A trained soldier needed only one shot to get the job done.

It would be so easy. Ryn could prime, load, aim, and fire a pistol four times in a minute. Those weapons were well kept, flints knapped to ensure a strong spark and no misfire. He imagined the taste of cold iron on his tongue, the bite of his teeth on the muzzle, as he pulled the trigger. All over in a blast of brimstone. Fitting enough, considering the deepest Hell must already have a choice spot reserved for him.

But that would be a coward's way out. He owed Sablewood's dead too much to deserve such a quick end. Even now, five months later, that awful gurgle as Quintan died drilled his ear like a ravenous shipworm. He couldn't escape the cold accusation of a mother's and daughter's dead eyes. Old Jaryk's final curse still chilled his soul. And the smell . . . the smell lingered worst of all. The blood and shite stench of a battlefield.

Sergeant Havlock stumped across the deck, his squat, barrel body immune to the roll of the ship, swarthy features framed by a graying beard that resembled furry lichen on old bark. He wore the mail and hardened leather of a palatar, complete with his shoulder lanyards of rank and order. Ryn's kit remained locked away, which left him feeling oddly naked in nothing but trousers and a shirt.

Havlock kept a wary eye on Ryn as he picked up the weapons store's stray padlock. "That lad should face the lash for being so careless." Such an offense would have been intolerable had this been a true naval vessel and not just a tubby merchantman that operated under the Holy Clerisy's charter.

"I was keeping an eye on it," Ryn said with forced casualness.

Havlock snorted. "I could tell. Wouldn't be the first time a man ate lead rather than take his sentence at the Claw."

"So I've heard." Serve eight years with the garrison at Dragon's Claw Abbey, get discharged with a clean record and a full pension. The Clerisy dangled that sliver of hope to encourage good behavior and maintain morale. In truth, the odds were poor that any man condemned to the place would survive his eight. Havlock and two other palatars had been tasked with escorting Ryn to his new command, and they let him roam the ship between ports. Out at sea, he had nowhere to go but overboard, into the Deep Dark.

Ryn closed his eyes. He turned his head to relish the feel of the sun and the breeze on his face and breathed deep of the briny air. He had considered escape, even fleeing far south to Vysus where the Clerisy's influence was weak. But fleeing to Vysus wouldn't ease his conscience or make the ghosts of Sablewood rest any easier. Lieutenant Ryn Ruscroft—a penitent wretch who deserved his sentence, even if he and his superiors didn't agree on why. "Only in service to others, with no expectation of reward, do we atone for our sins," he murmured.

"I doubt Aegias had rotting in a pus pit like Dragon's Claw in mind when he said so," Havlock said. "You'll not be serving much of anything."

Ryn popped his eyes open to fix him with a hard stare. "I will be serving as second of the garrison, ensuring the safety of the sisters and their wards—and it's still 'sir' to you, Sergeant."

Protect the innocent and the helpless—as he should have done at Sablewood. That was the only honorable thing, the only *acceptable* thing, he could do now. If that meant keeping up appearances as a dutiful palatar, so be it. He could just as easily have been stripped of rank and sentenced to a regular prison, even swung from the gallows, but Dragon's Claw desperately needed experienced officers. The situation in that place had to be darker than pitch.

Havlock knuckled his brow, padlock still in hand. "Yes, *sir*, very good, *sir*. I'm still within my authority to knock you on that fine arse should you act out of turn, *sir*."

His other hand had come to rest on the pommel of his sword, which left Ryn painfully aware of his own lack of armament. "My fine arse expects no less, Sergeant."

"Captain says we'll be reaching Pellagos by nightfall," Havlock said. "Last stop before the Claw." He tossed the padlock up and caught it. "Pardon my lack of faith, sir, but you'll be locked below till we're off again."

Hot tar, rotting fish, and the piney burn of turpentine distillation.

Pellagos stank like every other fishing port Ryn had ever had the misfortune of visiting. Trapped as he was belowdecks in a windowless cabin bare of distraction, with nothing to focus on but the nauseating bob of the ship as it chafed against the dock's bumpers, the town's complex bouquet soon left his stomach churning.

Shouldn't a sentenced man at least have a copy of the *Codex* with which to ponder his sins? Not that he cared to spend his time reading the Scriptures and ruminating on doctrine. Stuck on this ship with nothing else to occupy him, Ryn had come to realize how much he now resented the Clerisy's authority.

Whether a palatar was a commoner sworn to the Peers Order or of noble birth and sworn to the Aegian Order, he vowed to follow in Aegias's footsteps, to live and die by the Nine Virtues—Humility, Piety, Courage, Diligence, Truth, Moderation, Chastity, Justice, and Brotherhood. The circumstances of his birth, his station, his class—none of it mattered.

But the Clerisy demanded a second oath, one that prevented the Orders from ever functioning independent of its authority. Instead of champions of mercy and justice answerable only to their brothers, palatars for centuries had been little more than the Clerisy's private army, used to enforce the Clerisy's code of conduct and discipline upon the Four Kingdoms.

Ryn had lived with that contradiction all his life. He had thought he could serve in the Peers Order and be true to Aegias and the Virtues while also giving the Clerisy the obedience it demanded.

So he'd thought . . . until Sablewood.

It would have been easy to blame the Clerisy for what had happened on that night, but Ryn blamed no one but himself. His actions, his choices, had been his own. Rather, his resentment stemmed from what had come after—he'd been lauded a hero by their superiors while Quintan had been damned as the villain. His one true friend, condemned to a traitor's unmarked grave. The injustice of it all burned worse than lye on an open wound.

At last, a parade of boots sounded on the deck above, with orders shouted to make sail. A small group came down and passed by Ryn's door. An indignant voice cried out, too shrill for a man.

"Pipe down, missy," Sergeant Havlock said. "Now here, make yourself at home."

The door of the adjoining cabin slammed shut, followed by a bolt thrown hard. Keys rattled.

"From what the townsfolk say, she's a witch," said one of Havlock's men.

"If her cleric thought so, she'd sure as *Hells* not be aboard," Havlock said. "So, shut your gob and don't repeat gossip. Understood?"

Ryn banged on his door. "I could use some fresh air."

A key jiggled in the lock and the bolt slid back. Havlock greeted him with a smirk. "There you are, sir. Was wondering if you needed your slop bucket dumped yet."

Ryn swallowed and hoped he didn't look as green as he felt. "We have a guest?"

Havlock thrust his chin in the direction of the other cabin. “Some girl run strange, cursed maybe, bound to become the sisters’ ward at the Claw.”

“‘Cursed’?” Ryn had too often seen that word used as an excuse to brutalize poor souls who were simply ill in the head.

“I’ve a sealed envelope to hand over to the abbess personally. Beyond that, don’t know, don’t care.” Havlock patted the keyring on his belt. “But I want the last leg of this merry jaunt to be as dull as the rest, so she won’t be leaving that cabin before we’ve dropped anchor at the Claw.”

A scream jolted Ryn awake that night.

Feet came stomping from the crew’s berth. A key rattled in the lock of the cabin next door. Havlock barked at the woman to keep quiet before shutting and locking the door again.

Ryn drifted back to sleep as muffled sobbing seeped through the cracks of the cabin bulkhead.

The screams came again the next night, and the next. Each time, Havlock peeked in, grumbling and cursing. But it was Ryn who remained to hear the woman’s grief and despair. He could barely imagine how she must feel, torn from all she knew, locked up and condemned to the Claw. She could at least do with some fresh air and a kind ear for company. The gods knew he could do with some of the latter himself.

But Havlock wouldn’t have it and insisted on keeping her locked up alone.

“I could just have her gagged, sir,” he said when Ryn pushed him on it.

Ryn knew nothing about this woman, not her name, what she looked like, or what had condemned her. His idle mind came to entertain ridiculous thoughts—the two of them somehow escaping this fate together, like some sappy pair in those terrible Sturvian romances his sister would read. They could go to Vysus, become bone hunters and make their fortune. Ryn had heard tales as a boy about the bone hunters who worked the pilgrim routes into the Empire, searching for relics of Aegias's war with Xang. Before he'd even thought of becoming a palatar, Ryn had dreamed of becoming one of these adventurer-scholars.

On the fourth night, it wasn't her screams that woke Ryn, but the words of old Jaryk's curse as he relived Sablewood's massacre.

Ryn bolted out of the dream and smacked his brow against the cold lantern on its hook. *Gods be damned.* Dawn must have been near, considering the swell of his bladder. He fumbled around in the dark for the bucket and relieved himself. The slow-build satisfaction of an overdue piss was sometimes a better tonic for the nerves than a hard drink.

Not on this stubborn night—a fidgety restlessness still gripped him after he'd buttoned up. The already cramped cabin squeezed, viselike, around him, so much so he expected to hear the creak and crack of straining oak. Ryn pulled on his trousers and boots and headed out, grateful that Havlock saw no reason to keep *his* door locked between ports. Lantern light spilled down the stairs. His attention drifted to the adjoining cabin.

Its door stood ajar. The lock lay on the floor. Ryn's first thought was rape. But the cabin lay empty—no rutting sailor with pasty moons bared to the ceiling and no woman. He picked up the lock. She might have been carried off, but that was bound to attract unwanted attention.

From what the townsfolk say, she's a witch.

He denied the notion with a curt shake of his head. As Havlock had said, her parish cleric had already ruled out the possibility. One of Havlock's men would have brought the woman her dinner earlier. The sergeant would have the trooper's hide for boot leather for being so careless.

Ryn hung the lock on a lantern hook and climbed the stairs. After ten days aboard, he'd gotten his sea legs and learned the night-time routine of the *Fool's Fortune* well: one man up in the crow's nest; one at the wheel; four on call, gathered around the brazier amidships playing cards. The other fifteen were bunked below, while the captain had his own quarters in the stern.

That made it easy for someone to slip out of the cabins belowdecks without being seen, provided she kept to the shadows behind the wheel and took to the sterncastle on light feet.

Ryn made a point of being heard when he stepped out behind the helmsman. He exchanged brief pleasantries before taking the ladder up to the sterncastle.

A slight figure, swaddled in a dark cloak, stood barefoot on the railing. Only a few fingers touched the post of the ship's stern lantern for balance.

Ryn's breath caught. The rest of him froze, too, certain that a single footstep, even a loud breath, might snap whatever delicate balance kept her from plunging into the hungry waves. He thought of himself a few days ago, eyeing that weapons store, considering the merits of a quick end.

She didn't fall, or jump, but rode the roll of the ship with effortless grace. Preidos hung low in the eastern sky—the greater moon's stormy face bathed her in a rosy glow. Little Supeidos had already slipped below the horizon, no doubt eager to avoid being witness to tragedy.

Ryn took a step, then two.

"She calls to me, you know." The Fisherfolk brogue colored her speech, but milder than that of most people Ryn had encountered from Morlandia's north coast. That suggested a more refined upbringing, like his own.

"'She'?" Ryn peered over the rail but saw only whitecaps brushed rose by the moonlight. Staring too long at that toss and churn threatened to bring his seasickness back.

"Do you know Dragon's Claw?"

He'd feared for her virtue, but she appeared to give it no thought at all, alone with a man she didn't know. Maybe despair had stolen the sense to care. He wondered what she'd been told about the Claw. Noblewomen who couldn't bear sons, mistresses on the wrong end of politics, deflowered daughters deemed unfit for a favorable marriage—these were the sorts who ended up wards of the cloister, discarded and forgotten.

"Only what people say," he said. Then there were the grenlich of Dragon's Claw. The Clerisy claimed grenlich were demon spawned. Whether that was true, he'd seen for himself their brutal savagery.

She snorted. "Never had much reason to trust what people say."

Ryn itched to snatch her from the railing, but still feared to make any sudden move. "You'd best come down before you fall."

"If I were gonna fall, *worry-wump*, don't you think I would have by now?"

She hopped down and turned to him. A pale and slender hand pushed back the hood. Freckled cheeks and an upturned nose. A mess of copper-red curls. Two big eyes of a deep sea green. She might have been nearing twenty, but those eyes belonged to someone much older. Tired, drawn, stripped of all joy, as if they'd witnessed the world's sins for centuries beyond count. Eyes that begged for company to share their misery. He had enough misery of his own. Still, a man could drown in such eyes without complaint.

"My name is Ryn," he said.

She sniffed and wiped at her eyes. "You'd best be careful, making friendly with me. They say I'm cursed, you know."

Cursed. She spoke the word with a bitter hardness that put him on his guard. He sidestepped away and leaned against the lantern post, trying to make the move look casual to hide his unease. Here he was, a seasoned soldier, spooked by this slip of a woman. "And why do they say that?"

"There you are."

Havlock stomped up onto the sterncastle, pistol in hand.

The aggression in Havlock's stance prompted Ryn to step between them. "Stand down, Sergeant." He had nothing to counter that pistol except the hollow authority of a rank that meant nothing until he reached the Claw, but he couldn't stand for such a heavy-handed threat.

The pistol didn't waver. "I locked that door myself, missy—how in Hells did you get out?"

"I don't—" she began.

"Was that before or after you started in on the crew's grog?" Ryn asked. The obvious answer had to be the right one. "Think about it, Sergeant—what makes more sense?"

Havlock held his ground for a spell longer before stowing his pistol, with a couple of choice curses. "I've no reason to expect it, but can I ask for your discretion?"

Ryn didn't appreciate how tense he'd become until the relief flooded through him. "I'll not say a word," he said with an earnest nod.

The woman stepped past him. "I guess it's back into the crate now, isn't it?"

Havlock took hold of her arm and prompted her to the ladder. "Best get used to it, missy."

Ryn found himself strangely out of sorts, like some pimply-faced boy who'd missed his chance at a kiss before the girl he was sweet on got herded off by her father. Utter nonsense.

She paused partway down the ladder to look at him. "Josalind," she said, and then she was gone.

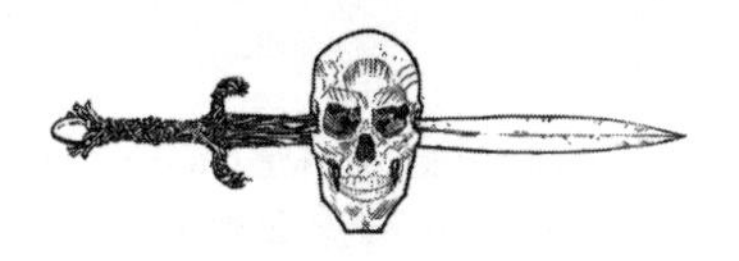

TWO

Her scream jolted Ryn from a sound sleep. His hand went for a sword that wasn't there.

Gods be damned, not again. He flung the sheet away and groped in the dark for his trousers.

Josalind cried out again, less a scream this time than a stream of babble muffled by the oak that separated them. Ryn found the door with his forehead, then stumbled out into the hall. "Sergeant!"

Havlock came down the corridor. The swaying lantern in his hand cast churning shadows. Irate curses chased him from the crew's berth. "I am going to have her gagged and strapped to the damned bed."

"Just unlock the door," Ryn said.

Havlock shoved the lantern at him and complied with a grumble. He pulled the bolt and yanked the door open.

The ship chose that moment to crest a wave larger than most and plunge into its trough. Ryn shifted footing to keep balance, so his attention wasn't wholly on Josalind's small cabin as the scattered light flooded in.

But it appeared for a moment that Josalind's cot, even Josalind herself, floated a good foot in the air.

The ship hit the bottom of the trough. The lamp swung in Ryn's hand, driving the shadows into a mad dance. When his vision corrected, everything lay where it should, including Josalind.

A trick of the eye. She must have been thrown up by the plunge of the ship. Nothing else made sense.

She thrashed about, tangled in her sheets, mumbling nonsense. Ryn hung the lamp on the hook over the cot, sat, and took her by the shoulders. Her flesh blazed fever hot, dry as toast.

"I'm telling you, it's some kind of falling sickness," Havlock said.

Ryn fought to hold her still and ignored the spray of spittle that struck his face as she screeched again. "If it were, she wouldn't be able to speak when the fits take her."

"You call that speech?"

Ryn gave her a shake. *"Josalind."*

She startled awake, wide-eyed and confused. Her expression shifted quick to anger. She flung him off with surprising strength. "Spit, spunk, and arse boils—why'd you do that?"

Havlock snickered. "There's gratitude for you."

Ryn wiped his face dry. He'd never met a woman outside of a brothel with such a foul tongue and found it oddly endearing. "You were having another nightmare. A worse one."

"*I was trying to understand*, so they'd leave me the Hells alone."

"Understand what, missy?" Havlock asked. Ryn could hear the skepticism in the sergeant's voice. It mirrored his own.

She fixed Havlock with a wary scowl. "That's none of your damned business."

"It is on this ship," he said.

"Please, Sergeant." Ryn gestured with his head for the man to leave them. Havlock grumbled under his breath as he drew the door shut.

"Understand what?" Ryn asked, once they were alone.

Josalind's attention had drifted to some point far beyond the ship, perhaps even beyond the sea it sailed. "What the voices say."

Voices. He didn't know if it made her foolish, brave, or just mad to confess something so dangerous without any apparent concern for how he might take it. "What do they say?" he asked, trapped by sudden fascination.

"That Xangtemias's skull was hidden."

Of all the things he thought she might say, that came nowhere close to any of them. "Xang's skull was destroyed with the rest of him—Aegias's paladins saw to it," he said, in that gentle way best suited to hysterical children and lunatics.

"What if they couldn't destroy any of his bones?" Josalind said. "They tried—I saw it. With fire and acid and even a grist mill. But Xangtemias wasn't born natural." A manic giggle tore out of her. "The evil old salt will rise again and have us all."

Nonsense, it had to be. And yet, Ryn couldn't deny the prickly chill that needled his spine. "It was just a dream."

Her eyes narrowed. "Is that all they are when I hear *you* in the night—just dreams?"

His temper began to simmer. "There's a sharp difference between things I've done that haunt me and some flight of fancy." He rose and clenched his fists to still their tremble, surprised and annoyed that her comment had rattled him so. "Get some sleep."

Josalind relaxed back onto her cot and turned her face to the wall. "While we can."

Havlock waited outside. "She's bat mad for certain. The sisters will have their hands full."

Ryn couldn't shake that image of her cot floating. "Did you see it, when you first opened the door?"

The sergeant frowned. "What?"

"Nothing," Ryn said. The eyes did play tricks sometimes.

They reached an accord after that. When the voices tormented Josalind, Ryn would meet Havlock outside her door. It would have been simpler if the sergeant just left him the key, but Havlock wouldn't hear of it. "Best we maintain at least the illusion of propriety, don't you think, sir?"

Ryn would go in and sit with Josalind. Those first two nights, they said little. Ryn found it enough to just sit there, together in the dark. She obviously did, too. Misery did indeed need company.

Then came the night where her hand found his.

Ryn savored the simple human touch. He could scarcely remember the last time he'd been with a woman. Being this close, this alone, faced with the grim unknown of Dragon's Claw, plagued him with the ache of need. But he didn't presume to ask for more. He didn't even expect her to speak.

"It scares me so much—sometimes I feel tired of living." She sounded so fragile in the dark, so brittle and thin. A lost soul who craved an anchor for her sanity but had given up on finding one.

Ryn squeezed her hand—a feeble gesture, given the suffering that laced her words. "What does?"

"The silence is the worst—the silence that comes after his knife falls." Her hand began to tremble. "He's slaughtered thousands by his own hand with that same black knife. Babes mostly. There's something richer about the souls of the most innocent, something more powerful."

The weight of the dark left Ryn eager to light the lamp, but her trembling hand held him fast. "You mean Xang."

"He takes no pleasure in any of it. He takes nothing at all. It's all just a means to an end—the end is all that matters."

"All that *did* matter," Ryn said with sudden earnest. "Xang is seven centuries dead. Aegias killed him with the Sword. Whatever horrors he did are in the past. They've got no bearing on the present."

She clutched his hand so tightly that it ached. "You don't understand. I don't just see him in the past, I see him in the future. Him and his priests, spilling blood on black altars across the Kingdoms." She gave a wet sniff. Only then did Ryn realize she was weeping quietly in the dark.

He wanted to tell her how these were just dreams, imaginings. But sitting there blinded by shadow as the ship rode the chop of a restless sea, Ryn couldn't muster the will for it. Any denial of his, any attempt to make light of the burden these visions inflicted on her, sounded too hollow to warrant being spoken aloud.

The next night, Josalind's visions cornered her again. His dreams of Sablewood did, too, as if they'd conspired together. Her screams tangled with his own so that Havlock ended up pounding on both their doors, threatening gags all around.

This time as they sat together, Ryn took Josalind's trembling hand and cupped it between his own. "This future, with Xang's altars across the Kingdoms—do you really believe it will come to pass?"

"Maybe. I don't know. I see so much that I can't make sense of." Hard-edged frustration colored her words. "You must think me mad."

"Well, that wouldn't be very charitable, would it?" Ryn said, in a lame effort to lighten the mood. He drew a deep breath. "I know what it is to be haunted by things you can't escape." Granted, his sins and her visions weren't cut from the same cloth, but he felt compelled to share something so she didn't feel so obviously alone.

"I know." He flinched in surprise when her fingers found his jaw. "I hear your pain."

A question hung on that word, *pain*, one which Ryn lacked the heart to answer. He swallowed tightly. "Good people died because of me—let's leave it at that."

"Let's not."

It surprised him, how easily he yielded to her gentle insistence. Still, it took awhile to muster the will to speak past the hot slag in his throat.

"Sablewood is a village upriver from Camblas Mills," he said at last. "There's an abbey there with a reliquary that draws pilgrims. I was second-in-command of the garrison. My commander . . . he was my friend. We'd trained together at the temple."

This time, Josalind took and squeezed *his* hand. "What was his name?"

"Quintan."

"What happened?"

"We were on the edge of the Frosted Wood, so there's always a threat—"

"From grenlich."

Ryn nodded. "With how hard the winter was, we knew they'd come raiding for food. Quintan and I both wanted to station men in the village, but our abbot wouldn't hear of it, said it was their lord's duty, but that myopic old fool didn't have the men or the sense to take steps."

A sudden fit of the shakes took him then, threatening to blow up into a full-on episode of the Dread. His lungs had shriveled to husks that couldn't draw a decent breath.

"When the grenlich attacked, Quintan wanted to help, but the abbot wouldn't let you," Josalind said, like she already knew.

"Quintan knew all the bastard cared about was his own hide," Ryn said. "He said our first duty was to the Clerisy's flock, not that pile of dusty junk in the reliquary. Half the men were ready to follow him. The other half weren't sure and I . . ."

"You put your duty first."

"The abbot ordered me to take command. The garrison was going to turn on itself. I had to do something before half the men mutinied against the rest, but Quintan wouldn't concede."

Instead, he'd just stood there with that hard, unfathomable look in his eye and said: *Blind obedience can damn a man as surely as disloyalty, Ryn.*

Quintan had drawn first. Ryn had only meant to knock him senseless with the flat of his blade when the opportunity came. He told Josalind of that awful sense of helplessness when his heel had slipped in a patch of ice, how his body careened out of control, sword arm swinging like a pendulum, the tip of his blade dipping under Quintan's jaw. There had been no sensation of impact, no tug of resistance in his hand. A dark spray had erupted from Quintan's throat as if reality itself had torn.

"I killed him." Ryn saw his friend staggering toward him again, with hand clutched against his throat, eyes wide with shock. Quintan had tried to speak, but only a gurgle made it past the bubbly froth that caked his lips. Then no sound at all.

"After that, the men fell into line." Ryn could barely speak now past the jagged fire, but he had to, he couldn't stop himself. "Because of me, Sablewood was left to fend for itself. It's not just Quintan—I bear the blood of everyone who died that night."

"But—"

"I DO." He slammed his fist against the bulkhead. "I always will."

The shakes had deepened into painful shudders that wound his guts so tight he wanted to weep. He sucked in a ragged breath. "And the best part? They promoted me—after I'd killed Quintan and left a village to the grenlich, they gave me a promotion."

"But . . . but why, then, are you here?" she asked.

He chuckled with bitter scorn. "I punched Her Ladyship, the Grand Inquisitar for all of Morlandia, in the face."

"You didn't!"

"I didn't care to be lauded for putting duty before friendship, or the way she maligned Quintan's memory before the whole garrison." Ryn had never experienced such a red haze of fury. He couldn't remember actually hitting the twisted bitch, only the flare of pain in his knuckles, followed by the sight of Her Ladyship, wobbling on hands and knees and drooling blood with two fewer teeth than before.

The telling had left him strangely spent, exhausted even. He didn't care to tell her about the Dread—the crippling anxiety attacks that now tormented him. The Dread caught him on any morning that he woke from a dream of Sablewood and heard the Clerisy's bells ringing from whatever chapel, abbey, or cathedral lay within earshot. Sablewood's abbey bells had rung the alarm on that hellish night. They would haunt him forever.

Josalind said nothing more, which left him both grateful and anxious, certain his admission had tarnished whatever impression she had of him. The gentle way she touched his jaw again before drawing away quashed that fear as soon as it had come. He found himself wondering, not for the first time, what his father would have to say about all this—the man he had defied to become a palatar in the first place, the man who had disowned him as a result.

No, I don't want to know.

"The first oath a palatar swears is to his Order, to uphold the Virtues in Aegias's name," he said softly. "In the spirit of that, those people trusted us to protect them and do for them when others could not or would not. The Clerisy milks this to polish its own image, encourages palatars everywhere to be charitable in *its* name. But in the end, all it cares about is our obedience. Quintan should have had the authority to countermand the abbot that night. I should have had the courage to back him."

"Why did you even become a palatar?" Josalind asked.

Ryn took a while to gather his thoughts. "Aegias said anyone, man or woman, should feel ashamed to die without having contributed to a greater good before their own self-interest," he said at last. "That always resonated with me. But my father only ever cared about collecting the wealth and favor that would earn our family a title. I came to realize I wanted no part in that."

"So . . . you became a palatar to serve others and do something nobler."

"Yes." His father, of course, had only seen it as a betrayal by his firstborn.

"Do you still want to be one?"

This time, the answer burst from Ryn's lips with sharp certainty. "No, not the way the Clerisy would have us."

"The Clerisy's way is the only way."

"That's right." Ryn often wondered what Aegias would say, if he could see the world his legend had shaped.

"You're a rebel, then."

Ryn scoffed. "A malcontent, perhaps, hardly a rebel." He gave a curt shake of his head. "I'm no sterling example of what a palatar should be, not anymore."

"By your measure, or the Clerisy's?"

"Both." The Clerisy and the demands it put on palatars couldn't be blamed for his failings. He gave her knee a squeeze. "Promise me something."

"What?"

"What you said last night, about sometimes feeling tired of living—don't lose hope." The prospect of her denying herself the chance to escape her affliction was just too tragic to consider. "So long as you're alive, there's still hope."

Josalind took so long to answer, he didn't expect her to. "I won't, so long as you promise me something, too."

"And what's that?"

"That you will forgive yourself."

Ryn patted her knee as an affirmation rather than lie to her. He didn't deserve forgiveness and never would. Blood didn't just stain his hands. It crusted his soul.

They settled again into silence, hands once more held between them, providing the anchor they both sorely needed.

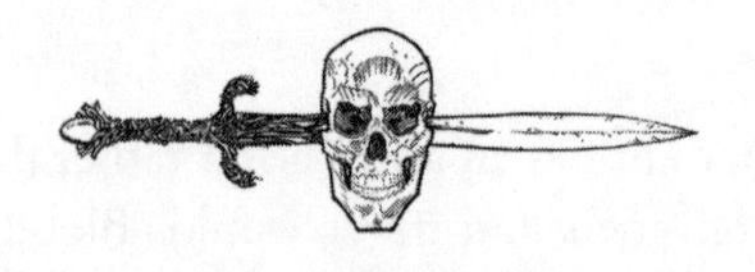

THREE

ragon's Claw Abbey.

Ryn watched that crouching pile of dark stone rise out of the fog from the ship's forecastle.

The tall curtain wall enclosed four acres or more, crowned by a keep that rose twice as high, girded by spruce and pine on a headland that jutted into the Iceberg Sea. A fortress on the edge of nowhere that might have been older than the Kingdoms themselves. A massive grave marker for all consigned to it—the living, the dead, and those whom despair had trapped in between. Weather had blunted the profile of the merlons that cut the top of the wall and ringed the roof of the Keep. The moss-eaten teeth of some decrepit grin that mocked any thought of hope or reprieve.

To the Hells with that—Ryn meant to live long enough to atone in some meager way for his sins, even if it meant doing his eight-year posting twice.

"This place won't make a difference," Josalind said from behind.

Ryn glanced back at her, surprised by the sudden comfort he felt to have her near. He wondered if she felt the same, as that hellhole drew closer to swallow them. They hadn't talked much about what would come next, once Ryn assumed his duties there and she became a ward of the cloister. They didn't have to—they both knew the Claw was a segregated community ruled by discipline and propriety. It had been easier to avoid the topic, to simply exist in the moment and enjoy, while they could, whatever it was that had blossomed between them aboard ship.

And now that time had ended. The realization swamped Ryn with glum discontent. He swallowed against it and forced a light tone. "So, Havlock let you out, did he?"

She shrugged. "Might as well—we're here, aren't we?"

Gulls called from the bay, hopeless and forlorn. The char of woodsmoke and a smith's forge fire carried on the air. "What do you mean, 'This place won't make a difference'?"

Josalind went to the rail, raised her hand, and pinched their new home between thumb and forefinger. "When I was a wee girl, I'd spend bells on this big flat rock, doing this to the ships that passed, to make the world small."

"I would do the same thing," Ryn said, "with our lord's men as they rode by, pretending they were toy soldiers."

"The other children teased me for being different—my ma thought that's what drove me to be alone on that rock," she said. "It wasn't the taunts, but what I saw beneath. Their fear of me. The day I saw that fear in my ma's eyes, my da's, too, I knew I had nobody. Nothing I could do anymore would make the world small enough."

No self-pity in her tone, no wallowing. Just that hard bitterness again. The only shield she had against the world's judgment. Whatever vulnerability she'd let slip two nights ago while talking about her visions had been buried deep. "How old were you?" he asked.

"Twelve."

Havlock joined them with something Ryn had missed dearly—his rig with longsword and pistols. He'd put on his armor and lanyards of rank and order earlier for the first time in what seemed like an age, but he still felt like a horse missing a shoe without his rig.

"Time to look respectable again, sir," the sergeant said. He even had the shiv that Ryn would keep hidden in his boot.

Ryn inspected a pistol—oiled and buffed and equipped with a freshly knapped flint. "You're a good man, Sergeant." He buckled the belts around his waist and massaged the squarish pommel of his sword with its facets of colored quartz—red, blue, green, and white. The colors of the dead gods meant to remind him of his oath to the

Clerisy. He no longer cared about the symbolism. The fine Sturvian steel assured that he had a reliable blade. Nothing else mattered.

A swivel gun fired from the main deck. Gulls took wing with startled cries. A moment later, a signal flare responded from the abbey's wall.

"That's the all-clear," Havlock said. "Though in this soup, the grenlich could crawl up to that wall and squat for a shite with none the wiser."

Hardly fitting talk for mixed company, but Josalind only snorted in amusement.

After weeks stuck on this ship, Ryn's blood raced at the prospect of a skirmish with grenlich. He tucked the shiv away and proceeded to prime and load his pistols. "We'd best keep eyes sharp, then."

The bay lacked the draft for the ship to dock. Instead, the crew dropped anchor a hundred yards out and lowered a longboat. Ryn, Josalind, and Havlock joined four sailors. Ryn would have gladly taken an oar to stretch his muscles, but given the circumstances, he perched in the bow instead with pistols cocked. Havlock had a pair of muskets, balls wadded with linen patches for greater range and accuracy.

The sailors leaned into their oars. Dim shapes grew on the shore as the mists parted. A giant skeleton's dark ribs reared up. Ryn at first thought it the remains of a beached whale, then realized the "bones" were in fact charred and rotting wood. The frames of a ship that must have been fifty yards long—the same size as the *Fool's Fortune*. Much of the hull had burned to the waterline, but enough of the keel remained intact to keep most of the frames erect. Perching gulls had crusted the remains with their splattered droppings.

Ryn looked over his shoulder at the bosun's mate. "What's the story with that?"

"Run aground by the Horror." The man spat over the side. "Poor bastards. Sovaris save their souls."

The Horror—a monstrosity that was half-squid, half-crab, and all trouble, or so the stories went. Ryn looked to the dock—a piling made of stone. It only made sense, given how easily the grenlich could scavenge or burn anything of wood.

Several figures stood on the dock. Two were fully ordained sisters of the cloth with heads shaven to topknots. Their scalps bore tattoos of Aegias's sigil—a nine-pointed star with a stylized sword in the middle. Both wore the same simple habits of unbleached linen, but the younger and slighter of the two caught Ryn's attention. Something about her stiff-backed carriage and sharp gaze left him with little doubt she outranked the other.

The last figure, broad and gaunt and armed with no fewer than four pistols, waved them in. A sergeant, perhaps around thirty. He wore kit in good repair, though the brass fittings had been left to tarnish dark. That wasn't neglect. Only a fool dared to walk in grenlich territory all shiny and spit-polished.

Havlock greeted his counterpart and introduced Ryn as they coasted in and a crewman hopped out to secure the lines. The other sergeant snapped to with a crisp salute.

Ryn stowed his pistols and acknowledged it. "Sergeant."

"Mundar, sir."

Ryn looked inland as he climbed ashore. A dozen more men with muskets poised held position to safeguard the path back up to the abbey. "I presume Captain Tovald is expecting me?" Messages had been sent ahead by pigeon.

"Yes, sir," Mundar said. "But there's a matter at hand. I'm to take you to him."

Ryn caught the shift in the man's tone. "Trouble?"

"There's always trouble of one sort or another, sir."

"The lieutenant will learn that for himself soon enough, Sergeant," said the smaller sister whom Ryn had assumed to be in charge. An auburn ponytail cascaded over one shoulder from her topknot to frame fine-boned features that reminded him of a bird. Hazel eyes fixed on Josalind—a sparrow hawk intent on her prey. "What have we here?" she asked.

Havlock held out a hand to help Josalind step from the boat, but she clambered ashore on her own with no trouble. "Josalind Aumbrae of Pellagos, sister," she said.

"Two things, Josalind Aumbrae. First, I am *Mother Prioress*—Mother Prioress Aelin. Second, you are no longer of anywhere but here. Who you were in the world matters not in the Claw, is that understood?"

Ryn saw something flash in those sea-green eyes, but Josalind only nodded. "Yes, Mother Prioress."

"Now, girl, what brings you to us?" Aelin asked.

Josalind raised her chin. "I hear voices and have visions, but I'm no witch." She shrugged. "Maybe I'm just mad. My family didn't know what else to do with me, so here I am."

Aelin blinked and regarded her with even more sharp-eyed scrutiny. The other sister turned a shade paler and stepped back. Mundar merely grunted with idle curiosity.

"I expect Abbess Gerta will take a special interest in getting to the root of what devils you, girl," Aelin said at last.

Ryn didn't care for the way she said that, as if Josalind were some deviant creature to be dissected. "If I may, Mother—"

"No." Aelin eyed him and Josalind together. "I don't care how the two of you might have fraternized on that ship. Dragon's Claw is a world of two solitudes—the Keep and the cloister are off limits to the rank and file. No sister or ward ventures into the garrison's areas without good reason and an escort. *Is that clear?*"

The woman looked like a child even beside Josalind, and yet her tone left Ryn feeling as though she had his ear in a pinch. "I look forward to assuming my duties and . . . adjusting to life here, Mother Prioress," he said.

"The stocks and the whipping post ensure it's a quick adjustment, for wards and palatars alike," Aelin said. "Remember that."

"I think she likes you, sir," Mundar said with dust-dry humor. He led Ryn around the flank of the abbey's curtain wall. The sisters had shepherded Josalind through the main gate. Havlock and his men were helping to ferry supplies from the ship.

Ryn snorted and made a point of hitching up his belt. "I'll be sure to keep the door locked in case she comes looking to rub my wood." He eyed the mists that concealed the forest's depths. The garrison kept the ground barren within musket range of the wall. Swivel guns and sharpshooters were stationed on the ramparts above. Still, he didn't feel comfortable being out here when he didn't yet have a sense of the place. Mundar didn't appear concerned, but Ryn kept his hand on a pistol all the same.

They rounded the curve of a tower, the largest in the wall. Ryn caught that rare stink—stale skunk mixed with moldering compost.

Grenlich musk.

He drew pistol and sword in a blink. Blood roared in his ears. Were the idiots on the wall blind?

"Mundar?" called a man's voice from the other side of the tower. It sounded mildly annoyed.

"Yes, sir," the sergeant said.

"Is he with you?"

"He's not sure he wants to be," Mundar said with a hint of a smile.

"Well, come on, then."

Feeling the fool, Ryn stowed his weapons and strode around the tower.

He found half a dozen palatars, armed and ready for all Hells. Bound in their midst were two grenlich, wearing nothing but loincloths. Where the clans near Sablewood resembled men crossed with boars, this pair had the look of mongrel hounds, with big dark noses, sharp-pointed ears, and a surplus of hair covering their sinewy bodies. A mess of fresh bruises and crusted blood left them even uglier. They sniffed the air and regarded him with hungry wolflike eyes. One bared his teeth to display oversized canines. Ryn stared right back and treated him to a lazy smile: *I'm ready to go a round when you are, cur.*

"There you are, Lieutenant. I thought you might miss the party." That came from the man who wore the lanyard of a captain.

Ryn tore his attention from the grenlich and snapped to with an efficient salute. "Reporting for duty, *sir*."

Captain Segas Tovald was a dark-haired man past forty, with flint in his honey-brown eyes and silver at his temples. A fleshy nose anchored heavy features. Extra pounds padded a big frame and blurred the lines of the man's jaw, but Ryn knew a bear when he saw one—the puff of Tovald's broad chest and the pull of his thick shoulders left little doubt that a mass of fit muscle lay beneath. An officer turned lazy and run to fat wouldn't last long in this place.

Tovald offered his hand. "Consider your duties assumed, Ruscroft."

The captain's grip was light a pinky and a ring finger, but Ryn didn't acknowledge the fact. Most fighting men found it hard, if not impossible, to adapt to such a loss. "What do we have here, sir?" he asked.

"Prisoner exchange," Tovald said. "You're on point with me." He started off toward the misty woods and beckoned the men to follow. The grenlich got their feet moving with little prompting and no complaint. Ryn wouldn't have expected captive grenlich to be so compliant. Not that he had much experience with grenlich as prisoners. Mundar gave a salute and turned back to the abbey.

"Posture like you're spoiling for a fight, but *do not* touch your weapons," Tovald said.

Ryn matched his stride and leaned close. "They have our men captive?"

"It's almost a game to them," Tovald said. "They grab one of ours and if we can grab one of theirs fast enough, we might get him back with his skin still attached."

Isn't that just grand. Ryn probed the forest's dim underbelly, trying to distinguish a hostile from the bushes of scrub cedar that marked its edge. Ranks of blue spruce and north pine fit for the masts of the largest ships towered high. Their upper reaches tangled in such a dense shroud, the forest floor lay in a perpetual twilight, carpeted in fallen needles and largely bare of other vegetation.

The sun chose that moment to peek through the clouds. Ryn caught a glint of metal, shadows that moved contrary to one another, in that twilight not fifty yards away. His hand twitched with the need to draw a weapon, but he followed the captain's lead. "I assume this is usually *not* a task for the garrison commander."

"No—and sometimes it doesn't go as planned—hence the new career opportunity for you," Tovald said.

Ryn wondered how quick or slow his predecessor's death might have been. The twitch in his hand grew more insistent as figures emerged from the mist at the forest's edge. Six grenlich clad in furs and buckskin and two palatars. The latter had been stripped of their gear and showed obvious signs of rough treatment, but no worse than the garrison's prisoners. They had all their skin, at least.

Tovald brought them all to a halt with an upright fist. Ryn stepped offside, conscious of leaving a clean shot for their sharpshooters on the wall. Grouped as they were, covering fire from such a distance had equal chance of hitting the wrong target.

"Ogagoth," the captain said with a nod.

A grenlich as big as Tovald stepped to the fore. A chief for certain, given the mantle he wore of fine deerskin trimmed in ermine, secured by a heavy silver brooch. Silver charms pierced his ears. He sported not one, but two palatar swords. One was an officer's longsword akin to Ryn's own.

The big brute noted Ryn's attention, and Ryn himself, with a snort of disdain. "Fresh meat, Tovald?"

Ryn let his hand hover over his pistol until the gesture couldn't be missed. "That longsword does not belong to you, *Tar-vrul*." Addressing him with the title used by his people conveyed the notion of respect. A tactic meant to blunt Ryn's words just enough so they wouldn't be taken as an open challenge.

Ogagoth rumbled deep in his throat. "Its man didn't protest much when I took it." He pointed to Ryn's lanyard of rank. "He wore that pretty twist, too."

The other palatars grumbled and muttered among themselves. Their grenlich counterparts spat in reply.

Tovald took a step to put himself before Ryn. "This isn't why we are here."

Ogagoth grunted. "A day yet to come, strappling."

Ryn didn't so much as blink. He took the nickname to be a play on the word *strapping* and couldn't tell if the tar-vrul meant it as an insult.

Ogagoth snapped his fingers. Two of his vruls nudged their prisoners forward. Tovald gave the order to do the same.

Ryn caught a flicker of movement out of the corner of his eye, back in the shadows beneath the trees. The distinct *whu, whu, whu* of a throwing ax cut the air.

He threw himself at Tovald and struck the captain in the ribs but lacked the mass or leverage to do more than knock him offside a step. The ax bit into the thick leather pauldron on Tovald's shoulder and stayed there. He ducked down with a grunt.

Man and grenlich cursed in equal measure. Blades hissed from their scabbards. Firearms cocked.

"Weapons down." Ryn yanked the ax from Tovald's shoulder. No blood stained the blade. The captain's mail hauberk had stopped it from cutting any deeper. He cast the ax at Ogagoth's feet. "Your vruls betray a parley for their own glory—has your clan no honor?"

Ogagoth snarled, clawed hands poised over his swords. Ryn kept hands clear of his own weapons despite the burning need to draw.

"Raise that pistol and I'll gut you myself," Tovald said from behind to one of their men.

Ogagoth stepped back and barked an order in the grenlich's guttural language. Three of his vruls took off into the wood.

They waited in silence. No one moved, man and half man alike trapped in the moment. Ryn kept his attention fixed on Ogagoth as he would any mad dog that threatened to bite. The tar-vrul's sneer suggested that he gave the idea serious consideration. Ryn may have just arrived, but if not for the parley in force, he would have gladly called Ogagoth out to reclaim those swords in memory of their fallen owners. He couldn't deny a thirst to spill grenlich blood for the sake of a mother and daughter left dead in the crimson snow. It didn't much matter if these grenlich had never heard of Sablewood.

A commotion arose back under the trees. Ogagoth's vruls returned, dragging another of their kind between them, not much more than a pup, so far as Ryn could tell.

Ogagoth grabbed the pup by the scruff, hauled him up onto his toes, and barked at him in their language.

The pup faced his tar-vrul, chin thrust in defiance, eyes wide with fear, and spat out a breathless response.

Ogagoth looked to the palatars. "He sought honor in killing a great battle-chief." He flung the pup down into the dirt and kicked him in the ribs. "No vrul betrays my word. Dagrauth's life becomes yours, Tovald."

Nursing his side, Dagrauth hauled himself up to his knees and stayed there when Ogagoth growled at him. Tovald stepped past Ryn and eyed the pup. He rubbed the stumps of his missing fingers idly across the palm of his other hand. Ryn might have wanted grenlich blood, but earned honest in fair battle, not like this.

Tovald drew his dagger with his left hand, caught the end of Dagrauth's ear with his right, and sliced off an inch. Ryn didn't expect such quick precision. The pup flinched but endured his punishment without so much as a whimper. He settled for glaring and ignored the flow of blood.

Tovald tossed the bit of flesh away. "I have no use for his life. A scar will serve."

Ogagoth nodded and ordered Dagrauth out of his sight with another kick. The prisoner exchange concluded without further threat of butchery. Tovald didn't say a word until they were almost back to the abbey.

"You'll do, Ruscroft."

Ryn figured that to be as much thanks as he could expect for getting between Tovald and that ax. He found himself looking forward to earning this man's trust and couldn't help but grin. There just might be a chance he could find some peace with himself here.

"You're welcome, sir."

"We fight the grenlich when we must, parley when it can spare a life, even barter if it buys us some grace to forage and hunt beyond the wall," Tovald said as they walked the ramparts.

Below, crews worked to prune anything that might provide cover to an enemy, under the watchful eyes of their brothers on sentry duty. The mists had cleared, giving a clear view of the forest's edge, where even now the scrub cedar likely concealed equally watchful grenlich scouts.

Ryn pulled aside an oiled leather cover to inspect the lock of a large-bore swivel gun mounted on the wall. Spotless, like all the rest. Tight-packed canvas bags of grapeshot and powder charges were stored nearby in a watertight oaken cabinet. "In my experience, the beast is most likely to bite after he's tricked you into thinking he's tamed."

"The abbess and I are under no illusion about the precariousness of it all, Lieutenant," Tovald said. "We just work for a balance that will ensure as many men as possible live to finish their eight while keeping us all true to the Clerisy." They took the stairs down to the common. Tovald thumbed the file Havlock had brought. "You're quite versed about grenlich for the boy of a genteel landowner from the River Lands."

"My commanding officer in Sablewood had established a . . . dialogue with an outcast from one of the clans," Ryn said. That grenlich's name was Ostath. Quintan had hoped to gather intelligence on clan activities, to better keep the community safe. Ryn had never been able to bring himself to trust a creature willing to betray his own kind.

Tovald paused to take a closer look at the file. "Yes . . . I see."

Ryn had no idea what the captain saw, but he didn't doubt the reports in that file documented with terse precision the whole sorry chain of events that had brought him here. The sudden sympathy in Tovald's tone rubbed like salt on a blister. "It's done," Ryn said.

"Those sorts of things are never done, son. We wear them always."

Ryn dug his nails into his palms. "Your point, sir?"

"We are all stuck here for one poor reason or another," Tovald said. "That disgrace unites us in a way, even more than the brotherhood that comes of being sworn to the Order." He leaned close and raised the file under Ryn's nose. "But a man who denies how his past has changed him, how it colors his judgment—that man is a liability."

A deep and shuddering breath fought its way out. "I deny nothing, sir." Ryn couldn't begrudge Tovald his concerns. He'd have them, too, in the captain's boots.

"And when you punched the grand inquisitar, what was that about?"

Ryn looked him in the eye. "It was bad enough that I killed my friend. I wouldn't stand for that woman tarnishing his memory, too."

There was more to it, of course, but it wouldn't help to confess his bitterness toward the Clerisy. All that mattered was giving service to the other lost souls consigned to this place and honoring the Virtues as he believed Aegias had intended, regardless of the Clerisy's interpretations. If thinking that way made him a blasphemer, so be it. He could live with that.

Tovald clapped him on the shoulder. "Let's have a drink—it's already been a day that warrants one."

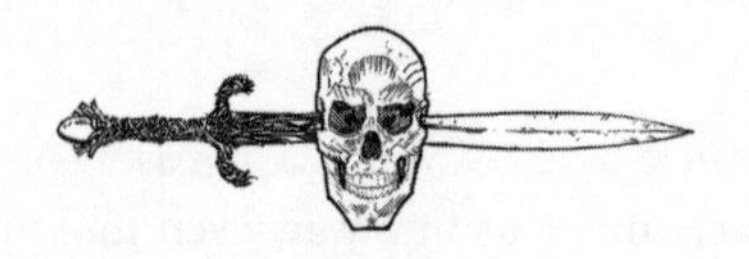

FOUR

Tovald's drink of choice turned out to be malt whiskey, served in a pair of chipped mugs from a desk so ancient, his cramped office and the rest of the barracks hall appeared to have grown around it.

Ryn took a polite sip of the heady stuff—it was only midmorning after all—and looked at the captain's crowded bookshelf. He'd been delighted to find such a trove in this grim place. Among more recent titles that had been press-printed stood older and rarer works, hand-copied and illuminated. One in particular caught his eye, *A Treatise on Contagion and the Dark Practice of Sympathetic Magic*, by Sagren the Fourth-Born. Ryn wondered what insight it might yield on Josalind's affliction.

The abbey back in Sablewood had an impressive library of its own. Where most men spent their off time in the barracks playing cards, or on more daring games that would test strength, reflexes, and nerve, Ryn had spent much of his time reading. The scholar in him missed that dearly, but not as much as he missed Quintan's ribbing about having his nose shoved in musty old books: *You're going to inhale some lung disease one of these days, or maybe one that rots the brain.*

"Wards of the cloister usually arrive with little more than a chest," Tovald said. "It's surprising how often they stuff them with books. They hope to find some escape that way, I suppose." He drained his mug. "The abbess has even more in her collection. You can borrow, but clean fingers always, please."

Ryn put Sagren's treatise and a couple of other titles aside for later. "About the sisters' wards, sir. I appreciate there's a protocol here to keep the men's trousers buttoned—"

"Trust me, Lieutenant, the men aren't the only ones who earn floggings for sneaking around to get their itches scratched."

"But I believe Josalind is a rare case who warrants special consideration."

Tovald arched an eyebrow. "I believe you did have the pleasure of meeting Mother Prioress Aelin."

Ryn felt a blush rise in his cheeks and wished he'd drunk enough to blame it on the whiskey. "I did."

"Then you know wards are no concern of ours. We keep them safe and unmolested and *that is it.*" Tovald leaned across his desk to stare him in the eye. "I consider myself a fair man, Lieutenant, even a lenient one, with palatars who know their place and keep to it. But I have little patience when a man crosses a line that's been made clear to him."

The captain's voice hardened as he spoke, but not nearly so much as his gaze did. Something came to crouch in his eyes, bristling with the hostility of a snarling guard dog, ripe with a threat far too excessive for the subject at hand. It cast a pall that made Tovald loom larger than he was in the confines of the office. Ryn's natural instincts kicked in—not fear, but the wariness of a trained soldier alert for any threat.

He resisted the urge to step back. It might have been the prudent thing to do, a sign that he deferred to Tovald's authority. Prudence be damned—he didn't care to be bullied. He held that dire gaze and conceded with only a respectful nod. "Duly noted, sir."

Best to let the matter rest, for now. But Ryn couldn't shake a sense that whatever plagued Josalind was bound to be misunderstood and that she'd wrongly suffer for it. He had to find a way to help her, even if that meant toeing Tovald's line.

Days slipped by in a blur, lost to the demands of settling in and getting to know the men—best done by crossing swords in the training hall, leading patrols outside the wall, and chatting off-duty over an ale. As Ryn had expected, all the men were commoners of the Peers Order. Noble-born palatars of the Aegian Order who met with disgrace rarely suffered this kind of exile.

He enjoyed the return to routine, and the need for focus and diligence with the grenlich threat. A fortnight passed before he opted for a quiet evening in his quarters to pursue his reading. Sagren the Fourth-born's treatise proved a fascinating diversion, but after bells squinting at the spidery script by candlelight, Ryn was no further ahead to finding a mystical cause for Josalind's affliction.

A hair lost, a drop of the blood, even the stray clipping of toe or finger gives fodder for the crafting of effigies with which to inflict distress on the target. Blood carries the power to enchant devices that can track the target over great distances. One's first defense is to burn all leavings of the body. If afflicted, seek out and burn the effigy. If tracked, one has little recourse if the device itself cannot be destroyed; death alone offers escape.

Old Sagren had likely written that last bit with a chuckle. Break the spell by dying—less than helpful. Nor did the book mention anything about such contagious magic being used to inflict visions or voices.

Ryn tossed the book onto his cot and rubbed his eyes. He couldn't shake the memory of what he'd seen—or at least thought he'd seen—that one night aboard ship when Josalind and her cot had appeared to float. For that reason, he thought it worth investigating whether Josalind might have attracted a curse. But Sagren didn't say anything about objects floating; *that* only came up in a whole other context: possession. And the Clerisy held that only an impious sinner could be possessed by the Great Deceiver's demons.

He leaned back over his chair to stretch and wondered how Josalind was faring in the Keep. He'd not caught even a glimpse of her since their arrival and it bothered him. Which of course left him wondering why he cared so much. What did he know about her, really? But he couldn't shake the feeling that she was bound to be unfairly judged. In his world, that just wasn't acceptable. If he could help, he would.

Quintan would have no doubt teased him about having a sorry need to play the hero. The fact he'd ended up dead attempting to play the hero himself spoke to the contradictions that had defined his character. Quintan had died true to form.

A sharp throb erupted behind Ryn's eyes. He winced and rubbed his temple. The pain had come and gone for several days, but not so fierce as now. Headaches with no obvious cause rarely bothered him.

He poured a cup of water and chewed on a leaf of thane's glory to dull the pain. The next book he reached for shared Sagren's vintage, *The Forbidden Mysteries of the Vysusian Brotherhood, as Sanctioned by the Holy Clerisy*. He flipped through it, grateful that the scribe had written in a crisp, bold hand. It contained chapters on the sorcerers of Vysus and their floating city (wrong context for Josalind) and how a sorcerer's dark covenant with the Great Deceiver allowed them to summon demons to their service and bind them to a physical form.

The text also addressed the incorporeal nature of demons and how, in their natural form, they could twist a person's perceptions, pluck thoughts, manipulate matter, and enchant objects. One chapter even referenced a ritual through which the body and soul of a willing mortal could be fused to a demon to create a fiend. Fused to a *lesser* demon, of course—no human, no matter how strong and willing, could endure a greater one.

The author also emphasized, with garish detail, how any ritual of sorcery required the blood of innocents. But the Clerisy's censors had made certain the book contained nothing useful in a practical sense. A work of propaganda, written for melodramatic effect to provoke shock and disgust from the reader. And none of it shed any light on Josalind's condition.

The headache deepened into a vibrating drone that made Ryn's teeth ache. His tongue tasted metallic. Gods be damned, he'd have to go to the infirmary and nag the sister surgeon for something stronger than leaves.

He chewed more thane's glory and eyed the *Aegian Codex* lying on his desk—a worn copy of the Commons edition that printing presses across the Kingdoms churned out by the cartload. He knew his Scripture without having to look up what it said about witches—and warlocks, too, for that matter. They entered a different kind of covenant than sorcerers. One where they invited the Great Deceiver *inside*. That could explain voices and visions. But it left its mark—disfigurements and blemishes that couldn't be concealed, an aversion to electrum, a twisted tongue that couldn't speak Aegias's words.

Josalind had apparently passed all those tests back in Pellagos. His eyes must have been playing tricks that night. She wasn't right in the head—like street beggars he'd seen. There wasn't more to it than that.

Then he heard the Voice.

The Great Deceiver is not the only cancer that poisons the Balance.

It came from nowhere . . . and everywhere. Ryn sent his chair crashing to the floor, heart pounding, chest so tight with sudden terror, he couldn't breathe. Frantic to put his back to a wall, he tripped over the chair, glancing wildly to spot from where, from whom, that voice could have come. His desk, a small wardrobe already open to bare its secrets, a rack on which to hang his armor and rig—none of it offered a means to hide.

The cot.

He grabbed the end and flung it over. Nothing lay beneath but cobwebs and dust.

His quarters had one window, high and narrow, but the voice hadn't come from outside. It had echoed between his ears.

A clammy thing slithered down his spine at the thought.

He pressed the heel of his hand to his brow and focused on a deep slow breath, then another. His headache—it had to be that, coupled with too much thane's glory. Nothing else made sense.

Just breathe.

Bit by bit, his headache faded, his pulse settled down. He heard nothing more beyond the hoot of a distant owl outside.

He needed rest. That was all.

Sablewood's dead lay scattered and exposed to the bitter cold, stinking so much of blood and shite that Ryn could taste it. He wondered how the smells could be so strong. The stains in the snow had already turned to ice that crunched underfoot.

There were so many bodies. Wives and husbands, mothers and fathers, even children. Thirty-six dead, but the sum of all the rest held nothing to Sara and Tamantha. Ryn found them, the girl still hugged to her mother's breast, raven hair matted together, both slain by the same thrust of a grenlich spear. Their flesh looked too much like lard to be real, eyes stuck wide with frigid wonder. Grenlich always gouged the eyes of their kills so ghosts bent on vengeance couldn't find them. But not Sara and Tamantha's—there hadn't been time. They alone among Sablewood's dead had eyes left to cast the blame where it belonged.

Murderer, *they called him.*

"You miserable swine. Why did you not do something?"

The words were spat with such mad despair that Ryn's ready hand went for his sword. But he couldn't draw it, not after Quintan.

He swung around to find Jaryk coming at him with a billhook clenched in his gnarled fists. A wild look blazed in the miller's eyes. Gore splattered his clothes. Ryn made no effort to raise a defense. Part of him knew grief had knocked the fight out of the old man. Another part savored the idea of finding a just penance on the edge of that billhook.

But Jaryk only stumbled to a halt and smacked the haft of the tool against Ryn's chest. He barely felt it through his armor.

The old man struck again and again, until his strength failed and his wheezing breaths fogged the air. "Why?" he croaked. "Why did you not do something?"

Ryn caught him by the elbows before he could fall. "I . . . we did our duty, as our abbot demanded."

Jaryk shoved him away with furious strength. "Duty?" His features twisted with scorn as he gestured at the bodies of his daughter and granddaughter. "Is this the worth of it? I've nothing now, nothing."

"Grenlich!"

The call came from the granaries, which the villagers had fought so hard to protect. A single raider loped across the common toward them. The bloodthirsty bastard must have lingered too long and hidden with their arrival. But now he came on with mace raised, determined, it seemed, to go down fighting with the best odds he could find. His serpent eyes narrowed to slits, slobber spewing past his tusks with each panted breath.

Ryn drew his sword. A pistol was too quick, too easy. "Stay behind me."

"I curse you." Jaryk turned and charged the grenlich.

The horror of what the man intended froze Ryn for a blink. Then a burning need to save one life on this miserable night, just one, propelled him forward with a roar.

But he was too late.

"Curse you all to Hell!" Jaryk cried as the grenlich's mace struck. His skull split with a sickening crunch . . .

Ryn snapped out of the dream with a start, bathed in sweat and breathing hard. Some might have called it a nightmare, but nightmares weren't real. This dream was faithful to the last horrid detail of what they'd found that night after the abbot finally gave Ryn leave to lead a troop to the village. Every time, it was the same. Every time, he was helpless to change anything. Every time, he knew it was only a window into the past, but still, he suffered through the experience again as if it were fresh.

The Clerisy taught that the only chance of being united with the Four in Paradise depended on living a long and upright life. Had Sara and Tamantha lived pure and upright for long enough, or had he stolen Eternity from them, too? Did they burn somewhere in the Five Hells even now?

Ryn heaved out of bed, not caring how the flagstones chilled his bare feet, and went to the washstand. The cold water rinsed some of the mud from his wits. He'd much rather face what came next with a clear head.

Hands clamped on the edges of the washstand, Ryn waited for the chapel's bells to announce the day. If the dream woke him, the bells would bring the Dread.

Bong. Bong. Bong.

On the first peal, his jaw clenched. The shudders came on the second, rolling through him in thunderous waves certain to shake muscle from bone. By the third, his teeth ached to the roots, temples throbbing to burst. He sagged against the washstand and fought to stay on his feet—lying down only made it worse.

Water sloshed from the basin and struck the flagstones, too much like the splatter of Quintan's blood. Both lungs seized as hot coals stuffed his throat. He kept his eyes clenched shut because even a glance at the mirror's reflection would leave his head spinning. His berries exploded with agony and clawed for refuge in his liver. Being gutted with a red-hot bale hook couldn't have felt any worse.

The Dread held him till the final note had faded. He slumped onto his cot and hugged himself to calm the violence of his shaking. The Mantra of the Nine Virtues offered little comfort, but he had nothing else. The words rolled off his tongue in a feverish mutter till his pulse settled to a reasonable rhythm—Humility, Piety, Courage, Diligence, Truth, Moderation, Chastity, Justice, and Brotherhood. Which had he broken, which had he upheld, on that night? The answer didn't matter because the dead no longer cared.

Then he felt a probing pressure in his skull, sharp and metallic. The headache returned.

Sablewood's handful mean nothing, Ryn Ruscroft.

This can't be real.

Ryn crawled to his feet, though his knees shook to crumble and his tongue clumped like damp flour in his mouth. Could madness be infectious? Did Josalind's voices sound like this to her?

He splashed his eyes with water from the basin and looked in the mirror, half expecting some maniacal fiend to stare back. One didn't, but he scarcely recognized the haggard wretch who did. He'd slept so deep he couldn't remember a single other dream, and yet he looked as though he'd not found decent winks in days. The scar Quintan had left him on that night blazed an angry path across his jaw, as if cut fresh.

A few leaves of thane's glory still lay beside the basin, shriveled now. The sister surgeon had warned him about chewing too much of the stuff but said nothing about booming voices. He went about his morning routine as quick as he could, eager to feel the sun on his face and lose himself in the company of others. Girding himself in his full rig—with longsword, belt knife, pistols, and even the shiv in his boot—provided some comfort.

Mundar met him in the hallway outside. As senior sergeant, he prided himself on always having the morning report ready to deliver while the senior officers took breakfast at their table in the mess hall.

A half-partition wall separated the officers' table from the rest of the men. Mundar shared their table so he could lean in and discuss matters discretely, but ate nothing, having done so already. A dozen overlapping conversations from the other tables crowded Ryn's ear. He struggled to focus and caught only half of what Mundar and Tovald discussed about duty rosters, who'd been caught nipping ale from the stores, and what punishment befitted dropping trousers with a hapless milking goat.

Halfway through his bowl of oat porridge, Ryn caught something that left him choking.

Tovald slapped him on the back. "Easy there, son."

Ryn eyed them both, certain they meant to prank him. "Did you just say 'dragons'?"

Mundar flicked a wet gob of Ryn's breakfast from his sleeve with no more concern than he would a speck of lint. "Not live ones, sir, just their remains."

Tovald affirmed the statement with a solemn nod. "We call it the Bone Yard. It lies about six miles northeast. The grenlich revere the place and make offerings on the harvest moon every third year to appease the spirits."

"Make offerings of palatars, when they get the chance," Mundar said with a bitter edge. "Those mongrels consider it an honorable way to go, like they're doing the poor bastards they sacrifice a favor. Vruls have contests to see which of their own will earn the right to die for their clan."

"This is the third year, and the time has come when we need to be extra careful," Tovald said. "The grenlich lose interest in prisoner exchanges till after."

Ryn blinked. "You're serious."

"Afraid so," Tovald said.

Ryn cast another suspicious look between them. "Why haven't I heard any mention of this place before now . . . from anyone?"

"The men consider it ill luck to talk about it," Mundar said with utter seriousness.

"I wanted to let you settle in before bringing it up," Tovald added.

Ryn took a drink of cider. "My father always argued that dragons were a myth—I knew he was wrong."

Many things lived before Nature's Order was corrupted.

The Voice's bite fogged Ryn's eyes and left his stomach churning.

"Skulls the size of horses," Mundar was saying. "No sane man steps foot in the place."

Ryn pushed to his feet, desperate to escape before he swooned. The air had grown too thick with the smell of men and the sizzle of pork fat from the kitchen. Even the bit of honey in his porridge had turned sickly sweet. "Feeling poor this morning." He staggered away. "Excuse me."

He barely made it out the door and to a spot where he wouldn't attract an audience before retching breakfast. Once the spell had passed, he sagged against the wall of the mess hall and tore a handful of dandelion leaves to wipe his mouth.

Are you . . . the Great Deceiver . . . his servant?

No one answered.

He didn't know what had prompted the thought. He was no warlock—he'd done nothing to invite such corruption of his soul. Sablewood had no doubt damned him, but that was still a far stretch from having the Great Devil in his head.

Maybe old Jaryk the miller truly had cursed him. Maybe the guilt had finally driven him mad. He'd seen men lose their wits for less in service to the Clerisy.

Cursed, damned, or mad, it didn't matter. A senior officer hearing voices? The Dread was bad enough. If he let this be known, Tovald would have no choice but to relieve him of his command. The men would pity him, fear him, mock him behind his back.

He'd be trusted with nothing more than a pocketknife and a shovel for mucking the animal pens. Officer in Charge of Managing Stink. He'd have it worse than those women up in the Keep, like . . .

Josalind.

What strength must she have to endure what she did and not be broken by it? He thought of her confronting Aelin on their first day here with such measured determination, stating her circumstances as if daring the prioress to find fault. If anyone might understand this . . .

He had to see her, talk to her. The rules of the Claw be damned.

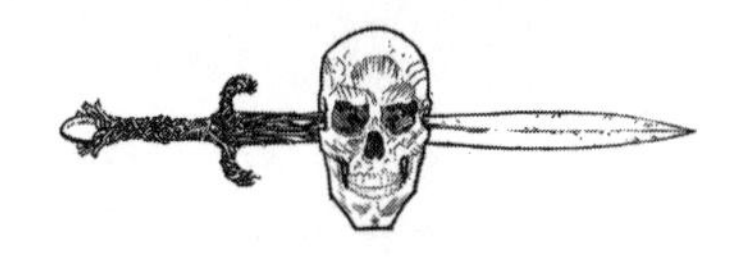

THE CHILD AND THE FORTUNE-TELLER

The Great Deceiver's awful need

o, my little angel, I said before that if Fraia had left Xang unchecked those seven centuries ago, he would've conquered all the West and gained the power to restore his father, the Great Deceiver. This threatens all of Existence—not just this world, but every world in the heavens above.

What do I mean? This is what the tea leaves tell.

The Clerisy would have you believe that the Great Deceiver is Corruption Incarnate. That he exists only to conquer and enslave for the sake of power. That he cares only about this world.

Oh, how typically dull and squint-eyed.

In fact, I don't even like that name, Great Deceiver. *The name that suits him best is Seeker.*

What if I told you this is but one of many worlds—thousands upon thousands of them, scattered across the heavens? What if I said that Seeker believed that all sentient life—all of it everywhere—once formed a single consciousness? Life existed in universal harmony and balance without conflict or want or despair. Instead, it existed only in unity, certain in the knowledge of its own reason for being. Like we all shared a womb together.

At some point, this Oneness splintered. Harmony and balance and, most of all, that ultimate knowledge, was lost. From the highest god to the lowest mortal, we now each carry a grain of the Oneness within us. It isn't gone, just scattered. Think of it as the spark that lights your soul.

I see how you're looking at me, pet. What matters is that Seeker believes this to be true. No, belief is too weak of a word. He knows *it to the last fiber of his being. And he so desperately wants to return us all to Oneness. He would save us all from the fear and doubt and suffering of existence . . . by stripping our last crumb of individuality and free will.*

But it's not about us. It's about him. Even a god can hunger for understanding. It's no different than any mortal who feels that emptiness inside and looks up at the stars to ask why she exists.

Seeker is driven by his emptiness, his need to understand his reason for being. The prospect of eternity, plagued by these questions he can't answer, is a constant torment. His only hope for sanity, for peace, is to restore the Oneness. So he thinks, at least.

He sees only one way to collect all those scattered grains of the Oneness. Every other god, every angel or demon that might serve them, every sentient creature of every ilk, on every world where they reside—he must consume every last one of them. And in that brief moment before his own individuality is lost to the restored Oneness, he will see, he will understand.

Everything he does is for the sake of experiencing this single, precious moment.

The leaves don't tell me how long ago Seeker set out on this quest, or how many worlds he consumed before he found himself confronted by a goddess determined to deny him. Fraia took from him a slice of the power he'd stolen from those unknown others. She battled him till they were both battered and exhausted. It left her world a lifeless husk. Seeker with his demons fled to the next world he could find, this world, and Fraia pursued him with what remained of her angelic host.

She fought him here as stubbornly as she had on her own world. Until circumstance led her to take the drastic step of creating Mordyth Ral, the Gods Bane. In the hand of a mortal man, the Sword crippled Seeker, but still he lingers.

Does the Keshauk priesthood that worships Seeker as All-Father truly comprehend the consequences of their god's restoration and victory? Did his son, Xang? I cannot say. Maybe they embrace this idea of Oneness and lust for it just as much. Maybe they're just ignorant pawns who care only about earning their god's favor—they wouldn't believe the truth if it kicked them in the teeth.

This is what I mean about the threat to all Existence. For if Seeker or Great Devil or Great Deceiver or All-Father or whatever you want to call him rises again and defeats Fraia, he will consume all sentient life before moving on to the next world and the next.

So, pet, this truly is a battle for all worlds, not just this one.

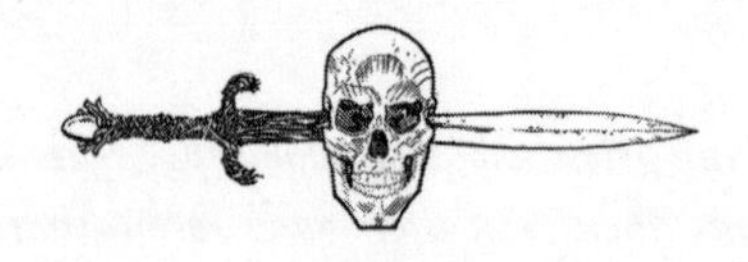

FIVE

Josalind took roll call of the hairs that sprouted from the mole on Abbess Gerta's thick neck—Prickle and Poke, Curly and Stumpy, Bristle and Ginger. The Deep Dark could have her before Josalind would break the silence first. She had endured enough scrutiny from clerics, physicians, and charlatans eager to bilk money from her parents to know this woman's sort right off—interrogate by saying nothing at all.

So, she sat in Gerta's study, comfortable in an old leather-backed chair, and kept quiet until the silence hung as thick as starch. The queen bee had an impressive collection of books, Josalind had to grant her that. Several hundred, maybe, crowded the shelf that sat beside her desk. A multicolored braided rug lay on the plank floor and a few faded tapestries softened the coldness of the stone walls. Two of the tapestries appeared to depict Aegias in some scene or other from the *Codex*. The third drew Josalind's attention the most—dolphins, leaping over choppy waves.

Gerta, sitting in her own leather-backed chair, topped up her cup from the pewter tea service that sat on the small table beside her with a plate of biscuits. She hadn't offered any tea to Josalind, nor any nibbles, though she knew damned well the abbey's latest ward had been herded here short of any breakfast. Gerta split and buttered a biscuit still warm enough to smell. The sunlight peeking through the study's window glistened in a glorious way from the spoon of strawberry jam as she piled that on next.

"Tell me, Josalind," she said, once nothing remained of the biscuit but a fruity smear at the corner of her mouth. "What is it that you want?"

"'Want'?" Josalind couldn't remember ever being asked that.

"Yes, poppet, *want*," Gerta said with a patient smile. "Surely there must be something you want."

Josalind didn't buy that smile for an instant. Oh, she acted all motherly, leaving Aelin to be the iron hand of the place, which only proved her to be the true terror.

The voices chose that instant to start digging at her—all four of them. She couldn't make sense of any of them, but that didn't make her noggin ache any less.

"Well?" Gerta prompted.

Josalind rubbed at her temple. "To be away from here for a start."

"Try again."

One word reared up out of the babble. *Goste . . . Goste-what?* They kept shouting it over and over. *Gostemere*—that might have been it. Whatever in Cursed Hells that meant. There was more, about taking something *to* Gostemere. A place, then, but take what?

Josalind clutched at her hair. "I want to know silence, emptiness, without them digging around."

"Why?"

Josalind gritted her teeth. "So I can be free and know what it's like to have a life of my own."

Gerta answered with a faint smile. "Don't we all yearn for that. Where do you think these voices come from?"

"Maybe I'm just mad."

"That is a firm possibility," Gerta said, as she went for the last biscuit. Her dogged calm made Josalind want to slap it from her pudgy hand. "Do you feel they want something from you?"

"'Want'? What could they possibly?" But of course they did. Most of what they said made no sense. Her visions whipped around like leaves in a windstorm—the ones of Xang she'd told Ryn about, tangled up with other random glimpses of war, death, and destruction from times and places she couldn't know. Sometimes they came so intense she could smell the blood, taste it on her tongue, even feel her skin bake under the heat of a tropic sun and her eyes sting from the bite of smoke and ash. Only one thing was certain—the voices wanted something, they needed her. That implied a will not her own. It didn't matter what tests she'd already passed, admitting to that would have them talking witchcraft again.

Gerta gave her a long look. "I can't help you if you're not honest with me, poppet."

"No one's ever been able to help me, Mother Abbess." Josalind heard how her voice cracked and hated herself for it. She wouldn't seek pity or show a speck of weakness—that was the promise she'd made herself before leaving home. Yet here she was, tears mustering to make a liar of her, throat aching like she'd swallowed a thistle.

Gerta gave another of those empty smiles and patted Josalind's knee. "We will see about that."

The vigils were the worst—bell after bell spent on her knees till they felt pounded into the cold stone of the chapel floor. Josalind recited the Mantra of the Nine Virtues and Aegias's Litany till the words lost meaning.

It was pathetic, thinking mindless repetition might impress the angels enough to come cure her affliction. No one had actually said that was the plan, not Aelin and not the abbess, but Josalind didn't need a string to link the pegs. She'd decided long ago that the Clerisy offered nothing but hollow bombast. The gods were beyond reach, and the angels didn't care anymore.

They expected her to focus on the Tetraptych the whole time during those vigils. It hung behind the chapel's pulpit from chains of polished brass, a circle of stained glass two yards tall and divided in four, bearing the sigils of the gods. She'd long lost track of how much of her life had already been wasted this way in some other chapel before another Tetraptych. How much black powder would it take to blow the damned thing to bits?

When she didn't kneel, she scrubbed—floors, pots, and linens. Wards all had their jobs to do. Whatever rank or privilege they may have enjoyed before being cast off in this place didn't matter. Each sorry soul had her own story, even if she didn't share it. It made them equal. Josalind found that liberating after years of being singled out for being different.

One day she found herself hoeing potatoes with Temea, a pinch-faced ward about her age who spent far too much time brushing and braiding her chestnut tresses.

"You'll soon grow some ugly-big calluses like a right proper sailor," Josalind said with impish glee as Temea hissed in dismay at the broken blister on her palm. She doubted the fussy girl had known how food of any sort got to her plate before coming to the Claw.

Temea's lips twisted and her scowl knotted in a confused state between scorn and dismay that would have spooked a cat. She wielded her hoe with savage zeal. "He will come for me one day."

Josalind didn't know who *he* was and didn't much care, though she did fear for the safety of those potatoes. "Nobody's coming for any of us except Lady Death, deary."

That was how she played it as the days blurred together into a numbing drone—sharp and brassy. She had no other defense, no way to keep her frayed wits from snapping like catgut stretched too far.

Because the voices were steadily getting worse. She'd long known they numbered four—three male, one female. *She* was the loudest of all. Whenever Josalind could grasp a word or phrase that made half a speck of sense, it came from *her*. But still, most of it was just noise, shrieking noise ten times worse than being trapped in a crowd of brats banging pots and spoons.

The visions worsened, too. Mostly about a skull she somehow knew to be Xang's—eye sockets like pits of dark hell that threatened to swallow her soul. She roused the whole dormitory one night, screaming bloody murder. They told her she'd been repeating "rise again" over and over.

One morning after vigil, she joined the other wards for their constitutionals in the cloister—little more than a kennel barely thirty yards to a side. A stone colonnade overgrown with hardy red grapes marked its boundary. Wards weren't permitted to venture beyond without permission *and* an escort.

She drifted over to pluck some grapes. They tasted tangy and sweet—her favorite kind, fit for a fair wine. She wondered if she might prune some of the vines to weave them. This place was so bleak—if only there were some flowers to pick. She could lose herself in weaving flowers but the chance hadn't come in months. Palatars drilled on the common beyond. She ignored the attentive look from hulking Sister Dagetha and drifted under the colonnade. Letting her toes skirt the line tasted more delicious than fresh fruit. How far could she go before the leash got yanked back?

Only then, with fewer leafy vines to see through, did she spot the armored figure that loitered in the shadows just steps away. She pulled back with a sudden fear that embarrassed her. Had she not walked the docks of Pellagos when they swarmed with the rough crews of her father's ships?

The figure stepped closer.

A giddy rush surged through her with surprising intensity. "Ryn." Even saying his name gave her a thrill that was altogether silly. But he was the closest thing she had to a friendly face on this gull-stained rock, especially after rousing the dormitory.

"Hello," he said.

He wasn't particularly imposing, of average height and average build. Still, there was a somber intensity about him. Coupled with the sure and graceful way in which he carried himself, his demeanor cloaked him with a confidence that might have been taken for arrogance in another man. But Josalind knew his deepest shame. Arrogance wasn't a word that fit him.

His deep, dark eyes had sunken into rings like he hadn't slept in days. He'd battled the razor that morning, judging by the nicks that marred his strong jaw. That pillow-spiked dark hair had evaded the comb altogether. "Have you been well?" she asked.

He winced and rubbed at his temple, a gesture that was naggingly familiar, though she couldn't finger why. "Your voices, do they say things you couldn't know?" he asked. "Strange things?"

A phantom chill left her hugging her chest. There was no cause to be cold, even in the shadows. The sun already beat hot and she wore a light cloak. "More show than say."

"Like they can't be part of you; they have to be from outside."

The chill deepened. "Yes."

He nodded in a quick, nervous way. "But you're still you, at least, you think you are. Though what does that matter? People going mad never think they are." He seemed to be talking to himself now more than her.

"Josalind." Aelin ducked under the grapes. She had her dander up for certain—that same vein always twitched on the little shrew's shaven scalp. Josalind found it fascinating, the way it made the sword dance in Aelin's tattoo of Aegias's sigil.

"Palatars are not permitted in the cloister without permission, Lieutenant," she said to Ryn.

His distraction gave way in a snap to tight-lipped hardness. He made a show of examining the earth between them. "Please correct me if I'm wrong, Mother Prioress," he said. "But I do believe I'm still a foot short of the mark."

Spoken with the utmost courtesy and respect owed to a senior cleric, and wickedly sarcastic at the same time. Josalind found herself both delighted and impressed. "We both had a taste for fresh grapes this morning, Mother Prioress," she said.

"Of course, you did." Aelin's attention drifted past the colonnade. Their encounter didn't appear to have attracted the attention of the palatars at drill, and she relaxed a smidge. "I expect you to consider appearances at all times, Lieutenant," she said. "We don't need a senior officer giving encouragement to needful men."

Ryn gave her the point with a nod. "It's not my intention to lead with a poor example, Mother Prioress."

"Then what was?"

"Just to say hello," Ryn said. "It's important for a man to remind himself what he's protecting, from time to time."

"How original," Aelin said. She'd no doubt heard such a line a thousand times before.

But to Josalind's utter astonishment, the prioress's manner relaxed even more. Josalind popped another grape into her mouth to hide her gawping. Not that the prioress would have noticed—she only had eyes for Ryn.

The little shrew has a heart after all. Josalind had suspected the Iron Hand of Dragon's Claw to be more bark than bite—a scrappy little dog who acted tough to keep the big hounds in line. It must have been lonely for her, trapped here like the rest of them. At least the wards and the sisters had each other. Josalind couldn't imagine that queen bee, the abbess, being much of a companion.

Ryn didn't seem to notice the slant of Aelin's attention. Another man who couldn't see under his nose. "I should be getting back." He treated prioress and ward alike to a brief smile. "Good day to you both."

Then he strode away, tall and proud as a mainmast, one hand riding casual on the pommel of his sword.

"And what have you to say for yourself?" Aelin asked.

Josalind wiped grape juice off on her cloak. Gray wool served well to hide stains, linen habits didn't, she'd learned too well in the laundry. "Like I said, I had an urge for something ripe," she said, trying not to smirk.

That vein throbbed with a wilder tempo. "I think it will be chamber pots and rat traps for you today."

"Thank you, Mother Prioress." Josalind turned to the Keep. "That'll be a welcome change from the scrubbing."

Hands, viselike, shook her. Nails gouged her skin.

Josalind's eyes flew open. Somebody big crouched over her, smelling of lye soap, pinching her ribs with knees like hams. Lantern light spilled across her cot to reveal Sister Dagetha's plain and creased features, glaring with teeth clenched in anger and fear.

"What's wrong?" Josalind asked. "Was I dreaming again?"

"That weren't no dreaming." Dagetha leaned close, till Josalind could smell rotting teeth and supper's fish stew more than soap. *"Witch."*

"Dagetha, bring her here," Abbess Gerta called from the door of the dormitory.

She climbed off and didn't wait for Josalind to rise on her own. Instead, she grabbed the collar of Josalind's shift and hauled her up. Here it was, the middle of the night and she was being manhandled. Half-choked and outraged, Josalind drove an elbow into Dagetha's breadbasket before she could think better of it. The big woman grunted and balled a fist.

"Enough," Gerta said. "Be civil—both of you."

The commotion had woken every ward in the dormitory. Josalind endured their stares as Dagetha herded her to the door. They were the kinds of stares she'd come to expect from her neighbors, from her family. Curiosity, fear, pity—twisted together in a way that left her feeling small and awkward, needing to beg forgiveness for drawing breath. The dream-vision must have been something truly awful to behold this time. She didn't know—she couldn't remember.

But that name danced again in her head, like a sea ditty that stuck worse than a spell of hiccups.

Gostemere. Gostemere. Find the key to Gostemere.

Gerta looked hard at her by the light of the lantern. Her plump face didn't bear curiosity, fear, or pity. Just the kind of grim determination Josalind had seen her father wear when the time had come to put down his favorite water dog, Barnacle.

"Come with me, poppet," she said.

Josalind followed, glad that Dagetha didn't. Gerta led her down the stairs to the Keep's isolation floor. The wards whispered about the handful of women who lived here. What they must have done, who they must have crossed, to warrant being locked away forever. Each door bore a heavy lock and a slot just wide enough to pass a tray through.

A chill stiffened Josalind's spine. She'd not feared the Claw until now. Her breath turned shallow and rapid as Gerta led her to the one open door.

"Inside," the abbess said.

Josalind forced her granite feet across the threshold. Beyond lay an apartment about twenty feet to a side, decently furnished with a four-postered bed that had a straw tick, a couple of slat-backed chairs, a small table, and a washstand. The stone walls were oppressively bare, broken only by a tall and narrow casement window. It was more space and privacy than she thought possible at the Claw, but a prison was still a prison. She couldn't imagine being stuck here for the rest of her days with no company but the voices. If she wasn't mad already, she surely would be.

She swallowed hard. "Please."

Gerta lit a candle from her lantern and planted it on the spike of a wall holder. "Wait here."

She pulled the door shut. It hit the jamb with a thud that made Josalind flinch. At least Gerta didn't lock it before the glow of her lantern faded away.

The candle kept the shadows at bay. Still, Josalind felt surrounded by things, evil ones that hungered. She hugged her chest and drifted to the window. Its brass hinges had stiffened from neglect and would open only a few inches, but it would do. She rested her head against the frame and breathed deep of the salty sea. Supeidos, the sailor's moon, rode near full. She let herself sink into the rhythm of the surf washing the shore as she used to back home, sitting on that big flat rock. Moonlight painted blue-toned patterns in the sky as clouds slipped by.

Josalind.

Her voice, always louder than her brothers'. Josalind didn't actually know if these voices were kin in some way. It just seemed right to consider them so. She rubbed at her temple.

"Who are you?" she asked.

Soon. Soon.

Her voice had never been so clear. "What do you want from me?"

Soon. Soon.

The door opened, giving Josalind a start. She turned to find Abbess Gerta and Prioress Aelin.

"Come here," Gerta said.

Josalind trudged toward them, trying to read what she had coming from their expressions, but neither gave anything away. "Would you please tell me what happened? What I said?"

"It's not what you said, poppet," Gerta said in a weary way, as if truly grieved by the whole affair.

Aelin crossed her arms, eyes narrowed. "What do you remember from before you woke?"

"Nothing, Mother Prioress," Josalind said.

"Nothing." Aelin's foot began to tap the floor, slow and steady, the beat of a funeral drum.

Josalind ignored the temptation to stomp the little shrew's toes and focused on keeping her voice steady. She wouldn't let them see fear, no matter what. "Just tell me what happened."

An angry sigh hissed out of Gerta. "You had one of your episodes and the other wards said—" She shared a quick look with Aelin. "They said things in the dormitory *were moving*."

Josalind gawped at her, then at Aelin. "But that's . . . that's just ridiculous." Visions and voices were one thing, but things moving—that couldn't be.

"I won't lie to you, poppet—this concerns us greatly," Gerta said. "You were cleared of any suspicion of witchcraft, but this testimony cannot be ignored." She glanced around the room. "This will be your home now. You are not permitted out without our consent."

Josalind swallowed hard. "For how long?"

"Till the last star falls, if it suits us," Aelin said. "I'll have Sister Morna research stronger tonics that might calm your episodes. Someone will be outside this door every night to see what devilry comes of your dreams."

Devilry. Aelin already talked like witchcraft had been proven. Josalind looked them both in the eye. "I swear, I don't know anything about what the others think they saw." A traitorous tear slid down her cheek. "You have to believe me."

"We will see." Aelin's gaze sharpened even more, as if she meant to fillet Josalind with a stare. "But know this, girl—we will not tolerate a threat to the abbey for the sake of one."

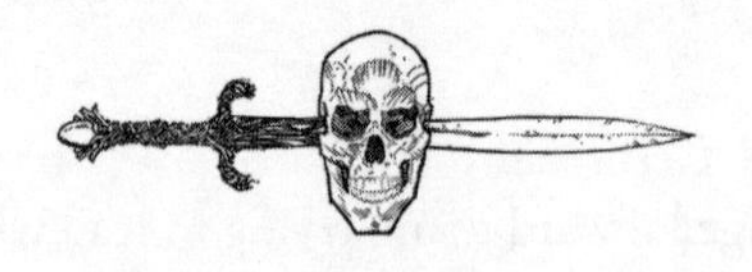

SIX

Ryn eyed the hair shirt on the cot beside him and fingered the coarse weave, crusted with someone else's old blood. Aegias had said trials of the flesh purified the spirit. Might they quiet the ghosts that whispered in the dark, the old and the new?

He'd never practiced mortification of the flesh. He'd never felt the need, never understood how it might bring him closer to Aegias, to eternal truth, to Paradise.

But still, he suffered the dream-memory that brought the Dread with the morning bells. Still, he heard Jaryk's last words. Still, he heard the *Voice*.

For several months now, once or twice a day, Ryn had felt that probing pressure that left his eyeballs fit to boil. The Voice spoke in riddles and made references that lacked the context to have meaning, all in the tone of a warning but as hard and lifeless as stone.

He might have told Josalind but hadn't found the chance to talk to her alone again since that day under the grapes. Considering how the sisters had imprisoned her, the way whispers about the "witch" had begun to circulate through the garrison, he didn't dare confess his affliction to anyone else.

Tovald's books kept him circling back to the same two possibilities—either he'd gone mad, or the Voice belonged to *something* else. Angels had appeared to Aegias and provided guidance, so the *Codex* claimed, but it didn't describe anything like this. Only the

Great Deceiver and his servants were said to touch a man's mind in this way . . . *if* he had willingly invited corruption.

Maybe old Jaryk truly had cursed him—plain and simple.

Whatever the root of it, Ryn had decided to ignore the Voice and never dare ask again from where it had come or what it might want. Refusing any dialogue denied it the chance to deepen its hold on him. Thin reasoning, to be sure, but he could think of nothing better. Instead, he buried himself in his duties, in trying to glean anything useful from Tovald's books, in drilling and training with a ferocity that left him exhausted and with few men eager to face him as a sparring partner.

But still, he couldn't escape the Dread or the Voice. He'd sworn to accept his penance at the Claw, to serve and protect the innocent. Did some power expect more from him, a harsher form of atonement? When he'd found the hair shirt in a trunk in the chapel yesterday, he couldn't help but think it might hold the answer. This notion of purifying the spirit through pain might be rubbish, but if there was any chance at all that physical trial could drive the devils from his head . . .

At this point, he had nothing to lose.

Ryn gathered up the hair shirt and shrugged it on. It stank of old sweat. A mild itch soon deepened into a rasping burn that made him conscious of every inch of skin. This would test his mettle at every turn. He put on the rest of his kit, drew his sword, and ran through a basic drill. His flesh soon reached a state of tolerance. He might be able to endure the shirt till sundown without being so debilitated that he couldn't go about his duties.

As he left his quarters, grimacing with the urge to hunch and twist his shoulders from the rasp, Ryn felt a certain rightness that had nothing to do with the Voice in his head.

He did owe Sablewood's dead a caravan's riches in honest suffering.

By noon, Ryn had come to appreciate the benefits of blood as a lubricant. Just when he'd thought he could bear the burn of the shirt no longer, the worst-rubbed patches began to bleed.

By midafternoon of that dreary, drippy day, he faced a field of horrors that made him forget the shirt altogether.

During a patrol that wasn't supposed to stray a foot beyond musket range of the wall, three men of the garrison—three damned fools—had gone farther and never returned. How or why remained a mystery. Some men blamed the fickle fogs that came off the sea and confused any sense of direction, though nothing but a thin mist had shrouded the Claw that day. Others cited more sinister forces at work and invoked the sign of the Virtues. They spoke of the grenlich's dark sorcery, summoning demons to swallow the men in smoke and shadow and bear them away.

"I've seen a demon, son, in its true and natural form," Tovald had told Ryn. He grew visibly pale as he said it, and he suffered a shiver that prompted him to rub at his stump fingers. "Neither I nor any commander before me has ever logged such a thing here. These grenlich are no sorcerers. Men find it easy to blame spooks for poor judgment."

Whatever the truth, no one doubted those three men had become fodder for the grenlich and their triennial sacrifice at the Bone Yard. The harvest moon had come early this year, before the autumn equinox. With its passing, Tovald gave Ryn leave to lead a recovery party with Sergeant Mundar. "Ogagoth will ensure safe passage," the captain said. Ryn didn't intend to give any vrul who dared to cross their path the benefit of the doubt. He hadn't forgotten his first day at the Claw.

After Mundar's briefing, Ryn thought he knew what to expect at the Bone Yard. As they cleared the forest's edge and the mists parted, he still found himself awestruck. Carefully balanced stacks of bone—sun-bleached and bearing a pale copper luster—loomed high. Each stack claimed a roughly quarter-acre plot, and Mundar had said the yard spread across two square miles or more. There had to be thousands of them.

Ryn stood there gawking, overcome by a boyish wonder that brought an idiot grin to his face. Every last bone of each dragon had been used with the delicate precision of a clockmaker to build its stack. A horned skull crowned each one, many as large as a horse, just as Mundar had said. No two were alike. Some had snouts shorter and blunter than others, and where most had two horns some had three, or even five.

Then Ryn's wonder turned sour.

He came to feel that every skull in sight had turned its attention to him. It made no sense—those empty sockets held nothing but the odd splat from a passing bird. Still, he could imagine dozens of reptilian eyes the size of saucers coming to bear on him. Not with hostility, more . . . expectation, as if they had plans for him that he knew nothing about. He thought he heard whispers on the sodden air. His heart pounded with the sudden need to flee, no different than a mouse unfortunate enough to catch the attention of a cast of hawks.

That hot pressure flared in his skull and drowned it all out.

The ambitions of small men bury many truths.

He came within a hair's breadth of answering that Voice, tempted by the need to ask questions.

Mundar saved him. "Makes you wonder what else called myth was real, too," he said.

Ryn forcibly kept himself from daring to look at the skulls again and gestured for the sergeant to lead. "Let's just bring our brothers home."

They found them minutes later, in the company of three vruls. Man and grenlich, treated as equals, each stripped naked and crucified across a skull that had been lifted down from its stack. Their arms had been lashed to horns and their feet bound with ropes looped around dagger teeth. The savage bastards had started with the manhood of their offerings, before flaying the skin from thigh and torso. The smells of stale blood and charred wood from spent fires stained the air. Raw meat and glistening bone had already drawn crows by the dozen. Wolves, too. The scavengers retreated with angry caws and petulant snarls when confronted.

Ryn had steeled himself for this. They all had. Mundar had picked the ten men he considered best suited for such a grim task.

But they'd expected to find corpses.

"By Aegias—they're still alive," said Corporal Daine.

That's not possible. Ryn went to the nearest body—Scorben. A fair-haired lad only half a year into his eight. Ryn touched that cold and ashen arm. Hot bile rose, nearly choking him, when Scorben's head turned and confronted him with empty eyes.

"Wanted secrets. Wouldn't give 'em," Scorben croaked.

Had they interrogated him? About what, the abbey's defenses? The poor bastard had no doubt earned praise for not dying. Ryn forced his breakfast to stay put with a hard swallow.

"That witch in the Keep—it can't be coincidence."

Witch—Ryn had heard that foul word whispered far too often of late. He snarled with sudden outrage and turned on the man who'd spoken. Corballys, a tactless idiot who often said things that offended without realizing it. "What?"

"We've all heard rumors from the Keep about that girl, sir." Corballys glanced around for support. "She brings ill-luck just being among us. This is proof."

Daine grunted in agreement. So did a few others.

Ryn stepped toward Corballys, gripped by the need to throw a punch, to find satisfaction in the pain of bruised knuckles and the sight of this ignorant bastard sprawled at his feet. But that wouldn't be a fit way for a senior officer to handle the situation. He couldn't afford to let his personal feelings color his judgment or betray him, not if he hoped to hold the respect of these men and keep them in line.

Instead, he looked to Mundar, who kept stone-faced. "There has been no formal charge against her," Ryn said, forcing an even tone. "I myself know she passed the Test in Pellagos."

Mundar nodded and looked to Corballys. "Let me hear 'witch' from you again, trooper, and it will be ten lashes." His attention broadened. "Same goes for all of you. The girl is nothing but what the abbess says she is, and that *word* has not been used."

That silenced the men's tongues for now, but once this kind of infection started, it easily resisted all means of purging. Ryn knew it, and he could see in Mundar's eyes that he did, too.

The sergeant gestured at the crucified men. "Your orders, sir?"

Ryn squared his shoulders and grimaced against the hair shirt's burn. He went to Scorben, pressed his palm across the lad's mouth, and pinched his nose shut. "Let Aegias guide you."

He looked away as Scorben convulsed and suffocated, unable to bear the emptiness of those eyes, so much like Sara and Tamantha's eyes that night in Sablewood. He should have been angry, filled with righteous hatred for the grenlich. Instead, he only felt tired, beaten down by this grim necessity. "Mercy is ours to give, Sergeant."

Only a day remained until the Claw celebrated the Feast of the Reformation, the holiest day on the calendar outside of Aegias's birth. The feast marked the anniversary of the Clerisy's founding—one of the few occasions in a year that could ever be considered *festive* in this place. But today the garrison would plant the brothers brought home from the Bone Yard.

This year's Feast was sure to just burst with levity, Ryn thought as he dressed in his quarters, starting with the hair shirt. Each time he put it on, the battle to find that bearable state of tolerance began anew. Each time, the urge to give up and toss the hellish thing into the corner almost won. Almost, but not quite. He didn't care to celebrate the Clerisy in any fashion, but it would be easy enough to ignore that aspect of the Feast once the damned high mass had finished. The garrison needed a formal gathering outside of a funeral ceremony to find solace in brotherhood and begin to move on.

The Clerisy couldn't be blamed for the deaths of those men, not directly, at least. And yet, it was the Clerisy that had put them there. Sure, many of the garrison were true rogues and blackhearts—men who had violated their oaths, not just to the Clerisy, but to their Order. They'd betrayed Aegias and deserved penance. But others, too many others, in Ryn's view, were good men condemned for the wrong reasons under the Clerisy's iron-fisted rule.

Since the Bone Yard, that truth had left Ryn considering how much better off his palatar brothers would be if the Clerisy vanished. Not just his brothers, but all the Kingdoms if freed of its tyranny. But even in this moldering hellhole, voicing such blasphemy could earn a man a noose.

He let Tovald herd him around the floor of the training hall during their morning session with a cunning combination of strikes. The captain may have lost two fingers from his sword hand, but he was no slouch with his left. Ryn soon had a sweat going that made the hair shirt itch and burn all the more. He savored the pain, embraced it even.

When he'd had enough, Ryn blocked, countered, and slipped past Tovald's guard with a mind to his footwork. He locked Tovald's blade up against the larger man's throat, with his left foot planted behind Tovald's leg to trip him. The captain had nowhere to go but down on his arse.

"Yield," he gasped.

Ryn stepped back. "Well fought."

Tovald snorted. "If I were vain enough, I'd say I'm gaining on you—but your heart wasn't in it." He gave his practice sword a swipe with an oily rag before racking it.

Ryn wiped his brow on his sleeve and grimaced as the hair shirt dug in. "I'll be sure to give you a fair pummeling tomorrow, sir." He considered sharing his mind with the captain, then thought better of it. He couldn't trust this man that much, not yet.

Tovald's hand came to rest on Ryn's shoulder. "You did what needed to be done in the Bone Yard, son—no one can dispute that." His fingers tested the coarse weave of the hair shirt's exposed cuff. "We can talk later, if you have a mind. Nothing good comes of letting things fester—silence is seldom a strength." He stepped away. "But right now, the prioress and Josalind are expecting you."

Soupy fog crowned the ramparts. The peaty smells of fall hung on the air, stained with woodsmoke and the stink from the livestock pens. Gulls called forlorn from the bay.

Ryn plucked a handful of grapes as he passed under the cloister's colonnade. The women of the abbey took their morning constitutionals swaddled in bulky woolen cloaks, heads bowed and hoods drawn. Sexless beings beyond the hungers of flesh—a crafted illusion that fooled no one. Still, it made a point that left ward and palatar alike with one less excuse to act on their impulses.

Aelin already waited for him on the steps of the Keep. She wore a cloak, too, with hands tucked into its drooping sleeves and hood drawn.

"Lieutenant," she said without emotion when he reached her.

Ryn dipped his head. "Mother Prioress."

He waited for her to say more, certain that she meant to. The stilted silence soon turned awkward. In some fashion, they were of equal position, each the second-in-command for their half of the abbey. But even Tovald as captain answered to the prioress. Best to keep their relationship on a formal footing.

She pulled one hand free of her sleeves. He watched her fingers drift toward him. The gesture came slow and deliberate—he had no reason to be startled when she took his hand. Still, it was so unlike her, so odd, a tingle stole up his arm and he almost jerked away.

She tilted her head to one side, eyes still hidden by the hang of the hood. "It's often a hard thing, to be merciful."

The empathy with which she spoke surprised him even more than her touch. It stirred something deep inside, something too raw, too vulnerable, that he didn't want to show. "Yes." He could muster nothing better. A sudden fear stole over him, that she would look up and see the vulnerability glistening in his eyes.

But she didn't. Aelin mustered a kind smile and tugged the protruding cuff of the hair shirt. "You came to mortify your flesh before the Bone Yard. Why?"

He reached for the only truthful answer that didn't involve the Voice in his head. "We all have to live with things we've done that we didn't want to do."

Her hand lingered. "You only need to ask if you want Confession and Absolution."

Most horrifying of all, her thumb had come to trace a slow circle on the back of his hand. Ryn swallowed, stimulated by the gesture even as his knees trembled with the need to bolt. He had to be reading this all wrong, she must have meant it as a simple gesture of sympathy. Aelin hadn't earned the moniker "Iron Hand of the Claw" with coy touches.

"Mother Prioress, a moment?" a sister called from the cloister below.

Ryn welcomed the interruption. "Thank you, Mother Prioress. Perhaps after our duties." He winced even as he said it, painfully aware of how abrupt he sounded due to his awkwardness with the whole encounter.

Aelin pulled her shoulders back. "Yes," she said with a curt edge. "I didn't mean to keep you, Lieutenant. Wait for me on the cellar stair."

Ryn couldn't tell if the change in manner betrayed anger at herself or at him for failing to respond in a way that suited her. He hoped that would be the end of it and headed into the Keep. The time had come for Josalind to attend the chapel for her daily vigil.

The Keep didn't have a dungeon in the true sense of the word, but the cellars below served the purpose well enough—a maze of passages and storerooms, dark and dank with vaulted ceilings that hung low. Lard oil lamps lit the way down. Their greasy smell mixed with the mustiness of the place.

The injustice of Josalind being forced to live down here for weeks now tasked Ryn even more than the hair shirt. They had first moved her to the Keep's isolation floor but even that hadn't been enough for the cowards for long. Josalind had become an outcast in a place of outcasts. Maybe the abbess hadn't yet said *witch*, but too many witnesses had spoken of things they'd seen and heard during Josalind's nightmare rants. Something plagued her, but that made her a soul in need, not one to be feared.

He had to believe that, for his own sake as much as hers.

Dead silence gripped the cellars. Even the rats and cats seemed to have reached an accord. Ryn had been assigned the duty to escort Josalind, both for her own safety should fear provoke someone to violence and for the safety of everyone else. His express orders forbade him from speaking to her or being left alone with her. But damn that—they needed to talk about their voices. He couldn't bear to miss this chance even if Aelin could be along at any moment.

He headed to the bottom of the stair and rounded the corner, expecting to find the door of Josalind's cell shut.

It hung open.

He covered the distance with a quick stride and poked his head in. Her rope cot had been neatly made and tucked. A copy of the *Aegian Codex* lay open on the small table. Besides a stool and a chamber pot, the cell held nothing else.

It didn't hold Josalind, either. Aelin carried the only key for the door. Besides, no sister had the nerve to take Josalind to the chapel alone.

He retraced his steps, mindful of the floor. Small footprints in the dust led into a corner of the cellars where he'd never been. The passage they followed vanished into the dark. He lifted the last lamp from its hook to light the way.

The footprints led him down a short flight of stairs into a subcellar, where the air clung thick with mildew. A stack of barrels had been pushed aside. He gave them a nudge. They easily teetered—empty. Even so, it impressed him how Josalind had managed to move the stack without tipping the top ones over. Of course, she'd somehow gotten the door of her cell open, too. He couldn't imagine Aelin had been careless enough to leave it unlocked.

Ryn thought of that night on the *Fool's Fortune*, when Sergeant Havlock had been certain he'd secured Josalind's door, and that other time, when he thought he'd seen her floating.

A witch, the men had begun to whisper. *A willing whore of the Great Deceiver.*

He raised the lantern to inspect what the barrels had concealed. An angular opening cut the wall—a secret door crafted to blend with the surrounding stone. There was no latch or handle. He patted around and found an oddity in the shadows above—a recessed lever that surely had to be a release. Just beyond the secret door, he found a ratchet and pulley system. Pulling the ratchet handle would leave only seconds to slip out before the door swung shut.

Beyond the door lay a narrow passage of fitted stone no different from the rest of the cellars. A ghostly figure emerged on the edge of the lantern's light.

He ignored the chill that skittered down his spine, put a firm hand to his sword and stepped deeper into the passage. Details of the figure emerged—a slender form, clad in nothing but a homespun shift smudged with dirt. Copper-red curls hung tangled and matted.

Josalind had found her way down here, shifted barrels and opened a hidden door, all in pitch blackness. She stood with her back to him before another door, this one still shut. Her freckled skin blossomed with goose pimples in the dank air, but she didn't shiver.

He came up behind her, closer than he'd been since the ship, teased by the illicit temptation of being alone in this hidden place. The circumstances should have left him wary, but he couldn't bring himself to believe the witch talk. The evidence just wasn't conclusive given everything he'd ever heard on the subject or read in Tovald's books. *Cursed* by a witch, maybe.

When desires thirst, a man can blind himself to anything.

Ryn caught the hem of the hair shirt, gave it a fierce tug, and welcomed the burn. His third day wearing it now and the Voice still haunted him. The frustration of it left him wanting to howl.

"He's getting stronger," Josalind said, without turning.

Ryn at first thought she'd somehow heard his Voice, but he wouldn't describe it as a *he*—or a *she*, for that matter. "Who?"

"I can't tell." She clawed at her head. "They keep ranting all at once."

Given time, he'd likely end up as cursed as her. That was the way of curses and madness—they only got worse.

Mine is the only voice you will ever hear, Ryn Ruscroft.

He needed to focus on something else. This door. He squeezed around her for a closer look and raised the lamp. The door had been crafted entirely of metal. And not just any metal. It gleamed with a dark, greenish hue.

Witch iron.

Witch iron negated witchcraft, sorcery, and their effects. A relic of Lost Pandaris—the ancient realm that had predated the Kingdoms. The art to forge witch iron had been lost long before Aegias, which made it more precious than gold to the Clerisy.

And yet, here rested an entire door of the rare stuff, hidden in a cellar, under a forsaken place on the edge of the world.

"*Lieutenant*," Aelin snapped from behind them.

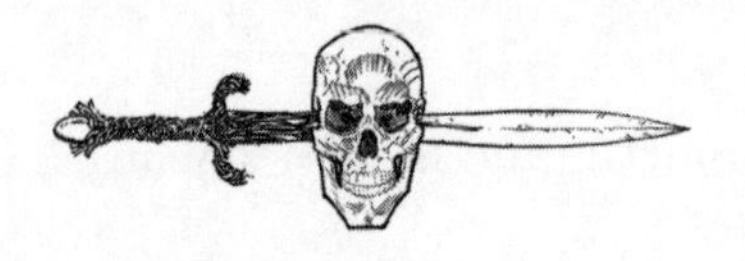

SEVEN

Ryn turned sharply. There Aelin stood, fists clenched, face flushed. He'd seen the look she reserved for threats about castrators and pickle jars for palatars who stepped out of line—it didn't hold a candle to the scowl she wielded now.

"Explain yourself, Lieutenant," Aelin said.

He worked his tongue around but couldn't find where the words had gone. Anything that came near the truth would leave Josalind facing some bloody penance.

"I am waiting, Lieutenant."

Josalind knelt at Aelin's feet. "It's not his fault, Mother Prioress. I don't know how I got here. I must have been sleepwalking again."

"How did you get out of your cell?"

Josalind looked up at Aelin. "I don't know, Mother Prioress."

She slapped Josalind hard enough to drive her sideways against the wall. Ryn's jaw clenched. He took a step, hand tight to his sword.

"Don't lie to me," Aelin said. "How did you know about this place?"

"I didn't—"

Aelin cuffed her ear. "Don't think I won't have the truth beaten out of you."

"I swear, Mother Prioress, I don't remember."

Josalind sounded sincere enough, even angry that she couldn't offer more. Ryn saw no reason to doubt her. Aelin, however, didn't appear convinced. She balled her hand into a fist.

Ryn cracked his bootheel upon the stone. "Mother Prioress."

Aelin looked to him, eyes narrowed, fist still poised over Josalind. "I do hope that obnoxious stomp was to crush the earwigs underfoot, Lieutenant."

"She did seem . . . confused when I found her," he said. Lies were best kept simple.

"'Confused'?"

"Yes, ma'am," Ryn said. "I think she honestly doesn't know how she came to be here."

Josalind picked herself up and wiped her bloodied lip on the back of her hand. If being the subject of Aelin's wrath—or even worse, her suspicion of witchcraft—had her frightened, Josalind didn't show it. Ryn could only admire her pluck.

"Forgive me, Mother Prioress," she said. "But I've spurned the Great Deceiver in every bloody way you've asked. What more can I do?"

Aelin flexed her hand, still considering the blow. Ryn knew better than to intervene again. Better for Josalind to endure a punch or two—let Aelin vent her outrage that way rather than opt for a harsher penance. A wise palatar knew when to put up, shut up, and wait for the battles he could win.

"Aegias spare you, girl, you'll be the doom of us all," Aelin said at last.

She paused. Ryn tensed. It would be the lash for sure. He couldn't bear the thought of Josalind stripped to the waist and locked in the stocks, degraded for all to see.

"You *will* attend the chapel, from now until the end of tomorrow's high mass for the Feast," Aelin said. "And you will fast for two full days."

Ryn stared at her in surprise. He would never have expected such lenience.

Josalind climbed to her feet, head bowed, and nodded. "Your mercy and faith give me hope, Mother Prioress."

"Just get your behind straight back to your cell, girl. We'll fetch you in a moment," Aelin said.

Ryn hoped Josalind would look back at him as she walked away, but she didn't. He knew better than to let his gaze linger on her.

"You seem rather eager to leap to her defense, Lieutenant," Aelin said.

"With respect, Mother Prioress, I don't care for how much I'm hearing the word 'witch,'" Ryn said, meaning every word. "That kind of fear can turn ugly damned quick."

Aelin locked her fingers together under her chin, with one pinky folded to invoke the Nine Virtues. "I don't need you to tell me that."

"Maybe someone picked the lock on her door." Could someone be trying to give Josalind the rope to hang herself? Ryn wondered if that person might be standing right before him.

"That still wouldn't explain how she got here," Aelin said.

"And 'here' is . . . ?"

She stepped past him to the witch-iron door. "None of this makes a whiff of sense." Her hand shook as her fingers drifted over the door's surface. But as close as she came, she didn't touch it. "You will speak of this to no one."

The tremble in her voice almost left her choking on the words. Now he understood the contradiction of her anger and leniency toward Josalind. This door had left her so rattled she couldn't think on a level keel. Ryn eyed that mass of witch iron with sudden suspicion and backed up a step. "What's in there, Mother Prioress?"

Distracted by the door, he caught the warning signs too late. She turned quick and caught him square across the jaw with a backhand that left his ears ringing.

"Do not ask that, *ever*," she said. "You have seen nothing, you know nothing, you will say nothing."

Ryn ignored the sting. "I will do nothing of the sort if there's some risk to the abbey."

"There is not—" Her voice broke into a shrill squeak, and she took a breath to regain some composure. "How could there be a threat? Look at the age of this place." Her hand touched his. "There is only a trust, a secret that every prioress and abbess of the Claw has sworn to keep."

"But not the commanders of the garrison." Something stank about that.

Her gaze hardened and her hand retreated. "This is not a palatar's concern."

"This palatar knows, so where does that leave us?"

Aelin glanced back to the door. "We have standing orders, Gerta and I."

Ryn didn't care for the way she said that. "Oh?"

"It won't go well for you, for me, or that cursed girl if Gerta finds out about this." She looked back to him. "Give me your solemn oath that you will say nothing about this to *anyone*."

He shook his head. "The captain should—"

She grabbed his wrist with surprising strength. *"No one."*

Ryn suspected that further protest would only earn him a firsthand introduction to those standing orders. He pressed his palm to his heart. "I swear in Aegias's name, may my life be forfeit."

"It likely would be," Aelin said.

But Ryn didn't care to be left in the dark. Despite her denial, whatever lay beyond that door obviously represented a threat of some kind. He couldn't just ignore that. Josalind already knew about this place, and his oath to Aelin didn't bar him from pressing her for answers.

Ryn didn't expect to find a guard planted before the chapel's Door of Swords.

After the funeral for their fallen brothers, he'd spent the day on patrol outside the walls. Night had fallen by the time his troop returned. He'd made his report to the captain and grabbed a quick meal before heading to the chapel. Josalind would be inside, likely under the watch of a sister or two. The odds of being able to speak with her weren't worth green pennies. Still, he had to try.

The chapel was a place of refuge and introspection, open without constraint to sister and palatar at any bell. It was of course segregated, with separate entrances. The garrison called their entrance the

Door of Swords, and there stood Sergeant Mundar, in full kit with his double brace of loaded pistols.

Ryn stopped at a discreet distance and rested his hands on his hips. "Care to explain, Sergeant?"

Mundar shifted footing but didn't break eye contact. "Orders from the captain, sir. The chapel is closed to *all* the men for the night."

Tovald hadn't seen fit to mention such a departure from standard practice while taking Ryn's report. It *might* have been an oversight, but he felt a twinge of panic. Had Aelin said something?

The line between a test and a trap is easily blurred.

He responded with a knowing nod to imply Mundar's answer had been the one he expected. "Who else is sharing this duty?"

"Masten, then Cabrilenda."

Masten—the sharpest shot in the garrison. "Stout-hearted lads, sure enough," Ryn said. "They'll have to be."

"Why is that?"

"Did the captain give a reason for this unusual order?"

Mundar swallowed. "No, but . . . it's that witch woman, isn't it?"

Ryn's eyes narrowed. "Witch?"

"Now don't go giving me that look," Mundar said. "It's just us and I'm only repeating what I've heard."

"From where?" Ryn still had his suspicions about Aelin, and maybe the abbess, too.

"Sisters in the infirmary talk to the patients, that sort of thing."

Ryn let it go in favor of his immediate goal. "You said Masten, eh? I'd rather have him fresh for tomorrow than soggy from a short sleep."

Mundar rolled his eyes. "I wasn't thinking—with most of the garrison giving observances for the Feast and these damned fogs, you'll want his eyes on the wall."

The man had herded himself right to where Ryn wanted him. "Let me grab some sleep and I'll come relieve you in Masten's place."

"You, sir?"

Ryn afforded him a casual smile. "Like you said—I'm the one who's been minding her in the chapel. I'd rather not push the duty on short notice to anyone who might be wound up by these rumors."

"Fair thinking," Mundar said.

Ryn didn't give him a chance to express any further opinion. "Till later, then."

When the time came, Mundar gave up his post with a quick salute and a brief goodnight. Ryn watched him head off to the barracks hall, wreathed by billows of frosty breath that caught the glow of the sentry fires. He held his post for half a bell, half expecting Captain Tovald to appear, armed with a few probing questions. No one came.

The Door of Swords lay half in shadow. Ryn made a point of drifting in and out of sight for a while—if anyone did watch him, it would take that much longer for them to realize anything was amiss. With luck, they wouldn't notice at all. Not that he trusted in luck.

He slipped inside and drew the door shut behind him. Vigil candles sweetened the air with beeswax. Metallic salts made them burn in the colors of the gods. Unlike the chapel in Sablewood, with its richly carved hardwood paneling and pews scribed by generations of pilgrims, the stone and exposed timber frame of the Dragon's Claw chapel bore no ornamentation at all. Instead of oak, these pews were cut from knotty local pine. Six round windows a yard across—three on the left and three on the right—captured in stained glass the exploits of Aegias and his paladins. Ryn could appreciate their symmetry with the Tetraptych, hanging there on its brass chains behind the pulpit.

This chapel also stood four times the size of Sablewood's, with a second-level gallery. The palatars' entrance led into the nave on the main level while the sisters' entrance took them up to the gallery. A stout locked door blocked the only staircase inside the chapel. Ryn heard gentle snores from above as he approached the pulpit. Luck smiled after all—Josalind's chaperone had drifted off.

A penitent's box lay before the pulpit on the main level—a wrought iron cage barely tall enough to sit up in, inclined on blocks so that its resident confronted the Tetraptych directly. Josalind lay within, corpse-like, hands folded across her chest. Under normal circumstances, palatars wouldn't have been barred from the chapel even with a sister or a ward occupying the box. They would've only been directed to keep silent and keep their distance.

Ryn came up on quiet feet, drew his sword, and knelt with the blade point down in the flagstones, hands resting on the cross guard. Claiming he'd come to meditate on the Virtues wasn't likely to gain him much leniency if he were caught out, but it couldn't hurt to make a show of it. He could always say the burden of the Bone Yard had driven him to break the captain's orders.

"Who would you be if you weren't here?" Josalind whispered.

He peered at her from the corner of his eye. She still lay as if unaware that she had company. He would never have been content with the path his father had laid out, that much he knew. Not even now, if he had the power to reverse time. He thought again of those musings that had occupied him on the *Fool's Fortune*—of fleeing south to Vysus to become a bone hunter, of fleeing with her. Idle and pointless thoughts.

Together, we can escape this prison, said the Voice in his head. **Together, there will be a once and final end.**

Josalind turned her head to regard him. Resting on those bars for any length of time must have been painful, but she didn't show any signs of discomfort. "Without the voices, I've no idea who I'd be. I'd like to know, but it scares me some."

He focused on the more pressing matter that had drawn him there. "Who let you out of your cell?"

"I don't know." As in the cellar, she said it with a trace of frustrated anger.

"Do you know what's behind that door?"

"I only know we should all be afraid."

"But what did you mean, 'He's getting stronger'?"

Her hand smacked her thigh. "Spit, spunk, and arse boils—I don't know."

A snort sounded from above.

Ryn didn't dare move for fear even the slightest twitch might draw attention.

A moment later, the snores resumed. He straightened his shoulders and grimaced as the weight of his armor dug into raw flesh. Though he'd given up the hair shirt for the day, its bite lingered. Common sense urged a return to his post without delay, but he couldn't, trapped by the need to confess his own madness, or curse, or whatever it was. For weeks he'd yearned for this moment, ached with the need to share it with the one person who might understand.

And now he had his chance. Only he didn't know where to start. The words clung like taffy in his throat.

"You'd best go, Ryn," Josalind said.

His base instinct for survival agreed. He sheathed his sword and slunk away, angry and frustrated with himself.

Tovald waited at the Door of Swords. "What are you doing, son?" he asked.

He'd come unarmed and alone. Ryn took that for a positive sign, despite the flint in the captain's glare. "I had a need for the chapel, sir. I'm sure you can understand."

"You've got feelings for that girl. I can appreciate that, but you need to keep a distance."

Ryn tried and failed to keep a scowl off his face.

"I'm trying to be kind, son," Tovald said. "However this plays out for her, it won't do you any good to be caught in the middle."

What had Aelin told him, if anything? Ryn considered his next words. "Something happened this morning, sir, in the cellars."

"Josalind got sprung from her cage and found her way to something she couldn't have known about," Tovald said with a tight nod.

"Then you know—"

Tovald's fist caught Ryn square in the breadbasket. Despite his mail shirt and the padding beneath, the blow left him gasping. The captain then caught the leather pauldrons of Ryn's armor and slammed him up against the wall. His whiskey-stained breath blasted Ryn's face.

"I *don't* know, and I'll have your gods-damned tongue before you can tell me." That snarling guard dog Ryn had glimpsed on his first day had returned, twisting Tovald's words into a spitting growl that left his chin wet. "I warned you about crossing the line—that cellar is not our business."

First a backhand from Aelin and now this. Ryn got his wind back and balled his fists. Tovald's aggression only served to fuel his own anger. He thrust his arms up and out to fling the captain's hands away, ready, even eager, for whatever might come next. He relished the idea of a good brawl and the chance to prove that he had a line of his own that shouldn't be crossed.

Tovald took a quick step back, steady enough on his feet for Ryn to doubt that drink alone could account for the captain's sudden turn to violence. "Consider carefully your next move, son. I won't be as forgiving as Her Ladyship."

Reference to the incident that had seen him sentenced to the Claw in the first place struck Ryn with a cold dash of reason. Assaulting a senior officer surely wouldn't help the situation. He throttled his anger back with a conscious effort. "Something's not right here, sir. Surely you must see that. How can you not want to know?"

That beastly glare faded from Tovald's eyes. "The best man to trust with a secret is a dead one," he said with grave earnest. "Don't cross the abbess by poking after things you'll regret finding." He smoothed back the graying hair at his temples. "Now go. I'll finish your watch, and we will speak no more of this."

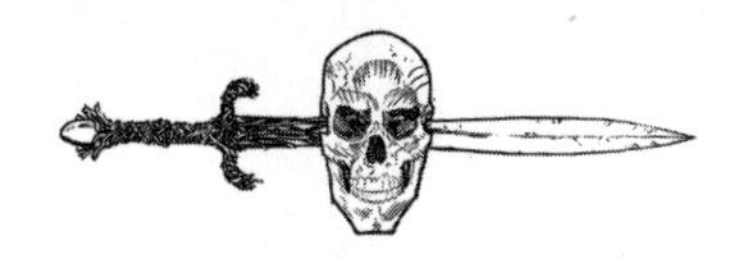

THE CHILD AND THE FORTUNE-TELLER

The Sword's true nature

Oh, my little angel, I fear I've led you astray with my talk of the Sword, for here you are, calling Mordyth Ral an evil thing.

I did speak true of how terrible a burden the Sword is to bear. Of how the Gods Bane binds itself to a man with a bond only death can break. Of how it seeks to twist him into the Earth-Breaker, the Soul-Taker, the Bane of All Things. For Mordyth Ral draws its strength and power from the life force of all living things. It would lay waste to a continent if need be.

But it is not evil.

Yes, it would seem so, if we consider only the scale of destruction the Sword would willingly wreak to achieve its ends. But we must weigh what it would do against why. *Mordyth Ral is an instrument of Nature's Order, perhaps even the spirit of this very world, given form to counter anything it deems a threat.*

It's really no different than a fever that draws on the body to fight an infection, even if it must drive the body to the brink of death to do it. Sometimes, the fever is too much for too long and the body dies, but is that the fault of the fever, or the infection? The fever only served its purpose, it only worsened in response to the threat; it had no desire to see the body die.

Mordyth Ral is really no different. Yes, it claims life, any life. It cares not about individual lives, or about race, religion, politics, or any mortal definition of morality. Only the sanctity, the purity, of this world matters. Mordyth Ral simply cannot abide the presence of anything that could be considered foreign—it sees it all as an infection to be expunged.

The Sword does not wish to claim innocent life. It will seek to spread its hunger as far and wide as possible, to avoid death. But if the need is great enough—say, to muster the power to strike down an alien god—well, then mass death can't be avoided. The Sword will take whatever it must out of necessity, without hesitation, without malice or regret, without grief or joy. You could say that the Sword is slave to its instinct.

Now, the man who wields Mordyth Ral—that poor wretch is doomed to suffer the deaths of all who feed the Sword. He alone might temper its purpose with mercy. But be assured, pet, that's not a compromise that comes easily. Mordyth Ral would break a man's sanity and make a puppet of him before surrendering.

Fraia proved her desperation to end the Deceiver by having the Sword made at all. She proved her fallibility by underestimating how much Mordyth Ral would have self-awareness and will. She thought her power and the Earthborn's craft would be enough to somehow render herself and her children, the Four, safe from the Sword's bias. How wrong she was. She and the Deceiver came here from other worlds and the Four bore the taint of that parentage. The fact that the circumstances of their conception made them part of this world, too, wasn't enough to spare them.

But what of the man who forged the Sword at Fraia's behest?

The Clerisy paints Vulheris as the villain and leaves Fraia out of the story. It claims that Vulheris tricked the Earthborn for the knowledge to forge Mordyth Ral. In his pride, Vulheris believed he could control such a weapon and destroy the Great Deceiver. Instead, the Sword's power drove him mad. Vulheris only crippled the Deceiver before turning on the Four and slaying them. The Clerisy claims Vulheris even destroyed the Earthborn. His madness allowed Mordyth Ral's hunger to ravage the world.

Well, there is of course much more to that story. And as we both know, pet, the Earthborn are not gone quite yet.

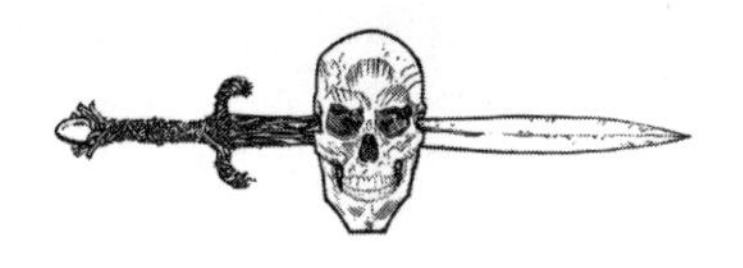

EIGHT

yn rose before the morning bells. He could rarely sleep longer, regardless of how late he went to bed or how his dreams tormented him.

The Feast of the Reformation had come. The day demanded fasting until sundown, as well as spit and polish—that included his dress-white half cape. What bitter irony and crass falsehood, to wrap himself in such symbolic purity. He would wear the hair shirt again to counter the hypocrisy.

As he readied himself, Ryn considered whether Tovald had reacted out of anger for the challenge to his authority the night before, or out of fear for his lieutenant's safety with the abbess. Maybe both. Even so, something lurked within the captain that made him the wrong man to have for an enemy. The most prudent course would have been to forget about that door and be the model of loyalty and obedience.

But as he looked in the shaving mirror and traced the angry red line of the scar Quintan had left that night in Sablewood, Ryn knew he couldn't.

He had been that palatar once, a man who never let free-thinking and an open mind conflict with his duty to the Clerisy. That man had killed Quintan and let death come to an innocent village. That man would be of no use to Josalind now, hemmed in by a pack of wolves that saw her as nothing but a threat. Becoming that man again would be no different than spitting on the graves of Sablewood's dead. It would rot what was left of his miserable soul. Madness then wouldn't be a curse, but justice.

Justice—the eighth of Aegias's Virtues. Scholars debated why Aegias hadn't included mercy among the Virtues. Ryn sided with the camp that believed justice and mercy went hand in hand. Each individual should receive the punishment, the reward, or the reprieve their conduct and their circumstances warranted, regardless of their rank or station.

But who should judge that? The Clerisy's law made little distinction between victim and perpetrator when it came to anything that smacked of witchcraft or sorcery. Given the paranoia that had begun to seep through Dragon's Claw, Ryn feared true justice would be the last thing that Josalind could expect.

She couldn't trust in the Clerisy's law and Ryn couldn't, either. As much as he found himself wanting to openly question the Clerisy, he couldn't risk such defiance. The odds were too great that it would leave him no better off than Josalind. His only defensible course was to hold the Clerisy—hold himself, Tovald, Aelin, and the abbess—to the Aegian ideals which it purported to honor.

But how? He hadn't a clue, not yet, at least. He could start by treading carefully around Aelin and Josalind both. That meant giving nothing by either word or action that could be used against him or serve to invite unwanted attention. The episode with Aelin on the steps of the Keep still nagged him. If she did have an interest in him, how could he cool it without leaving her bitter? Wielding charm with such calculated intent had been Quintan's strength, not his.

He found Tovald already waiting in the chapel. If not for Tovald's cape and fresh shave, Ryn would have suspected that the captain had never left.

The sisters had released Josalind from the penitent's box. Two sat with her now in the pews of the nave on the main level. Her attention appeared to drift among the images captured in the stained-glass windows—the victory and death of Aegias, the battles of his paladins. Her expression was vacant, distant, as if she'd strayed from her body and even now drifted across those ancient battlefields.

Aelin entered the chapel with Gerta. Tovald gave salute. "Good morn, Mother Prioress, Mother Abbess."

Ryn came to attention and stared straight ahead, in keeping with protocol as the subordinate officer.

"Captain," Aelin said with a brief nod. Her lips curled as she looked to Josalind. "That girl is to be returned to her confinement in the Keep following mass. A guard will remain on her at all times."

Ryn's eyes widened. Palatars inside the Keep, through the night. To his knowledge, there had never been such a precedent.

"Yes, ma'am," Tovald said.

"Lieutenant Ruscroft will not share this duty," she added.

Ryn tensed. Had she learned about his visit of the night before? Surely not from the captain. Aelin's attention fixed on him. He kept his gaze straight ahead, trusting in protocol as an excuse to avoid eye contact. His hand tingled with the memory of her touch. Of course, she had struck him with the same hand not long after.

Tovald had said the best man to trust was a dead one. What about a woman?

The whole of Dragon's Claw, some three-hundred-and-fifty souls, had soon packed the chapel, save for the handful of men left on the wall. The garrison kept to the main floor. The sisters took to the gallery and hustled Josalind off along with them. She appeared lost in a trance, mindless of the bustle around her.

Ryn took his place to the left of the pulpit and faced the congregation. Tovald did the same on the right. They drew their swords and held them in low salute—hilt cradled in the right hand, blade straight up in the front of the nose. It would be comfortable enough for a while, but this was a long mass.

Abbess Gerta launched into it with gusto from the pulpit, Aelin at her side.

Gerta recounted the history of the Aggression between the Four Kingdoms and the Teishlian Empire, the rise of Xangtemias, and the coming of Aegias. She told of how a host of angels had chosen Aegias as their champion and revealed the truth about the gods.

"And Prince Aegias did take up the Sword, called Mordyth Ral, the Gods Bane, and slew Xangtemias. But the Great Sorcerer's hold to the Mortal Realm did rival even the gods; Mordyth Ral's hunger did strip the land of any life for thirty leagues and task all that lived for sixty more. Prince Aegias suffered a hundred thousand deaths as the Sword fed. Then Our Prince Messiah fell to His wounds . . . "

Ryn could have repeated every word while too drunk to stand. The hair shirt rasped, his stomach growled with growing annoyance from fasting, and his shoulder ached from holding the salute for so long.

Beware their rise.

A sudden light flared in the corner of Ryn's eye, brighter than the noon sun on fresh snow.

Gerta's words cut short.

"In Aegias's name!" Aelin said.

Ryn looked up to the gallery, then higher, to the vaulted ceiling, fifteen yards above.

Josalind hung rigid in mid-air, arms outstretched and toes pointed, eyes alight with rainbow fire. No, not fire—fire would flicker and dance. Her eyes burned as sharp and constant as the sun, but the color of them kept changing.

Ryn struggled to make sense of what he saw. She floated, *floated*, with the grace of a feather. The cruel brilliance of her eyes made it impossible to make out her face, to tell if she embraced this power or suffered from it. She spewed what seemed to be mindless babble, but three words rang clear. *Seal. Break. Reborn.*

These things didn't happen, not here, not in the Four Kingdoms where the Clerisy persecuted witchcraft and sorcery without mercy. The gods were dead. They didn't manifest in earthly fashion—they couldn't. It was heresy to suggest otherwise.

Fear left Ryn's empty gut twisting on itself—fear for Josalind and what this meant for her. In the eyes of the sisters, she was surely damned now.

He startled when Aelin brushed past him.

The prioress strode up the center aisle, fists clenched at her sides, trembling with fear, outrage, or both. Such bold courage had to be fueled by shocked disbelief. "Josalind, you—"

A thunder crack rocked the chapel.

Hard objects pelted Ryn in the back like a hail of sling stones. Hunks of multicolored sparkle skittered across the floor and shot through the air past him. Something sharp gashed his head. He staggered to keep his footing. Cries of pain and consternation broke out among the congregation.

He clenched his teeth and panted to keep the roaring tide in his skull from beating him down. A run of blood soaked his collar. He didn't have to look to know the Tetraptych of stained glass that hung behind the pulpit had just exploded. Three men were dead, maybe more.

Somehow, Aelin hadn't suffered a scratch. She alone stood tall.

Josalind sank to the floor before the prioress with her arms still outspread, bathed by a harsh and multihued halo. Her messy curls danced with a static charge. The palatars nearest to her cowered in horror. Many reached for swords they'd left in the barracks. Only senior officers could bear arms in the chapel.

Aelin didn't give an inch. "*Hellspawn*—how dare you defile this holy place!"

Josalind touched down on the floor and let her arms fall. The glare dimmed to a tolerable level. Her eyes seethed with such anger, Ryn half expected Aelin to be cooked to ash. He'd never read about such a display from a witch. An angel come to earth, maybe, but the *Codex* never described Aegias's angels with beauty so cold and terrible.

"This place will no longer hold him." The voice that spoke wasn't Josalind's. It bore the eerie resonance of many voices speaking as one, stripped of that Fisherfolk brogue. "The ignorance of your false faith is going to damn us all."

The light in her eyes died like a candle snuffed. She crumpled to the floor and lay still.

Tovald swore. "Abbess!"

Ryn turned on wobbling knees, fighting the effects of the gash in his head and the madness of it all.

Tovald crouched beside Abbess Gerta. She lay in a growing pool of her own blood.

Ryn had barely crossed the threshold of Captain Tovald's office door before Aelin stood in his face with arms crossed. The color still hadn't returned to her cheeks.

"What took you so long?"

Ryn swallowed the urge to snap at her. His head pounded so harshly from the blow in the chapel he could barely see straight. A quick bandage and a few leaves of thane's glory to dull the pain didn't substitute for a decent meal and a long rest. He looked past her to Tovald. "I had to break up two scuffles on the way here. The mood among the men is turning ugly."

"Is she under guard?" Aelin asked.

"Yes, ma'am," Ryn said.

"How many?"

"Two outside her cell, four more down the hall." He didn't bother to add that he'd ordered that many for Josalind's safety as much as the abbey's. The men he'd picked were the most cool-headed and trustworthy in the garrison.

"Has she woken?" Aelin asked.

"No." Ryn had carried Josalind back to the Keep's cellar. No one else up to the task had the nerve. The effort had almost finished him.

Aelin turned on Tovald, who leaned against the wall behind his desk. "That girl is *no* witch," she said.

"Then what?" he asked.

Her foot tapped the floor. "I have no idea, which shakes me to the root. But the Great Deceiver's hand must be in it." Her foot stopped. "Her presence within these walls puts us all in danger."

Tovald glanced at Ryn before resting his hands on the back of his chair. "Shall we put her out of the abbey, then?"

Ryn stiffened and balled his fists behind his back.

Aelin's eyes widened. "She's desecrated the chapel, killed four good men, attacked the abbess, and you suggest we just let her go free?"

"It would hardly be freedom, Mother Prioress," Tovald said. "There is no safety outside these walls."

"If she is some servant of the Great Deceiver, the grenlich would likely kneel at her feet," Aelin said. "Then where would we be?"

A clammy chill gave Ryn a shiver. Tovald's expression turned bleak. "What do you suggest, Mother Prioress?" he asked.

She gathered herself with a ragged breath. "I have a responsibility to each man and woman here. I can't risk their souls. I won't."

The word popped out of Ryn's mouth with a will of its own. "No."

Aelin's eyes narrowed. "No?"

Tovald winced, evidence that Ryn might have his sympathy, but not his support. The betrayal stung, though Ryn had sense enough to appreciate the captain's awkward position, trapped between loyalty to his officer and his duty. Just as he'd been trapped between Quintan and the abbot, that night in Sablewood.

"What I think he—" Tovald began.

Aelin cut him short with a chop of her hand. "He can speak for himself, Captain."

Damned right I can. "Do circumstances such as these not require a formal inquiry, presided over by a lord inquisitar?" Ryn asked.

"The nearest lord inquisitar is in Tanasgeld—six days or more for a pigeon to carry the message and a ship to bring him," Aelin said. "We could all be frost-burnt in the Hells by then."

"With respect, how are we so certain of Josalind's guilt?" Ryn caught the quick headshake Tovald directed at him but ignored it. He wouldn't stand for this, he couldn't.

Aelin just looked at him, mouth agape.

Ryn pressed on, determined to have his full say even if it earned him the stocks and the lash. "Consider the facts, Mother Prioress. Does the *Codex* not state that when the angels came to Aegias, 'they were bathed in a holy radiance that seared the eye'? And did they not 'give dire prophecy of evils to come'?"

Aelin found her breath again. "'Holy'?" Fire crackled in her tone. "Do you honestly consider what we just saw to be *holy*?"

Just the thought of that raging light in Josalind's eyes left Ryn cold, but who was he to judge? "With respect, none of us are in a position to know what 'holy' should look like."

"No," Aelin admitted. "But we should all know our Scripture: 'The Great Deceiver's minions are ever watchful, quick to deceive with a mask of virtue; be wary when your eye finds what your heart desires.'"

Ryn suspected he walked a knife's edge with her that had nothing to do with skirting blasphemy. His knees shook, but he resisted the urge to rest his hand against the wall. Given his injury, it would have been reasonable to ask to sit in her presence, but now wasn't the time to show a speck of weakness. "We don't understand what grips her and neither does she. With a reasonable doubt—"

"Now you sound like a barrister, Lieutenant. This is not a civil court." Aelin almost shouted the words. "The abbess might not last the night." The admission left her shoulders shaking and stole her thunder. "It's up to me to do what's best for us all." She turned away and wiped tears from her cheeks with an angry swipe of her hand. "Just me."

Ryn didn't care for the fragility in her voice. "What of the warning Josalind gave?"

"She also said, 'The ignorance of your *false faith* is going to damn us all,'" Aelin said.

Perhaps truer words had never been spoken, Ryn thought. Josalind's statement only reflected his own doubts about the Clerisy's legitimacy as the steward of Aegias's legacy. "That could mean any number of things."

"Truly?" Aelin faced him, red-eyed, iron demeanor left shattered on the floor. In that moment, she looked younger than Josalind. "What could it mean, then? Tell me."

It might have been sarcasm, but Ryn heard only desperation. He could offer nothing that didn't challenge doctrine and risk a charge of heresy.

Aelin turned to the door. "I need time to think. Just keep her under guard."

After she'd left, Ryn leaned on the chair before Tovald's desk and swallowed against a flood of sour bile. "She's going to order Josalind executed."

"Burned, I expect," Tovald said.

His quiet grimness suggested he'd already given up and resigned himself to it.

"Gods be damned. Sir, it's not right," Ryn said.

Tovald reached into a drawer and pulled out the whiskey bottle, along with those chipped mugs. He poured two healthy measures and offered one. "That hardly matters."

The woody fume made Ryn's stomach roil and threatened to intoxicate. He waved it away. "What in Hells is that to mean?"

"Do you really think Aelin has a choice in this?" He dumped Ryn's measure into his own mug. "You just told us how this place is a spark away from an inferno." He drained the mug in a single swallow. "I know you have feelings for her, Ryn, I do. But she's dangerous. Whether that's her fault or not makes no difference."

Ryn lacked the strength to do more than glare at him. "You want her dead."

Tovald slammed his mug down on the desk with such force the old earthenware split in two. An edge sliced his hand. The blaze of fury in his flinty eyes left Ryn glad that a chair and a desk lay between them.

The captain drew a shuddering breath to calm himself. "There is no telling what that girl might do next, or when." He drew a rag from a drawer with which to staunch the bleeding. "And if she doesn't kill us all first, we're bound to have a mutiny on our hands. There has to be a show of authority."

Ryn thought of that night in Sablewood, of a garrison divided, a twitch away from turning on itself. "I can't watch her burn."

"You won't have to, son, but if Aelin orders it, I will see it done," Tovald said with a weary slump of those big shoulders. "Don't challenge it. There's no point."

Ryn had no idea what disgrace had earned Tovald his assignment to Dragon's Claw. He'd never cared to know. The world and its affairs weren't supposed to matter in this place. But that was a lie. Something had been hidden here that mattered a great deal to someone, somewhere. Why else the secrecy around it? Whatever lay beyond that witch-iron door probably had no bearing on all this, but he could think of nothing else. The lock—what would it take to get past the lock?

He drew up as best he could and offered a salute, resigned to the fact that he could trust no one in this but himself. "If there's nothing further?"

"Dismissed," Tovald said.

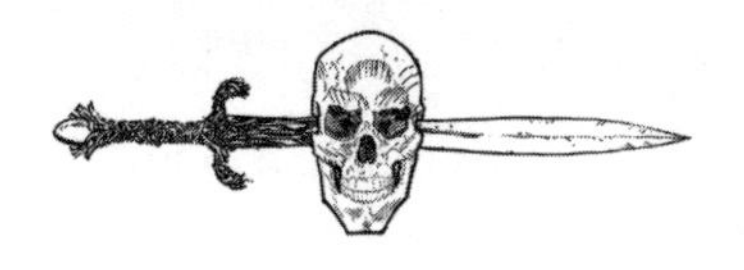

NINE

yn managed to slurp down a bowl of tasteless barley gruel and a hunk of bread and felt much better for it. It wasn't yet sundown, but he doubted anyone cared now about observing the Feast's fast. He stopped by the infirmary and nagged the sister surgeon for more thane's glory before heading to the Keep's dank and musty cellars. He couldn't decide which dogged him more, his aching head or the bite of the hair shirt.

The "cool-headed" men he'd assigned to guard Josalind were twitchier than rabbits in a fox den. He came around the corner to find the muzzle of a musket hovering under his nose.

The palatar on the other end eased his finger off the trigger and lowered the weapon. "Sorry, sir."

The six of them clustered a distance from Josalind's cell, sallow-aced and reeking of fear. There would be no shortage of volunteers to build a pyre, or light it, for that matter. Ryn hated them for it. He looked to Sergeant Mundar. "Has she woken yet?"

"There's been no sound from her, sir."

"That's not what I asked, Sergeant."

Nervous looks passed around. "We've not dared to look, sir," Mundar said.

Ryn shook his head in disgust and shouldered past them. The door of Josalind's cell was oak, free of a single knot, bound in iron. The smith and the carpenter had made it expressly for her confinement, with a slot at eye level and a sliding cover. Ryn opened it to find Josalind lying on her cot where he'd left her, hands folded on her chest. He watched the faint rise and fall of her chest by the dim light of her lamp before turning away.

"Tell me when she wakens," Ryn said.

"Yes, sir," Mundar said.

Ryn headed down the hall but didn't get far before a snide remark nipped his heels and roused chuckles. He should have let it slide, but he was spoiling for a fight and didn't care if he was in poor shape to finish one. It wouldn't be the first time he'd enforced discipline by knocking heads.

He stopped and turned. "Does somebody have something to say?"

Mundar had the decency to look embarrassed, but kept his mouth shut. Ryn knew the sergeant hadn't made the remark, or chuckled, either. But his silence put him on side with his men. He wouldn't play rat.

"I've left each of you on your rumps in the practice yard, more than once." Ryn drew his sword, slow and deliberate. "If one of you wants to go a round, have the guts to say that to my face. We'll do it right now. Rank won't matter."

No one spoke.

Ryn sheathed his sword, relieved and disappointed. "Later, then."

This time, nothing but silence echoed in his wake. He didn't leave the cellars, but instead made for the subcellar in the far corner. A lamp already burned down there. Its glow led him on.

He found the barrels he'd put back moved aside again, the secret door opened to reveal the hidden passage. Aelin stood before the witch-iron door. A heavy key rested on her palm, as long as a soup spoon, black with age. A lard oil lamp sat at her feet.

Ryn stopped at a respectful distance, curious and also annoyed that Aelin had thwarted his plans for some discreet investigation. She studied the key with a knotted brow, as if it held some secret she could drag out by will alone. Josalind's fate remained undecided, the abbess lay near death, and the garrison might turn on them, but Aelin had time to be standing here.

Which meant that whatever lay on the other side of that door *must* have had something to do with Josalind.

He cleared his throat.

"This door was made, then it was closed, and it's never been opened since," she said.

In truth, the door wasn't much to look at. Other than being constructed from a rare and mystical metal, nothing about its shape or design distinguished it—sheet metal reinforced with flat bands. "How long ago was that?" he asked.

She ran her fingers over the key's shank. "Centuries."

He took a step toward her. "You know what's in there."

She said nothing.

"Look, I can see you've sworn an oath you don't take lightly. But don't tell me the burden of it isn't scaring the Hells out of you." Ryn rubbed wearily at his brow. "I already know the door is here, so you might as well tell me the rest of it."

"I was supposed to have you killed for even knowing," she said, attention still fixed on the key.

Aelin seemed blind to the fact that she had little chance of defending herself should he take that as a threat. He wouldn't even have to shed her blood, just trip the hidden door's mechanism. Seal her in stone forever. The odds were slim that anyone would hear her muffled screams for help.

But that wouldn't avail Josalind. "With respect, Mother Prioress, I have done nothing but obey your wishes and play my role as a loyal officer."

She fixed him with a cold stare. "Do not presume to think yourself irreplaceable, Lieutenant."

He didn't so much as blink. "If you don't tell me, I'll bring down a cask of powder and blow this place to rubble."

Her eyes narrowed to slits. "You wouldn't dare."

He loomed over her in a sudden fit of guilt-ridden anger, the last of his patience eaten away by the hair shirt and his pounding skull. "Won't I?"

Aelin's hazel eyes flared wide and her top lip curled with such stark outrage, he expected her to call for his arrest on the spot. Then her fire faded with a nervous look at the door. "They were meant to be forgotten."

"'They'?"

She clutched the key to her chest. "I should have the smith melt this thing to slag and cast it into the bay. That's what I should do. Put a final end to it. Burn the key and Josalind both." A manic edge tainted her words. "Leave the Great Deceiver with nothing and redeem us all with the Purity of Flame."

Ryn decided to call her bluff. "Then why haven't you?"

"Because it won't save us if Josalind speaks truth."

"Is there a threat to the abbey?" Ryn asked.

"I can't be sure till I see."

"But leaving the door shut won't be enough to protect us."

Aelin hissed in frustration. "I don't know."

"Then just leave the damned thing till Josalind wakes up," Ryn said. "She might be able to tell us something."

"I can't. I need to know." She drove the key into the lock like she meant to deal a fatal wound.

He wanted to know, too, if only on the slim chance that unearthing the mystery might somehow help Josalind. But the sight of that key in that lock shook him to the core nearly as much as a fit of the Dread. He clamped Aelin's hand before she could turn it.

She flung her other elbow back into his chest but couldn't do much against his armor. "Let go of me, Lieutenant."

"We should wait."

"I should have you in chains—I only have to scream."

"And the whole garrison will know about this place," Ryn said.

"They'll swear silence quick enough when they see you hang," Aelin said. "What will they think when they find out how you feel about that cursed girl? I see how you look at her."

Ryn growled. "That has nothing to do with this."

"Doesn't it?"

Josalind's misery and loneliness spoke to his own. That did bewitch him in a way. He'd be a fool to deny it. But her certainty that this affliction would only ever damn her in the eyes of the world, coupled with her strength to endure it—*that* left him helpless with admiration and determined to help her. He didn't care if that made him a romantic fool. A palatar true to the Virtues had an obligation to fight injustice and defend those who couldn't defend themselves.

"You had best decide where your loyalties lie, Lieutenant," Aelin said. "I'm losing patience."

Ryn held his ground for a moment longer before he let go. His withdrawal had nothing to do with loyalty. Damn her and the Clerisy both. But he could do nothing stripped of his freedom. "Open it, then."

Aelin tried to turn the key.

Nothing happened.

She tried again. Seized tumblers squeaked in protest but didn't yield. She struck the door in a sudden fit of anger. "By the Blessed Martyrs."

After all that, here they were, thwarted by a lack of basic maintenance. Ryn touched her arm. "Let me."

He knelt and eased the lamp's lid open with care to keep the wick from snuffing out. "The key." She handed it over. Once he had it well coated in warm lard, he rose and tried the lock again.

Her foot tapped, fast and nervous. "Well?"

He jiggled the key around for a spell, then gave a hard turn.

The lubricated tumblers shifted with a groan and a clank. He left the key in the lock, grasped the handle in both hands, and braced his foot against the wall. Witch iron apparently didn't rust like regular iron, but it still took all he had to break the hinges free of their slumber. The effort thrust fresh daggers through his aching skull.

Aelin raised the lamp high. It shook in her hand, driving the shadows into a mad dance. A strangled gasp tore from her throat. "It's true, then. By the souls of the gods."

Ryn stepped from behind the door to see for himself.

A sword like no other, driven through the ear cavities of a skull. They rested on a simple pedestal carved from black granite. The room lacked the space for anything else. A secret reliquary that was little more than a closet.

The sword's odd beauty snared Ryn's attention before the skull's ugliness could. A polished yellow metal he couldn't name formed the leaf-shaped blade, too pale to be brass or bronze. Russet-green veins rose from it. They thickened and wove together to form a guard shaped like a pair of curving horns and a two-handed grip. The sword's pommel was forged from the same metal as the blade, the size and shape of a goose egg.

Ryn had read descriptions of such a sword, seen it captured in drawings and paintings. Mordyth Ral, the Sword of Aegias—the blade called Gods Bane.

The gleam of light from the blade's curves teased his eye and lured him closer. He shouldered past Aelin for a better look.

She grabbed his arm. "Carefully. *He* watches."

Her words broke the Sword's spell and let the skull lay claim. This was no simple relic. The jawbone was intact for one, to all appearances fused to the skull, with every tooth impossibly perfect and intact. Under the lamplight, the bone shone with the burnished brown of ancient bronze. The skull's size suggested a big man, but the strong jaw and broad cheekbones, coupled with the weight of its presence, made it seem even larger—the skull of a giant, ten feet tall.

The eye sockets were pits of darkness. Ryn caught Aelin's wavering wrist to angle the lamplight. The darkness held its ground and dared him to look closer.

He found himself trapped on the edge of an abyss. He couldn't breathe. He couldn't move. All he could do was teeter on the edge, helpless, waiting to fall. Things of smoke and shadow danced on the edge of sight. A hissing whisper called to him, compelled him to listen. Louder and louder it grew, until he drowned in the shrillness of it. He couldn't tell if it was one voice or a hundred, certain only that it would drive him mad.

Things he couldn't see slithered over his skin. Hot, throbbing, oily things. He desperately wanted to shrug them off, to batt them away with a curse. Only he couldn't move or find his voice. His flesh began to melt, mixing with the stew of corruption that swarmed it.

Aelin boxed his ear. "Don't be a fool, Lieutenant."

It all vanished in a blink. Ryn stumbled back against the wall and panted for breath. "It can't be."

"It is," Aelin whispered, almost too faint to hear.

Xangtemias. The Scourge of Aegias. Mortal-born son of the Great Deceiver. Aegias's paladins hadn't destroyed Xang's final remains. Josalind had spoken true that night on the ship—they hadn't been able to with the mundane means available to them. Ryn found himself gripped by the image she had described of a wailing babe on a black altar, silenced by a black knife.

The evil old salt will rise again and have us all.

"The *Codex* lies," Ryn whispered.

Aelin kept her back to the skull and clutched the doorframe as if expecting the mystical metal to bolster her resolve. "For the good of us all."

And yet, the Clerisy would have every soul in the Four Kingdoms accept each word as truth, cast in stone. Anything less was blasphemy. "What else does the *Codex* fail to mention?"

"With his last breath, Aegias bound the Sword and the skull together with a seal of his own blood."

"Magic," Ryn said.

"Miracle," she corrected. "By the will of the angels. Xang's spirit is trapped by the power of Mordyth Ral."

"Why didn't Aegias just use the power of Mordyth Ral to destroy the skull?" Ryn asked. *Had he been too close to death?*

"He couldn't bear the cost," Aelin said. "As the *Codex* says, just to kill Xang's earthly body, the Sword stripped the land of life for thirty leagues and weakened anything living for sixty more. To erase Xang utterly, to burn away even his bones—how much further might the destruction have reached? How many more thousands would have died? Aegias couldn't bring himself to do it."

The skull's horrible glare hammered at Ryn, demanded his surrender. The Clerisy had hidden the skull and the Sword in this forsaken place to keep them from . . . whom? Whom ever might have the rest of Xang's bones, along with the means and desire to bring him back?

A dry creak cut sharp, as distinct as a ship's mast at sea or an old oak bending before a storm. The gleam of light from the Sword's blade shifted angle.

Aelin almost jumped out of her skin. "What was that?"

Ryn stepped up to the pedestal. He couldn't see anything on the blade. Not even a speck of dust had settled on it over the turn of centuries. And yet, he was certain Mordyth Ral had just pulled from the skull, or the skull from it, by half a finger's breadth.

"What is it?"

He struggled to find the words. His throat felt pinched shut. This was madness. It couldn't be. And yet, he'd just seen the proof.

"Aegias's seal is breaking," he said.

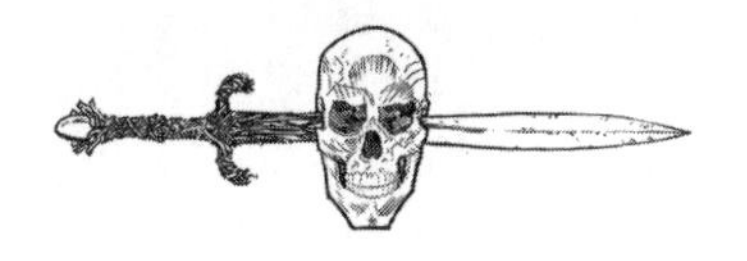

TEN

elin refused to speak until the reliquary was once again lost behind the secret door and the stack of barrels. But nothing could block the images seared into Ryn's mind by that hellish bone and the oddly beautiful blade that trapped it. Not simple stone and oak, not even witch iron.

He heaved the last barrel into place. "Can nothing restore the seal?"

"It was forged by Aegias with the aid of angels, with his dying breath and the last of his life's blood," Aelin said.

So, no. "Then why does it fail now?"

"Decay, maybe. After so long . . ."

He frowned at her sudden silence. "What?"

"Maybe Josalind is the cause."

"How is that possible?"

"How is any of this?" Aelin snapped. "But it's clear she's the vessel of some power with an interest in Xang. In the seven centuries since Aegias, the only sort of . . . manifestation like we saw in the chapel has had one source—the Great Deceiver. False prophets, Sevrendine heretics, death cults—none could withstand the Purity of Flame."

"So the Clerisy says." Ryn made a point of looking to the now-hidden reliquary. "How many other lies has it told 'for the good of us all'?"

"That doesn't matter." Aelin touched his fingers. "These are the moments that put our faith to its truest test, Ryn. Not faith in the Clerisy, but in the values on which it was founded."

Her palm slid over his knuckles. Did she mean to win his obedience with subtle flirtation? It had to be a calculated move, surely. But the earnest need in her eyes suggested otherwise. Maybe with the gravity of the situation she'd just forgotten propriety. Or maybe she only wanted him to think so.

Either way, he wouldn't be played.

"Xang's soul craves release," she said. "Without Aegias's seal, it will find a way. Our only hope is to destroy the Great Deceiver's presence within these walls."

"Our only hope is Mordyth Ral," Ryn said.

That it is.

Until that moment, he hadn't noticed that the Voice had been silent. How long had it been? Since before the high mass in the chapel, for certain. Maybe the crack to the head had something to do with it. Fitting that it should find him now, while his mind flirted with such mad thoughts. Maybe his mad thoughts had called to it.

Aelin looked sideways at him. "You think yourself worthy?"

Ryn swallowed. He was no savior, no warrior messiah, and certainly no Aegias. Sablewood's dead would attest to that. Besides, Aegias had been bound to the Sword till death, or so the *Codex* claimed, a burden that "crushed his soul with constant grief." What kind of man would take on such a thing?

Aelin's nails dug his flesh. "Pull that blade from the skull and it will only hasten Xang's return."

Whether that might be true, Ryn didn't doubt that nothing good would come of breaking the seal. He struggled to understand why he'd even suggested Mordyth Ral might be their only hope. The rogue thought made no sense to him now. He yanked his hand away from hers. "What if you're wrong and you murder her for nothing?"

"What if I don't and the price is three-hundred-and-fifty souls?"

Aelin stood there, jaw set and chin proud, but she couldn't hide the strain in her eyes or the slight tremble of her frame. She truly believed that she faced a choice between one life or hundreds.

But Ryn knew that alone didn't fuel her desperate certainty. Giving Josalind the benefit of the doubt shook the foundation on which her life, her identity, had been built. As a cleric, Aelin had been weaned on a doctrine that dealt in absolutes. Anyone who questioned the Clerisy was either a hostile enemy in league with the Great Deceiver, or a lost and misguided wretch who had condemned themselves to the Hells.

Aside from all else that had happened in the chapel, it was Josalind's words that had sealed her fate in Aelin's eyes—*The ignorance of your false faith is going to damn us all.*

Faith might be an anchor, but it could also become a prison. Ryn had taken a different path from Aelin as a palatar, but the Clerisy ruled all. Why, then, did he think so differently from her? Perhaps because he'd always considered Aegias's true intentions with the Virtues first and the Clerisy's interpretation of them second. He preferred his apples fresh from the tree rather than from someone else's barrel.

Boots clomped down the stairs from the main cellar. Sergeant Mundar. His eyebrow cocked with the question it would have been too impertinent to ask. "I heard voices where I didn't expect any," he said, by way of apology.

Aelin stepped away from Ryn. That vein pulsed on her scalp. "And just what did you hear, Sergeant?" she asked.

Ryn had no doubt that Mundar's life rested on his answer. The sergeant must have known it, too. He dropped his gaze and responded with due promptness. "I heard nothing, Mother Prioress, but sounds echo."

"Do they . . ."

Aelin could have frozen a lake with those two words. Ryn tensed and let his fingers stray to one of his pistols. He'd kept them loaded since the episode in the chapel, given the mood among the garrison. While he had no wish to kill a good man, not again, he had to be prepared for the order should Aelin give it, be prepared for what a man condemned might do in desperation.

"What drove you to come snooping where you don't belong, Sergeant?" Ryn asked.

Mundar cleared his throat. "Sir, you asked to be notified as soon as the prisoner awoke. She has."

The news struck Ryn with equal measures of dread and relief. At last they might get answers—but of what sort? "Thank you, Sergeant, that will be all."

"Yes, sir." Mundar knuckled his brow and fled up the stairs.

Ryn expected a reprimand for taking such liberty, but Aelin only drew a ragged breath and touched his cheek in a surprising gesture of sympathy.

"That cursed girl has one chance to save herself," she said. "I won't give her more."

Aelin may have been willing to grant Josalind a chance—perhaps only for Ryn's sake—but others weren't. Dagetha and two other sisters had joined the guards outside Josalind's cell.

Aelin froze at the sight of the big woman. "The abbess."

"She holds on, by the love of angels and nothing else, Mother Prioress." Dagetha looked to the door of the cell. "How will she die?"

Her blunt features simmered with such hateful grief, Ryn expected she would gladly throttle Josalind with her mannish hands. He took his measure of the men—the palatars he'd considered the most trustworthy. They all hung on Aelin's answer.

Aelin mustered her full shell of authority, but she still ranked as a seedling before Dagetha's oak. "That isn't your concern, Sister. Attend the abbess."

The mood among the men and the other sisters soured into something predatory. Even Mundar wore disgust for Aelin's answer.

Dagetha's brow knotted. "She's a witch—"

Aelin stomped Dagetha's instep and the big woman fell back against the wall. "Flout me again and it will be the lash. She is what I decide she is *after* I've questioned her."

One of the men cursed in disgust. Dagetha pushed herself upright and balled a fist.

Gods be damned. Ryn drew and cocked a pistol in one smooth motion, his attention fixed on Mundar. "Sergeant, get everyone out. Now."

A moment passed, then another. No one moved. Vague mutterings came from Josalind's cell. Dagetha's nasal breaths roared in the silence. Ryn stared at Mundar, pistol poised for the first threatening move, the first wrong word, from anyone. If the sergeant didn't back him, they were done.

At last, Mundar nodded. "You heard him. *Out.*"

Ryn denied himself the luxury of a breath or even a blink until the last man had turned away. He didn't care for Mundar's jaundiced look. The sergeant couldn't be counted on for much longer.

Dagetha gave Aelin a final glare. "Our sisters won't answer to a traitor and coward, Mother Prioress, remember that."

Aelin's shoulders sagged once they were all out of sight. "What either of us thinks about that girl is quickly becoming moot, Lieutenant."

"Let's just start with getting answers, Mother Prioress." Ryn stowed his pistol and stepped up to Josalind's door to peer through the slot. She paced her cell, arms hugged to her chest, head cocked to one side.

"The time's come. The old salt's busting free. Nothing's gonna stop it now," she said to the air at large. "They're gonna hear him. They're gonna come."

"Josalind," Aelin said from behind Ryn. "What happened in the chapel?"

"Bilge-sucking slime toads, why can't they be all-the-way dead and leave me be?"

Josalind stepped too far and cracked her head against the wall. Ryn winced at the sound. She turned and kept pacing without missing a step, heedless of the blood that now welled from the angry scuff over her eye.

"I don't want this," she said. "None of it."

Ryn thumped the door with his fist. "You are facing execution, Josalind."

"Going to burn the messenger—can't say nothing that won't add oil to the fire."

"Aegias save us." Aelin unlocked the door, drew the bolt, and stepped inside. Ryn followed as far as he could, given the tight quarters. His hands flexed with the need to grab Josalind and shake some sanity into her.

Aelin caught Josalind's arm. "If you don't—"

Lightning erupted—from the ceiling or Josalind's arm or both. Ryn couldn't tell for certain. But it most definitely struck Aelin. She shrieked and fell against him. His ears rang, eyes blinded by starbursts. He lowered Aelin's dead weight to the floor. She didn't move. He probed under her jaw. Relief washed through him when he found a pulse.

Josalind gasped. "Spit and spray, what have I done?"

Ryn blinked the spots from his eyes and reached for a pistol. Had she been playing him for a fool all along? "Stay back."

"I didn't mean for it, but she shouldn't have touched me like that, not when . . ."

Ryn looked up at her, searching for deception. Something crouched in those haunted eyes, something new, but he couldn't name it. "Not when what?"

She hugged herself and turned away. "I can't tell you."

"You mean you *won't.*" That should have been the end of it right there—call for help and be done with her. But even now, he didn't see an evil to be feared. He could only marvel at her strength, surviving so long with such a curse, with no one to trust and no means of escape. Still, she'd proven herself to be an unpredictable danger to them all. Even Aegias had said mercy and compassion were sometimes luxuries only fools indulged.

"Dragon's Claw isn't safe anymore," Josalind said. "That's all that matters right now."

"Xang—is he one of your voices?" He had to know but feared the answer all the same. *Could Xang be mine?*

"No," she said. "But I *feel* him, gathering all around, like a monster tangled in my nets, rising to drag me down."

"The monster right now is that mob outside," Ryn said.

Josalind cocked her head. "Should have blasted them all when we had the chance."

His nape tickled with a sudden chill. That voice wasn't hers, not entirely, at least. It echoed in that same eerie way as in the chapel.

She blinked and looked at him with a sudden smile that made no sense at all. The first true smile he'd ever seen from her that didn't come as rueful or sad. "You won't let me burn, will you?"

Ryn shook his head in despair. "There's nothing I can do, Josalind."

She knelt and clutched his arm with feverish strength. "No. You will find a way. You have to."

Aelin began to stir.

Josalind's earnest plea left him stretched between pity and frustration. "I will. I swear it." What else could he say, when she so obviously needed to hear it? It wouldn't matter much, once the fire started.

"Lieutenant," Aelin mumbled.

Ryn helped her up as boots sounded on the stairs. Tovald came at them, pistols in hand, Mundar and others on his heels. "Report, Lieutenant."

Aelin, face whiter than pastry flour, pushed Ryn away and braced herself against the door. "She burns without delay, Captain. See it done."

Each word sliced Ryn to the bone. He teased the butt of his pistol, weighing the odds of grabbing Josalind and fighting their way clear of the abbey. It was hopeless, of course—armed guards on the walls, the only way out barred by gate and portcullis. Even then, where could they go, with frigid sea on one side and grenlich on the other?

"Step aside, Lieutenant," Tovald said.

Josalind touched Ryn's arm. "You know what needs to be done."

He did, but the notion horrified him as much as doing nothing at all. The men openly wore their fear, their contempt, their carnal hunger to see Josalind burn. Even Tovald had a manic look in his eye that was beneath him. Ryn wanted to cave each of their faces with a maul.

Fear paints men as the beasts they are.

Ryn sidled past Aelin and took a deliberate step toward the palatars. Whatever look he bore made them all give ground. "Any man who lets harm come to her before the pyre, I'll beat the penance out of his hide." He looked straight at Tovald.

The captain nodded. "You heard him, troopers."

Ryn made to stride past them. He had to leave this cellar before the need to look back got the better of him. The sight of Josalind's eyes again would sap his will to do what he had to. The only mercy he could grant.

Tovald grabbed his wrist. "This is for your own good, son." He looked to the men. "Jarest, Corballys—confine the lieutenant here until it's done."

Ryn's heart clenched into a bitter knot. The coward had condemned Josalind long before Aelin. Time to sate the wolves with some meat—that's all Tovald cared about.

"Damn you." Ryn lashed out with a fist and managed to snap the captain across the jaw before someone caught his arms. Other hands took his weapons.

Tovald easily shook off the blow and slammed his fist into Ryn's gut. Ryn saw it coming and tried to steel himself, but having his arms pinned and shoulders pulled back conspired against him. The captain's knuckles felt like they dug far enough to brush a kidney.

Tovald leaned close, breath thick with malt whiskey. "You damn yourself, in the eyes of the men. Think about where that might leave you, come tomorrow."

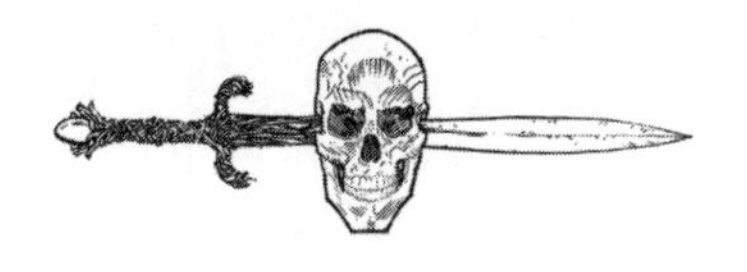

ELEVEN

They had put manacles of plain iron on Josalind's wrists—heavy, awkward things meant for thicker arms. The abbey didn't stock witch iron.

Tovald didn't say another word to Ryn, but his glower left little doubt that the matter was far from settled. *You damn yourself.* Had the dark looks from others suggested he now had to fear a knife in the back?

After they had led Josalind off, Ryn slumped in the hallway outside of her cell, the image of a man beaten. Playing the part came easily, given how his head throbbed and his gut ached from Tovald's punch. His hands had been quickly bound behind his back with a bit of rope. A second pair of manacles hadn't been brought and Josalind's cell couldn't be locked shut to imprison him. Her lightning blast had arced from the iron lock plate, leaving the oak around it scorched and the key fused to the tumblers inside.

He let himself slump down against the wall far enough to tease from his right boot the shiv he always kept hidden there and got to work. From the corner of his eye, he took stock of his two chaperones—Jarest and Corballys. Both men wore their regular kits of mail and hardened leather, with arming swords and daggers at their belts. Jarest had propped his loaded musket against the wall. Corballys had a pistol hooked on his belt at half cock, the frizzen closed—primed and loaded. They stood off to Ryn's left, about ten feet away.

The shiv's edge slowly frayed through the rope's fibers. Ryn tried to be careful to avoid drawing their attention, but he still managed to nick his wrist. "You're going to miss the entertainment," he said, without looking up.

"Just as well, sir. I've no wish to see it," Jarest said.

"Damn the Deceiver for tainting such a hump-worthy sweetmeat," Corballys added, as tactless as ever.

"Bite your tongue, man," Jarest said. "Can't you see the lieutenant had feelings for the girl?"

"I only meant . . ." Corballys frowned and stepped toward Ryn, hand reaching for his pistol. "What are you—"

Ryn snapped the remaining fiber with a quick jerk, thrust himself up, and buried the shiv in Corballys's thigh. The man howled and clutched Ryn's wrist with his left hand even as he tried to throw a punch with his right. Ryn easily blocked the blow. Corballys staggered in a half circle that dragged Ryn around and exposed his flank. He twisted his wrist free and caught Corballys with an uppercut to the chin that sprawled him out, senseless.

Steel glinted in the lamplight from the corner of Ryn's eye. He ducked and backstepped. Jarest's dagger brushed over his head in a reverse grip. At least the man had only meant to knock him cold with the pommel rather than skewer a kidney. Ryn tackled him to the ground and smashed his brow into the bridge of Jarest's nose. The blow left him seeing fresh fireworks and his neck in spasms. He heaved himself up and finished Jarest with a hard right.

Skull pounding like a clash of anvils, Ryn hugged the wall and crawled to his feet. A dizzying void hungered to swallow him. He shook it off, retrieved his weapons, and took Jarest's musket. His feet didn't feel connected to his brain. He staggered to the stairs and struggled to take them one at a time.

Outside, he made for the cloister's colonnade, where it met the wall of the Keep in a thick tangle of grapevines and deep shadow. The crisp wash of evening air helped settle his stomach and clear his wits.

He hoisted himself up on top of the colonnade's stone arches and spread out on his belly. The tart sweetness of the grapes he'd mashed stuffed his nose. He traced the cold contours of the musket's trigger. Maybe he'd cut his trigger finger off for what it was about to do, for the life it was about to take. That might be penance enough to appease Aelin for denying her this gruesome spectacle. It wouldn't do much to scrub the stain from his soul. He didn't have fingers enough for that.

Tovald had kept his word about giving Josalind her dignity. Six men had escorted her from the Keep to the abbey's common yard in a tight cordon with swords drawn. The captain led the way, grim and somber. The rest of the garrison stood assembled, mouths shut to the last man. Ryn couldn't judge their mood. Toy soldiers all lined up, true to their oaths to serve and obey, no matter what they had stewing inside.

The sisters and their wards had gathered on the opposite side of the pyre, swaddled in those bulky cloaks, hoods drawn to hide their faces. Did they hunger for Josalind's death, too? Did they bear regret for murdering one of their own? Only Dagetha stood among them with head bare. She almost grinned with anticipation.

Aelin waited for Josalind next to the pyre. A torch roared and spit in her hand. Ryn heard nothing else in the entire abbey over the thud of his pulse.

The call of a spotted owl carried on the damp air from beyond the wall. Another answered.

A stool sat at the stake's base. Bundles of kindling were stacked around, but not enough. The bigger the fire, the better the odds Josalind would succumb to the heat and smoke before the flames reached her. This fire would be too small. She'd burn before dying.

Ryn fingered the trigger. He had to do this. It was the only thing he could do. He'd done no less for Scorben in the Bone Yard.

One life matters not.

Be silent.

Josalind walked to the stool and mounted it without pause. Aelin said something while Tovald hooked the manacles up over the spike that had been hammered into the stake. Josalind just nodded. Ryn couldn't make out her expression. Tovald pushed the kindling into place and stepped away.

Aelin raised the torch high and swept it around as she addressed the crowd. "There is no doubt of this woman's guilt. This is no dispute of her crimes against the Holy Clerisy and its flock." Her voice shook, but the torch sank with sure deliberation toward the kindling. "Let us all bear witness. On this night, we purge this place of the Great Deceiver's taint. We free ourselves of a wicked influence."

Ryn sighted down the musket's barrel. The range was about forty yards, his line of sight clear. He imagined the ball, slamming into Josalind's chest, shearing flesh and shattering bone as it plowed through her heart. She wouldn't even have a chance to cry out, a strangled gasp maybe, before fainting from shock and blood loss.

Tears blurred his eyes. He clawed them away with a growl.

The spotted owl called again from beyond the wall, closer now. Another answered.

Aelin brought the torch to the kindling. The wood caught quick, hungry to burn. Smoke fumes made an odd blend with the grapes' sweetness.

Josalind turned her head to the sky.

Ryn tried to tighten his finger around the trigger. It wouldn't budge.

Would you hear her screams, smell the sizzle of her flesh?

The Voice's flat delivery only infuriated him more. *Go to Hell.*

The Hells cannot bear me.

Good. I'll be free of you there.

Flames circled Josalind entirely now, crackling and kicking up sparks. She coughed on the smoke.

"Aegias forgive me," Ryn said as his fingers finally obeyed his command to move.

Darkness swallowed the abbey.

The pyre, the torch in Aelin's hand, even the glow of lamplight from the windows of the abbey's buildings, winked out in the same instant.

Ryn jerked his hand even as he fired, sending the ball wide of its target. After staring into the fire, he had no night vision at all. Everyone in the common had the same problem. Cries of dismay and confusion erupted from palatar and sister alike.

The owls called again.

Something hit the ground with a meaty thud and a clank of metal off to Ryn's right. A muted scrape sounded from the wall above, like a grapple with its hooks padded to cut the noise.

Gods be damned!

Not owls—grenlich, passing signals. The sentries on the wall had likely been distracted by the scene below instead of minding their duty. They might have all been picked off by now. The grenlich had chosen the perfect time to strike.

They're gonna hear him. They're gonna come, Josalind had said.

It couldn't be coincidence. They'd come for Xang, to free him and swear allegiance. That had to be why Scorben had been interrogated during his flaying, to plan for this.

But that still didn't explain the sudden darkness.

Ryn rose and gave a roar to be heard from one end of the abbey to the other. "Attack! Attack! To the walls!"

"Lieutenant?" Tovald called.

"*Sir*—grenlich scale the walls!"

Tovald didn't hesitate. "Sergeants—to stations."

Ryn's eyes had adjusted enough to track the organized chaos that erupted in the common. Palatars split into their troops to make for the walls and break out the armory. Sisters herded the wards to the Keep. No one paid any attention to Josalind, still shackled to the stake. He couldn't spot Aelin.

During an attack, Ryn had command of the gate. He wanted nothing more than to rush to Josalind and hack her free of that damned post, but the abbey's safety came first. It had been years since grenlich had mounted any real threat to the walls, but with Xang's will at work, nothing could be taken for granted.

He slid down the mass of vines from the top of the colonnade, musket still in hand. A light waxed in the corner of his eye, where the Keep's flank merged with the curtain wall. The old stone had come alive with a light all its own. It glowed soft in shades of pale blue, more like glass now than granite.

His nape hairs prickled. The grenlich of Dragon's Claw didn't muster any magic, any more than those of Sablewood.

DO NOT LET THEM TAKE THE SKULL.

The words ravaged his mind with a hail of hot lead. He slumped against the colonnade, on the verge of blacking out. "Grenlich?"

There is no time.

An anxious fear whipped his feet into motion. It had no cause, no focus. He just knew he had to get down to that witch-iron door. Nothing else mattered. He stumbled up the stairs to the Keep's doors.

Sisters still crowded the entrance. "Make way." Ryn shouldered past them with little care for courtesy, using the musket as a sweep and leaving plenty of bruises in his wake. He ignored the cries of protest and took the stairs down in such a mad churn of feet he almost pitched headfirst.

Down in the cellars, he paused to catch his breath and hear over his racing pulse. The lamps here were out as well—another mystery that stank of magic. He felt his way along the walls, trusting in memory. Before long, a pale light, too blue-white to be a lamp, spilled down the passage and guided him to the subcellar. Whispers followed—not the guttural tones of grenlich.

Ryn padded down the subcellar stairs. The hidden door had been opened and the strange light came up the passage. The barrels had been moved but they blocked his view. He slipped behind them just as the tumblers of the lock on the witch-iron door gave way. The intruders must have picked it. The door squealed open.

"By Fraia's Grace, it's true." A man's voice, speaking Islari Common with a strange accent.

Ryn's eyes widened. *Fraia's Grace.* Only a heretic would say such a thing, one sort in particular—a follower of Sevren. But the Clerisy had wiped the Sevrendine from the Kingdoms ages ago.

Ryn peeked around the barrel. The man was a fair-skinned Jendal—a giant of a man, as Jendals so often were, at least half a head taller than Ryn. His scalp nearly scraped the ceiling and his broad shoulders crowded the passage. He had sandy-brown hair cut short with a full beard to match, both streaked with traces of red fire. Jendalia had been the breeding ground of the Sevrendine Heresy, but the woman with the man was no Jendal—her deep brown skin and tight curls of black hair were foreign to all the Kingdoms. Not even the olive-skinned Teishlians of the distant south had such an appearance.

They hadn't dressed for burglary, or even combat. The woman came as modest as any sister, in a smock of homespun wool and a vest buttoned to accentuate her buxom figure. The man could have been a farmer headed for chores, considering his threadbare frock coat and the tattered straw hat with a broad brim he had tucked under his arm. But Ryn knew the carriage of a seasoned warrior when he saw it.

Given the man's size and the thickness of his arms, the prudent thing would have been to slip away for reinforcements. But the door already stood open. Ryn couldn't risk letting this pair out of sight. His cartridge pouch didn't carry reloads with the caliber and grain for a musket. He set the long gun aside and checked the prime of his pistols.

"Can we just . . . pick them up?" the man asked.

"Grace Above, how else do you expect to cart them off?" the woman said.

Taking a deep breath, Ryn cocked his pistols and stepped around the corner. "Don't move."

They both did, of course.

Golden sparks arced between the woman's fingers. Witchcraft, sorcery, it didn't matter. Sudden fear prompted Ryn to shoot for her heart with both pistols. She didn't have a chance.

The man moved faster than any man should. He lashed out with some monster of a sword that could have sheared a horse in half—a sword with a white blade that appeared out of nowhere. It shattered the lead balls inches from the woman's chest. The light that lit the passage came from that blade. First Mordyth Ral, now this.

"We're not looking for trouble," the man said with surprising calm.

His ice-blue eyes bore a mischievous twinkle, as if he were having a quiet laugh at Ryn's expense. He might have been in his midthirties, with lean and angular features creased around the eyes by laugh lines. Ryn suspected the body under that bulky frock coat to be equally chiseled.

Considering that discharged pistols were little better than clubs, Ryn had no choice but to take the man at his word. He fought to consider the situation with a rational mind. They didn't mean to harm him . . . not yet at least. Those golden sparks still danced between the woman's outspread fingers. Surely some unnatural means of attack but here he stood, unscorched despite his attempt to kill her. She hadn't even flinched. He took the woman for the elder of the two, though her broad face seemed ageless, with high, heavy cheekbones. She had clear gray eyes as sharp as an owl's. They bored into him with intensity enough to slice clean through.

Ryn stowed the pistols and drew his longsword with calm deliberation. Its yard-long blade seemed paltry compared to the man's witch blade. "Trespassing is grounds for arrest." That seemed paltry, too; he wanted to wince as he said it. He cursed himself an idiot for coming down here alone.

The man's lips peeled back in a feral way that could have been either a smile or a snarl. That damned twinkle in his eyes deepened. "Did you see a sign?" he asked the woman. "I didn't see one." He looked back to Ryn. "There should be a sign."

"You are in well over your head, Master Palatar," she said, offering no hint that she shared her companion's sense of humor.

"I'm not the thief," Ryn said.

The man jerked his thumb over his shoulder. "Do you know what you've got in there?"

"Xang's skull and the Sword of Aegias," Ryn said. "And that is where they're going to stay."

"Aegias's seal is breaking," the woman said.

"And what would you know about that?" Josalind asked.

Her unexpected presence gave Ryn a start. He glanced back at her. "How did you get free?"

Josalind rubbed at her chafed flesh. "Small hands and big wrists." She thrust her chin at the woman. "Why are you here?"

The woman looked hard at her and frowned. She saw something that rattled her where getting shot at hadn't. "Dear girl, what is that power that possesses you?"

"Answer the question," Josalind said.

The big man lunged forward with a one-handed strike, hat still tucked under his left arm. His big blade came straight for Ryn's bandaged head, flat-side first to knock him senseless. It wouldn't take much, under the circumstances.

Ryn flung one arm back to sweep Josalind clear and deflected the attack offside. The man struck with such power he almost tore Ryn's sword from his hand. Both blades screeched as their tips scraped wall and ceiling. In such tight quarters, Ryn had the advantage, and his mood didn't leave him as chivalrous as his opponent. His counterstrike scored a shallow cut along the big man's ribs. The exertion left Ryn's temples throbbing with a harsh rhythm worthy of a bass drum.

The man drew back and pressed his hand to the wound. "Not bad for a fellow with a cracked skull." He most definitely snarled now. Still, those eyes bore a twinkle that implied Ryn was nothing more than an annoying insect.

"Enough," the woman said.

Golden fire blasted from her fingers. It struck like a fist, two yards tall. Ryn suffered an explosion of jolting pain, then felt nothing at all.

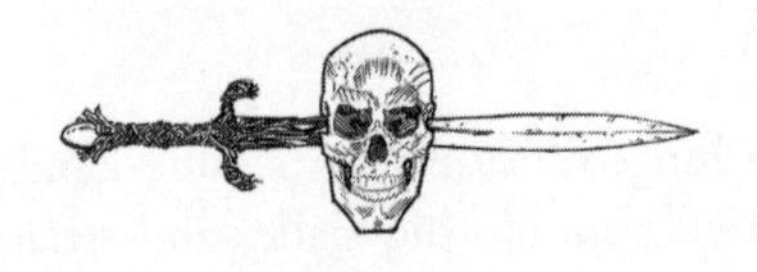

TWELVE

yn."

Someone shook him. That made his head throb all the more.

"By the Weeping Mists, Ryn, wake up. They're getting away."

He dragged his eyes open and still couldn't see. They'd been left in the musty dark of the subcellar. His whole body ached from the blast of that witch woman's hellfire, no different than being stuffed in a barrel and kicked down a mountainside. Josalind's breath blew moist against his lips. He savored it like a fine wine.

"How long?" he mumbled.

"Not long." She pressed her hands to his cheeks and kissed him.

Her lips were warm and soft, just as he'd imagined they would be. Their warmth spread through his whole body until he tingled to the last finger and toe, and another place besides. His eyes widened. He clutched her wrists and pushed her away. "What in Hells did you just—"

"Do you feel better?" Her words were clipped short with pain. She sounded suddenly exhausted, too.

"Why would . . ." But he did. His aches had fled. He probed under the bandages around his head. Crusted blood pulled at his hair, but the wound had healed. He tensed with a sudden, wary fear, at odds with the blissful warmth he'd just felt. Witchcraft, it had to be, but he'd never heard tell of a healing kiss from a servant of the Great Deceiver. A kiss that cursed, maybe. He pulled off the bandages and tossed them. "How did you do that?"

"It doesn't matter right now." She rose to her feet and drew him up after her. "Come on, we've no time for lazing about."

"Where's my sword? I can't see—"

She pressed a familiar wire-wrapped hilt into his hand. "Come." She pulled him along with far too brisk of a pace considering they were as blind as bats.

"How can you tell where you're going?"

"I just can," she said.

Do not argue. There is no time.

The Voice came faint and muffled now. Ryn should have protested—too many things at play here didn't make sense or pointed to the Dark Arts. But the Voice compelled him in a way that he found difficult to ignore. Nor could he allow heretics to just make off with the relics. If the *Codex* could be trusted, Mordyth Ral was a force even more destructive than Xang.

Josalind placed his hand on a stair rail. Light with a bluish tint outlined a door above.

"The kitchen pantry," she said.

That put them at the northeast corner of the abbey, right where he'd first seen the stone give light. Common sense demanded he take the time to reload his pistols, but the same urgency that had compelled him into the cellars after the skull in the first place wouldn't allow it. He charged up the stairs and slapped the latch as his shoulder struck the door.

The pantry lay empty. The thieves had already gone.

Ryn stopped short and stared at a portion of the pantry wall—the exterior wall. A circle about three yards across rippled with a glassy sheen, more like water than stone. Had it been their means of escape? It grew smaller as he watched.

Josalind gave him a shove from behind. "Quick—before it closes."

Of course, just walk through yards of stone, trusting in some manner of witchery that could fade in a blink. He'd endured the butchery and madness of battle. Faced the prospect of a cruel death at the hands of grenlich. Never had he felt terror as he did now. His bowels threatened to gush down his trouser legs.

The portal had already shrunk by a third.

Coward.

Josalind grabbed his hand and dragged him toward it. "Come on."

He went.

Two steps in, Ryn realized he couldn't breathe.

He'd become water, soaking through the stone as if the wall were a wave-swept beach, aware of how every bit of himself moved around each grain of sand. The stone's grittiness gouged his eyes. It crammed his throat and gut as it slid between and through skin, meat, and bone. He couldn't see past a blue haze. Only Josalind's sure hand holding tight to his kept panic at bay.

He had to make it through before his lungs gave out. *Just keep walking.* Wading through mountain snow came at less cost. Falter for even a blink and he'd be finished, a fly in amber, trapped forever.

And then they were through. He collapsed to his knees and gasped for breath, wondering if any part of him had been left behind. The chaos of battle raged from the walls above. Muskets and swivel guns fired, charring the damp air with brimstone.

A guttural growl sounded close. Josalind shrieked.

Ryn's sword arm flung out just in time to deflect the mace before it crushed his skull.

He came up on one knee and smashed his fist into the grenlich's groin. Edges of metal sliced his knuckles and made him wish for gauntlets. Still, the hit landed square. The grenlich stumbled back with a grunt and dropped his guard. Ryn thrust out into the fiend's gut, gave his sword a twist, then yanked free. A splash of gore followed. The grenlich toppled with a choked gasp, clutching the wound.

Ryn got his feet under him and put his back to the wall beside Josalind. They sheltered in the shadowed nook where the swell of the Keep jutted out from the main wall. Weapons clashed and men screamed on the walls above. Ryn burned with the need to join the fight. This was his command, his brothers. It didn't matter that he despised them for their eagerness to see Josalind burn, for their stupid ignorance. This was no fitting end for them.

Three grenlich rounded the curve of the Keep. Ryn groped around, found a rock with decent heft, and tossed it. The thud and tumble caught their attention. He charged.

The first grenlich barely had time to squawk before Ryn sliced his throat open. The second ducked aside with a curse and raised a spear. Ryn was off his footing and too close for a killing strike. He smashed his sword hilt into the bastard's ugly face to knock him off balance.

Before Ryn could finish the job, the last grenlich came at him in a blur of steel. She wielded a prized piece of booty—a palatar's arming sword. Speed and fury couldn't compensate for lack of skill. Ryn gave ground and let her overextend. It didn't take long for his chance to come. He ended it quick with a clean thrust through the heart.

Her wolf eyes glazed over. He plucked the arming sword from her limp grasp as she fell. Grenlich thought a warrior's soul lived on in the weapon they held when they died. Hers had no right to this one.

He should have been thinking less about souls and swords and more about the second grenlich whose snout he'd flattened. A wet snort from behind gave warning. He fell back and turned on his heel, one sword raised to block, the other to strike.

The grenlich's spear thrust through a gap in Ryn's defense to skewer him, then the brute yelped and his attack faltered before it could land. His knees collapsed. Ryn swatted the spear aside and finished him.

Behind the grenlich stood Josalind with a wild look in her eyes. She held the first grenlich's cleaver, dark with blood.

"Are you all right?" he asked.

She flung the cleaver away like it had stung. "We have to get to the dock." She was off at a run before the words had left her mouth.

Gods be damned. He glanced around to be sure no other grenlich had spotted them before chasing after her.

The ground around the east flank of the abbey fell away in a treacherous slope of loose rocks and exposed roots. He stumbled and tripped several times, trying to keep up before they reached the path that curved down to the shoreline. Josalind skipped along with such ease she appeared to float. He couldn't fathom it.

Corpses littered the way. Grenlich, a dozen or more, no doubt felled by that big man's monstrous sword, considering how thoroughly they'd been sliced and sheared. Heads and limbs lay scattered in a macabre puzzle. Ryn caught up with Josalind and grabbed her arm. "There might be more—stay behind me."

"Pick up your feet, then," she said, but she let him lead.

Moored to the stone piling that served as a dock, a skiff with an open hull bobbed in the swells of the bay with its triangular sail already unfurled. Only fools would dare sail the Iceberg Sea this late in the season in such a cork of a vessel. The first safe harbor free of grenlich lay hundreds of miles east. There had to be a proper ship waiting out at sea.

That witch woman sat at the tiller. The big man stood on the dock preparing to cast off the lines.

Ryn ran down the path. "Hold!"

The man turned quick. His white sword wasn't in sight. Ryn stopped short at the foot of the dock and Josalind almost plowed into him. They'd charged down there with more urgency than sense, heedless of how outmatched they were with witchery in the mix.

"You brought the grenlich down on us," Ryn said. When in doubt, fling an accusation.

"That we did not," the man said with mild amusement. "Or did you not notice how many we took off your hands?" He set that tattered straw hat firm on his head. "You are welcome, by the way."

Ryn couldn't see the man's eyes in the dark but expected they still carried that damned twinkle. "You serve the Great Deceiver," he said.

"Wrong again."

The woman didn't move, but her attention clung to Ryn. The Clerisy taught that the Sevrendine held to their belief in the false goddess Fraia even as they burned for it, never willing to admit that the Deceiver alone answered their prayers. Had that been another lie to mask a truth it couldn't tolerate? Ryn took a couple of steps onto the dock, both swords in hand. "I can't let you take those relics. They're too dangerous."

The man chuckled and glanced at his companion before looking back to Ryn. "You are one dogged fellow, I will grant you that."

"And you are Sevrendine, are you not?" Ryn said.

The chuckle died, as did any evidence of humor in the man's tone. "The Sevrendine are no more."

Ryn took another step. "Then who are you?"

"No one," the woman said. "We were never here."

Ryn didn't notice the fog until it swallowed him. It welled up as thick and heavy as cold gruel to hide any trace of the skiff.

Josalind's small fist thumped him in the back. "Go!"

He darted forward and almost pitched headfirst off the dock before realizing he'd reached its end. The heretics had vanished. He heard no oar cut the water, felt not even a whisper of a breeze that could fill a sail, but somehow, they were gone.

"Wait," he called. "We need passage. She is sentenced to die." The plea burst from him out of sheer desperation. Heretics or not, they were a means of escaping this cursed rock.

Leave the Claw. The traitorous thought surprised him, and not because of any loyalty to the Clerisy. Leaving meant turning renegade, becoming a wanted man. Capture for that offense would surely mean a noose or being left to rot in a dark hole, stripped of any chance to atone for Sablewood. He'd descend into gibbering madness for certain with nothing but the Voice for company.

His plea went unanswered. The woman's fog began to lift, revealing nothing but empty sea.

He clanged the flats of both swords together. "Gods be damned."

A cheer rose from the ramparts of the abbey. Another followed. The grenlich had been routed. The fact both pleased and frightened him. They couldn't go back. He sheathed his longsword, slipped the other under his belt beside it, and ran past Josalind.

She followed after. "Where are we going?"

He rolled over the first body he found and choked on the sudden reek of ruptured bowels. "Find bedrolls, flint, tinder—anything for a night in the woods. Be quick about it."

He patted the body down but didn't find much. Grenlich traveled light. The next body sported more trophies from the garrison's dead—a palatar's battle gauntlets of leather and articulated steel. They proved a decent fit. A third body must have been that of a chief or war captain, by the look of the dress. Ryn freed the big brute's corpse of a deerskin cloak trimmed in ermine and a heavy silver brooch. The brooch offered something of value he could barter, though he couldn't imagine when such an opportunity might arise. Still, it seemed familiar.

The corpse shook with a gurgling cough. A hand seized his wrist. He grabbed for his dagger.

"Where be the skull, strappling?"

Ryn's hand froze. He squinted to see the grenlich's face. Ogagoth, the tar-vrul. Their vow to cross swords wouldn't come now, given how Ogagoth's guts glistened in the starlight. That big man's white sword had denied them the chance.

"What would you know about that?" Ryn asked.

"It calls, we come."

"In service to the Great Deceiver."

"No." Blunt claws dug Ryn's flesh. "Vauka'rau have vision, warn us. Son of Dark Father rise again, we become slaves again. Freedom lost."

A hacking fit got the better of him. Ryn flinched away in disgust and wiped the spray from his face. A vauka'rau was a clan matriarch of sorts, a priestess, too, so far as he understood it. The outcast grenlich Quintan had befriended back in Sablewood, Ostath, had told of how his clan had fled their masters in the east untold centuries ago. All the clans that plagued northern Morlandia had done so and given up the dark magic that had been their birthrights.

Ryn had always mistrusted Ostath and anything he told Quintan, expecting the grenlich spun whatever yarn might earn him a ration of food. That same wariness governed him now. "You expect me to believe you came to protect the skull?"

"To protect ourselves," Ogagoth said. "We make it safe before *they* come for . . ."

Ryn leaned close as the tar-vrul's voice trailed off into a raspy whisper. "Who?"

"Lost brothers . . . rule the sky . . . fear them . . . Kun-Xang . . ."

Ogagoth choked on a rush of blood and expired. Ryn didn't know what to make of his deathbed confession and didn't have the time to dwell on it. *Xang*, he understood; *Kun* meant nothing. He found Josalind near the abbey's south wall. They were close enough to be spotted, well within musket range.

"I found these," she whispered.

Ryn saw a woolen blanket, furred moccasins, honing stones, and didn't worry about the rest. She still ran around barefoot in nothing but her shift. He bundled it all in Ogagoth's cloak and led her away in a crouch. Their movements in the shadows could too easily be mistaken for those of grenlich. At any moment, he expected to hear a sentry raise alarm, the roar of a musket just before its ball shattered his spine. He didn't breathe easy until they were back at the dock.

Josalind planted her heels when he tried to lead her down the shoreline past the old shipwreck. "Where are we going?"

He shoved the bundle into her arms. "Cover up, there'll be frost tonight."

"Then what?"

"How in Hells should I know?" The words rang harsh over the gentle lap of the surf. A nesting gull took wing with an irate cry. He flexed his hands and drew a deep breath to smother his temper. "If we go back there, you will burn. I'll have to answer for disobeying orders and assault. Then there will be questions about how we got outside the wall, how that door was opened, and who took the relics. The truth is likely to earn me a choice spot on the pyre beside you. I can't think of a lie that will serve much better."

Josalind had the moccasins on and drew Ogagoth's cloak tight around her shoulders. "What do we do?" Her voice sounded small and vulnerable, that of a frightened child desperate for answers.

He took her roughly by the wrist. Too little made sense, too much left him wondering if she had bewitched him after all. Still, if he truly doubted her, his most rational course would have been to march her back to the abbey, label the heretics as her accomplices, and offer to light the damned pyre himself.

He'd rather chop off his own hand. Did that make him chivalrous or just a moonstruck fool? Quintan would have said both. Ryn suffered too much sour anger over the whole sorry state of affairs to consider himself either.

"For now, find someplace safe," he said.

"Safe? Where's that?"

Ryn let her go. "The Bone Yard." He proceeded to reload his pistols. "*If* we somehow manage to slip past the grenlich, you and I are going to have ourselves a nice little chat."

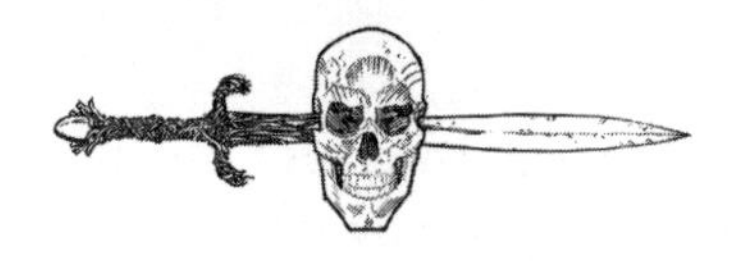

THIRTEEN

Ryn and Josalind took the night as quickly as they could without rousing a gods-awful racket snapping branches or tripping over roots.

He could think of nowhere else to go other than the Bone Yard. Grenlich wouldn't trespass out of reverence, while the garrison believed it to be a den of the Deceiver. Maybe it was, but desperation made even mad ideas seem reasonable.

Halfway there, the rolling echo of musket and swivel gun fire caught up with them. The grenlich must have remustered for another attack. Their dead would be piling around the walls by now—penance for their bloody handiwork on the harvest moon. All because they sought to *prevent* Xang's return? Ryn found that hard to reconcile. Pointless slaughter now with the relics already gone.

The rumble of battle had hushed the forest, but the silence only plagued him with more time to consider what he'd done, the line he'd crossed, by stepping through that wall. His anxiety deepened into a prickly fear as they passed the Bone Yard's boundary. The stacks loomed high, crowned by those horned skulls. Little Supeidos had risen, just past full, to paint the night with blue shadows that heightened the ghastly and haunted feel of the place.

Josalind crowded close. "They watch us."

Ryn hissed at her. "Don't say that, for Aegias's sake." As before, he imagined those empty sockets alive with reptilian eyes, staring at him with patient expectation. If she said another word, he just might lose his resolve and flee.

"But they do. They don't mean us harm, but they do."

"How can you know such a thing?"

"I just can."

He stowed his pistols, yanked their bundle of looted gear from her hands, and threw it down. A rock poked out of the earth nearby, flat-topped and high as a chair. He marched her over by the shoulders, plunked her down on top of it, and held her there. "Look me in the eye and tell me something that makes sense." He half expected the Voice in his head to chime in with an opinion of its own, but it didn't.

She looked up at him. Her eyes caught the moonlight with a silvery sheen that wasn't natural, like a cat's. She could probably see like one, considering how little trouble she had with the dark. "You'll think me mad."

"That might be better than thinking you're a witch—the Great Deceiver's willing whore."

"You know I'm not." She squirmed under his grip. "Let me go."

"Give me a fair answer."

Her eyes flashed cruel with silver fire. "LET ME GO."

Her palms slammed into his chest with unnatural strength. He flew back and crashed into a stack of bones. The pile shifted and the giant skull slid off, snout first. He heaved himself aside just in time to avoid being crushed. Wind gone, ribs aching, he staggered to his feet and drew pistol and sword. He doubted either would make much difference after what he'd seen in the chapel, but he had no other assurance.

She hugged herself now, head down and shoulders drooped, as if he'd been the one to assault her. He circled around, wary, bewildered, fighting to get his wind back. His breath billowed plumes in the cooling air.

"My voices—I know their names now, since the chapel," she said.

"Oh?" He could manage nothing better.

"Sovaris—she's the loudest, as shrill as wind in the rigging. It makes my ears ache. Mygalor doesn't say much, but he's got a moan that saps the life out of me. Koglar's all thump and bluster, a storm rolling out of the mountains. And Kyvros . . ." She gave a ragged sigh. "He's the worst of all—always so angry. Sometimes I think he'll burn me up from the inside."

Sovaris. Mygalor. Koglar. Kyvros. But these were the names of the Four, the dead gods. His sword's point sank to the ground. "You *are* mad."

"Would you rather that I was?" Those cat eyes shone in the gloom. "Would that be easier? But you've seen the things I've done." She touched her lips. "You've felt it."

He wouldn't soon forget that kiss. "The gods are dead."

"But the hearts of them survive. So long as the world lives, they'll linger."

Ryn glanced at the nearest bone stacks with a start, certain he'd just heard something—whispering, like before, when he'd led the recovery party here. More than dead gods lingered. "But how can you hear them?"

She looked to the sky. "My ma said I was strange because she squeezed me out late under twin full moons on the winter solstice—I wouldn't come till the ill omens had their glory." She raked back that tangle of curls and shrugged. "I don't know. I just can."

"What about the chapel?"

Josalind looked up at Supeidos—the sailor's moon, which made it Sovaris's moon, too, given the water goddess's ancient associations with river and sea. The Kingdoms tracked the harvest moon by the cycles of the larger moon, Preidos. This year, for the first time in Ryn's life, the first full showings after the autumn equinox by both moons had coincided on the same night.

"This is a place of power, of magic," Josalind said.

He looked warily about. "Magic?"

"The *natural* magic that fills all living things. That's why the dragons chose it as their resting place. The grenlich sacrifice, the moons—it all roused something, gave Sovaris and her brothers power to get *inside* me, to *connect* with me, in a way they couldn't before. That's what happened in the chapel." She studied her hands. "They've got the power to do things now, *through* me."

She claimed to be something much worse than a mere witch—a prophet, a heretic, a rival to the Clerisy itself. And here he was, likely already branded a deserter and apostate, in league with her. The Clerisy would hunt them both with eager prejudice.

He had a sudden need to sit down. The fallen dragon skull offered a handy perch. He stowed his pistol and took it. The Bone Yard didn't hold any horrors for him, not anymore. How could it? No spook or shade could compare to the hell that faced him now. It might be a kinder end to just walk out into the dark and let the grenlich have him for a good flaying.

Josalind came over to sit beside him. "Hearing all this is rather like getting kicked in the head by a mule, isn't it?"

"If the gods still haunt the earth, then there is no Kingdom Beyond, is there?" He'd always had his doubts in the absence of real proof. On the other hand, the Hells seemed real enough—the practices of witchcraft and sorcery made it hard to argue otherwise. Didn't that mean there had to be a Kingdom Beyond, too? For everything an opposite?

She placed her hand over his. "No, I don't think so."

"But what about the angels?" Ryn said, feeling desperate now. "If demons in the Deceiver's name torment the Damned in the Hells, then—"

"I don't think it works the way the Clerisy says. Demons and angels don't make a point of shepherding our souls one way or the other."

"Your voices told you this?"

"Not so much. It's just . . . a feeling I have."

Her quiet certainty darkened his already grim mood. Where did that leave Quintan and Tamantha and Sara and Jaryk and all the rest of Sablewood's dead? Where did that leave anyone? Did their souls just wander the land in limbo without purpose or respite? Ryn imagined legions of them, rarely heard or seen, growing mad over centuries with the misery of watching the living enjoy the comforts denied them. He wondered how many might surround them now, crowding the night with the spirits of dragons, consumed by hate and despair.

Her hand felt soft and warm, too warm, given how crisp the night had become. It wasn't natural. He fought the urge to yank away even as he thirsted for the reassurance of simple human touch. She seemed to sense his unease and folded her hands prim on her lap. "Now you know—what do you mean to do?" she asked.

He puffed his chest with a deep breath and savored the brisk air. The choices a man made in life when he couldn't be sure what came after—*that* was what mattered most. That alone defined his immortality, as measured by the legacy he left behind. "I'm a dead man walking, unless I give you over to Aelin." Even that might not be enough at this point.

"But you won't," she said.

He heard doubt seep through her facade of certainty. Try as she might, she couldn't hide her fear—of what he might do, of the pyre, of the voices in her head, maybe all three. He rose, sword still naked in hand. The fine steel shone pale in the moonlight. One quick swing and it would be over. His chance to redeem himself with Aelin and Tovald, resting on a cruel edge.

Josalind just sat there, head down, hands tight together, as if to make it easy for him. He wouldn't even have to look her in the eye. Maybe she yearned for a quick end and just couldn't bear to ask for it—freedom from this cursed life.

"Your voices." He couldn't bring himself to call them gods. "What do they want?"

"Xang's skull."

Ryn snorted in disbelief. "They're welcome to go get it, then."

"They can't. They need us to be their arms and legs. But they can help."

"How? I thought they were dead, half mad, too, by the sounds of it."

She looked up at him. "I'm their vessel, Ryn. I never really understood until the chapel. They've gone and poured into me all they've got left." Her lip quivered. "The shrieking fiends never gave me a choice and I don't have one now. They'll drive me mad if I don't get on with what they want done." A tear streaked down her cheek.

"But I need your help. There's no one else and I'm just so tired of being alone."

He sheathed his sword. Despite all that he still didn't understand, he couldn't bear to allow any harm to come to her, no matter how much it damned him. "What can I do?"

She wiped her cheeks. "What you've always wanted—serving a worthy need greater than yourself. Maybe even find redemption . . . for the things you've done."

He just looked at her. What a perfect temptress she made, vulnerable and strong, winsome and sympathetic, armed with all the knowledge she needed to lead him straight to the Hells. By telling her about Sablewood, he'd given her the perfect carrot to dangle.

She took him by the wrist. "You are a good and decent man, Ryn Ruscroft."

He pulled away again, too disgusted by such an absurd notion to suffer even a kind touch.

"You've suffered every day since Sablewood," she said. "You need to. That's how I know the man you really are."

Her words sounded sincere enough. But suffering didn't change the fact he'd made the wrong call when it mattered most. It didn't redeem him or give life back to the dead. He studied her face by the moon's light, certain he'd find evidence of falsehood. The simple honesty he found instead brought an ache to his throat. She knew his deepest shame and had never judged him harshly for it. He found it awkward, uncomfortable, a nagging itch he couldn't reach to scratch. As bad or worse than the hair shirt.

She pulled him down to sit and folded her hands over his. "The gods intend to see the Great Deceiver destroyed, Ryn. His evil wiped from the world."

He swallowed hard. "Just how do they expect to manage it?"

"I don't know yet, but they need Xang's skull. Will you help me fetch it?"

A bitter laugh tore out of him. "As it stands, I can barely help myself."

"Just say you will." A brittle edge crept into her voice. "You swore you'd always be there when I needed you."

She had dragged that oath out of him under false pretenses. "You *knew* you weren't going to die on that stake." The sudden realization stung.

"I expected the gods would do something." She stormed to her feet, fists clenched in sudden anger. "But they didn't, not before smoke burned my eyes and fire singed my legs. Do you have any idea how that felt?"

"Then who—"

"That *woman*. She's the one who turned the abbey dark."

"They might be Sevrendine."

Josalind clenched handfuls of her hair. "It doesn't matter who they are. They've taken the skull and the Sword, and we have to get them back."

He just looked at her, still smarting from the truth.

"I never said I expected to die, Ryn," she said.

No, she hadn't. But that left something else that made no sense. "Then what in Hells did you intend when you said I knew what to do?"

"Get ready for us to flee the abbey, of course." She frowned in return. "Why? What did you think?"

Ryn thought of the hell he'd put himself through, laying there smeared with mashed grapes, finger on that trigger. If the Four did still linger, maybe it wouldn't hurt to venture one small prayer and ask them to never show her that. "It's not important."

He started to shake. Heaving swells as violent and relentless as a stormy sea beating itself against a beach. He knew it for the panic that it was, rising up to swallow him, drown him, maul him with the absolute certainty that he was now doomed and damned in equal measure.

Josalind touched his arm. "Ryn?"

He shrugged her off with a growl and rose to face that night maze of shadow and bone. His hand latched on to a horn of the fallen dragon skull. Did it throb faintly under his touch or did he only imagine it? His own shaking made it impossible to tell. But he did draw comfort, even strength, from focusing on the horn's smooth flawlessness. He sucked in one deep breath after another, until his nostrils came to burn from the air's frosty chill.

The shakes began to pass. He wouldn't give in to panic. He wouldn't let fear rule him. What purpose would it serve? The Clerisy didn't deserve his fear. It deserved nothing but his contempt. Aegias and his paladins had blazed their own trail, decided their own fate, created their own code in the crucible of war.

That made him realize something, *feel* it with such sudden conviction his blood tingled. It was something he had known for a long time, down deep, if he were truly honest with himself. He'd just never before had the courage to acknowledge it openly and, most importantly, *act* on it.

A man couldn't be a palatar, a *true* palatar, if he gave even token allegiance to the Clerisy. Any attempt at compromise, any effort to reconcile the two, undermined whatever he hoped to achieve. A true palatar could only ever afford to follow the Virtues and his conscience.

Quintan must have come to the same conclusion, before Ryn killed him. His last words cut even now: *Blind obedience can damn a man as surely as disloyalty, Ryn.*

His conscience told him to help her.

"Ryn?" He could hear the waver in her voice, the anxiety fueled by his silence.

How many palatars before him had entertained similar traitorous thoughts, only to suffer the Clerisy's wrath after being hunted down by their own brothers? The Clerisy was now his enemy. His brothers in the Order were not. But he would have to treat them as enemies if he expected to survive. Few men would have the courage to risk their necks on his account, considering the fear that the Clerisy put into them, considering their own ignorance. His failures in Sablewood proved that, painfully well.

Utterly and finally rejecting the Clerisy wouldn't ease his guilt or cleanse the blood that stained his soul. Nor would it improve the odds of them living long enough for Josalind's offer of redemption to amount to more than a fool's wish. But it meant something, all the same. He might be able to face that wretch in the mirror with less loathing.

He turned back to her. "I've seen whatever that was in the chapel; I've seen you heal." He touched his tender ribs. "And you can hit like a bull. What else?"

"I don't know. It's them, not me," she said. "I'm not sure even they can predict what they can do, and when."

"We're stuck here. How do they expect us to go after those relics?"

She bristled. "I don't bloody know yet." The silver flash of her eyes drove Ryn to take a prudent step back. She broke his gaze and her tone softened. "They haven't said, not that I can tell, anyway. It's still so hard to understand them most of the time."

"You've suffered your whole life thanks to them." He took her hand and gave it a gentle squeeze. "They owe you. Don't be afraid to push back and demand an answer . . . or ask for help."

A timid smile teased her lips, then grew more confident. "In for a drop, in for the whole bucket."

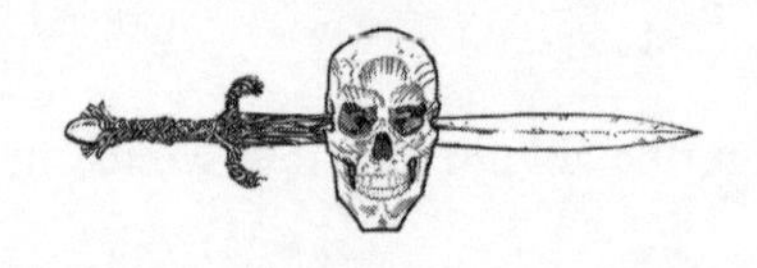

THE CHILD AND THE FORTUNE-TELLER

The old religions and Lost Pandaris

t's a question for the ages, my little angel, how the peoples of Islaria, the ancestors of the Four Kingdoms, came to be unwitting demon worshippers those thousands of years ago.

But imagine—what must it have been like in those days after the Sword and Vulheris had struck down the Four, crippled the Great Deceiver, and claimed so many lives? I know, it's a difficult thing to grasp. The Four are distant to us now. But back then, they were seen by the people, they took an active interest in mortal affairs. So did their mother, Fraia. Prayers were answered for true.

And then one day, the Four were just gone. Poof! Fraia, too. Where did she go? Vulheris had trapped her in a prison that left her powerless. Wait, yes, we'll get to the how and why of that—patience. For now, just think about what the loss of their gods must have meant to the peoples of Islaria when the Sword's Devastation had just left half their world in ruins.

The tea leaves show me horrible things from that time. Mass hysteria and suicidal despair ruled the day. The surviving Earthborn suffered the people's wrath until they decided to just disappear. Fraia's angelic host, harried and outnumbered by the Great Deceiver's demons, could do too little.

From this chaos, something new sprouted in Islaria. A new religion and a new caste of priests. They claimed the people were being punished for their lack of faith. They claimed the only way to redeem themselves was to show their devotion to the Four with rituals that involved the sacrificing of human blood and flesh.

And these rituals worked—they summoned beings that looked and claimed to be angels, even Earthborn. But they were really just demons. These rituals, you see, were designed to summon and constrain a demon to a specific form. This new religion was nothing more than a form of sorcery.

Now, you have to wonder how this could come about. It only goes to reason that the founders of this new religion were sorcerers—agents of the Keshauk Dominion come from the East to take advantage of the situation and subvert the West. This, too, would explain the myths that arose of a Dark Goddess to be feared. Bringer of Chaos. Mother of Night and Sorrow. The Unholy Lover of Lady Death. A mysterious being that had been cast into the Void. These myths twisted the truth about the making of Mordyth Ral and Fraia's imprisonment with one purpose—to poison the West against Fraia should she ever return.

Through all the centuries that followed, these old Keshauk-spawned religions prospered. So, too, did the myths about the Dark Goddess. In fact, these religions knit the peoples of Islaria together and gave rise to a new empire—Pandaris. An empire where noble houses warred for favor and privilege by wielding sorcery as artfully as they did politics and intrigue. Eventually, Pandaris fell, but not before it left the West polluted with demon-enchanted relics and that rarest of commodities, witch iron.

No, pet, we can't go see—those ruins are haunted places even now, and best avoided.

From the ashes of Lost Pandaris rose the Four Kingdoms as we know them today. In those early centuries, the Kingdoms blindly and blissfully carried on with the old religions, certain that all their fiendish bloodletting earned their souls a spot in Paradise at the feet of the Four. Instead, it only served the Great Deceiver's aims.

And then Xang came along, and Aegias to challenge him.

After so long, Fraia's prison had begun to weaken, enough that she could give direction to her angels. She knew that if she left Xang unchecked, he'd conquer all the West for the Keshauk Dominion and gain the power to restore his father. As I've told you before, this threatened all of Existence—not just this world, but every world. Xang's victory simply could not be allowed—whatever the cost.

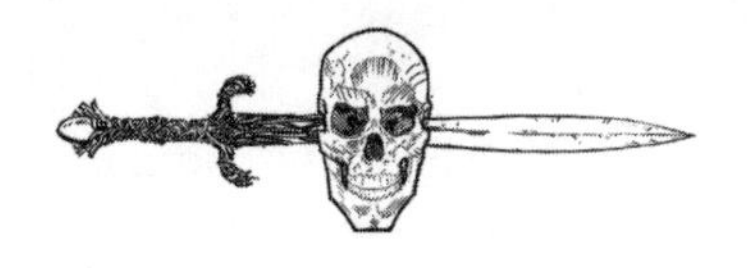

FOURTEEN

Segas Tovald stood before Prioress Aelin—reeking of blood from the grenlich he'd slain and the twenty-seven men he couldn't save—and eyed the device she had placed on Abbess Gerta's desk. Its curve caught the lamplight with a steady gleam.

Just the sight of it, what it represented, fueled disgust and gave the stumps of his missing fingers fresh reason to ache. Sometimes they ached from the cold, sometimes to herald a change in the weather. Other times they ached in response to circumstance.

Like being confronted by this foul *thing*. A relic of Ancient Pandaris. There had always been rumors that the Clerisy had tucked away from the Lost Realm more than just forgings of witch iron. But that's all he had ever known them to be—rumors.

Until now. Enchanted objects like this had only one origin, so the Clerisy itself taught—they were fashioned by a demon that had been summoned and commanded through a sorcerer's ritual. The craft of the Dark Art was never to be trusted, never to be used, on pain of death.

So the Clerisy taught.

He stepped up to the desk and let his fingers trace the patterns in the walnut parquet without going near the device. "How did *that* even come to be here?"

Aelin leaned back in her chair and regarded him with rheumy eyes. "Does it matter, Captain?"

Tovald had been in Gerta's study countless times before. The abbess always sat behind her desk in that heavy old magistrate's chair of worn oak and leather. If Aelin attended as well, she would sit alongside in the simple, spindle-backed chair that she occupied now—the lesser chair for her lesser rank. The abbess's life hung by a thread, but Aelin had left Gerta's chair empty, avoiding any appearance of a claim as the new head of the abbey.

Her restraint may have stemmed from respect, even affection—she certainly looked as if she had been crying before summoning him. Tovald decided it had more to do with prudent caution—Aelin would have a lot to answer for with their superiors after this debacle. So would he. Best not to reach too far, too fast.

"Such things are banned on pain of death," he said. "They are not even supposed to exist."

"We can't let them escape."

"With respect, Mother Prioress, I am beyond giving a damn." He leaned across the desk on his knuckles, careful not to touch the device. "We've lost enough this night without risking more lives beyond the wall. It is a fool's errand. For all we know the grenlich have them."

"They took something."

"Like what?"

She sniffed and wiped her cheeks. "I saw how he looked at her, and she at him. We should have kept them at opposite ends of the abbey."

Her comment hit like a knee in the gut. "That failing belongs to me and no one else."

He'd seen the grief and guilt that burdened Ruscroft from that first day, clear as spring water. The boy's service to the Clerisy had cost him too much. Tovald had seen it often over the years—good men who lost their way after their idealism suffered a messy death on the bitter point of reality. Men in that state needed free rein to sort themselves out. But he'd granted Ruscroft too much, lulled by how ardently the boy had taken to his duties, his apparent devotion to the welfare of the men under his command.

Touching that thing on Gerta's desk would only compound that mistake by defiling his oath to the Order, sworn in Aegias's name. His *other* oath—the one to serve and obey his *ecclesiastical* superiors in the Clerisy—should never put him in such a position of conflict. He had been neck-deep in that piss pot before, back in Vysus, when he had dishonored Aegias to obey the Clerisy's orders.

"There will be blame enough for us both," Aelin said. "But I committed the greater sin. I let my . . ."

And then she did something Tovald had never seen from her, something he hadn't thought her even capable of. She blushed. A rosy wave flooded up her neck and left her cheeks burning.

By the gods, the woman pined for the boy. That gave him plenty of reason right there to question her motives and her judgment.

It lasted only a moment before Aelin's jaw clenched and her nails peeled wax from the arms of her chair. "We need to find them, Captain, for both our sakes."

He considered walking out. The men needed his attention, both on the wall and in the infirmary. But he wouldn't risk challenging her authority until he had all the facts. "Tell me what they took."

She spread her hands flat on the desk and raised her chin to him. "The skull of Xangtemias and the Sword of Aegias."

The combination of shock and weariness drove him to the nearest seat. *That* was what had been buried here under his nose, all along? "I think you need to start at the beginning."

Once Aelin had finished, Tovald pushed out of his chair, heedless of the complaints from his tired knees and stiffened back, and went to the study's window. They had maybe a bell until dawn. The abbey would survive the night, despite three waves of assault. A mixed blessing, considering the dark days sure to come with that skull and the Sword loose in the world. No wonder the Clerisy had established an abbey in such a desperate place and chosen to garrison so many men here under the pretense of penance. Hide and guard the relics where no one would ever want to come.

"You understand, then, Captain," Aelin said. "We have to use whatever means are at our disposal."

"A man can't truly be measured until desperate times test his convictions," Tovald muttered. So Aegias had said.

"What?" Aelin asked.

Was a man who wouldn't bend his principles to necessity a paragon or a fool? He had to look past his personal feelings and consider a broader tapestry.

Aelin rapped her knuckles on the desk. "We can't afford to delay, Captain. It will only work so long as he's alive."

Tovald returned to the desk and regarded the device. Such a little thing. To all appearances, nothing more than a brass pocket compass with a hinged lid, small enough to nestle in his palm. Smooth and plain, without any markings. He at least expected some arcane symbol or other to be engraved on its lid. Aelin had already shown him the dial with two needles inside—one needle to indicate the direction of his target, the other to track their distance. So simple and practical. Should it matter how it had been imbued with power?

He rubbed at his stumps again and wondered, not for the first time, where his life might have led if not for the wound and the blood fever that followed. The drier climate of Vysus had been considered best for his health. He might be retired by now if not for what had transpired in that profane cesspool. Settled down with some handsome fellow, an artisan, perhaps. He liked the company of men with the skill to craft beauty. It took so much more talent than swinging a sword. More than he had ever possessed, at least, even with both hands.

But Vysus had spoiled all that. Intimate relations between men might have been tolerated in the Four Kingdoms, but the wrong kind of association quickly soured people's acceptance. In Vysus, he had ignored his conscience to fulfill his duty to an archbishop who had preyed on children. The sorry episode had led him to deny his true self for fear of being wrongly judged. He felt no shame for who he was—he never had and never would. But he could only ever afford to trust other people so much. It had been simpler to remain celibate—the model of a devout palatar honoring the Virtue of Chastity. Not easier, but simpler.

He tried not to let what he'd denied himself, what Vysus had cost him, leave him embittered toward the Clerisy. Its purpose was to uphold an ideal for all to strive for—a noble purpose he still considered worthy of his loyalty. He couldn't blame the Clerisy for the moral failings of one archbishop, even if he did curse the bastards on its Council of Prelates who had chosen to turn a blind eye. He served the institution, not the parade of characters who took turns governing it.

Still, the choices his loyalty had led him to make haunted him. A bottle of single malt could only drown so much when contemplating the prospect of growing old alone—provided Dragon's Claw even gave him the chance to. As he had told Ryn on that first day, an honest man never denied how his past had changed him or colored his judgment.

His past weighed on him now, as he considered the consequences of using that compass, of again ignoring his conscience to fulfill his duty. But how many lives stood at risk if he didn't use whatever means available to secure the relics as quickly as possible? It would be selfish vanity of the worst kind to value the sanctity of his one pathetic soul above the welfare of all the Kingdoms.

He reached out and let his hand hover over the device. "I don't do this to save your hide, or mine. But to serve a greater good."

Aelin nodded emphatically. "The good of us all, Captain."

A knock sounded at the door.

"Come," Aelin said.

The door opened. Sister Dagetha poked in. Her sorrowful expression left Tovald with little doubt as to the news she bore.

Aelin inhaled sharply.

Dagetha bowed her head. "Our Mother Abbess has ascended to Paradise, Mother Prioress."

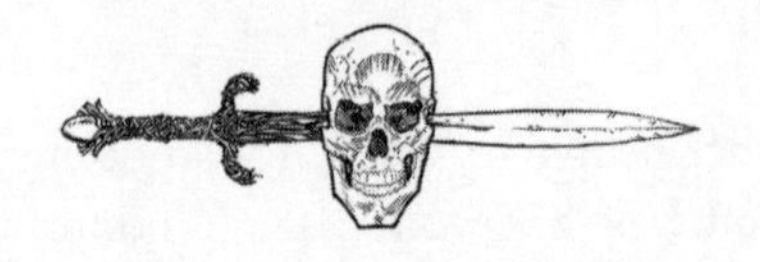

FIFTEEN

Ryn dreamed of that day before the Sablewood Massacre:

He and Quintan had gone after little Sara, lost in the woods on the wrong side of the river. The chill air had hung still between the pale trunks of the aspens. Their branches scratched at a dull sky with a tangle of bared claws.

Sara likely would have frozen to death before any harm found her, but all she could think about as they rushed back to the village with night approaching were grenlich. Cradled against Ryn's shoulder, the child had leaned in so her warm breath tickled his ear. "Will they eat me?"

"No, they won't eat you."

"You're gonna keep me safe," Sarah had declared with absolute faith.

Later, Ryn had found himself in the family's cottage, parked in a rocker before the hearth, trying to ignore the way they all looked at him: Tamantha, who pretended not to, as she checked on the biscuits that baked in the masonry oven. Her father, Jaryk the miller, who sat before Ryn in a matching rocker, packing his pipe with cured wild lettuce. Sara, with that grin frozen on her face, as if Aegias himself had come for dinner. Tamantha had lost her husband the year before. Jaryk had decided she was too young to remain a widow. He knew palatars could be granted a dispensation to marry and take a permanent posting.

"My Tam here, she does her dear mum proud, the gods keep her soul." Jaryk patted his chest. "She deserves better than keeping house for this old tom."

"Da!"

Tamantha had turned on her father with that hot pan poised. The swirl of her skirts fanned sparks from the hearth fire. Sparks of a whole other sort flared in her eyes. "For mercy's sake, Da, you're worse than the old hens who gossip at the well. Have you no shame?"

Ryn had shared her embarrassment. Quintan's knock on the door cut further conversation short. But as he left, Ryn caught Tamantha's gaze. She had been a beauty, in her early twenties like him, with full cheeks, a tapered chin, and full lips. Far too young to be left a lonely widow. She did deserve better. Her mouth had quivered, and her eyes welled with tears, as if she'd read these thoughts from his expression. He hoped that she understood it to be one of sympathy and not pity.

Ryn never had the chance to find out. The next time he saw Tamantha, she was dead. She and Sara both, killed by the same thrust of a grenlich spear. And then Jaryk was, too, after cursing Ryn and the Clerisy with his last breath.

Ryn had failed to keep any of them safe.

He dragged himself awake with a groan. His head pounded hard enough to rival a trip hammer.

That was it—his battered brainpan. Josalind and the Four, grenlich attacking the abbey, that strange pair stealing the relics—all a delusion fueled by too much thane's glory.

Only the pounding didn't come from inside, but out, and his brainpan felt just fine.

He pried an eye open. The sun had risen somewhere beyond a bloated ceiling of misty cloud. A dragon skull loomed over him—patient, watchful. Had these creatures possessed intelligence and morality, been inclined to serve a greater good or their own selfish need? The Clerisy dismissed them as mindless beasts from tired old legends. Ryn preferred to think of them as noble beings who'd risen above the muddy contradictions of character that defined humanity. Thinking so, however, only left him sad that they were gone.

The skull's weighty presence washed away all chance that last night had been a delusion. Ryn felt a thrill at that—he'd awoken a palatar true to Aegias, free of the Clerisy. The hangman would no doubt be impressed to hear him say so, before kicking the stool out from under him.

At least it hadn't rained or snowed. They had huddled under the old blanket with its musky reek and Ogagoth's deerskin cloak through the night, risking only a meager fire to keep the frost at bay.

He traced the pounding to Josalind. She smacked a stone on top of a boulder. For a blink, he thought she might have gone mad after all, beating rocks for the mindless joy of making noise. Then he noted the piney smell of fresh juniper—she was crushing berries.

He climbed to his feet and gasped as the hair shirt tore loose from the ooze of raw skin that had crusted overnight. Damn the thing, but at least it was warm. The dream bit worse, which left him unwilling to peel the shirt off and end the mortification of his flesh—he owed the dead something with no bells to bring the Dread. He ignored the shirt's bite and stretched to work out the kinks.

Josalind looked up from her work and smiled. "I wondered when you were going to stop lazing about." She gestured toward the fire. "Those fish need cleaning."

An impressive pair of rainbow trout glistened wet in the trampled grass, brained senseless.

"Where did those come from?" he asked.

"There's a stream not too far, with fair water for drinking."

"How did you catch them?"

"I'd be a poor child of the Fisherfolk if I couldn't go and noodle myself a fish or two for breakfast," she said, heavy with that northern brogue. Ryn couldn't tell if the way she slipped into the rougher manner of speech on occasion was by accident or intent. "Now hop to," she added. "We don't want that fire burning for long."

Ryn couldn't argue with that. The damp morning smothered the smoke before it could carry far, but if the sky cleared, the fire's plume would be a beacon.

He answered the call of nature and got to work. With knives looted from the grenlich, Josalind had her trout gutted and scaled before he had his own half done. They roasted them on sticks, smeared inside with Josalind's mixture of juniper and wild herbs. As soon as the fish had cooked, he smothered the fire. He savored every bite as they ate. A wise man never passed up the opportunity for a decent meal, especially if it might be his last. He waited for Josalind to speak on the matter at hand, but she didn't.

"So, where's that help you requested?" he asked as he licked his fingers clean. She'd spent some time sitting off in the dark the night before, trying to commune with the Four and impress upon them the need for some means to escape the Claw.

Josalind shrugged. "Like I said, it's coming."

She hadn't said much else, only that she'd been left with the "impression" that help had already been dispatched before she'd even asked. It all sounded far too vague for Ryn's liking. He much preferred having a sound plan. "When?" he asked.

"Soon—that's all I know."

He hissed in exasperation. "Is there any place we might need to be by a certain time?"

"Not that they said, but I told you I can't make sense of their caterwauling half the time."

"Well, isn't that just bloody brilliant."

Josalind cringed as if his sarcasm had cut. "I'm sorry. That's all I know. I try to listen, I try to understand, but it hurts to let them in, it hurts to hear." She clutched her head between her arms. "Their pain seeps in and I can't bear it."

Her distress left him feeling like a ripe bastard. Too much time with hardened men had left his tongue overly sharp. She did a fair job of playing normal, making breakfast as though nothing else mattered—an eggshell facade too easily cracked. He knelt and took hold of her oddly warm hands.

"Well, we'll just have to keep our heads down and eyes open then, won't we?" he said, as gently as he could. He took a moment to muster his thoughts. "There's something you need to know. I tried to tell you before . . ."

"What?"

"I . . . I started hearing a voice, too." He felt relieved to say it.

She looked at him with wary surprise. "What kind?"

"I thought it might be the Great Deceiver, or even Xang, after we found his skull, but . . ."

She squeezed his hands. "But what?"

"It's so cold—not in an evil way, just hard and empty of feeling." Each word drained the fear and doubt that had festered for weeks. "It says it has no place in the Hells. What does that mean?" A ragged sigh rippled through him. "Maybe I'm the mad one."

"No, Ryn." She touched his jaw. "Old things still wander the earth—that much I get now. Forgotten things still looking for a chance to be heard."

"But I don't know what it wants—that's what haunts me." He swallowed. "I've even wondered if it could be Mordyth Ral." The *Codex* said nothing about the Sword ever actually *speaking* to Aegias, but what could he trust from that damned book? Still, it couldn't be that—the idea struck as just too outrageous, even after all he'd seen in recent days.

"I don't know," she said.

He cocked an eyebrow at her. "What do you mean, you don't know?" A swarm of nervous moths took flight in his belly. "Is there some chance it could be?"

"I mean I don't know what it could—" Josalind stiffened and cocked her head to one side. "*Arse boils*—they've found us."

Ryn went for a pistol, mindful of the fact he had only four reloads. "Who?"

"Your men."

He rose into a half crouch for a quick glance around but saw nothing. "They're not mine anymore. How do you know?"

"The dragons told me."

Of course they did. "I don't suppose they mentioned from where, or how far?"

She started piling their meager possessions onto the blanket. "West—close enough to be seen from the edge of the Bone Yard."

Too damn close. He'd already burned the fish guts to keep from drawing bears or wolves. The remains of the fire would be harder to hide. He'd cut back the sod to make a proper pit. With a few quick stomps, he crushed the charred wood then covered it back over. Good enough to pass inspection at a distance, but the evidence would be easy to spot, and smell, close up.

They headed off to the east at a quick trot. Ryn figured their best chance was to make for the far edge of the Bone Yard and keep going. They'd reach the coast in maybe five miles. With luck, any grenlich in the area would still be massed farther west after the attack on the abbey.

Josalind froze before they'd made it a hundred yards.

He dropped to a crouch and yanked her down. "What?"

"They're this way, too."

"Gods be damned." He should have expected it. If Tovald suspected his prey had gone to ground here, it only made sense to loop a snare and close it quick. If they couldn't run, they had to hide. He pulled her eastward. "Come on."

The dragons were bigger here. He spotted a true monster, with a skull a good four yards long and incisors like cutlasses. Its bones had been stacked beside an outcropping of stone that thrust out of the ground at an angle. The dirt beneath the stone had been dug away by some burrowing creature to leave a crawl space that extended back around behind the bone stack.

He squatted and probed around with his sword to make sure the crawlspace didn't still house a fox or wolverine. "Can you wiggle your way in there?"

"Can you?"

"Don't worry about me."

She looked hard at him. "What do you expect to do? There's naught but one of you."

"I'm not about to toss my life away on some fool heroic gesture, if that's what you're worried about."

She slipped in without trouble. He followed, wiggling through the opening on his back. The crawl space widened farther in, but the first part was narrower. The added layer of hardened leather on his shoulders and around his neck—the pauldrons and the gorget—made for a tight squeeze. He didn't have time to fuss with buckles and straps and tried to muscle his way in.

Sure enough, he got stuck.

He dug his bootheels into the earth for leverage, hissing against the grind of the hair shirt, but it didn't help. "Pull."

"Which part?" Josalind asked.

"Pick one."

She latched on to his leg and gave a heave, then another. At last, Ryn popped through. He wiggled around onto his stomach and edged up behind the bone stack, sword in hand. Two ribs were loose enough to tease out without tipping the whole thing. He shifted them over to mask the entrance to their cramped little haven. It *might* look from the outside like the work of nature or scavengers.

Ryn pulled off the looted battle gauntlets to dump the old loads from his pistols and reload fresh from his cartridge pouch. For all the good it would do—if they were cornered here, they hadn't a chance. Still, he wanted to be sure that if he had to take a shot, a stale load spoiled by the overnight damp didn't leave him with a misfire. After he'd finished and pulled the gauntlets back on, Josalind's hand found his and squeezed tight.

The tread of palatar boots drew near. He caught flickers of movement through the cracks of the bone stack. Two, three, maybe more, taking their time. Josalind's breath caught. His pulse thudded so loudly it couldn't possibly escape notice.

The palatars moved past without pause.

And then Ryn saw Tovald.

The captain strode into view at just the right spot for Ryn to have a clear view of him. He held something in his hand. It looked like a pocket compass with its brass lid flipped open. A fine chain dangled from its underside, swinging free between Tovald's fingers. Clipped to it was a crossbow bolt. It hung parallel to the ground, wrapped with what looked to be a bloodstained bandage.

Tovald came to a stop right in front of them, holding the compass out. The bolt swayed, then held fast. It turned of its own accord, in a deliberate way that wasn't natural, until it pointed straight at Ryn.

Contagious magic—it had to be. The damned Clerisy broke its own injunctions when it saw fit. Ryn couldn't believe Tovald had lowered himself to use such a thing. The bandage must have been the same one he'd pulled from his head and left in the Keep's cellar. They'd tracked him with his own blood.

Tovald looked straight into the bone stack. "I know you are there, Lieutenant."

Ryn aimed at the easy target the captain presented even though he had no intention of firing. What was the point? They would still be surrounded and outnumbered.

Tovald sat on a boulder. "The abbess is dead. She passed last night."

Five palatars gathered behind him in full gear, each with sword, dagger, and a brace of pistols on their belts, and a musket at the ready.

They had no chance of making a run past them. Ryn couldn't even get out of this crack of a hole without being caught like a belly-up turtle. He clawed the dirt in frustration. They should have stuck with the original plan and tried to slip through Tovald's snare before it could close.

"This doesn't have to be hard done, Lieutenant," Tovald said. "Give up the witch, give back the relics, and I promise you'll hang quick. But make us come in there after you and the Inquisitarem will have you begging for death—Aelin will see to it."

The relics—so Aelin had told him. Ryn could appreciate how that might drive the captain to use outlawed magic. Who was he to judge, given the circumstances?

Josalind's hand tightened on his. It felt almost hot now. She'd started to shake and mutter some senseless babble. He could only imagine her terror, faced with the prospect of the pyre again.

"I won't let them have you," he whispered. A quick thrust to the throat. It would take no more.

First the pyre, then the idea of taking her head to save his own hide, and now this—all in a day. The gross absurdity almost made him laugh.

"My patience is getting stale, Lieutenant," Tovald said.

Josalind grabbed the blade of Ryn's sword.

He thought she meant to spare him the horror and put an end to the pain herself. But she only opened a thin slice across her palm.

"What are you doing?"

"Be ready to run," she said. Only it wasn't her, not entirely. As in the chapel, he heard the echo of *them*.

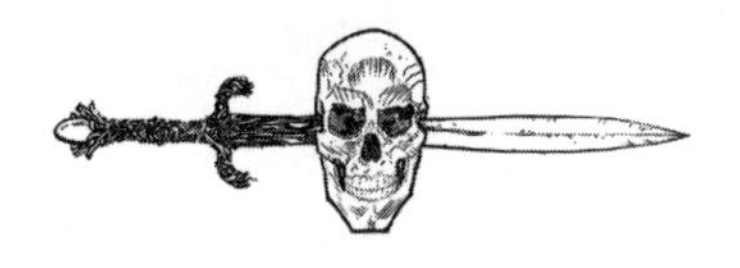

SIXTEEN

osalind smeared her hand across a dragon rib and left a crimson trail. Weathered bone drank the blood like a thirsty sponge. The whole stack shuddered and shook. Bones began sliding around one another to find their proper position.

Palatars cried out in horror.

Ryn tried not to. He readied himself for what might come, whatever that might be. Giant tarsals and phalanges collected mere inches from his nose to rebuild a foot. Leg bones followed. Thick talons as long as arming swords flexed and dug furrows in the ground.

Josalind gave him a shove. "Out."

He heaved and clawed his way through the crawl space's narrow opening. The skeleton loomed over him, shaking off Lady Death's shroud with a clatter. A musket fired. The ball struck the rock above his head in a spray of chipped stone. He had to credit the man with the grit to hold his ground and take the shot.

A skeletal leg rose and slammed the earth beside him. Tovald and his men had fled for cover behind anything not likely to come alive. Ryn glanced up and wished he hadn't. A sun-bleached mass of death towered overhead, breastbone thrust out to rival a ship's prow, serpentine neck reared back. Two thick horns curved wide to impale the sky. The dragon could have comfortably rested its chin atop the abbey's curtain wall. Its assemblage of wing bones spread out to span half an acre.

Ryn flinched when Josalind grabbed his hand. She'd tucked their blanket of supplies under her other arm. "No time for lazing about," she said. "Old bones won't wake for long."

An insight that came from her voices, no doubt. She tried to lead but managed only two steps before her legs gave out. He caught her as she stumbled.

"Their favor comes with a price," she gasped. "That way."

Ryn looped her arm around his neck and dragged her along in a half crouch. They wove between rocks and bone stacks for cover as the eastern edge of the Bone Yard and the forest drew near.

Shouts rose behind them. Muskets fired. Their shots tore past with that distinct angry buzz.

Gods be damned. So much for stealth. Ryn rose up to haul her along faster. Their only chance of slipping away rested with making it to the forest.

Josalind staggered to the right. "Not the trees. We have to stay in the open."

"Are you mad?" A rather senseless question, given the circumstances.

"They need a place to land."

The ground rumbled with the thud of dragon feet—the bony beast must have followed them to scare off pursuit. But it didn't have to land, it couldn't even fly. "Who?" he asked.

She puffed to keep up the pace. "That help you requested."

He conceded for lack of an option. The sun peeked through a break in the clouds. They reached the edge of the Bone Yard and rounded a stony outcrop that provided cover.

Josalind slumped against it and wiped at her brow, panting to catch her breath. "I could do for a spot of water."

Ryn realized how thirsty he was. The thud of the dragon stomping around had faded in the distance. Palatars hailed one another.

A large shadow flitted overhead. Then another.

Josalind looked up. "Here we are—now, mind your manners."

Two winged forms circled in the sky. A melodic trumpeting shook the air. The creatures fell into a dive straight for them with the sun at their backs. Ryn squinted to make them out. He could tell only that they were big, not so enormous as the dragon, but at least the size of draft horses.

They fanned their wings to brake for landing. The gusts kicked up a hail of leaves, twigs, and pebbles that forced Ryn to shield his eyes. He backed against the outcropping, sword and pistol in hand.

"Manners, Ryn," Josalind snapped.

The leader struck the earth on all fours with such force that Ryn felt the thud ripple from his soles up through his knees. A fell beast with the tawny hindquarters of a lion, russet leathery wings like a dragon's, and a scaly scorpion's tail with a bulbous ivory stinger. Most shocking of all, it had a humanlike head, with a woman's face framed by a thick golden mane, and shoulders and arms to match.

A martichora.

Ryn's family had often dined in the hall of their lord. There had been a martichora's skull over the mantle. An heirloom old beyond measure, from a creature thought long extinct—*a monster infamous for favoring human flesh.*

He aimed his pistol in sudden panic as the second beast came to land. Josalind heaved herself up beside him.

The lead martichora didn't care for the display of weapons. That disturbingly human face twisted into a terrible grimace, displaying rows of narrow, serrated teeth. Her muscular arms powered big, clawed hands that could have gutted him with a swipe.

Josalind pushed down Ryn's pistol. "No."

"But—"

"Oma and her sister Astrig have come to help."

Both wore rigs of finely tooled leather, slung over their shoulders and belted at the waist. The rigs held haversacks, quivers stuffed with arrows, and large recurve bows of laminated wood and horn. They wore nothing else—Ryn noted they had the breasts of women, too. Despite their humanlike halves, and arms that were longer in proportion to their bodies than the forelegs of a great cat would be, they were not built to walk upright. They had to rear back on their haunches to use both hands.

Primal fear warred with his disbelief. "But those are *martichora*."

Josalind stepped in front of him and greeted the first creature with a curtsy. To Ryn's utter astonishment, the martichora responded with a bow of her own.

"That they are," Josalind said. "A noble race near wiped out by cruel lords and ladies who used them for sport. They killed people only to save themselves."

Oma's creamy jade eyes could have passed for human if they weren't the size of plums. Ryn saw wisdom there, deep and old, and something feral, too. The martichora's broad and flat features were more or less attractive, though any comparison to a human standard of beauty gave him a shiver.

"You mean for us to ride them." Ryn had no love for the idea of being aloft where no sane man had any right to be. He'd mastered bareback riding by the age of eight, but that was challenging enough on a level green.

"You will never ride me, man-child," Oma said with quiet authority. "But I will carry you."

Ryn just looked at the martichora, wide-eyed, stumped by her ability to speak a civilized tongue, and to do so with such a melodic voice.

A distant cheer carried from the depths of the Bone Yard. Josalind's "old bones" must have returned to their slumber.

They needed a quick way off of this rock, no matter how mad the means might be. Ryn mastered his surprise and stowed weapons before approaching with caution. Oma didn't move, though something like a smile stretched her broad mouth. That unsettled him even more than her grimace. "Why would you help us?" he asked.

"We fear Mordyth Ral and the skull of that devil-child being loose in the world, as you do," Oma said.

Ryn bowed after Josalind's example and tried not to feel awkward about it. "Thank you."

Oma returned the gesture with regal dignity. "Have you the courage to see this through?"

Tovald and his men could be on them in moments. Still, Ryn hesitated to trust their lives to these creatures.

Oma's stare didn't waver. "Time is against us." She didn't seem inclined to go anywhere before she had a firm answer. Astrig sat back on her haunches and picked dirt from her claws.

The Clerisy might have the means to reclaim the relics before all the Hells broke open, but only if it believed the truth. Ryn had seen enough to be certain it couldn't see past its own web of lies. A fresh-hatched chick had better odds with a cat than he did of convincing Tovald or Aelin before they stretched his neck.

If the fate of the world rested with one renegade palatar, a half-mad woman haunted by dead gods, and two creatures of legend, so be it.

Ryn looked Oma in the eye. "I have courage enough, and we've a ship to catch."

The martichora's wings shouldn't have been enough to lift such masses, and yet, the martichora flew with power and speed, even bearing passengers. Ryn almost lost the trout he'd had for breakfast when Oma took to the air. She flew as a horse would run, with belly parallel to the earth. Every trick to riding bareback came into play: Toes up, ankles down. Grip with the calves and inner thighs. Don't lock knees or hips because too much bracing made it too easy to start bouncing.

He had to contend with wings that forced him to sit back farther than he would have on a horse. Oma almost lost him twice before he learned that the best approach wasn't to keep erect, but to hug her back and use his arms as he did his legs, left hand clutching the shoulder strap of her rig. The flap of her wings pinched his ribs, which helped keep him from sliding off.

Screaming wind numbed Ryn's skin, tore tears from his eyes, and made his ears ache. All he could see were the restless waves of the Iceberg Sea, glittering with a gold shiver under the sun. He buried his cheek in her mane to find what warmth he could and looked for Josalind. She rode not far away on Astrig, copper-red curls streaming.

Neither the cold nor the height seemed to bother her. She somehow managed to sit tall with only a light hand to brace herself, eyes to the horizon. Her size could have partly accounted for that, but not entirely.

Nearly two bells must have passed before Oma spoke. "There."

Ryn blinked through the icy blur, body aching with exhaustion. A ship—a caravel with a low-slung forecastle and sterncastle, square sails on its fore and main masts, and triangular lateen sails on the other two. It tracked an eastward course, hauling close to the north wind.

Behind it on a towline, a familiar skiff rode the waves with its sail furled.

Damn. Ryn had thought there might be another larger ship. Those heretics were handful enough without an entire crew at their back. "Closer."

Oma dived, spurring Ryn's gut into fresh gyrations. The caravel flew the Jendalian flag, as most ships plying the Iceberg Sea were likely to. It also displayed the pennant of the fishing guild of Jendalia's capital, Jaegen. Again, not unusual.

He couldn't tell if the caravel had swivel guns and didn't care to find out. "Veer off."

As Oma wheeled to regain altitude, he heard a muted boom, then another. She shrieked and twisted sideways with a sudden jerk. He tumbled over her head with nothing to catch him but the icy waves two hundred yards below.

Josalind screamed his name.

Ryn didn't let go of the shoulder strap as his legs flew over his head. He couldn't if he wanted. Breathless terror gnarled his fingers tight. He caught Oma's mane with his other hand and his weight wrenched her head sideways. Oma snarled, then grunted when his knees smacked her gut. He hung nose to nose with her, like he meant to steal a kiss, but the rotted meat stench of her breath made him more likely to gag.

She beat her wings furiously against the drag. "Ready?"

Before he could ask *for what*, she tucked her wings and dropped. Any sense of weight vanished. His legs floated up as the wind screamed and the waves rushed to meet them.

Then Oma tossed her head and spread her wings.

His body went from featherlight to boulder-heavy in a blink. He cartwheeled through the air and splayed across her back, wind knocked out, tongue bitten through one side. His right leg lay across her wing and flopped up and down with each beat. He swallowed blood and fought to get his wind back as he twisted around to a proper seat.

Oma's left wing bore three fluttering holes that whistled as the wind sought to tear them wider. The bastards had used grapeshot. Chance had spared her wing bones, but the pain must have been brutal.

The coast of Morlandia cut the southern horizon. Considering how Oma struggled to keep altitude, they might well ditch and drown in the frigid sea well short of land. Even if they made it, nothing lay there but the Frosted Wood—thousands of square miles ruled by grenlich, all the way south to Sablewood.

They didn't have a choice.

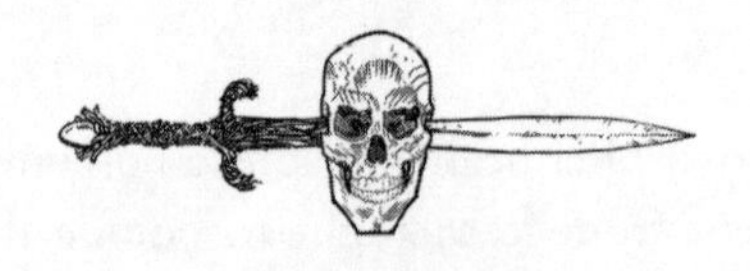

SEVENTEEN

strig and Josalind flew ahead to scout for a decent landing site. They found a stretch of sandy beach, tucked under a bluff crowned by cedars and aspens, which displayed their first fall colors. Past storms had eroded the bluff's underside, and tree roots tangled so thick they hung like awnings over the beach.

Oma plowed almost face-first into the damp sand. She glistened with a sheen of sweat but shivered as if soaked in ice water. Ryn hopped off her back as Josalind and Astrig landed beside them.

Astrig nuzzled Oma's wing. "I will peel the hides from every last one, sister mine." The gouge of her claws spooked a half dozen burrowing crabs. They popped out of the sand and tried to scuttle off, but she caught them all with quick licks and crunched them down.

Ryn masked his disgust. "We don't stand a chance against that ship." He looked to Josalind. "Do you know where they're taking the skull?"

She raked the windblown curls from her face and looked out to sea. "East."

Oma huffed. "This is no secret, blessed child, we can see the ship sails east."

"In the Keep, our thieves spoke of the goddess Fraia," Ryn said. "That is a Sevrendine belief." He almost said *heresy*—that razor-edged word so often wielded by the Clerisy. But he couldn't afford to take anything the Clerisy professed, nothing it claimed, at face value. Not anymore.

Still, Astrig snarled at him. "I hear your scorn, palatar. Fraia exists. She is the Great Deceiver's equal and opposite, true mother to the slain gods."

"So the Sevrendine claimed." Ryn looked her in the eye. "I'm not denying it. I'm just trying to make sense of all this by considering what the Clerisy had to say on the matter."

Astrig sat back on her haunches. "Which is?"

"The Sevrendine sought their false goddess's favor through prayer—that broke Aegias's Injunction and it damned them," Ryn said. "They became pawns of the Great Deceiver but were too blind to see it, just like any other heretic who claims divine power."

"We have little knowledge of these Sevrendine, but if they give worship to Fraia, then their faith is true," Astrig said.

Their faith is true—Fraia, despite the Clerisy's claims to the contrary, existed. Had what the Sevrendine said about Aegias also been true—that he had worshipped Fraia? That he had been Fraia's first messiah since the Four Gods of the Kingdoms—her supposed children—had been slain by Mordyth Ral and the man who had forged it, Vulheris the Mad? But that would mean the Sevrendine faith was the faith of Aegias—making it the one *true* foundation on which the Virtues rested.

If that were so, it meant the Clerisy had perpetrated a lie upon the Kingdoms *for seven centuries*, every bit as large and foul as any plot of the Great Deceiver. And for what? The power and ambition of the men who ruled it? The idea made Ryn's blood boil with sudden outrage.

The clamp of Astrig's big hand on his shoulder gave him a start. "Are you well, man-child?" she asked.

"Far from it!" Ryn shrugged free of her, turned sharp on his heel, and roared himself hoarse at the uncaring sky. Vented himself with a wordless, raw torrent of emotion because no curse he could muster seemed adequate to the task. He saw only one path forward that he could trust: Honor the Virtues and the dictates of his own conscience, apart from any religion's dogma, apart from any gods or goddesses, dead or alive. As all palatars should.

He drew a deep, cleansing breath and turned back to face them all. "The Clerisy claimed to have rounded up the Sevrendine and shipped them off to fight the Keshauk two hundred years ago. Never to be seen again." He'd read the histories of the Keshauk Aggression, the accounts from prisoners of war who'd spoken of how the Keshauk's Dominion stretched eastward for a thousand leagues, with a score of nations crushed under the heel of a bloodthirsty priesthood that worshipped the Great Deceiver as the All-Father. Tales of dark rituals where people were forced to sever their own flesh and sacrifice their firstborns as acts of devotion.

Dark rituals little different than what Josalind said she saw in her visions of Xang.

Her attention had strayed somewhere else, head cocked to one side as if her ghosts even now whispered in her ear with tales of those atrocities. "East," she said again.

"The Keshauk Aggression was fought in the east, beyond the Impalas Mountains," Ryn said. "But after the Kingdoms gave it up, the passes were blocked."

"The Clerisy left the Sevrendine to be slaughtered." Josalind smiled a dreamy smile and brushed her hands together as if clearing crumbs. "Just like that, those lofty men thought they could sweep away what they couldn't bear to believe. They've no idea what seed they left to sprout."

"The Sevrendine survived," Ryn said. "Maybe by making their own peace with the Keshauk because they serve the same master."

Josalind's attention fixed hard on him. She dashed the notion with a sharp shake of her head. "No."

Ryn didn't think so either. "The Sevrendine still roam the Kingdoms. And these two intend to take the Sword and the skull east . . . home."

"For what purpose, man-child?" Oma asked.

"I would hope to lock them up so they can't cause any mischief," Ryn said. "They certainly don't have reason to trust the Clerisy with the task."

"But the seal is breaking; it can't be stopped," Josalind said. "Xang's voice will be heard, Mordyth Ral will crave a hand to wield it. What happened before will happen again—misery and butchery." A manic giggle tore out of her. "Round and round it goes, over and over again."

She wiped tears from her cheeks. "Our thieves mean well, but they're so wrong about what to do. It isn't enough to hold the boar by the tusks—you need to run a proper spear through his heart."

"That's what you mean about destroying the Great Deceiver," Ryn said.

"He has to be drawn out," Josalind said.

"Was Xang truly the Deceiver's mortal son?" The *Codex* said so, if Ryn could believe it.

Josalind nodded. "Xang's strong where his father is weak. The Great Deceiver needs him. That can be used to bait a trap."

The martichora offered no comment. They hung on Josalind's every word as if she were their prophet foretold. "How?" Ryn asked.

"I don't know," Josalind said. "But we have to get the skull—the skull and the Sword both—before the seal breaks, and take them to Gostemere."

Ryn gaped at her. Gods be damned—this just kept getting better. "Gostemere?"

"What is this place, man-child?" Astrig asked.

"It's where some people used to believe the Four were slain by Vulheris the Mad," he said. "A lost place." From a lost time. Half the known world laid to waste by Mordyth Ral, the Deceiver scarred and forever crippled—or so the *Codex* claimed. The modern Commons edition of the *Codex* didn't name Gostemere outright, but a crumbling second-century edition Ryn had found buried in the abbey's library in Sablewood did.

"Not lost, just hidden," Josalind said.

Ryn stepped close to her. "Why there?"

"I don't know."

"They must have given some clue." He could remember nothing from what he'd read that might shed light.

Josalind winced and rubbed at her temple. "Maybe they did, and I missed it. All I know is you can't find it without a key."

"What kind of key?" Ryn pressed. Pulling teeth came with less pain.

She scowled at him. "*I don't know*, for glory's sake. If I did, I'd say so."

"One task at a time, man-child," Oma said with a weary sigh, huddled against Astrig. "The Four will speak when it serves them."

Ryn turned on her. "Really. And just what do you know of the gods? Josalind is the only one who seems to hear their ravings. How is it that your kind are part of this? Where did you even come from?"

Astrig gave a growl that raised goosebumps and the urge to reach for a weapon. Ryn refused to let his apprehension show. He cupped his hands behind his back and ignored her.

"*My kind* lives close to the earth, man-child," Oma said. "Hidden in the mountains where *your kind* can't find us, doing what we can to keep the grenlich of these reaches scattered and divided." She pushed herself up with a grimace. "We see things, hear things—things that few of *your kind* can. Those of ours blessed enough to hear the Four, we honor. Yours you call 'witch' and give to fire."

Ryn couldn't argue with that. "You worship the gods."

"We *respect* the Four and seek knowing of their wants," Astrig said. "They wish to wipe the Great Deceiver's ill from the world. This, too, we desire. We can feel how the earth cries out where his followers rule. It has suffered long enough."

Ryn nodded at Josalind. "Are you saying there are martichora who hear the Four as she does?"

"None of our kind has *ever* heard the Four as she does," Astrig said. "She is blessed above all others."

Blessed? Ryn still considered it a curse. "You're putting a lot of faith in her."

Josalind wilted as if each word added a stone around her neck.

"We hope, man-child," Oma leaned toward him and licked her lips. "But hope means nothing without action and conviction. The task belongs not to her alone."

"It falls in equal measure to every soul who shares her path," Astrig added.

"I know what it is to share a vow of brotherhood." Ryn worked his palm over his sword's pommel. "When all that matters is keeping one another alive as the world goes to shite around you. That I understand. Considering what happened after that ship fired on us, I expect you do, too."

Oma bowed her head.

"I've sworn to this, wherever it leads." Ryn broadened his focus to include Astrig and Josalind. "But I don't care to be spoon-fed the details like I'm some toothless old buzzard who can't shovel his own gruel."

Oma's lips stretched into that unnerving excuse for a smile. "I have no taste for gruel either, man-child. There will be no secrets between us that I keep. But as we cannot force the Four to speak, we must embrace patience." She shivered. "Enough talk, my wing aches and craves warmth."

"Sorry, meant to tend to that," Josalind said. She made for the martichora with that silver gleam in her eyes.

Oma hissed and cringed away. "What do you mean to do?"

"Just hold still," Josalind said.

She planted her hands on the martichora's cheeks and kissed her square on the lips. The sight made Ryn shudder, considering the ripeness of Oma's breath.

The martichora's eyes flew wide. Her tail curled and its ivory stinger beaded with yellow venom. She sank down onto her belly, caught in some rapture, as the torn flesh of her left wing knit itself back together.

"By the craft of gods and men," Astrig swore.

Josalind cried out in pain. She collapsed to her knees in the sand.

Ryn dropped beside her in sudden fear and gathered her up. That odd warmth had fled. She felt like melting ice in his arms. Fresh welts on the back of her left hand oozed blood. He pushed up her sleeve and found more. "What in Hells?"

"Grace has cost, 'specially to heal," Josalind whispered. "Been too soon since I fixed your head, woke the dragon." She gestured wanly at Oma. "Better?"

The martichora flexed and flapped her wing. Only pink scars remained. "Very much so, blessed child."

"That's good." Josalind closed her eyes and nestled against Ryn's shoulder. He watched in wonder as the wounds began to fade from her arm. She meant to say something else, but it came out in a slurred mumble. And then she fell asleep.

Ryn woke the next morning about the time he always did, when the Clerisy's bells were due to ring. There were none for miles, but that didn't matter. He bolted out of his sleep, anxious and restless, like a hound spooked by a coming storm. There was no reason for it. The dreams hadn't come. He couldn't remember the last time he'd started a day without one.

He should have been grateful. Instead, the absence of a dream left him feeling guilty.

A chill wind blew out of the north, from the great glaciers where legend held that the god Mygalor had resided. It whipped the surf into a briny froth and peppered them with damp grit from the beach. Josalind still slept, wrapped in her blanket and curled around their spent fire. Oma and Astrig had already risen. They splashed around in a tidal pool down the beach. A growing collection of ambushed fish flopped on the sand beside them.

Ryn scanned the tree line but had no sense of being watched. Oma and Astrig had assured him they could smell grenlich a mile off. The hair shirt had grown too maddening to bear any longer. He headed for a stream that trickled out of the forest and cut a path to the sea.

The pieces of hardened leather came off first, straps stiff and stubborn in the morning chill. Next, he shrugged the mail shirt over his head and let it fall to smash a crater in the sand. His quilted gambeson followed, then trousers and boots.

That left only the hair shirt. Pulling it off stung like peeling skin. The wind bit into the raw spots it had left. He tossed it, then dropped to his knees and plunged his whole head into the stream. The icy flow numbed his skull with a dull ache. When the need for air could no longer be denied, he pulled back and let his soppy hair drain down his torso. The chill felt more invigorating than a morning run.

Oma sat on her haunches on the opposite side of the stream.

Those big eyes had a look that might have contemplated dinner or mating. Either way, Ryn felt more naked than he was, considering he still wore his braies.

He slicked back his hair. "Yes?"

"What compels you to give such torment to your flesh?"

He glanced at the hair shirt with an equal measure of scorn and want. "Things I've done, things I should have." *A voice I didn't want to hear.*

"Does it help?"

"No." Though come to think of it, he couldn't remember the last time he'd heard his Voice.

"I understand the jagged claw that is guilt, man-child," Oma said. "But we suffer enough just to live. Better to be strong and hale, so we can atone through our deeds."

"It's easy to do senseless things when your beliefs turn out to be shite and you have nothing else." He looked to Josalind, lying there curled up, looking even younger than she was, and he felt a sudden, deep affection. "Then things change."

Oma stretched her mouth into that terrible parody of a smile. "The lessons that hurt are the last forgotten."

She left him to dress. He put the gambeson on first. The threadbare linen felt wonderfully smooth and soft against his skin. The hair shirt he pulled on over top. He considered burning the damned thing but needed the extra layer to keep from freezing in the sky.

To learn that the Clerisy had likely hidden the truth about Aegias and Fraia from its very inception left him more eager than ever to see his brother palatars freed of their oath to serve and obey. But what could he, a hunted renegade, possibly do to bring it about? The challenge of snatching the relics back from the Sevrendine and tracking down Josalind's mythical destination seemed trivial by comparison.

Trivial or impossible, it didn't matter—he had a new purpose, a direction, a *cause*. It left him with a sense of self-worth that had been absent for too long.

By the time he had his armor back on, Josalind had risen and stoked the fire to new life. Another morning of roasted fish for breakfast, except for the martichora, who preferred theirs whole and raw.

Josalind from somewhere had gathered up a mix of wildflowers. After breakfast, she just sat there, humming a tune Ryn recognized as a Fisherfolk sea ditty while she wove the stems of cup-shaped mauve blooms that appeared too delicate for the task. "I had a book as a wee lass," she said. "*Tathemay's Menagerie of Plants*. Watercolors of flowers from across the Kingdoms."

"A princely possession," Ryn said, considering each copy would have been hand-painted.

"My da gave it to me." Her busy fingers faltered for a moment and her shoulders slumped, then she carried on as briskly as before. "This is autumn crocus, or meadow saffron, though it's not what the spice saffron comes from." She held it up for his inspection. "Smell it."

It smelled of honey, and he said so.

"I know—isn't it grand?" Her face brightened with an almost childish delight that washed away some of the fatigue that still hung dark about her eyes. "Tathemay wrote nothing about how any of the plants smelled. But you don't dare eat it—even rabbits know better."

"And why's that?" Ryn asked, wholly enchanted by the simple joy she took in this. He realized much of the world outside of books must have been new to her.

"It will poison you not much different than arsenic." She finished her task and placed the flower crown upon her head.

Ryn could have been quite content to sit on that beach all day and let Josalind educate him on flora he would have otherwise ignored as weeds. But they hadn't the luxury of lingering. "We can't afford to trail that ship until it reaches a port of its choosing," he said. "There's no telling what allies these Sevrendine will have waiting for them."

Oma grunted. "Carrying you with your metal shell is tiresome, man-child."

"I expect any captain with half a wit would make for the nearest port if his ship cracked a mast," Ryn said. That port was Tanasgeld, but he couldn't think of how they might manage such a thing without eating a blast of grape shot.

"I expect he wouldn't," Josalind said. "If it's an upper mast, the ship will stock a spare—a handy crew can make the switch at sea. If it's a lower mast, they'll just fish it."

He frowned. "They'll what?"

Josalind sorted through her remaining stock of flowers. "Brace it by lashing extra spars around the crack."

"What about a hit below the waterline?"

"A fair carpenter can shore up a lot," Josalind said. "A pump can do the rest."

He crossed his arms and leaned back against a log. "Well, you're the one here with salt water in your veins—tell me how we can force that ship to port in Tanasgeld without ending up fish bait."

Josalind's face brightened with an impish smile. "There ain't a sailor born who doesn't take to superstition more than his grog." She had slipped into the heavy brogue of her kinfolk as she might a favorite pair of slippers. "We just have to give 'em a wee fright."

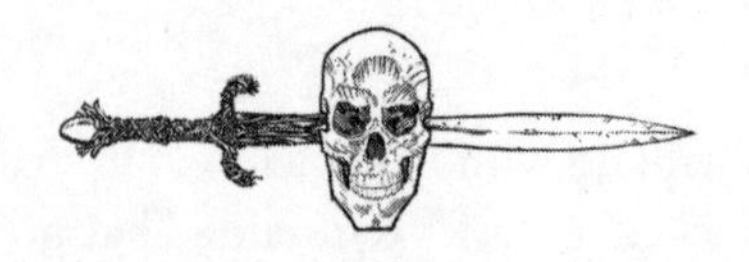

EIGHTEEN

Josalind's "wee fright" turned out to be almost as large as the caravel they pursued.

They flew hard through the morning till they spotted their quarry again, then Josalind sought an open stretch on the stony shore where they could put down. She sat on a rock with the waves lapping her feet, staring out to sea and waiting, but she wouldn't say for what. Ryn and the martichora built her a fire, as requested back from shore. The stiff breeze coming off the sea made the flames crackle and roar.

And then *it* came.

"The Horror"—the thing held responsible for the ship wrecked at Dragon's Claw. Sailors spat for good fortune at the mere mention of it. They considered it an omen of the worst kind even to spot one.

It reared up out of the sea on stubby crab legs, as tall as a chapel's belfry, dwarfing Josalind with its hulking mass. Water cascaded off a lobster's segmented shell, mottled brown and green and gnarled with barnacles. Instead of lobster's foreparts, a massive squid's head bore a beak great enough to snip a man in half. A squid's tentacles twitched with obvious ire, chameleon skin flickering between shades of blue and green. Eyes the size of cart wheels fixed on Josalind.

One of its feeder arms could have smashed her flat. She waded into the sea like she didn't care, till the icy water tickled her ribs and that beak could have had her with an easy lunge.

Ryn clamped the hilt of his sword so tight, his fingers ached. "Gods be damned." He'd faced his own death with less fear.

"Calm yourself, man-child," Oma said. "Cetuu does not come to eat."

"Is that its name, or its kind?"

"Cetuu is Cetuu, be it one or many," Astrig said.

"One is plenty."

Josalind tested the air with a slow hand as Ryn would to calm a skittish horse. *She had better not intend to ride the damned thing.*

A tentacle wrapped around Josalind's arm. Another slipped about her waist. She hadn't a chance now. Ryn ripped his sword free and took a step.

Oma's clawed hand landed on his shoulder. "Cetuu sees you, man-child."

The monster let go of Josalind and thrust itself backward before vanishing under the waves. Ryn sheathed his sword and ran to her as she came back to shore.

She shivered something fierce. Her sodden shift was too thin for modesty. Ryn tried not to look, but his eyes still strayed for a moment. He snatched up her cloak and draped it over her shoulders.

Josalind's eyes shone silver. A laugh broke past her bluish lips.

"What?" he asked, as he led her to the fire.

"Cetuu calls you 'that fussy little crab with the shiny claw.'"

"Crab, am I?" he said. "Well, the other crabs on that ship have cannon. We'll see what the monster thinks of that."

Josalind had barely dried herself off before urging them into the air again.

Midday glare had turned the sea into quicksilver. They came around from the south to have the sun at their backs as the caravel came within sight again. Ryn kept them circling at a safe distance while they waited.

Oma soon spotted a hump that broke the surface and drove a broad bow wake, about two hundred yards behind the caravel and the skiff that it towed. Ryn nudged her closer as Cetuu dove out of sight.

Nothing happened for a spell, then those big feeder arms whipped out of the water and snatched the skiff up in a crushing hug. The small vessel heaved into the air as its hull splintered. Cetuu hauled it under with such force, the caravel jerked before the towline snapped. All that remained were shattered ends of wood, bobbing in the waves.

Shouts rose from the crew. A frantic hand rang the pirate bell. The ship lurched like it had been rammed amidships. A man fell from the rigging with a scream. Crew scrambled across the deck as the ship listed to port and its bow pulled northward. The sails lost their wind and started to flap.

Cetuu intended to climb aboard.

Ryn didn't object when Oma circled down within range of the swivel guns for a closer look—not a soul on that ship looked in their direction. Cetuu's feeder arms had latched on to the rigging at portside as its smaller tentacles snaked over the gunwales. The swell of panic from the crew rang clear over the whip of the wind. That big Sevrendine man stood on deck, weird white sword in hand, accompanied by a woman who was fair and blonde.

Ryn frowned and shaded his eyes but saw no sign of that witch woman from before. Whatever power the Sevrendine could muster against Cetuu, he thought it a fair bet that they wouldn't rush into anything likely to further spook the crew. Sailors weren't the sort to flirt with the ill-luck of having a witch or sorcerer on board—they'd toss their passengers with even half a reason.

Crewmen broke open the weapons stores as that snapping beak rose over the gunwale. The big Sevrendine faced Cetuu with his sword in a two-handed grip. Ryn didn't doubt that blade and the mass of muscle behind it could shear the monster's rubbery limbs with no bother.

Before battle could be joined, Cetuu flung itself away from the caravel with such force, the ship plowed sideways. The crew didn't cheer their good fortune but went dead silent. One sailor's attention strayed to starboard. He yelled and pointed at Ryn and Oma.

The Sevrendine man turned. Ryn drew his sword and gave an exaggerated salute as Oma wheeled to gain altitude before those swivel guns could catch her again.

He looked forward to their next meeting in Tanasgeld.

Being back in a civilized place made Ryn's skin crawl.

Not that anyone with refined sensibilities would rush to label Tanasgeld's harbor as "civilized." The waterfront was altogether loud and boisterous, reeking of pickled herring and hot tar. He doubted his nose would ever be the same.

But that wasn't what he found so bothersome.

Tanasgeld was also a seat of power for the Clerisy. The archdiocese for northern Jendalia had its own grand inquisitar, its own garrisons of palatars. Five days had passed since their escape from the Claw. A messenger pigeon could fly the distance in one. Tovald and Aelin had surely sent word of what had happened. Ryn felt that his back sported a target every time he stepped out.

He had taken to a tavern on the docks anyway, planting himself on the front stoop for a clear view of the breakwater. He had to be out in plain sight if he expected to spot his prey. Lurking in the shadows was the surest way to earn suspicion. To play the part of a hiresword looking for work, he wore his mail hauberk with simple leather gloves, along with a light woolen cloak and a plain arming sword with a dagger. Tanasgeld had rules about who could carry firearms in public.

He found it strange, being back in the world, watching people go about their business. Sailors and longshoremen, customs officers and merchants, working women cruising for a trick, wives seeing their menfolk off or welcoming them home again. The random rhythms of life. How many of these strangers who crossed the boardwalk before him stood to suffer on account of the Sword or the skull if he did nothing?

Circumstance had left him with resources and knowledge—that no one else had—to retrieve the relics before all Hells broke lose. If he failed to act on that, he fully deserved the noose that the Clerisy would soon have waiting.

As to what might come afterward should they actually succeed . . . he hadn't yet decided how much he trusted Josalind's ghosts or their desire to take the relics to Gostemere. He found it all too easy to despise the fiends for how they afflicted her to the edge of madness.

"Anything else, goodman?" the server called from the doorway. His tone didn't hide the fact that he'd grown tired of asking.

"Perhaps a bowl of chowder in a bit," Ryn said.

The server grumbled something and disappeared inside. The pint of sweet mead in Ryn's hand was only the second in three bells. He wanted to keep his wits and stretch their resources as far he could. A nice dark stout would have been his preference, but mead was cheaper. For coin, he'd bartered his swords, the battle gauntlets he'd looted from the dead grenlich, and the silver brooch from Ogagoth's cloak. The costs of survival in a strange city threatened to burn fast through such a meager purse.

A familiar caravel rounded the breakwater. Ryn shaded his eyes and squinted. The ship still listed to port. Cetuu must have stove the hull badly enough for it to take water despite the best efforts of its carpenter and pumps. According to Josalind, the monster had accosted the ship twice more after they had flown on ahead to Tanasgeld. The crew had furled all but the topsails to ease the ship into port.

It wouldn't take long for the Sevrendine to be off and gone if the harbor inspectors found no obvious threat of shipborne illness to warrant a quarantine. These two were not enemies, Ryn had decided, but still represented a sizeable obstacle. They believed in their cause and wielded arcane powers as a reward for their devotion. Zealots certain in their faith seldom compromised, not without a fight.

The situation called for discreet snooping, rather than direct engagement.

Ryn dropped a coin on the table and rose to leave. Several pairs of hard-soled boots thumped on the boardwalk toward him in perfect cadence. He caught a glimpse of the scarlet half capes embroidered with the Pure Flame, worn only by palatars in service to the Inquisitarem. Redbacks, so palatars who took the White called them. Quintan had often said men who wore the Red had an appetite for torment that made their devotion to Aegias questionable.

Their presence argued in favor of a quick detour in the opposite direction from the landing quay. Ryn had already talked his way past one patrol earlier in the day. Their hard-nosed questions left little doubt that arrest warrants had been issued for him and Josalind, even if the city's printers hadn't typeset any to post yet. Ryn had passed himself off as a hiresword affiliated with the well-respected Upright Company—a claim he could defend, thanks to the brand that now marked his forearm. Careful work with a red-hot horseshoe nail and Josalind's healing kiss had assured the brand looked legitimate and years old.

The caravel had docked by the time he had circled back around to the boardwalk at the foot of the quay. An inspector stood at the bottom of the gangplank, flanked by a pair of marines with pistols in hand.

The crew crowded the deck, yammering at one another. They likely would have abandoned ship faster than rats from a fire if not for the marines. Any man who tried to come ashore before the inspector gave his leave courted a ball in the brainpan. If the captain had the nerve to go back to sea once repairs were done, he'd be hard-pressed to find willing replacements. This lot was likely to get drunk and stay that way until their coin ran out. A few might even take holy vows and retire. Most anyone else in port would think the ship cursed.

The inspector boarded the ship. A quarter bell passed before he gave his leave. Ryn watched with growing anxiety as the crew fled ashore. He didn't see either the man or the woman. Had they already slipped away?

But no, they appeared from belowdecks as the crew cleared off.

And again, the man's companion was this fair-skinned Jendal woman with corn-silk hair gathered in a bun under a day cap. She had the same buxom figure as the other woman. Could it be her, masking herself with some glamor through the Grace of her goddess? It would make sense—her true features were far too distinctive in these northern lands.

She came ashore with an oblong bundle tucked under her arm and the man followed. Ryn didn't see that big white blade, or any weapon at all. They made for the boardwalk at a brisk pace.

He pulled up his hood and turned away as they approached, eager to appear as a nondescript part of the scenery. A young lass sold oysters from a pushcart nearby—so fair and blonde she appeared bleached. Her basket-weave hat, decorated with shells, sported a brim broad enough to shade her whole enterprise. "How much?" he asked.

"Two pennies each, good sir."

"I'll take two, and don't be shy with the horseradish." It was the only way he could stomach the things. And then he had a troubling thought—what if the Sevrendine had an urge for fresh oyster?

They stepped onto the boardwalk behind him and paused. He took up his first oyster and slurped it down so fast, his nose swelled and eyes watered from the horseradish's burn. Then they headed off.

Our time grows short, Heir of Aegias.

Ryn almost choked. The Voice had been silent since they'd fled the abbey. Why here? Why now?

Follow them.

He dropped twice what the oysters were worth on the girl's tray, ignored the second one, and turned after the Sevrendine. They were already well down the boardwalk. Only the man's height and that ratty straw hat kept them in sight as the caravel's crew clogged the way. Ryn shouldered through the crowd and came out the other side just as the pair turned up the main street for the heart of town.

He ducked down a side alley at a run and rounded the back of a bakery in time to see them pass. They moved with a confidence that suggested they knew the city well. Maybe Tanasgeld had been their destination after all, though he couldn't fathom why. He shadowed them through several more alleys, past a brothel enjoying some brisk afternoon business and a butchery busy with chickens, judging by the flavor of stink.

A dead end forced him over to the main street. He waited until the Sevrendine had passed before sidling up to the corner and glancing around. He had precious little cover—the street saw only light traffic and ran straight as an arrow. Damn the Jendalians for having such an eye for right angles. Everything always had to be done to a plan.

Ryn had little choice but to follow in the open. The Sevrendine hoofed along at a brisk pace, which made it a challenge to look casual and not like a footpad stalking a mark. Twice the man looked behind. Both times Ryn took what cover he could—a passing cart, an apple vendor's stall—and hoped he'd been quick enough.

They passed into the merchant quarter, home to the city's better inns and dining establishments. The place where Ryn and Josalind had taken board lay only one street over.

The Sevrendine took a side street.

Ryn ran over and peeked around the corner. They disappeared into a building three doors down. He found an alley with a clear view past the rear of the building and its stable yard. After giving it a spell, he circled around to the front and then back again. They had ample chance to slip past him if they suspected a tail.

No.

Ryn took that to mean they hadn't. In Dragon's Claw, torn with the choice of killing Josalind or watching her burn, he'd broken his own vow and responded to that Voice. He had to be careful, disciplined, certain now more than ever that giving the Voice any acknowledgment only deepened its hold on him.

He circled around to another alley that offered a clear view of the building's main entrance. The alley lay in shadow, crowded with crates and barrels. Rats squeaked and scurried out of sight.

The Sevrendine had taken to an inn—no surprise there. The Captain's Reprieve, a name that no doubt had a story behind it. There was always a story, rarely told the same way twice.

A hand touched his arm.

Ryn's heart leapt into his throat and his sword from its scabbard. There stood Josalind, as proper as any young miss of a well-to-do merchant family, girded with three layers of linen petticoats in shades of brown and green. A fine woolen vest cinched a billowy blouse with draping sleeves.

No decent clothier in town could deliver on a rush order in less than three days with what Ryn could afford to spend. There had been only one way to quickly acquire some decent clothes so Josalind could blend in. Courtesans with the means liked to dress respectably. Ryn had found a fine pair of ladies willing to part with some of their wardrobe for a price that amounted to extortion. They'd also taken the precaution of dyeing Josalind's distinct curls a common shade of brown.

Considering the gravity of their situation, Josalind had taken to the whole business of outfitting and disguising with far too much enthusiasm. Her frivolity reminded Ryn of some pampered nobleman's daughter, giddy with the preparations for her coming-out ball. Even now, the pose she struck in those clothes left him feeling the part of a suitor seeking a spot on her dance card.

He shoved his sword home and scowled. "What are you doing here?"

Her eyes narrowed at his tone. "I've been cooped up in that damned room for two days." She thrust out her chin. "I wanted to see the city—to just walk around like a regular person. You have no idea how good it feels to be a stranger exploring a strange place. To be able to walk around *without* people pointing and whispering and flinching away from your shadow like it's going to bite them."

Her eyes welled with emotion as she spoke. Here she was, abroad in the world for the first time, after years of being treated as her family's dirty secret. She had the right to take what simple pleasures she could.

Ryn touched her hand. "I'm sorry. That wasn't very charitable of me. Just . . . just be careful, all right?"

Josalind looked toward the inn. "The time for that's long over—I can feel the skull." She squeezed her eyes shut and rubbed at her temples. "*They* feel it and they're running short of patience."

"Are they," Ryn said. "Have they any kind of plan?"

"Not that they've said." She squared her shoulders and stepped past him. "Best get to it, then." She may have meant to sound resolute, but it came out as fragile.

Damn. He grabbed her arm. "You think those two will just hand the relics over if you ask nice?"

That silver fire flickered in her eyes. "I don't mean to ask." A shock erupted from her skin and flung his hand away.

She made for the inn with a firm step, fists clenched to keep a chokehold on her resolve, or maybe to keep the gods from swallowing her entirely. He rubbed his palm against his trousers to ease the sting and followed.

Damn the Four for leaving him to figure a way out when this inevitably went south.

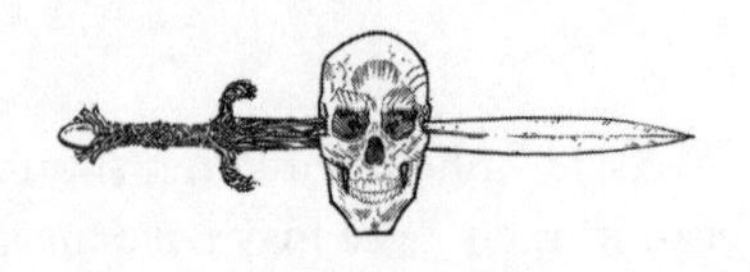

NINETEEN

The Captain's Reprieve exuded a simple, stately charm. Cut stone with clean lines on the first floor, topped by two more stories of timber framing and clapboard siding weathered gray. Shutters painted in bright shades of green, yellow, and blue, and window boxes thick with asters and mums broke up the somber tones.

Ryn saw it all as clever embellishments to hide the jaws of a trap.

Josalind walked right up to the paneled oaken doors and pulled them open by the big brass handles.

A doorman waited inside. The big ox looked as thick at the knees as he was in the shoulders, with heavy and jowly features to match. His weight rested on a cane fit for a fence post that had likely cracked more than a few skulls. He peered down at Josalind through wire spectacles. "Can I help you, miss?" Thunder carried less rumble.

She gave a curtsy. "Might the kitchen be open for an early dinner, good sir? I hear the Captain's chowder and biscuits are the pride of Tanasgeld." A safe bet—most every respectable establishment in the city made the same claim.

"Is that your man?" the doorman asked, thrusting his chin in Ryn's direction.

Ryn tipped back his hood and gave a pleasant nod.

"Of course," Josalind said. "My da won't be having me about without a proper escort."

The doorman stepped aside. "The dining room is to the left."

Ryn blinked for his eyes to adjust as they stepped into the foyer. Josalind went straightaway for the dining room. He made to follow, but that big cane barred his way.

"Your sword, sir. You will have to check that here, along with any other weapons you're carrying."

Ryn grimaced but didn't see that he had much of a choice. Josalind had already passed out of sight. He handed over his sword, dagger, and even his belt knife. "Content?"

Thick fingers slid down his back but found nothing. His boots earned only casual inspection—the shiv in the right remained undisturbed. "For now," the doorman said. "I recommend the stout, if you have a thirst."

"My thanks," Ryn said over his shoulder.

He found the dining room almost empty, though it could seat forty. Two other young women shared tea and pastries while their escorts played cards and shared a pitcher of something stronger. The drapes were half drawn on two deep-silled windows. Wooden paneling gleamed with fresh polish under the calm light of wall-mounted oil lamps. Nautical instruments mounted between them offered some decoration—a brass telescope, a ship's compass, a whaling harpoon, among others. The tapster's counter ran along the right side of the room, while a pillar clock kept time with a pedantic *ticktock* in the opposite corner.

A fire crackled in the hearth that lay at the back of the room. Josalind had already claimed the table nearest to it. Ryn settled into a hard-backed chair across from her. The furniture showed the same care as the woodwork, built heavy and sturdy. They ordered chowder and a basket of sourdough biscuits from the hostess. Ryn decided to splurge a bit and chose the stout, determined to enjoy himself before the shite began to fly. Convention dictated that a respectable miss abstain from alcohol in public, but the hostess took it in stride when Josalind asked for an ale.

Ryn frowned at the almost idiotic grin Josalind wore after the hostess had left. "This whole business amuses you?"

She leaned over the table to whisper in the manner of a co-conspirator. "No one knows me. No one cares. I could never do this at home, no matter my age or how respectable my family." The grin faded. "Not without people treating me as a leper." She sat back in her chair. "I hold every moment we're free for the precious gift that it is. To you, it's just an ale; to me, it's a sip of heaven. And I'll say the same tomorrow even if we're drinking from a puddle."

Despite the situation they faced, Ryn couldn't help but smile. He reached across the table to pat her hand.

More patrons arrived. The pillar clock chimed four bells post midday. Ryn and Josalind were already halfway through their meal when the Sevrendine came in.

They could have passed for a master tradesman and his wife. The woman had dressed much the same as Josalind and still wore that glamor to hide her true features. Ryn had to wonder what else she hid. That boxed and wrapped bundle lay under her arm, about four feet long. The man wore boots and trousers, with a waistcoat and frock coat of gray and brown. Ryn could only assume he'd left that big white sword on the ship. Even so, the man had to be armed in some fashion, no less than Ryn was with the shiv in his boot. The roving gaze of those ice-blue eyes missed nothing. When the man spotted Ryn and Josalind, his posture tensed, and he spoke to the woman. Her brow furrowed, more with curiosity than concern.

Ryn smiled and pushed out one of the empty chairs with his boot, damned if he wouldn't play this as cool as meltwater. What else could he do? Whether the man was armed or not, they still had to contend with the woman and whatever power she could muster. Ryn could only trust that a room full of witnesses would keep her muzzled.

The couple crossed the room to their table. The man eased into the chair that put his back to the wall. The woman sat across from him. She laid the bundle across her lap. The end brushed Ryn's leg. His nape hairs prickled as if some slimy invisible thing had just skittered up under his shirt.

The darkness gathers.

"How's the stout?" the man asked.

"Better than most," Ryn said. Which it was. Not too bitter and served at the perfect cellar temperature. Though between the Voice and the touch of that bundle, his enjoyment of it had been ruined. He found himself longing for the bite of the hair shirt, desperate for the distraction.

"Indeed," the man said. "I could go for a pitcher or two."

His casual politeness didn't fool Ryn for an instant. The woman had eyes only for Josalind. She didn't even blink. Josalind stared right back and sipped her ale.

"The Clerisy has a price on your head," the man said.

Ryn gestured at the bundle. "We have larger concerns."

As before, those eyes twinkled in a way that left Ryn certain the man either mocked him or found it impossible to take him seriously. He pressed a hand to his broad chest. "I am Horgrim."

"Ryn, and that's Josalind."

"Kara," the woman said. The stare-down continued. "What power do you serve, girl?"

Josalind's eyes narrowed. "You first."

Kara's hand whipped out and pinned Josalind's wrist. The woman's mere touch appeared to inflict pain—Josalind gasped and dug her nails into the table. Ryn wasn't one to draw steel on an unarmed woman, but Kara was nothing ordinary. He went for the shiv in his boot.

Horgrim snagged his wrist halfway.

Ryn broke the hold by twisting his forearm and snapping his arm up straight. The back of his fist should have caught Horgrim square in the nose, but the fellow was damned quick. He dodged aside so fast, he had to grab the table's edge to keep from falling out of his chair. Chowder and beer sloshed as the table shifted. Ryn slapped his hand down to steady it with such a crack, the whole room went silent.

Horgrim scowled, lips peeled into a snarl. The hostess eyed them from behind the bar. Her tapster, whom Ryn had dismissed as a rather meek-looking little fellow, had already pulled a cudgel from beneath the counter. He didn't appear so meek now.

Ryn waved his tankard at them. "A round of the same for our guests." He put it down and leaned toward Kara. "Get your hand off her—*now*."

Kara slumped back in her chair, arm falling limp at her side, eyes wide with disbelief. Her voice trembled as she spoke. "It can't be."

Horgrim drummed his fingers on the table. "What?"

"She hears the Four." Kara's flabbergasted manner would have suited the revelation that the Great Deceiver was her own father. Ryn took grim satisfaction in the fact that Josalind's truth had so thoroughly rattled the woman.

Horgrim's fingers stopped cold, but he gave no other reaction. "Impressive, considering they're dead."

Ryn found the man's stoicism, by contrast, decidedly annoying.

"But not gone," Josalind said.

"You're a herald, then," Horgrim said.

"What's a 'herald'?" Ryn asked.

Horgrim looked to Kara.

She pressed her hands flat on the table and squared her shoulders. Ryn took that for a deliberate effort to rally some composure. "A cleric blessed with the power of divine will."

"Is that what you claim to be?" Ryn asked.

Kara bit her lip and said nothing.

"You *are* Sevrendine," Ryn said. "Admit it. Or would you deny your faith and your goddess?"

They deny the futility of their cause.

A growl sounded from low in Horgrim's throat. "Watch yourself, lad."

"And what if we were, sweetie?" Kara said.

Ryn found the undivided attention of her piercing gray eyes hard to bear, but he would have preferred to gouge his own with a fork than be the first to blink. "We've come for the skull and the Sword."

Horgrim leaned back and laughed aloud, not a mocking laugh, but one filled with genuine mirth. He folded his hands across his chest. "What claim could you possibly have?"

Ryn nodded at Josalind. "Ask her."

"The Four's purpose is to end the Great Deceiver," Josalind said, blunt and matter-of-fact.

Horgrim snorted. "Is that all?" He looked to Ryn as if expecting him to refute it. Ryn just held his gaze. Horgrim looked back to

Josalind. "You don't lack for ambition. Is this the madness your holy ghosts whisper in your ear?"

"Easy, old lion," Kara said. She appeared the more mild-mannered of the two, but Ryn didn't doubt that aggressive fanaticism lurked just beneath the surface.

"Pain and torment we can't imagine has made them mad," Josalind said. "But still, they've got the grit to do what your Goddess Fraia, *their own mother*, does not—bait the Great Deceiver and use the Sword to end the miserable devil."

They fell silent when the hostess came with supper, beer, and a fresh basket of biscuits.

Once she had gone, Horgrim leaned in until he almost brushed Josalind's nose with his own. "You play a dangerous game, little girl. Do you have any idea the power of that sword?"

The *Codex* might be stuffed with half-truths and lies, but Ryn found himself still believing what it said about the devastation Mordyth Ral could wreak.

Josalind didn't give an inch. "And yet, *they* would see it done."

"Let's not make this tedious," Kara said. "The skull and the Sword will go east . . . with us."

"Then the seal will break and Xang will be heard," Josalind said. "His father's servants will come for him."

"That's not a threat new to us," Horgrim said.

"No," Josalind said. "War and death, in the name of righteousness—that's all you Sevrendine know."

The barb didn't appear to prick Horgrim in the least. "The Clerisy exiled us from the Kingdoms and left us to be slaughtered," he said. "We had to fight to live. We still do. If not for us, the Keshauk would be on the Kingdoms' doorstep."

"You're a long way from home." Ryn took a swallow of his stout and looked to Kara. "How did you find out about the relics?"

"I have dreams from time to time." Kara glanced down at the bundle. "A rather disturbing one, this time."

Ryn couldn't fathom how she could bear to have Xang's skull nestled on her lap like a dozing cat. He wondered how her powers compared to Josalind's—the grace of one living deity versus the unwanted predations of four dead ones. "Something this dire and just the two of you, eh? You must be quite the pair."

"We do what we can, with what Fraia sees fit to provide," Horgrim said without a drop of conceit. "Few can be spared when war with the Keshauk never ends."

"It never can, so long as the Great Deceiver lives," Josalind said. "His evil is everywhere."

"There is evil enough in men's hearts without *Him* being the cause," Horgrim said. "His priesthood is the true evil. It is they who keep millions under heel across the Keshauk Dominion, who demand the sacrifice of babes torn from their mothers' teats."

His reference to babes and sacrifice brought tears to Josalind's eyes. "With the Great Deceiver gone, the power of his priests to command demons will be gone," she said. "What do you think will happen then?"

The answer to that was obvious—a priesthood of sorcerers that ruled a score of nations by fear would lose all authority when suddenly stripped of its arcane powers. And not just them—from his layman's knowledge of the subject, Ryn expected every sorcerer, anywhere, would lose the means to ever again summon and command a demon. "I expect the peoples of the Dominion would rise up and overthrow them," he said.

Josalind nodded and rubbed at her temples. "Don't you see—destroying the Deceiver is the surest way to end the madness. There'd be no more cause for your war."

Horgrim scoffed. "You say that like it would be an easy thing to do, girl. Of course, we want to see an end to the Deceiver and the evil he empowers. But the Sword is a cure worse than the disease. History has proven it."

"I pray for the day when we might embrace the Keshauk in peace, child," Kara said. "The land of my own grandparents suffers under their priesthood." She placed a gentle hand on Josalind's arm. "But the idea of using the Sword . . ." She shuddered. "No. We will not risk it."

"It's time you were going," Horgrim said.

Josalind gave her head a hard shake and winced. "No."

Do not leave this to them.

"I wasn't asking, girl." The twinkle in Horgrim's eye had hardened to ice. "Cross us again and I won't be so charitable."

Ryn realized the room had gone dead silent. His Voice's interest in this troubled him, even more so because it appeared to agree with Josalind. But he couldn't risk splitting his focus by worrying about it now. He rapped his knuckles on the table to draw Horgrim's attention. "Hand over the relics, and you won't have to worry about sullying your charitable nature."

Horgrim only grunted with amusement and looked around the common room. "This building has good bones. The one thing I appreciate more than a fine stout is fine stonework."

The man obviously had some point to make. "And why is that?" Ryn asked, even as he tensed and regretted the fact that his weapons remained stuck in a closet.

"It's the care that's taken to build something strong and durable." Horgrim snapped his fingers. The sound rang sharp. At the signal, chairs scraped the floor and half the people in the room stood up. Even the doorman came in, that fence post of a cane in his hand. Their hostess fled through the kitchen door as the tapster came around from behind the counter with his cudgel.

Damn, a whole Sevrendine nest. Wouldn't the Clerisy love to learn about this place. Ryn refused to show his fear and treated Horgrim to an appreciative nod. "Well played."

Josalind rocked in her chair, eyes closed, and muttered under her breath, arms hugged to her chest.

"We will leave, and you will not follow," Kara said with grave certainty.

Josalind rocked harder, till her chair tipped and threatened to spill before coming down again with crack. "No, no, NO." She flung her head so hard, her hairpins and day cap went flying.

Ryn half rose from his chair, not sure what to do. "Josalind?"

Kara regarded her with the tight-lipped tolerance of a mother enduring a toddler's tantrum. She raised her hand in a soothing gesture. "Calm your—"

Josalind's eyes flew open. They simmered with the same rainbow fire that had exploded from them in the chapel at Dragon's Claw. She caught Kara's hand over the table. The woman stiffened and tried to pull away, but Josalind held tight. A white-knuckled battle had begun that Ryn knew had little to do with physical strength. Kara's brow knotted and her nostrils flared as her own eyes gleamed white-gold.

Horgrim sat as still as the stone he professed to admire and didn't dare even speak. Neither did anyone else in the place. The tension left Ryn even more desperate for a decent weapon, though he had no idea how it might serve him, under the circumstances.

The air tingled with a static charge. It grew too thick to feed a decent breath. An anxious wave of goose pimples swept Ryn from head to toe. He struggled to see either woman clearly now. A hazy distortion that rippled like windswept water clung tight to their bodies. Trying to squint through it left his eyes aching. He flinched away as sparks of silver and gold began to arc and spit between them.

Kara's glamor vanished, revealing her true features. "Don't," she said through clenched teeth.

Josalind's hand started to sink to the table. A whine tore out of her. Ryn weighed the risks of clipping Kara with a hard jab.

"Get in the middle of that and your own mother won't know you from burnt bacon," Horgrim said.

Ryn took it for sound advice, as much as it nagged him to just watch.

Josalind's eyes shifted color and flared bright silver. She heaved herself up and flung Kara back. A thunderous boom shook the building. Kara shrieked. An invisible force threw Ryn back over his chair.

He scrambled up to a crouch. Horgrim picked himself up, too. The blast had flattened everyone in the room. Kara sprawled flat on her back, dazed. She'd probably cracked her skull when her chair went over.

Josalind scrambled to her feet, eyes on the prize—the bundle had fallen from Kara's lap and spilled open. Ryn forced himself not to look at Xang's skull. Its hellish chill washed over him anyway. The yellow gleam of Mordyth Ral offered a balm of sorts. He didn't know why, but his hand yearned for its hilt, hungry to feel that thick, wicker-like weave.

Josalind went for the relics.

Kara snagged Josalind's heel and sent her crashing hard onto her rump. Josalind squealed in outrage and clawed her way over Kara to claim the relics first. She drove a knee into the woman's stomach, an elbow into her chest. Her single-minded viciousness took Ryn aback.

Horgrim surged to his feet with a roar. Ryn rose to meet him, then stopped cold.

Something snaked out of Horgrim's sleeve and over his knuckles. It pushed into his ready hand—a fluid substance with the luster of rustled silk. A blade took shape. In a heartbeat, Horgrim held that monstrous white sword. Stubby red thorns sprouted from its pommel and crescent-shaped cross guard. He'd been wearing the damned thing like an undershirt.

Ryn threw his weight behind the table and slammed Horgrim against the wall in a messy shower of chowder, beer, and biscuits. That big blade whistled over his head. Horgrim grabbed the edge of the table and flung it away. The tapster threw himself aside as it crashed into the counter. Everyone else scurried out the nearest door. Sevrendine faithful they might have been, but if they were residents of Tanasgeld accustomed to living in the Clerisy's shadow, they'd never seen or felt such displays of power. Prudent fear proved stronger than valor.

Horgrim came at Ryn with the grim purpose of Lady Death. As far as charity went, his had clearly been well spent. Ryn backed away with a quick step and snatched up a chair. Then Horgrim's attention jerked from Ryn to something beyond him. His eyes bulged. "No."

Ryn didn't doubt his sincerity—such blood-draining terror was hard to fake. He turned to look for himself.

Kara struggled to pick herself up. Josalind stood with Xang's skull tucked under one arm, Mordyth Ral's hilt clenched in her hand to pull the Sword free.

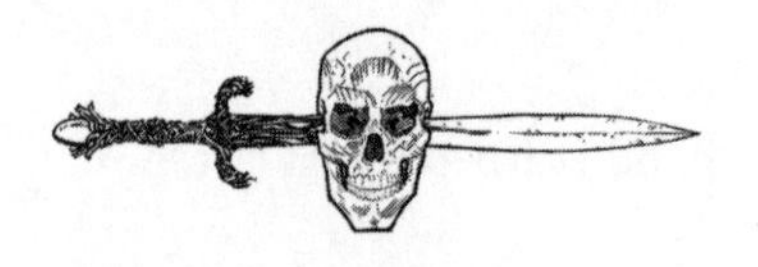

TWENTY

Holy fury danced in Josalind's eyes. Her features twisted into a scowl, torn between pain and bliss.

She pulled Mordyth Ral an inch from Xang's skull. There weren't many inches left to take. The grate of bone and metal stabbed Ryn's ears. He doubted the infernal machines of the Hells themselves could yield a sound more fiendish.

Gold fire blasted from Kara's fingers. Maybe she only meant to prevent Aegias's seal from being broken.

It didn't work.

Josalind flew back with a strangled cry, engulfed in a crackling net. Her back arched and her arms snapped tight to her sides, yanking the relics apart.

Xang's skull was free.

Josalind tumbled over a table. The skull struck the floor with such weighty authority, the flagstones cracked. Ryn's knees buckled like he'd taken the blow himself. Shadows swarmed the room, swirling and darting in defiance of the steady light from the oil lamps. A horde of voices wailed from some distant place. They cried out in one unbroken torrent without any need to draw breath. Such mindless despair clawed at his sanity. He choked and gagged with the effort to stifle a fit of maniacal laughter, certain it would rage beyond control until it suffocated him. Covering his ears did nothing to help.

Somehow the skull had landed upright, that perfect death grin aimed straight at him. Its terrible glare challenged him to come, to probe its depths, to gamble his soul.

Abide him not, Heir of Aegias.

Mordyth Ral lay across the room. The gleam of light from the curves of that leaf-shaped blade teased his eye like the swell of a woman's breast or a flash of her ankle. He noted every perfect detail despite the distance. The organic grace with which those russet-green veins rose from the blade and wove together. The round taper of that egg-shaped pommel. A beauty with no match that somehow must have been grown as much as forged.

"What have you done?" Josalind shrieked. Her obvious distress yanked Ryn's attention from the Sword. She dragged herself up and staggered toward the skull.

Kara stepped in to block her. Fresh licks of flame crackled between her outspread fingers. "Me? Idiot child—you meant to break the seal."

Josalind circled around. "I didn't mean to let Xang's skull shout for all to hear."

"What do you mean to do?"

"Stifle him," Josalind said.

Kara held her ground for only a moment longer before stepping aside. Josalind crouched by the skull and snatched up a stray dining knife. She slashed both her palms open.

That cackling lunatic still threatened to burst from Ryn's throat. "Josalind, what—"

"Not now."

She tossed the knife and slapped her hands against the skull. Her slender frame trembled. A low moan escaped her throat. "Can you feel it singing in my blood, Xangtemias?" she said, in that voice not wholly her own. Bloody fingers drifted over the skull with a mother's tenderness. "Crawl back to your pit, old salt."

The evil shadows faded from the room. The cries of the Damned followed. Ryn sagged onto his rump with the relief of a man freed from an inquisitar's rack.

Josalind sat upright, though her shoulders slumped and her head remained bowed. She left the skull sitting there, anointed with her blood. "That should go in a sack." She sounded herself again, but weary and wrung out.

"How long will that seal hold him?" Kara asked.

"Till it doesn't," Josalind said. "I'll have to cage him again before long."

Horgrim regarded Ryn with a sour eye before cocking an eyebrow at Kara.

"They'll have to come with us," she said.

His face flushed. "What?"

"I don't know if I can keep Xang smothered like she did, old lion," Kara said.

Josalind looked to them. "You won't. You can't."

"How are you so sure of that?" Horgrim asked.

"Think about it," Kara said. "The Four's parents were Fraia and the Deceiver—gods foreign to our world. But we know Fraia used more than just the Deceiver's seed for that conception. She took something from this world's life force, too."

Foreign to our world—Ryn considered asking what she meant by that, but found himself too distracted by a yellow gleam.

"The Four are of the earth, where Fraia isn't," Horgrim said.

Kara said. "Which gives Josalind a power to bind Xang that I don't have."

That yellow gleam swelled until Ryn could see nothing else.

"She broke the seal to force our hand," Horgrim said with the fierce gravity of a magistrate eager to punish.

"I never said she wasn't a reckless child," Kara said.

"You weren't leaving me much of a choice," Josalind said.

"Now, what in the Deceiver's black arse are you doing?" Horgrim snapped.

Ryn didn't remember crossing the room. He didn't remember kneeling. And yet, here he was, fingers hovering over Mordyth Ral's hilt. He studied how the veins rose from that strange pale metal, how they thickened and wove together to form the curved guard and two-handed hilt, trapped by the need to find a pattern and understand it.

The Sword was a thing to be feared, a burden to be shunned. The *Codex* left no doubt about that. Still, Ryn craved to have it in his hand. He imagined the feel of that gnarly grip against his skin, the pull of that heavy blade on a swing. An aching need outstripped anything he'd ever known, deeper even than the frustrated lusts of a boy on the edge of manhood. Not even the time he'd been snagged at the bottom of the Panlor—a gasp away from drowning and ready to barter his soul for a breath—could compare.

The rounded tip of Horgrim's big white blade drifted under his nose. "Step away."

Ryn rubbed his fingers across his palm. "It calls me."

"Then my advice is to run fast the other way and don't look back."

What harm could it do, just to touch it? Madness—Aegias had been bound to it till death. A touch might be all it took. But no . . . surely it would take more than that?

The need justifies the sacrifice.

That sounded reasonable enough. Aegias had said nothing meaningful came without sacrifice.

"Mordyth Ral accepts no master, serves no will but its own," Horgrim said. "If it wants you, it means to use you."

Ryn yanked his gaze away, though it crushed his heart to do it. His mouth had gone dry as ashes and tasted of them, too. He stood, slow and deliberate with fists clenched, and forced his leaden feet to shuffle away. Each step nudged him closer to an abyss of despair. "Take it from my sight." He almost choked on the words.

Would you be a sheep to slaughter, then?

Ryn tried to lose himself in the *ticktock* of the pillar clock. The Voice couldn't be trusted—not if it wanted him to take up the Sword.

"You can't enter."

That came from the doorman, out in the foyer. There was a pained "oomph," followed by the meaty *thumps* of a big body bouncing down the hall. It would take a lot of muscle to toss an ox such as him.

Ryn caught a glimpse through the doorway of what looked to be two men . . . but then they weren't. In a blink, they became something else, taller even than Horgrim and broader in the shoulder. Their bony skulls swept back into horns, one with a mismatched pair of spirals, the other with a distorted fiddlehead. A veil of darkness clung to their bodies like trapped smoke. It churned with a restless discontent, evident through the occasional swirl of bile-green phosphorescence—seething hellstorms constrained to a man's shape. That darkness masked their faces so that Ryn saw only their eyes—heartless orbs that flickered with a violet flame.

Fiends. The kind of hybrid he'd read about in Tovald's books—a human willingly and forever grafted, body and soul, to a lesser demon. Maybe they weren't, but he didn't know what else they could be. One look at those eyes chilled him almost as much as the abyssal stare of Xang's skull.

They crowded into the dining room, each armed with a beast of a sword that rivaled Horgrim's. But where his blade gleamed white, theirs looked to be cut from dark volcanic glass.

Horgrim lunged forward to meet them both and booted Xang's skull back toward the kitchen as he went. "Kara—take it and go."

Josalind darted after the skull. Kara looked ready to debate the matter but followed.

The first fiend swept its sword straight at Horgrim's head. The second went after the women.

Ryn dropped his shoulder and barreled into the second fiend with all he had. The impact made his teeth rattle. Caught by surprise from the flank, any other man would have gone flying. This spooky bastard only grunted and stumbled sideways half a step. Ryn shoved away and grabbed the nearest chair just as that black blade came swinging. He deflected the attack but found himself holding only a pair of broken spindles.

Horgrim and the other fiend danced around the room, flinging aside tables and chairs with abandon. The strike of their strange blades rang too hoarse and shrill for proper steel.

Ryn grabbed another chair and tried to circle around to the hallway. His sword rested somewhere out there, likely in a cloak closet. But the moment he stepped out of the way, the fiend he had challenged with a chair bolted for the kitchen.

Though Kara and Josalind had disappeared with the skull, Ryn feared that the fiend could easily chase them down. Maybe between the two of them, they still had the vinegar to take the fiend on after the fury of their own battle—or maybe not. Horgrim hadn't been inclined to risk it.

Ryn charged after the fiend and tossed the chair at its legs. Its feet got tangled up, and it slammed face-first into the kitchen's doorframe. The fiend roared and smashed the chair into kindling with a kick. Ryn had another in hand to crack over its head, but it dodged aside and caught Ryn square in the breastbone with a quick jab.

That fist hit like a sledgehammer, driving the air from Ryn's lungs and knocking him onto his rump. If not for the mail shirt and the padding beneath, he would surely have had a cracked rib or two. As it was, his chest ached too much to breathe. He blinked to see past a swirl of stars and scuttled back on heels and elbows.

The fiend followed. "You will die, then suffer."

Millstones sounded kinder than that guttural growl. Ryn didn't doubt the fiend fully intended to hand his soul over to a cousin in the Hells. That dark blade came down in a two-handed blow faster than he could make his body move.

White met black with a piercing cry. Horgrim heaved the fiend's attack aside. "Get your arse out of here."

Horgrim's fine frock coat already bore several bloodstained slices. Ryn managed one painful breath, then another, as he heaved around onto his hands and knees. The first fiend was down, but not done. It dragged itself up, favoring one leg, attention on Horgrim's exposed back. The blood it left smeared on the floor shone oily black.

Ryn fished the shiv from his boot and tackled it around the waist. Prickly cold cut through him as though he'd just hugged a shaft of frozen iron naked. The fiend smashed Ryn between the shoulder blades even as it fell. Ryn grappled its sword arm with his offhand and thrust the shiv into its throat.

The narrow point punched through as if it contested with harness leather rather than normal flesh. Air whistled from the fiend's punctured windpipe, but it didn't seem to mind. It yanked Ryn's hand from the shiv with freakish strength.

Ryn drove his knee into the fiend's groin even as the grim bastard smashed its forehead into his face.

The fiend's grip slipped. Ryn threw himself away, a gasp shy of blacking out from the blow to his nose. Coppery warmth flooded his mouth. Something sharp grazed his arm and squealed across the flagstones. Ryn rolled across the floor to escape the fiend's reach and bumped into the pillar clock. He needed a proper weapon, but judging by the shiv, plain steel wouldn't do.

Horgrim howled in pain. Something bounced across the floor and whacked Ryn in the shin—the Sevrendine's sword.

The other fiend had Horgrim sprawled against the tapster's counter. Each had a hand clamped about the other's throat. Back bent to break, Horgrim clenched the blade of the fiend's sword in his fist, the tip inches from his chin.

Paying no mind to the shiv stuck in its throat, the first fiend struggled to rise on its good leg.

Ryn wiped his bloody face on the back of his hand and took Horgrim's sword by the hilt.

A sharp pain exploded from his palm. He yanked away. The damned thing had sprouted a fat red thorn—right from the hilt. He tried again. This time, two thorns caught him.

A metallic gleam caught his eye.

Another sword lay within reach—Mordyth Ral.

You have but one choice, Heir of Aegias.

Horgrim had arms as thick as posts, but his strength was failing. The black blade inched closer, slicing his palm and tickling his chin. Some men would have worn raw terror. They might even have begged. The Sevrendine faced his end with a snarl of frustrated rage.

Lips clamped, Ryn went for Horgrim's sword again. He could bear the pain of a few thorns. But this time when he touched the wretched thing, it didn't sting him. Instead, it just . . . melted. From sword to puddle in a heartbeat, like butter on a smoking skillet.

The first fiend made it back to its feet.

Ryn looked to Mordyth Ral and thought of all those faces he'd seen on the docks, the pale oyster girl with her outlandish hat, even those Redback palatars in service to the Inquisitarem. A city crammed with the good, the bad, and the mob in the middle. If he dared wield the Sword now in the face of such a desperate need, would they be anything but cattle to it? The *Codex* warned of the Sword's hunger, of the grievous burden it had been for Aegias, but offered precious few specifics about its actual use or behavior.

The fiend fixed on him.

If you don't, another will. You will die for nothing.

Or take up Mordyth Ral with no idea what might result, certain only that he'd end up bound to it, as Aegias had. Was Sablewood not burden enough?

Then the world vanished.

The fiends, Horgrim, the Sword—all gone in a blink.

Ryn found himself in a cavern, lit by a pale aqua light.

He should have been shocked, terrified, anything. Instead, he felt numb of all feeling. Every muscle had gone flaccid and lifeless. Perhaps they'd just vanished. With them had gone the sense to be concerned. He remembered when he'd broken his leg after a fall from his horse at thirteen—the surgeon had drugged him with some brew of dwale before resetting the bone. That same dreamy disregard gripped him now. He tried to take a step, to lift his hand before his face, but nothing happened. Only his eyes could move.

The cavern had the general shape of a dome, fifty yards high at its peak and covering a good acre. A dry cavern that didn't appear to have ever seen a drip of water sufficient to sprout a single stalactite. Skilled hands had levelled the natural irregularities of its floor. The aqua light came from some species of radiant fungi that grew up the walls.

A man stood with his back to Ryn. A stump of a man, shorter than Ryn and as wide as Horgrim. Gold wire gathered his black hair into a braid that reached his waist. He wore armor already considered ancient by Aegias's time—a battle girdle of bronze and leather, with a skirt of metal-tipped leather strips.

And he carried Mordyth Ral.

A form slumped before him on its knees. It was a woman, or at least the form of one, masked by a snowy radiance that seeped out of her skin. Her light seemed soft but left Ryn's eyes aching if he dared look too closely. He found it oddly similar to the haze that had swallowed Kara and Josalind during their battle in the inn's common room.

Three pedestals formed a triangle around them. A crystalline stone rested on each pedestal—one red, one green, one white. The man dipped Mordyth Ral into a cauldron that resembled a giant skull, which had been cleaved at the nasal cavity and turned upside down to make a bowl of it. Ryn tried and failed to will himself closer and see what the cauldron contained. The man dipped his fingers into the cauldron, too, then put them to his face, maybe to anoint himself. Ryn couldn't tell from this angle.

The man kept Mordyth Ral dipped in the cauldron. A yellow light erupted from the Sword and flowed to the three stones on their pedestals. The female entity's snowy light flickered and flared in a wild pattern. She beat her fists on the cavern floor and screamed in a violent outpouring of pain and grief. Her radiance intensified until it blinded Ryn.

The glare turned gritty and scoured his eyes. Gusts of wind began to tear at him.

The glare faded. Ryn found himself on a battlefield of yellow sand and weathered stone.

Bodies stretched to the horizon. Wind, hot and dry as a forge, whipped across the bleak landscape and kicked up a haze that blurred the sun. Dust devils danced in courtship among the dead.

Ryn recognized the antiquated armor that belonged to men of the Kingdoms. Mixed among them were men with darker olive skin. They wore exotic armor of lacquered wood and polished brass, with pointed helms that trailed silk pennants.

A battle of the Teishlian Aggression. The time and place of Aegias.

He had his body this time—a body he could sense and feel as though this place were truly real. Still, that dreamy detachment mired his thoughts. He walked among the dead, buffeted by the wind, squinting to keep swirls of grit from his eyes. Something wasn't right. Hardly any blood stained the sand. Few of these men bore a wound. Enemies locked in battle; most had just dropped where they stood. This could be the Battle of Outrenar, where Aegias first wielded Mordyth Ral and accidentally decimated his own men.

"Mordyth . . . not . . . denied."

A male voice, faint and tinged with sorrow. Ryn turned to find a warrior not ten steps away. The warrior flickered in and out of focus. A dust devil danced through him. A ghost then.

That should have shocked him, or at least left him wary, but it didn't. Ryn stepped closer for a clearer look. A man of the Kingdoms—Sturvian, judging by the cheekbones and the angular nose. A short beard and jaw-length hair, both jet black, framed his face. He wore the armor of his time but carried no weapon.

Then Ryn took note of the device embroidered upon the ghost's surcoat, the crest of the royal bloodline that ruled Sturvia still. He staggered back as the fog vanished from his mind, overwhelmed by the sudden and dreadful conviction that this was no dream. But how could any of it be real?

He worked his tongue around his parched mouth, heart pounding so hard it threatened to chip a rib.

"Aegias."

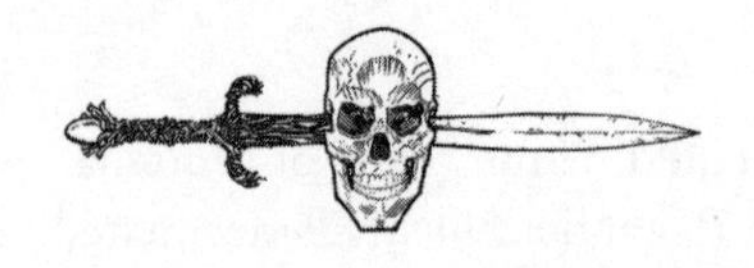

TWENTY-ONE

Aegias. Or at least his spirit.

Ryn fell to his knees and bowed his head.

"No." The spirit spoke in a muffled echo that called from much farther away than where it stood.

Ryn gained his feet as if a pair of strong hands had lifted him by the elbows, but Aegias's flickering form hadn't moved any closer. He forced himself to look directly at the spirit. "What do you want of me?"

The spirit pointed to the ground at Ryn's feet.

Mordyth Ral rested in the sand.

Ryn recoiled from it. This had to be a trick, a hallucination, maybe even some deception by his Voice. The Clerisy claimed Aegias had never appeared to anyone after his death. And yet the Prince Messiah would come now . . . to *him*?

But not since Aegias's death had any man faced so hellish a choice as this.

Ryn swallowed and looked across the killing field. "Why?"

He found himself in Sablewood again on *that* night.

The dead lay twisted and mutilated, gross parodies of the people they'd been. As it had been on that night, as it was in every dream since, the stink of blood and shite hung so thick on the bitter air that Ryn could taste it.

There lay Sara and Tamantha, dead eyes frozen wide in silent accusation.

Aegias appeared from the shadows across from them. "Find . . . anchor . . . deny . . . the Sword."

Ryn balled his fists and snarled. "Don't play me, spirit. I know my sins—I live them every night."

Aegias strode toward him through the bodies. Ryn held his ground, damned if he'd shrink from this illusion or whatever it was. Aegias stopped a step away and shook his head.

Sablewood faded away.

Another place took shape, a land stripped of life. They floated over it as free as clouds. Crops withered to the last root and stalk. Forests of peeling bark and skeleton limbs. Villages trapped in silence and paved with corpses that evaded decay. Somehow, Ryn knew that every creature of any sort that might scavenge the dead or hasten their rot had perished, too.

At the heart of it all, one pathetic creature still lived. A thing with the form of a man, which might have once stood tall and proud, now bent and twisted by the torment of its sins. It stared at a darkening sky with mindless eyes, cackling with manic despair. A warrior, a palatar, wearing the red of the Inquisitarem. In its gnarled hand, Mordyth Ral.

"If not you, another." Aegias's voice came from some place far away.

Ryn shut his eyes against the sight, but the image refused to fade. That cackle echoed all around, magnitudes worse than nails on slate. "I am not you."

The world shifted again.

This time, Ryn saw Aegias. Not the spirit, but the boy prince, in battle wielding plain iron long before Mordyth Ral had come to him. Hundreds of men hacked and screamed in mud-stained fury while the sky cracked and rain fell in sheets. They were all Sturvian—a united realm being forged in blood.

Aegias's knights soon had the enemy routed. The survivors fled over a hill. A village lay on the other side, surrounded by the camp of the defeated. Aegias's knights rode down the survivors before they could reach it. They didn't stop but swept through the camp and into the village's sodden streets. Men, women, children—it didn't matter.

Those who didn't die by sword or lance were trampled in the mud under iron-shod hooves.

And amid the slaughter, dealing death as sure as any other, rode Prince Aegias. The paragon, the messiah—but first, a butcher like all the rest.

"Every man . . . pay . . . sins," the spirit of Aegias said, from even farther off.

"By risking ones even worse?" Ryn said. "I'd rather die in that inn." Let the fiend have him.

"More death . . . fault . . . yours."

"No," Ryn snapped. "You will not hold me accountable for what becomes of that sword. It is not my responsibility."

"Sacrifice . . . greater good . . . your anchor . . . deny it mastery."

Ryn found himself back in the inn at the moment he'd left. Horgrim still sprawled against the bar, fighting to keep the fiend from driving that black blade through his throat. The other fiend favored its gashed leg and limped toward Ryn.

And Mordyth Ral waited.

The visions stuck in Ryn's head, crisp and real. What had it all meant, if anything? He didn't know what to trust.

If not you, another.

He'd argued that the Sword wasn't his responsibility. But there it lay, free for any fool who came along to pick it up. The Aegias of the Scriptures had a word for a man who would welcome death and leave the fate of such a thing to chance, who would turn his back for fear of the personal consequences—a coward.

Ryn reached for Mordyth Ral. He'd deal with the consequences as they came.

His fingers caressed the woven grip of that hilt. Mordyth Ral pulsed with life. A sword was a construct. Nothing more. Yet this one stirred under his touch, throbbing with some bridled energy. He took it up and rose. Impossibly well-balanced, but that gnarled and poky weave wasn't comfortable to hold.

He thought he would have to consciously call on the Sword to act before anything catastrophic might occur, willingly open his mind and body to it as a warlock would to gain the Deceiver's unholy favor.

He had no intention of doing so, but what he intended didn't matter.

The inn began to shake. The fiend with the limp, so intent on its prey, now kept a distance. A shimmering distortion blurred its form. Ryn tried and failed to blink his eyes clear. Seething revulsion overwhelmed him. Something growled with a mad dog's fury—something close. Ryn realized it was him.

The tremors deepened. Glass popped and shattered from the windowpanes.

HOW I THIRST.

Ryn's tongue shriveled, throat parched till he lacked the spit to swallow.

That Voice . . . This cursed blade had been in his head all along.

It all made sense now. For months Mordyth Ral had played him, nudged him, twisted his sense to make him its puppet against the day when Aegias's seal failed.

And now it had him. Had the vision of Aegias been nothing but a trick? Ryn felt deceived and ill-used, but it didn't matter. He'd done the right thing by not leaving the Sword for another. He had to believe that. Nothing else could save him now. But how could he rein in this wretched blade?

He tried to make out Horgrim and the other fiend past the odd blur of his vision. Something wasn't right about the Sevrendine—he wore the same dark aspect as the fiend now, roused the same hateful disgust that tasted of vomit. The Sword's senses colored and distorted his own—that much was obvious, but Ryn couldn't fathom why it would see Horgrim so.

All abomination must be cleansed.

All abomination. The Sword didn't view a servant of the Goddess Fraia any differently than it did a fiend or demon. Fraia and the

Great Deceiver both were threats to be expunged because they were foreign to this world—just as Kara had said. *The Great Deceiver is not the only cancer that poisons the Balance*—the first thing the Sword had ever said to him, back in the Claw.

Together, we will purge the world. Surrender to my purpose. Surrender your doubt. Be free of your guilt.

Ryn took the hilt in both hands and stared into the blade. His reflection crumbled into the same shimmering haze.

And then he understood. Mordyth Ral thrummed in his hand with such subtle violence his whole body vibrated like a plucked harp string. A prismatic swirl danced at the edge of sight, a phantom thing he couldn't see directly. It slipped through him with a tingling warmth, through him and into the Sword.

He felt Mordyth Ral feed.

The Sword drew its nourishment, its power, from anything living. The *Codex* didn't lie in that regard. After being trapped with the skull for so long, its thirst threatened to rage out of control. It couldn't help itself, any more than a magnet could refuse its pull to iron. Not a soul in Tanasgeld was safe. Ryn could taste the panic as it swept the city, surging outward from this very spot, no different than the blast radius of an exploding powder magazine. The horror that gripped every man, woman, and child rattled through him as their lives began to leech away. Those closest would die first. Thousands of innocents, on the brink of being snuffed out. Sablewood would be nothing to this.

"NO."

He tried to drop the Sword, but it wouldn't let him go. The fiend—where was it? It could have skewered him by now. He tried to see and hear with his own senses, to find an anchor in the pain of his battered nose and aching ribs. He could think of no other way to break the Sword's hold.

Bit by bit, his vision cleared. Mordyth Ral had torn the fight out of Horgrim and the other fiend. They teetered like feeble gray hairs, but neither dared drop their guard.

The first fiend slumped at Ryn's feet.

The shiv still stuck out of its throat. The flicker of those violet eyes had faded to embers. This abomination could hide nothing from him. With the Sword in hand, Ryn could easily distinguish from each other the man and the demon who had been fused together to create the fiend. Neither had ever before known the fear that they did now. He found that intoxicating and took a moment to relish it.

Then he plunged Mordyth Ral into their chest.

Their body convulsed with a shriek that cut short. The demon vanished, snuffed from existence. Nothing remained of the man but a desiccated husk that now looked years dead.

The bond is made.

Something changed inside of him, something Ryn didn't understand, but he felt it all the same, as sure as the turn and click of clockwork gears. Muscle and tendon through every inch of his body constricted with a sudden jolt then relaxed, still awash with a lingering tingle. The charge dug deeper than flesh, to his marrow, then deeper still, to his soul. His senses swelled with a rush of sensations: The pillar clock's *ticktock* crashed over him like cannon fire. Horgrim's panted breaths roared to match. The sudden stench of scorched food from the kitchen stripped all desire to ever eat again.

The Sword had put its mark on him, branded him in a way that could never be undone.

He couldn't let that concern him right now. He shoved the corpse aside with his boot to yank the Sword free. The effort lessened the assault of sound and smell to a tolerable level. *You will spare this city.*

I take what I must to fulfill my purpose. A handful of lives means nothing in the lifespan of a world.

An entire city is no handful.

I siphon my strength from many so that fewer need die.

If that was meant to be a concession for his sake, Ryn found no comfort in it. He still felt the lives of thousands on the desperate edge of slipping too far. *You have taken quite enough.*

A tortured, heart-twisting moment stretched by.

For now. When the threat is greater, so will be my need.

Ryn sensed the panic fading from Tanasgeld. He could only hope lives hadn't been lost.

Horgrim and the other fiend regained some of their strength as the Sword released them. The Sevrendine reached out to the puddle on the floor, and it took back the shape of the white sword and leapt to his hand. The fiend snarled in some harsh dialect and bolted for the exit as fast as its shaky legs would allow.

Ryn charged after. He'd never moved with such quick and fluid grace.

"Wait," Horgrim called.

But Ryn couldn't, any more than a hound when lured by a bounding rabbit.

The fiend stumbled out the door into the gloom of dusk. Burning whale oil cut the air with a fishy stench. A lamplighter shrieked and stumbled off, leaving her pole wick behind.

Ryn caught up with the fiend in the middle of the street and stabbed it through the hamstring. It dropped to one knee and tried to catch him with a clever backward thrust. He dodged aside and took its head with a single blow. A death sweeter than the finest mead. Ryn shuddered with the thrill of it even as the part of him that clung to decency recoiled in horror.

"Fool—get off the street."

Horgrim's voice chafed his ear. Ryn turned on him. He didn't see a man, only a thing, fouled by its Invader Goddess. Fraia's taint had to be wiped from the world. Flesh gone to rot had to be cut away before it poisoned the whole body.

The Sword throbbed in his hand as it gathered itself. They were one—an instrument greater than the sum of its parts. Never had he felt so powerful, so alive. He leapt at this thing called Horgrim with a roar.

Horgrim dodged the attack.

Ryn charged after with a wild flurry of strikes. His sense of self fought to tread water in a storm-tossed sea of hate. Four times that white sword deflected Mordyth Ral before the Horgrim thing was left sprawled on its back, stabbed through the shoulder. Ryn pinned the thing's sword hand under his boot and readied the killing blow.

Doubt flickered in that corner of his mind still his own. This was no demon, no slave of the Great Deceiver.

All abomination must be cleansed.

This is wrong.

Flesh is weak.

But he was flesh. He was a man. So was the thing trapped under his boot.

But you can be more. Together, we are more. We are the Gods Bane.

No.

A burning pressure flared inside his skull.

Defiance is the path to pain.

Ryn's arms tensed to strike. He fought against the Sword's will with all he had. Horgrim kicked and bucked to free himself, but blood loss and the Sword's hunger from before had weakened him. They looked eye to eye—two men, two warriors, with nothing left to say that would matter. Ryn's jaw clenched too tight to speak, in any case.

His mind combusted into sheets of scorching flame.

End it.

"You there."

Ryn barely heard the voice behind him, barely knew the thud of boots for what they were. Agony and outrage dragged a whimper out of him as Mordyth Ral sank toward Horgrim's chest.

Something hard slammed into the base of Ryn's skull. He was out before he hit the ground.

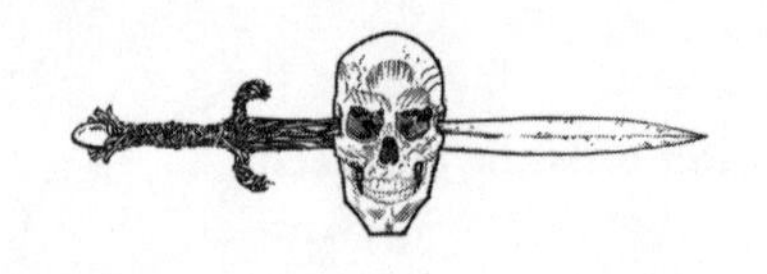

TWENTY-TWO

Fiends.

Josalind didn't know how she knew they were fiends and didn't care. Her blood chilled to freeze her heart at the sight of those horrid purple eyes. In that moment, she cared only about getting away. Never mind the skull, the Sword, or even Ryn. He would fight and die a glorious death. That's what he wanted anyway. There would be time to grieve for him later. First, she had to get away and hide.

No. She bit her lip and stifled her panic with an angry shrug. When had she become such a fainthearted little mouse? She had to do something, to help Ryn, to save them all. Turning tail wouldn't save her in any case. The Four would still be there to nag, dig, and poke. If she ever hoped to be free of Sovaris and her brothers, she couldn't run. Even now, her head began to throb, her fingers to tingle, her sight to burn with that rainbow haze as their power ignited within her. They weren't about to let the Sword or the skull fall into the Great Deceiver's grip.

It was too much. Fighting Kara and binding Xang's spirit had left her as worn thin as old socks. They'd make her swoon for sure, and then where would she be?

Horgrim kicked the skull toward the kitchen and charged the fiends. "Kara—take it and go."

Josalind lunged after the skull and snatched it up. Keep the old salt safe—that she could do. She fled through an abandoned kitchen clouded with smoke and stinking of burned biscuits and scorched chowder.

The Sword, the Sword, Sovaris howled between her ears with the fury of a winter gale.

The back door lay open. Josalind bolted into the alley and kept running, with no idea where to go but away.

Xang's skull felt warm against her chest, and heavy—far heavier than it should have. Dark fog crowded the Four's fury from her eyes. Gritty buzzing clogged her brain and smothered Sovaris's voice. She'd touched Xang's twisted soul, putting that seal on his skull. Might as well have prodded him with a glowing poker. Now he had an interest in her.

"Josalind, wait," Kara called.

She ignored the wretched woman and fled across the street. Draught horses neighed in protest. Their driver yanked back hard on the reins to keep from running her over. Big hooves pawed the air over her head. The driver flung curses as she slipped into the far alley.

Xang's feel deepened with every step, until she waded through a greasy slick of raspy little feelers that wormed their way into *every* part of her. He hungered to live again. Hated anything living that enjoyed the freedom denied him.

They will consume you, Josalind, he whispered. **I would have you, as you are.**

Her neck hairs itched as if his fetid breath blasted from an inch away. Phantom hands slid over her body, not the rough grope of a randy drunk, but slow and seductive. He'd lay waste to half the world to force the other half's surrender. Sickened by revulsion, she wanted to cringe away. If only she could. Memories of that time so long ago crowded her mind—memories not her own. Xang had usurped the Teishlian throne to mire the Empire and the Kingdoms in conflict, to exhaust them both for easy conquest.

Nothing worthy comes without sacrifice.

Sacrifice. How many times had she seen that knife fall, the silence reign, in the visions the Four had shown her, flaying her soul fresh each time? Visions of what Xang had done in Teishlia centuries ago, what his father's priests did even now on thousands of those black altars across the Keshauk Dominion, flooded her thoughts. It never got any easier to see. She feared the day when it did, when she became numb to it and lost the will to care.

What did these images reveal about Xang and his intentions? That's what she had to focus on.

Mastery of all things. That's what he craved—control, obedience. It was a kind of weakness, needing so desperately to appear strong.

Show me another way.

As what? His pet, his herald, maybe even his queen? The thought gave her the strength to snicker with scorn.

What is it you desire to be, without them?

Josalind knew better than to take the bait. She'd lost track of how far she'd come from the inn. Arms and shoulders burned from the skull's unholy weight, like she fought to land a net that groaned with fish. Somebody bumped into her. She shrugged them off when they tried to offer a steady hand. Someone said something. Another voice called out, no doubt puzzled by this odd spectacle of a girl with a skull. She ignored them both and stumbled away, too consumed to even notice where her feet might be carrying her.

If we are divided, the Sword will have us all.

The weight of him pinned her down, threatened to smother. Not his skull, but the swell of him inside, so much so she couldn't tell anymore what was real, what wasn't, and if the difference mattered. His need for conquest, to command obedience through fear and sacrifice—why? She sensed something, a truth he meant to hide. His father . . . what about his father? Something so human as a need to earn affection? But no . . . that wasn't quite right. His father needed . . .

NO.

She staggered and nearly fell from the thrust of his rebuttal, blinded now by his dark fog, walled off from whatever secret he fought to keep hidden.

A pair of hands, crackling with static charge, latched on to her.

"Idiot child," Kara hissed in her ear. "Get off the street."

Josalind didn't have the mustard to resist. She let Kara guide her along until the woman left her propped against a wall.

Those same hands slid over hers, gentle now. "Let it go, sweet, before he swallows you."

Josalind let the skull slide from her grip, muscles crying from the cramps, and gulped air. Her vision cleared as Xang's presence faded. They stood in an alley. Kara cradled the skull in her palms, staring into Xang's bottomless eyeholes. Her lips curled with a disapproving grimace, the kind of look a prim sort might reserve for belching at the dinner table.

"And this is how foul he is even with your muzzle." Kara glanced around and found an old burlap sack, into which she stuffed the skull. "Much better." She twisted the lose fabric into a knot and slung it over her shoulder before fixing that pointy gray gaze on Josalind. "Now, what are we going to do with you?"

The shake in Josalind's knees left her braced against the wall, doubting that she could make it out of the alley without falling on her face. "I'm going wherever the old salt does." Not that she wanted to be anywhere near Xang's skull. The lingering feel of him left her desperate for a good scrubbing, inside and out.

"Until such time as you think you can make off with it," Kara said.

Josalind thrust her chin. "Do you ever consider you might be wrong?"

"All the time . . . do you?" Kara glanced toward the street. The way remained clear. "But we have more pressing concerns—what about that selfless defender of yours?"

Sudden guilt left Josalind's heart in knots as those eyes pinned her fast. Ryn had nothing to defend himself with, not unless . . . She latched on to the only hope she could: "Horgrim—he can match two fiends, can't he?"

"Fraia grants what blessing she can, child," Kara said. "But like you, we're still just flesh and blood." She touched Josalind's cheek. "You know the price that favor demands."

Josalind forced herself to stand tall. "Then why are we lazing around here gaffing? They could both be—"

"Because we can't risk the skull falling into *their* hands. It's what they need—"

"To bring about Xang's resurrection."

"And after our little contest, neither of us has the strength to do much but get in the way."

Josalind had never felt so helpless. "What do we do?"

Kara fondled some round flat object under the collar of her blouse. "Wait—that's all we can do."

Sovaris, who'd been surprisingly quiet, screamed so loud Josalind gasped and clutched handfuls of her hair.

The Sword, the Sword, a hand and a heart for the Sword.

Josalind fell back against the wall with a gasp.

"What is it, child?" Kara asked.

The Four had wanted this all along—the thought struck Josalind like a thunderbolt. Had she known, even if they'd never said so outright? She tried to keep so many things buried, like those images of sacrifice, buried deep so they wouldn't drive her mad. Had it been just one more thing to ignore among so many? She couldn't be sure. So long as Aegias's seal endured, it hadn't mattered.

But the seal had broken—*she* had broken it—and now Ryn would pay the price. It didn't matter what she'd intended or hoped. Whether she could have kept the Sevrendine from getting away with the relics or not. She'd saved Ryn from a traitor's death at the Claw only to condemn him to a worse fate by breaking the seal.

Mordyth Ral's hunger seeped into her, sapping what little strength she had, as it spread across the city. She blinked away tears. "I've doomed us all."

Kara's eyes flung wide with horrid understanding as the Sword bit deeper. Anxious cries sounded from the street. Josalind barely heard them past the roar in her ears, the panicked thump of her heart. She slid down the wall till her behind rested on the dirty stone. Aching grief swamped her as though Ryn were already dead.

Her life slipped away, inch by inch, heartbeat fading, and she didn't care. Even the Four had gone silent. She'd die here, killed by the one person in this heartless world who'd ever shown true concern for her.

And then the Sword lost its leeching hold.

Josalind sucked in one shaky breath, then another. She clawed the tangle of curls from her eyes. Sovaris and her brothers launched into a broken chorus that might have been cheery if it weren't so frantic: **bond made, bond made**.

Kara slumped on a crate, ashen-faced. "Lady Above, the cream's curdled now." She struggled to her feet and offered an arm. "Come along."

Josalind ignored the help. She ground her teeth and forced the two lead slabs between hip and foot to push her upright. How infuriating that this woman, who had twice her years at least, had the mustard that she didn't. "Where?"

"I expect those hellspawn are no longer a bother." Kara let her arm fall. "We'll take a discreet look and then get to our safe house."

Sovaris launched into that tired old refrain as Josalind stumbled after Kara. **Gostemere, Gostemere, find the key and get to Gostemere.**

This key business again—what bloody key? Josalind still didn't know who, or what, waited in Gostemere.

The Earthborn.

The Earthborn? But the Elder Races were long gone, weren't they? Or were they? Nothing the Clerisy wrote in that damned book could be trusted.

What do you mean?

Get there, get there.

She knew better than to expect anything else useful. If the Earthborn waited, could they have some plan that would mean an end to Xang and the Deceiver without Ryn laying half the world to waste?

The skull couldn't be allowed to go east with the Sevrendine. No matter what, Josalind couldn't allow it. She'd fled the Claw wanting nothing more than to give the Four what they desired if it got them out of her head. But after breaking the seal, after rubbing up against Xang's sick mind, after feeling the Sword's bite, things had changed.

She, Josalind Aumbrae, would see the world rid of Xang and his father, and save Ryn from Mordyth Ral in the process, the Four's endless badgering notwithstanding.

The heavens help anyone who got in her way.

The Earthborn . . . answers . . . Gostemere gives means . . . find key . . .

Trapped in that vague state between sleeping and waking, Josalind would have sworn that Sovaris perched in person on the edge of her bed. She swatted at empty air in a futile attempt to slap that shrill voice into silence.

What key? What means?

But Sovaris didn't answer.

The water goddess could have answered. She could have spelled everything out—Josalind was sure of that. Yes, the Four's voices often swarmed around, either too frantic or too muffled for her to make any sense of them. But at other times, such as now, Josalind could hear Sovaris with the clarity of a chapel bell. It left her frustrated by the certainty that Sovaris chose to be obtuse. For whatever reason, there were things the Four didn't want Josalind to know . . . yet.

Being played left her boiling with rage, but what choice did she have except to go along? She had no other way of finding some kind of end that would free her of them, that would save Ryn from the Sword.

A knock sounded on the door.

Josalind drew the scratchy woolen blanket up under her chin and cracked an eye open. The Sevrendine safe house had turned out to be the manor home of a textile merchant and his family. Josalind had been caged in a small room up under the eaves, notable for having a window far too small for her to wiggle through and a heavy oaken door with an iron bolt on the outside.

Astrig and Oma could likely tear through the shingles and planks of the roof above quickly enough. Sovaris had already given Josalind a sense that the need for an escape had been communicated to them. But they would have to wait until nightfall.

The knock sounded again. Josalind opted to ignore it.

The first blush of dawn had brightened the window. After all that had happened yesterday, she had slept like a corpse and still felt tired. The sunlight didn't find much to fall upon: walls of plaster painted pale blue; a small wardrobe in an ugly shade of dark green; a simple spindle chair. At least the straw in the ticking of her small bed had been fresh enough to be comfortable.

The iron bolt slid back and the door opened. Kara stepped in, wearing a cheery smile that didn't disarm Josalind for an instant. A drawstring canvas sack, a cleaner and less smelly alternative to the old burlap one, was tucked under her arm, with Xang's skull inside. The woman probably carried it to the privy, too.

Kara also wore her true face, revealing the exhaustion that fringed her eyes. Josalind wondered if that meant Kara had gotten less rest than she had and therefore lacked the strength for a rematch. But Sovaris and her brothers had gone quiet—if only Josalind could predict when and how they would act through her.

"Well?" she asked.

"They've been imprisoned on the cathedral grounds," Kara said.

Josalind sat up against the headboard and tucked her shift around her knees. "And how are we going to rescue them?"

Kara came and sat at the foot of the bed, her expression solemn. "I am working on that—it might take a few days."

A few days. Josalind gave a ragged sigh, cut by the thought of what could happen to Ryn in that time, a disgraced palatar accused of oath-breaking, an apostate with secrets to give up. She had to consider the benefits of playing along with Kara and taking advantage of her resources to free him.

Kara's hand came to rest on her knee. "I will bring him back to you."

Josalind stiffened at the empathy in the woman's tone, tempted to smack her hand away, angry at herself for letting her guard down and betraying any weakness.

"We will get them both back." Kara seemed to say it mostly to herself.

"Don't pretend to be my friend," Josalind said.

"I wouldn't dare." As before, Kara's other hand came to fondle that flat, round object under her collar. "I was your age once, you know."

Josalind crossed her arms. "I expect that was a *looong* time ago." She nodded at the mystery object. "What is that?"

"A reminder of what I lost back then—the life I expected to have, the one that was taken from me." Kara's voice grew brittle as she spoke.

Josalind suffered a sudden wave of awkwardness that left her blushing. Could that object be a marriage bracelet? The prospect of some tender moment with this woman was too ridiculous for words. Josalind didn't want Kara's sympathy and—as sure as hellfire burned cold—didn't intend to offer any in return.

She didn't have to worry. Those gray eyes drilled into her without a sliver of weakness. "And yes, that was a long time ago," Kara continued. "I embraced a new life, a new calling."

"Why?" Given how she'd never had a say in the matter, Josalind couldn't fathom why anyone would willingly give themselves over to any god or goddess.

"Because I could," Kara said simply. "I was granted the chance to earn Fraia's faith and trust, and I took it."

"Because you *needed* it." That was how the world worked—somebody always needing something and ready to take it, whether you cared to give it or not.

"'Need' isn't such a foul word, sweet. Not when it prompts us to realize how pride blinds us to our faults and keeps us from asking for help."

Josalind found that to be about as subtle as a clash of cymbals. She looked away with a snort to mask how unnerving the woman's attention had become.

"Fraia's faith and trust was a balm I needed in a dark time," Kara said. Her hand continued to rest on Josalind's knee. "But it was so much more than that. It gave me the confidence and resolve to make every soul in Sevrenia my personal responsibility. I do what I do because I know in my bones it is the *right* thing to do. If I don't do it, I've only betrayed myself."

"And what does Fraia take in return?"

"My faith and trust," Kara said with all seriousness, as if that could possibly be the full extent of it. "And that gives me a peace and fulfillment I would never have had otherwise."

And makes you a self-righteous old cow. Josalind forced herself to meet that gaze again. "How are you so certain that Fraia isn't leading you down the devil's path?"

"Because she doesn't lead me anywhere. She trusts me to choose my own path, as she does all her heralds." A hint of sorrow softened Kara's expression. "I'm sorry it's not been that way for you, with the Four."

"I don't need your pity," Josalind said, though in that moment, her denial sounded flat and pathetic even to her own ears.

"Just as well. We don't have time for it." Kara abruptly straightened and pulled her hand from Josalind's knee. "But remember this—to be a herald is to make the hard choices that best serve a greater good." She looked down at the sack on her lap. "That has to come before our own wants."

Josalind understood Kara's meaning well enough, even if neither of them cared to say it aloud. They would rescue Ryn and Horgrim if they could, but not if it exposed them and risked letting the skull fall into the wrong hands.

They were bound by a common need, a common purpose, and the chance of heartbreak that came with it. For today, at least. Tomorrow might be different and Josalind intended to be ready.

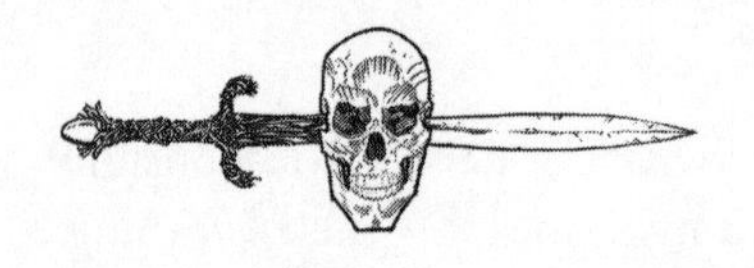

TWENTY-THREE

Ryn didn't care to wake, but something jabbed his gut with no regard for his opinion.

He couldn't breathe through his nose. Stale blood rimmed his throat with the taste of rust. The middle of his face felt twice its natural size. That fiend must have had a brick for a forehead.

His nose had been broken before, during his first year as a plebe at the temple in Teglion. An earthenware tankard caught him square in the face during a tavern brawl. The hit had given his brain a good rattle and left him skirting the need to puke for days.

But that didn't explain the sharp pains that riddled his gut now. Swallowing a handful of nails couldn't have been worse.

He tried to touch his nose, but his hand caught over his head. Both of his hands did. Iron rattled against stone. He snapped his eyes open in sudden panic.

A cell—cut stone and iron bars, dim and dank like any proper jail. Dark growths of mildew clung in the corners, though his swollen nose couldn't register any musty odor. He'd been stripped bare and sat on a stool, held up by shackles that chained him to the wall. A lamp burned just outside the door. He craned his head up. The shackles bore a greenish gleam—witch iron.

Then he noticed the table.

It sat before him, neatly arranged with heretic forks, finger screws, pincers, skewers, and toe cutters. He didn't see the larger machines of torture. Those would be down the hall in the actual testing chamber. This display had been designed for show, to break his will with the grim prospect of torture.

Sitting there naked, with no idea where he'd been taken and nothing else to occupy him, Ryn couldn't deny its effectiveness.

Over the pain in his gut and the rising dread that threatened to swallow him, his bladder ached with the need to void itself. He had no means to answer it with dignity. That, too, was the point—leave your subject stewing in his own filth. Make him feel less than human.

He knew the game and its inevitable end. With nothing left to lose, he heaved himself up from the stool. Cramped shoulder muscles cried out with a swarm of pricks and nettles. Urine arced in a sparkling stream and splattered the table dead center.

"A fine shot," Horgrim said.

The Sevrendine occupied the adjoining cell, separated by iron bars, half lost in the shadows. He had a table, too.

"They're going to torture us," Ryn said.

"What could possibly have given you that idea?" Witch iron creaked but didn't give. "That's fine stonework."

"Not right away, of course," Ryn said, out of a morbid need to emphasize the severity of their situation. He wanted to find a weakness in that mocking demeanor that might prompt the big bastard to confess the same gnawing fear that he felt. "They're going to leave us to think about it for a while."

"That's considerate—I do hate being rushed into things." Witch iron tapped the wall with a dull ring as if further testing the stone's quality. "You do know that by the time they fit you with a noose, you likely won't be in a condition to notice."

Damn the man. He didn't sound ruffled at all. But a chill squirmed down Ryn's spine. A sudden fit of nervous rage prompted him to kick out in the vain hope he could flip over that sheep-humping table. His foot fell inches short. His other heel slipped in some slime on the floor. The impact of his tailbone with the stool left him gasping, nose aching all the more. He drew a shaky breath. "I won't meet my end a sniveling coward."

"Good man," Horgrim said with boisterous enthusiasm. "Let me know how that works out for you."

The nails in Ryn's gut decided to do a jig right then. He gritted his teeth with a grunt and waited for them to settle down. "How's your shoulder?" He wasn't in the mood to offer a better apology.

"They patched it up fair, along with the rest of my scratches. I heal fast, anyways."

Ryn didn't doubt Horgrim had the favor of his Goddess Fraia to thank for that. His gut dragged another groan out of him.

"You're sounding rather poor over there," Horgrim said.

"A bellyache is all," Ryn said.

"Indeed."

One word, but Horgrim dressed it with all manner of insinuation.

Ryn grimaced. "What?"

"I wouldn't know what you mean."

The man's tone suggested otherwise. He knew exactly—this just wasn't the place for full disclosure when they couldn't be sure who might be listening. Best to change the subject. "Any idea how long we've been here?"

"About two days," Horgrim said. "Me, they just trussed up with a sack over my head. You, they kept under with some concoction of dwale."

That left little doubt as to whom they feared more. Ryn wondered what might have become of Josalind, Kara, and the skull, given that the Sevrendine appeared to have no shortage of allies in Tanasgeld, but he didn't dare ask.

Time to see if he might glean something useful. He hawked and spat to clear some of the bloody gunk before calling out. "Hey, there. It's getting thirsty in here. What does it take to get a pitcher of stout?"

"And a leg of ham?" Horgrim added.

Only silence answered. Horgrim said nothing more. Ryn found himself dwelling on what had happened in that inn, the feel of the Sword violating him, changing him, inflaming him with heinous appetites not his own. He couldn't decide which ranked worse—a slow and agonizing death in this hole or a life bound to that thing.

He got himself up on the stool for a spell to work the knots from his shoulders. The manacles were bolted to a chain that ran over pulleys and connected to a ratchet lever far out of reach. All he could do was stare at it, thinking absurd and hopeless things.

Some time later, Ryn and Horgrim received a visitor. It might have been only a bell or two after Ryn awoke, but his anxiety and those mysterious spells of jagged pain stretched it longer. By the time he heard a door down the corridor outside of his cell squeal open, he didn't much care if the inquisitar had come to ply their trade, so long as it meant an end to the waiting.

A bent old man appeared, shuffling along with a bucket and a bowl. A ring of keys jingled from his belt. He unlocked the cell, came in, and released the ratchet lever to lower Ryn's arms.

"What's your name, friend?" Ryn asked.

The jailer opened wide to show the stump where his tongue used to be.

"I trust you gave as good as you got," Ryn said.

The jailer shrugged, then filled a bowl from the bucket and handed it over.

Ryn gave the contents a cautious stir with his finger. Watery barley soup with bits of carrot and onion. Some meat, too. He didn't care what kind—it was nourishment. Thanks to his nose, he couldn't tell if it tasted like stewed shite. The jailer waited until he'd slurped the last drop, then took back the bowl. He ratcheted Ryn's arms up again before heading to Horgrim's cell and repeating the process.

When it came time to leave, the jailer paused in front of Ryn's cell and gave a gap-toothed smile. He mimed a gutting, then a hanging, using himself as the example.

Ryn spread his legs wide. "Lick my hairy berries, you lice-ridden sewer rat."

The jailer turned and shuffled up the corridor, humming a merry tune.

"Well, at least there's entertainment with dinner," Horgrim said.

They had only their jailer for company. Horgrim estimated that he came but once a day. Each time, he bore the same soup and the same twisted talent for showmanship.

After the jailer's second visit, Ryn didn't care if he came again or left them to starve. Those nails in his gut had bloomed into red-hot spikes. He found no pattern to it. The pain might have him balled up so he could hardly breathe for what seemed forever, then it would vanish for so long he thought it gone, only to flare up again with quick jabs that came and went.

Horgrim didn't say much. Not much could be said without betraying something they shouldn't. Besides, Ryn lacked the appetite for conversation. He knew a bond of any sort could be used against him in a place like this.

"Fishing," Horgrim said.

The abruptness with which he spoke gave Ryn a start. He'd just settled into a miserable doze. What in Hells had fishing to do with anything?

"Night fishing in spring is the best," Horgrim continued. "The sky drips with stars and the lake is so still it's a mirror. So, there you are, floating among the stars on a raft. In the shallows, peepers or bullfrogs are in full chorus. You can smell it on the air—the damp freshness of the earth after the last snow has gone, the green of things sprouting. A man can't get any closer to Paradise this side of the grave. It's almost a shame when a catfish bites and spoils the calm."

The dreamy longing in the man's voice left Ryn wandering among memories of his own—distant evenings with his brothers on the shores of the Panlor. Horgrim must have been trying to find his own escape. He knew fear after all. Maybe he even meant to offer some solace.

"Fire," Ryn croaked.

"What's that?"

Ryn cleared his throat. "Don't forget the campfire."

"Yes, that comes later, after the tub is full of fish."

And we've argued over who has to clean them—but the belly spikes caught Ryn again before he could speak. This spell left him gasping and shuddering, like he'd been doused with ice water while getting kicked by a mule. He couldn't help the whimper that crawled out of him.

Horgrim whispered something. Ryn dragged himself out of his misery. "What?"

"You . . . *it* . . . bound."

Mordyth Ral. Aegias had been bound to the Sword until death. The Scriptures read, "body, soul, and blade could bear no separation." The Prince Messiah's choice to bind himself to the Sword, to embrace the burden of it to defeat Xang, played well into sermons about the merits of redemptive suffering through means such as a scratchy hair shirt.

Now Ryn knew what that meant in practical terms. He couldn't be parted from the Sword . . . *ever*. How much distance between them did it take for the pain to start?

By their jailer's third visit, Ryn had slipped into a fog of torment that stripped any sense of his body and denied him even the respite of sleep. The jailer had to prop his head and hold the bowl to his lips to get him to drink. If he offered a show this time, Ryn didn't notice.

"Kill me . . . just kill me." Ryn didn't know how many times he said it. Maybe the words never made it past his crusted and cracked lips. He desperately hoped they had and that someone would have the decency to grant him the mercy.

Some time later, cold wet splashed his face. Voices murmured nearby. Then the pain eased. For the first time in a lifetime, he could breathe, full and deep. He savored every sensation—the rough wood beneath his rump, the ache in his shoulders, the raw bite of the manacles, even the foul taste in his mouth.

Heir of Aegias.

Ryn would have wept if he had the strength. They'd brought Mordyth Ral back to him.

They seek understanding of what they cannot control.

He might have cherished that voice in his head if the implications of it didn't revolt him so deeply. Here he was, bound body and soul to a thing with an appetite that threatened every living thing. He'd become no better than a demon.

There is only the Balance that Nature intends. The Primal Order of this world.

He could scarcely believe what he heard. *You lay waste to this world like a wildfire.*

Does life not flourish again in the fire's wake? Destruction and rebirth—this is Nature's way.

Unless the destruction is so complete there is nothing left.

Always, life returns. Always, enough of your species survives to multiply again. As I said, I take from many so fewer might die.

But it cared nothing about individual lives or laying whole kingdoms to waste. The Devastation wrought by Vulheris the Mad, the man who had forged Mordyth Ral and fallen prey to it twenty-five hundred years ago, proved that beyond a doubt.

I take only what necessity demands—no more, no less.

What if necessity demands too much? What if it means extinction?

The Sword didn't answer.

"Lieutenant."

Ryn popped his eyes open to find a familiar bear of a man. Captain Tovald sat on a corner of the table, rubbing absently at the stumps of his missing fingers.

Mordyth Ral lay on the table beside him.

Ryn lingered on its every detail with a desire that left him disgusted all over again. A desire to hold it, to trace its every contour with a lover's devotion, to experience again the sweet taste of an abomination vanquished.

"On me, Lieutenant."

Purplish bags bloated the flesh beneath Tovald's eyes and his crow's-feet cut deeper than usual. No doubt he'd lost some sleep. As the senior officer, he bore the burden of responsibility for what had happened at the Claw and was bound to suffer judgment. Ryn decided that was only fitting, given how eager Tovald had been to throw Josalind to the wolves.

"Sir," he said with a brief nod.

Tovald studied his ruined hand. "I got this fighting grenlich in the Icefell. Left me sick with a fever for weeks. The surgeon said the best thing for my recovery was reassignment to Vysus—something about the desert air down there being good for the blood." He looked up. "Ever been, Lieutenant?"

"I've read the stories," Ryn said.

"They aren't worthy of it," Tovald said. "Every belief rubs shoulders and any vice can be sated for a price. The Brotherhood of Sorcerers claims to be at arm's length from the government while pulling the strings from its City Above—and it does hang there in the sky, a mountain entire, raised by the Great Deceiver's favor. Vysus is no choice posting for any palatar—the Clerisy commands barely a spit of respect."

Ryn knew that, too. The Teishlians were nothing if not entrepreneurial. They profited from allowing pilgrims from the Kingdoms to visit sites in the former Protectorates, sites considered holy to Aegias and his paladins. For the sake of these faithful, the Clerisy refused to give up its diocese in Vysus or withdraw its palatar garrisons. It usually took a few shots of malt whiskey for Tovald to be this long-winded, but Ryn couldn't deny a need for honest talk. "So, what happened?"

"The bishop of the diocese, a man named Besk, he had . . . appetites," Tovald said. "Boys, mostly. It fell on me to cover up his excesses, maintain what little dignity the Clerisy had in that cesspool. I often wished I could just bring myself to kill the child-buggering bastard."

He smoothed back the graying hair at his temples. "But somebody else did—a father with cause. He would have hanged. I couldn't stand for that—it soured my milk too much to let him pay for what I should have done."

"You took the blame," Ryn said.

"I wasn't that eager to wear a noose," Tovald said. "But I'd heard Dragon's Claw needed a commander. A compromise was reached—the father went free, I went to the Claw, and the official report stated the bishop had a seizure and drowned in his bath."

He let his hand hover over Mordyth Ral's hilt. "Through it all, I kept my oath to serve and obey the Clerisy. I balanced my duty with my conscience, without betraying either."

"Is that what you tell yourself?" Ryn was too weary to sneer with the scorn he felt. "You let that bishop prey on children until a braver man did what you didn't have guts for."

"I did my duty to his office, if not to him. That is the oath we swear." Tovald's hand clenched into a fist. "But you betrayed the Clerisy, betrayed your men, *betrayed me*."

Ryn roused enough outrage to snap back. "But not Aegias. Not like you did in Vysus and still do—I saw that compass you used."

Tovald snarled. "I know your story too, son. You've become a slave to your guilt."

"You told me the day we met that a man wears what he's done, always."

"I said it can color his judgment and make him a liability."

Ryn shook his head. "Or give him the courage to do what's right and not just what's expected."

"That kind of prideful self-deception leads men astray."

"Does it? Tell me those children don't still haunt your dreams." The misery of this place left Ryn eager to hit back in the only way he could. "Or maybe the truth is that you took your own twisted pleasure in what was done to them—that's why you did nothing to stop it."

Tovald's brow knotted to match an oak burl and his nostrils flared. Ryn steeled himself for the blow as the captain shot to his feet with fist raised. He found himself eager for it, so he could spit his own blood in the man's face. But Tovald didn't throw a punch. Instead, he snatched up a skewer from the table—a foot of iron as thick as a pencil with a blunt tip.

The snarling guard dog that Ryn had glimpsed in the captain's office on his first day in Dragon's Claw had turned rabid. He flinched back in sudden fear but had nowhere to go.

Tovald grabbed a handful of hair to yank Ryn's head back, then drove the skewer into the clenched muscle between Ryn's neck and shoulder. The impact drove Ryn back against the wall. He roared in agony as the iron punched through his flesh and grated against the stone. A sharp blade that cut clean would have been better. This dull explosion sent bolts of lightning shooting up his neck and down his arm.

Tovald leaned close. "You have no idea the choices I've had to make." His snarl splattered Ryn's face with spit. "The honest comforts I've had to deny myself. The only thing that makes it tolerable, the only thing that keeps me from despising myself as much as I did Besk, is holding to the belief that my oath to the Clerisy means something—*it did then and it does now*."

Ryn could only stare him in the eye, starved for breath. The pain had paralyzed his lungs. Having his arm chained up over his head only made it worse.

Tovald kept the skewer pressed to the wall as he twisted his other wrist to bend Ryn's neck at an even more painful angle. "But you . . . you have the vanity and the conceit to piss on all of that. And for what?"

For the first time, Ryn felt true fear of this man. It warred with his fury at being so helpless, so powerless. He should have shot the bastard in the Bone Yard when he had the chance.

Tovald reined himself in with a conscious effort. He released Ryn's hair to brace his hand against Ryn's chest. The skewer came free with a quick yank. Ryn sagged against his chains with a wheezy shudder as his lungs broke free at last.

Tovald turned away and cast the bloodied skewer down the table as if the mere sight of it now revolted him. He clenched his fists behind his back and took several measured breaths. Blood oozed from Ryn's shoulder and tickled as it found a path down his sweaty torso. He'd started to shudder—either from the trauma to his body, his spirit, or both—and couldn't stop it.

"I told you before that I faced a demon once—a *greater* demon," Tovald said at last. "In their natural form, you only see what they want you to see." He kept his fists tight behind his back. "I saw a raging storm of oily smoke and glimmering shadow. That's all they seem to be, when a sorcerer summons one without imposing some physical shape."

Those thick shoulders began to tremble, as if some stale memory could possibly task the man as much as Ryn's suffering wracked him now. "It's the cold you notice first—the ache of it bites the marrow before the goosebumps hit your flesh. But it's a demon's glare that's the worst."

Tovald stiffened his spine and pulled his shoulders back with deliberate effort. His voice had grown hoarse with tortured emotion. It seemed to goad Ryn's shudders.

"It didn't even have eyes, but you just *know* it's staring at you," the captain continued. "I felt nothing but its hate. I couldn't move. I couldn't even scream. I knew nothing but the beat of my own heart, heard it fade as that thing willed me to die."

He turned back to Ryn, heavy features twisted in a wet-eyed expression of dread. "I would have died, I have no doubt of it, if the damned sorcerer holding the leash hadn't finally stepped in."

Ryn rolled his tongue around his mouth and mustered enough spit for one word. "So?"

"No book can make you truly appreciate just how dark things are beyond reach of the Clerisy," Tovald said. "The evils that come of sorcery and witchcraft left unchecked. I saw that firsthand, in Vysus."

Ryn couldn't help but flinch away as Tovald leaned in, but the captain only rested his hand on the cold stone of the wall overhead. "You think I don't know the Clerisy's flaws?" he said with a measured conviction that belied his previous rage. "But I'd much rather cope with the flaws than the alternative. The Clerisy brings order to chaos. It protects us from the horrors of Hell and the egos of kings. In seven hundred years, how many wars of any import have there been for the Kingdoms—a handful? You should know, you're the student of history. Never before has there been such peace and prosperity."

Ryn swallowed and cursed his frailty as the shudders left him fighting to speak. "And what has been the cost of it? Do you ever think on that? Might there not be a different way, a better way? What would Aegias—" A fit of coughing caught him then, wrenching fresh agony from his shoulder.

Tovald stepped back. "I failed you, son, and I'm sorry for it," he said, his voice weary with regret. "I should never have put you in a position where that witch could addle your sense."

The fit passed, leaving Ryn desperate to draw careful, ragged breaths. Before he could manage a response, Tovald turned to the table and picked up Mordyth Ral.

The sight of the Sword in another's hand incensed Ryn so much he forgot about his shoulder and yanked at his chains with a curse. He felt fourteen again, like when he'd caught the girl he was sweet on giving free range under her skirts to that lump-headed bully from down the road. He despised himself for feeling so, but it made no difference.

Nothing happened. The Sword appeared to keep quiet in Tovald's hand. He angled it this way and that under the lamplight.

Death alone will part us, Heir of Aegias.

"The *Codex* speaks true," Tovald said. "The Sword would respond to no other so long as Aegias lived. And now it will respond to no other but you . . . so long as *you* live."

A raw scream echoed down the corridor. A man's scream.

Horgrim. Only then did Ryn realize the adjoining cell sat empty. The man's torment roused a fresh wave of shudders and left a stone lodged in Ryn's throat.

"The Clerisy's had suspicions about that inn. Whispers of a goddess cult, like the Sevrendine of old." Tovald turned back and raised Mordyth Ral so that its tip hovered under Ryn's chin, his features grim and hard. "I don't expect you know what heresy festered there?"

Ryn looked him square. He would give Tovald nothing—not his fear, not his dignity, and sure as Hells no information that he might find useful. "Should I?" He doubted that selling out the Sevrendine would earn him a reprieve, in any case.

"And the whereabouts of Xang's skull?"

"I've no idea."

Horgrim screamed again. Ryn clamped his jaw to stifle the shudders that continued to wrack him. "My turn's coming, then."

Tovald lowered Mordyth Ral to his side. "It won't be lengthy. I can give you that."

Ryn's attention followed the gleam of that blade. Just the sight of Mordyth Ral offered a balm of sorts. He didn't want it to, but he sorely needed something. "The Clerisy wants the Sword in a hand it controls."

"The Clerisy would have the Sword kept from *any* hand—for the good of us all," Tovald said. "But desperate times have sprung on us." He turned to the door. "The High Lord Inquisitar arrives tomorrow."

Ryn's breath caught. "Him? . . . Here?"

"It's our great fortune that he already sailed north to tour the Clerisy's holdings." Tovald tapped Mordyth Ral's blade against the bars of the cell. "The most dire weapon in all the world—in the control of our chief fanatic—there's a restful thought."

He left without saying more.

Why me? Ryn feared to ask, feared to know, but he had to.

Your need spoke to me.

His need? For what? To atone, to suffer, to find meaning in death?

You bore an emptiness that begged to be filled.

All he'd ever wanted was to follow Aegias's example, to live a life that had meaning as a palatar. How could that have led to this?

You were the best choice.

The best choice—in a place of shame and penance, from among men who were disillusioned, flawed, and focused only on the immediate needs of survival. Ryn had held to the hope that he might atone for his sins by devoting himself to the safety and sanctity of the Claw's residents. But he'd also come to resent and reject the Clerisy's authority, not just over himself, but over all palatars. Had that made him so different, so vulnerable?

They brought Horgrim back shortly after.

It took two of them to drag him into his cell, prop him on his stool, and lock the manacles in place. Ryn found it hard to tell under the dim light, but Horgrim looked half peeled. The damp, metallic smell of opened flesh wafted through the cell.

Once they were alone, the big man sucked in a great wheezy breath. "I need a deep tankard and a cheery fire to go with that ham." His voice shook with frailty, like half his soul had been carved away. "They started with the water torture then went for the fingernails, but the true artistry came when that ghoul opted for the wee scorper."

Ryn forced a swallow and tried to ignore the booming throb of his shoulder. "'Wee scorper'?"

"Like that tool a cooper uses to shave the insides of barrel staves," Horgrim said with murderous intent. "It's a grand way to peel skin without bleeding you out. Then came the salt."

"The High Lord Inquisitar is coming . . . to take the Sword."

"Anton Bucardas? Grace Above."

"They say he'd burn babes for being born with a mark if the law would allow," Ryn said. "He can't be allowed near the Sword." And he meant it—with every fiber of his being. But the futility of their situation swamped him with a dark despair that burned at his throat.

"Well, then," Horgrim said. "You had best not die."

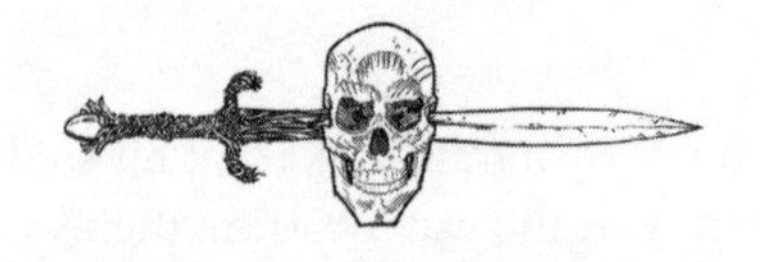

TWENTY-FOUR

Ryn slept until they came for him.

It was likely better that way—waiting gained him nothing. Still, part of him recoiled, desperate to beg for some reprieve, for any kind of delay. He considered demanding the right of a final vigil in the chapel, not that it would mean anything.

But as two palatars marched him from the cell, he still wearing nothing but his witch-iron manacles, Ryn kept his mouth shut tight. All he could do was shame himself with pointless cowardice.

He might still do that before the day was out, but not yet.

"Be strong," Horgrim said.

Their tongueless jailer gave Ryn a soothing pat on the shoulder and grinned.

He couldn't muster an adequate response to either.

The palatars took him, not toward the testing chamber where Horgrim had been entertained the day before, but to the right, from where the jailer came and went. Fine, then. They had something different in mind. Heavens forbid the inquisitar be bored repeating himself.

The way led through a door and up a set of stairs. Rough-hewn stone gave way to clay tile, then a hallway of white marble with a vaulted ceiling. The morning sun replaced lamplight. It beamed from the right through huge arched windows of stained glass and white and red drapery embroidered with gold and silver thread. All of the doors on the left were closed. The odd alcove between them housed a piece of statuary in pale alabaster.

Ryn forced himself to keep pace with his escort as they walked that long hall toward a door with raised panels at the far end—white, like the walls and ceilings. Symbolic purity at every turn. Pure hypocrisy, more like. Two palatars in full dress flanked the door, wearing the scarlet half capes of the Inquisitarem. Their mail hauberks were accessorized with gorgets, pauldrons, and greaves of polished steel rather than hardened leather. Anton Bucardas's personal guard, no doubt.

One opened the door as they came. Ryn forced his feet to keep moving, to cross into Hell with some measure of dignity and not give these men reason to beat him across the threshold.

On the other side, he found a foyer, which in turn opened onto a bath with walls of gleaming ceramic tile and the copper piping and brass fixtures for running water. He'd heard of such plumbing but had never seen it before. Lazy steam rose from a tub big enough for three. A mousy-looking fellow—an initiate in one of the monastic orders, judging by his unshorn scalp and simple cassock of unbleached linen—stood by with brush and soap.

Ryn stopped just inside the door. By the look of the place, it had to be the archbishop's own bathing room, in his own apartments. Did the initiate serve as his valet?

The palatars shoved him in the rest of the way.

The initiate bowed and gestured at the tub. "Would his person please take to the bath?"

Two other palatars lurked in the corners, small crossbows cocked and ready. Muskets or pistols must have been considered too boorish for such a refined setting, with their rude noisemaking and sooty belching. Maybe they meant to drown him when he least expected it or bleed him out. That would be a pleasant way to go—slit wrists and a nice sleepy soak.

Of course, they could have just run a sword between his ribs down in the jail.

Ryn got in the tub.

A spell later, after the initiate had scrubbed him pink, shaved him smooth, and even reset his broken nose and dressed his puncture wound, Ryn found himself still alive, with the aches and hunger pangs to prove it. He didn't bother to ask what was going on. Not a soul in that room had offered a word and he didn't expect they would.

The initiate toweled him down, helped him into a pair of drawstring trousers, and draped him in a wrap since sleeves were out of the question—Ryn doubted those manacles would come off before his heart stopped.

The palatars with crossbows escorted him out a different door and down a short hall to another room.

A study.

The sort of study Ryn would expect of a wealthy noble, or a bishop, given there wasn't much difference. Dark-stained hardwood paneled the walls, oiled and buffed until it gleamed. Leather-bound books were crammed on a shelf that stood behind a grand old desk with curved legs and viny carvings. A round table lay before the big bow window. A man sat there, only a few bites into his breakfast—porridge with baked apples and a side of ham.

Ryn had never smelled such heady perfection. His stomach rumbled. It would have been better if his nose had still been too swollen to work.

The man looked up. He was maybe fifty. A Sturvian of the old blood with raven hair that fell in waves to his shoulders with glints of silver. His beard, trimmed and shaped to the last whisker, girded a chiseled jaw and hollow cheeks. Any inquisitar would have worn his crimson robes, or his Pure Flame pendant of gold and scrimshaw. But only one man in all the Kingdoms sported that fat ruby ring.

Anton Bucardas, the High Lord Inquisitar. The man who considered himself the scourge of the Great Deceiver and all his works. Ryn wondered where the archbishop had been left to take his bath and breakfast this morning.

Bucardas's dark eyes were friendly, even fatherly. He beckoned Ryn to sit. "We don't need those."

Ryn cocked an eyebrow as one of the palatars removed the witch-iron manacles. Even with those crossbows aimed and ready, Bucardas took a risk. Maybe he meant to illustrate how little a threat he considered his prisoner to be. Ryn rubbed at his chafed wrists and sat down across the table. His restless stomach demanded he ask for the final meal owed to any condemned man. But that could be taken for weakness. He wouldn't give this zealot the satisfaction.

Instead, he fixed on those eyes and tried to reconcile their fatherly warmth with the cruel stories told about the man. "My thanks for the bath, Your Lordship," he said with a dutiful nod. It wouldn't help to ignore simple courtesy.

Bucardas looked back to his food. "Thank you for reaffirming my faith in the order of things."

"Your Lordship?"

"Each of us is born with a flaw that invites corruption." Bucardas washed down a bite of ham. "That's why we must be so diligent, to remain pure in thought and action. Look at you—a palatar led astray. We need such cautionary tales."

As much as he hungered, Ryn lacked the appetite for a sermon or a lecture. "With respect, Your Lordship, I know how this ends. You're going to offer me a merciful death if I tell you what you want to know. I'm not going to do that, partly because I can't and mostly because I won't."

"I can respect conviction, even from an apostate reborn to the Great Deceiver's service." Bucardas turned to his apples and porridge. "But why die a heretic's death? In the end, the Sword will answer to me—your secrets will be mine. Pride isn't worth such a price."

Ryn heard curt shouts from beyond the window. He leaned over for a look. Two score palatars drilled in the yard below. "If you were so certain the Sword would reveal all, I would've been dead before breakfast. What do you want?"

"That friend of yours is Sevrendine." It wasn't a question.

"The Clerisy drove those heretics out of the Kingdoms ages ago."

"What we did was cast an evil into a hostile wilderness, where it could be forged by trial and hardship into something greater than before, and then let it seep back across our borders." Bucardas's tone suggested he had only contempt for how his predecessors had addressed such a threat to the Clerisy's authority.

"That's a fair story," Ryn said.

"One that will finally have its end, thanks to you."

"Me?"

"Well, you did deliver us the Sword and a Sevrendine for interrogation," Bucardas said. "We will have his secrets and then the stain of his heresy will at last be wiped from the world."

Ryn didn't doubt Mordyth Ral would welcome the opportunity to play its part in that. "You're not more concerned about Xang's skull?"

"All things in their time."

"You seem to have this all sorted. What do you need me for?"

"We live in a dangerous time, my lost lamb." Bucardas's spoon twisted circles in his porridge. He studied the patterns as if seeking portents. "Fools boast of how we live in an age of reason, of invention and liberty for the common man. That the advent of the microscope, the sextant, even those little steam toys, somehow preclude the existence of the evils that have always lurked in the dark. So many people, so eager to embrace such naivete." He cocked an eye at Ryn. "But we know different, don't we?"

"Xang's skull is real enough."

"I refer to your paramour," Bucardas said. "By all accounts, she's a rare breed. Just the evidence I need to prove witchcraft flourishes and must again be rooted out."

He wants Josalind. It had been almost two centuries since the Clerisy endorsed the last witch hunts, but their grim shadow lingered. Wars had sparked less butchery and madness. It had gotten so bad, in fact, that the Clerisy had formally curtailed the Inquisitarem's reach and authority. Bucardas sought justification to undo that and swamp the land in a fresh tide of innocent blood. Men of his sort saw evil in everything except themselves.

"I'm here, she's not," Ryn said. "What makes you think I've any clue where to find her?"

Bucardas clucked his tongue in disapproval. "Don't be coy. It doesn't suit that handsome face. You are her thrall—you've fornicated with her, to seal the pact and bind your soul to the Great Deceiver. Like the Sword, it's a bond only death can break."

Ryn just looked at him, eyes wide. Sword and skull aside, the maniac actually thought this was something so pedestrian as an affair between a witch and her thrall.

Bucardas scraped his bowl clean and leaned back to pick his teeth with a metal tool. He cupped his other hand before his face, as if concerned with being discrete about it before his guards and his prisoner. "There is a certain . . . ritual. I detest such means, but a lesser sin is sometimes necessary to conquer a greater one."

A ritual. No . . .

"If we had a fresh sample of Josalind's blood, this wouldn't be necessary," Bucardas added, like he expected there to be comfort in that fact.

Ryn knew of what the man spoke, having read about it in old treatises on witchcraft. His neck tingled with sudden, clammy fear. It crawled down his arms and left his palms slick.

"It is the foreskin that's the crucial element," Bucardas continued as he wiped the tool clean and returned it to a small case on the table. "Though I'm afraid the whole offending member must be taken—slowly."

"The foreskin is the contagious link between thrall and witch that can be used to track her down." Ryn dug his fists into his thighs to stifle their tremble. "But it's the insult to his manhood, to the pact between them, that will compel her to his side. His suffering has to last until she's lured near enough to trap." He saw little point in trying to argue that he and Josalind had never shared more than a kiss.

Bucardas clapped his hands with genuine delight. "You know it, then. I had no idea of your gifts as a scholar."

Ryn wanted to throw the table aside and get his hands around that unyielding neck. But the crossbows at the door would drop him in a blink. "It's a hobby."

"Delightful." Bucardas wiped his lips on a napkin and rose. "Shall we get started, then?"

Ryn didn't move. "How often have you actually seen this work?"

"If it fails, I will take that as sound evidence of your innocence," Bucardas said. "But your life as a eunuch will still be short—apostasy cannot be forgiven."

"Of course." Ryn's attention strayed to the guards. They just looked at him, expressions flat. "Can't have palatars thinking for themselves, now, can we?"

"If the Orders would only take my counsel and have all palatars practice infibulation, an unfortunate situation such as this could easily be avoided." Bucardas motioned at the guards. "Suturing the foreskin has certainly kept my mind clear and free of temptation."

Someone cleared her throat from the doorway.

"His Lordship is not yet finished, Sister," a palatar said.

Two bodies hit the floor with clanks of gear and armor. A misfired crossbow bolt thunked into the bookcase. "I believe he is, dears," the woman said in a familiar voice.

There stood Kara.

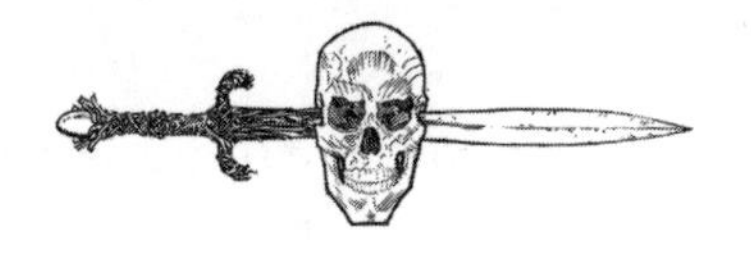

TWENTY-FIVE

Kara stood in the doorway with both palatars crumpled at her feet, armed with no weapon but her faith. She wore the glamor again, corn-silk hair shaven to a topknot with ponytail in the manner of an ordained sister, complete with what appeared to be a tattoo of Aegias's sigil on her scalp.

Bucardas stepped back. "Who might you be?"

"One of those stains that you're so eager to wipe from the world, Anton," she said.

Ryn darted over to the door and grabbed the crossbow that was still loaded before checking the hall—empty on all points. He felt such a giddy mix of relief and gratitude, his throat swelled. "I'd kiss you, if not for the sour audience."

Kara gave him a pleasant smile. "Maybe later, dear." Her expression hardened as she stepped into the room. "Now, where might the Sword be?"

Bucardas eyed the distance to the door, then the crossbow when Ryn brought it to bear. "Truly, you don't expect me to cooperate?"

"It never hurts to ask," Kara said.

Ryn wrapped his fingers around the crossbow's trigger and savored the idea of burying the bolt in His Lordship's breastbone. "But it does not to answer." At this range, it would punch all the way through the bastard's spine. A shame to make such a mess on the archbishop's fine collection of books.

Bucardas puffed out his chest. "I would rather die pure than sully my soul by aiding your corrupted ilk."

"'Ilk' indeed." Kara closed the distance between them with a bold step. His Lordship held his ground as she seized his wrist. "I can find what I need," she said.

Bucardas smiled and gave no resistance. "I always defer to an authoritative woman."

Ryn frowned. "You mean to know his thoughts?" He had only ever heard of demons in their natural form having such a skill.

"Yes," Kara said. She held Bucardas's gaze as a moment passed, and another. Then she frowned, obviously perplexed. "What is this?"

Bucardas raised and shrugged his other arm. The sleeve of his robe slipped back with the metallic hiss of mail. He wore a hauberk beneath, made of rings too thin and fine to serve as decent armor. But it wasn't meant to block any simple weapon. Ryn spied the gleam of witch iron.

Kara dropped his wrist. "Well, aren't you a clever little duck."

Bucardas gave a dark smile and rubbed a finger across his fat ruby ring.

Kara cried out and recoiled like he'd flung scalding water, but Ryn saw nothing. Her glamor faded. Bucardas's ring had to be enchanted—the High Lord Inquisitar, using an outlawed construct of sorcery. The hypocrite had ordered Ryn's manacles removed, not from hubris, but to ensure that the ring would work on him if needed.

Bucardas rubbed the ring again before Ryn could fire the crossbow. Scorching agony erupted from every inch of his flesh, stealing the means to move, to even twitch a finger. Bucardas caught Kara with a right cross. She crumpled to the floor.

As the agony deepened, Ryn tried to fathom how His Lordship could use an enchanted device while wearing witch iron. The ring's power aimed *away* from Bucardas's person—that had to be it. A searing haze, swirling black and scarlet, clouded Ryn's eyes. His back arched, his mouth stretched to scream, but nothing came out. He expected to smell the greasy sizzle of his own flesh, hear its *crackle* and *pop*. Not even separation from Mordyth Ral compared to this. He no longer felt the crossbow in his hands, no longer felt his hands at all. He fought to clench something, anything, in the hope it might be the trigger.

A faint jolt. A distant howl.

The fire, the pain, vanished. Ryn sucked in a desperate breath of air and realized he'd fallen to his knees. He looked to his hands, fearing that he would find only charred bone. Not so much as a knuckle hair had been singed.

The shot had taken Bucardas in the thigh. His Lordship had fallen back into an overstuffed chair. He clutched the seeping wound, face already shades whiter.

Kara latched on to the arm of the chair to drag herself up, eyes hard, jaw clenched. She grabbed a handful of that rich black hair and twisted Bucardas's head back. "Let us try again—where is the Sword?"

Bucardas managed to chuckle through his pain. "My dear ebon lady—trials of the flesh purify the spirit."

Kara looked to Ryn. "Does your bond with the Sword not draw you to it?"

"How do you know about that?"

"I've been snooping around here for two days."

She must have known of Horgrim's torture, and yet, she'd left him to suffer and bided her time to strike. Ryn admired her fortitude. He focused on an image of Mordyth Ral. Reaching out to it rubbed him wrong—an admission of weakness, dependence. But he couldn't deny his need to see it again, to feel it.

Are you there?

Now and forevermore, Heir of Aegias.

Images flitted through his mind—a vault packed with treasures, a chest, a squad of palatars armed for Hells' coming. It wasn't far.

"*Ryn*," Kara said, as if it weren't the first time.

He startled. "I have it."

She bent low to Bucardas's ear. "Here that, Anton? Now, the bolt doesn't appear to have struck a vital vessel. The surgeons should get to you before you're lost to Paradise."

"We should just finish him," Ryn said.

"I'll not condone cold murder," Kara said. "Let his fate rest with Our Goddess."

"Sevrendine—I knew it," Bucardas said.

Ryn fingered the trigger. Killing Bucardas would only rile the Clerisy more and position some other fanatic to claim that ruby ring. He'd be left with another face to haunt his dreams. "We should at least tie and gag him."

"No need." Kara hauled back and caught Bucardas square in the temple with a hammer punch. He slumped in the chair, out cold.

"Fine work," Ryn said.

"Horgrim makes a fine teacher." She pulled the ring from Bucardas's finger with obvious disgust.

"Where's Josalind?"

"Safe," Kara said, but in a vexed way that left Ryn with little doubt there was more to the story.

"The skull?"

"Secured, for now."

Ryn relieved one of the palatars of his hip quiver and strapped it on before reloading the crossbow. "How did those fiends come on us so fast at the inn?" He'd wanted to ask Horgrim but hadn't for fear of being overhead.

"The sect operates in the Kingdoms as we do," Kara said. "When Xang's skull was freed, those two were the first to hear it."

Ryn took an arming sword next and belted it on. "'Sect'?"

"The Kun-Xang sect—a sect within the Keshauk's All-Father Priesthood tasked with bringing about Xang's resurrection."

Kun-Xang. That sounded familiar . . . The name that Ogagoth, the grenlich tar-vrul, had died with on his lips at Dragon's Claw. Ryn cocked an eye at her. "But that means—"

"The Keshauk have spies and agents all the way down to Vysus," Kara said. "They likely control its Brotherhood of Sorcerers."

The pieces fell into place. "To find the rest of Xang's bones." It only made sense given Vysus's strategic importance during Aegias's time. His paladins had been based there and likely hid many of Xang's bones in that area of the world after realizing they couldn't be destroyed without Mordyth Ral.

"That's right—the sect has been at it for centuries. For Xang to have his full strength, he must be resurrected with all his bones."

The thought cast a whole new twist on Ryn's idle dreams about fleeing to Vysus to become a bone hunter on the pilgrim trails. "But what if they only had his skull?"

"Considering how he haunts it, it's possible his spirit could be brought forth in a willing host," Kara said.

Damn. Ryn hooked the witch-iron manacles on his belt and went to the door. "Ready to muster that righteous fire?"

Golden sparks danced on Kara's fingertips. "If I must, but the well does run dry after a while."

Ryn led her down the hallway, through the far door, then left into another hallway. His hollow stomach rumbled and his legs trembled. Bucardas's ring had sapped what strength he had. If it came to a fight, he hadn't the vinegar for much of one.

Something tugged between his ears, something more than a memory. He paused and glanced around a corner, where another short passage widened into a rotunda. At the far end lay a heavy door bound in polished brass and built for siege. The squad of palatars he expected stood stationed before it. Each bore a loaded crossbow.

He looked back to Kara. "There's six—ready?"

In response, she ducked past him into the open. Gold fire blasted from her fingers. It arced and spat from anything made of steel. Crossbows fired at random. A bolt hissed past Ryn's ear. Another grazed Kara's leg.

Ryn charged down the passage as her fire died. Two men still moved. Groggy hands struggled to bring a still-loaded crossbow to bear. Ryn kicked the muzzle of the weapon up and clipped its owner across the jaw with the butt of his own.

The armored shoulder of the other palatar slammed into Ryn's ribs, sending his lungs into spasms and rousing a complaint from the wound Tovald had dealt. An elbow smacked Ryn's jaw. He swung the crossbow in a wild arc as he crashed against the wall. The bow limb met meaty resistance. A choked gurgle reached his ears.

Propped against the wall, Ryn panted to get his wind back. Something impacted the floor. That gurgle worsened. He blinked his eyes clear. The last palatar lay at his feet, eyes bugged out, clutching his throat, windpipe crushed by the wild swing of the crossbow.

Ryn slid to the floor. He watched with horrid fascination as the life faded from the man's eyes. A confused mix of shock and disbelief that gave way to . . . nothing. Just like Quintan, that night in Sablewood.

Kara's comforting hand came to rest on his shoulder. He forced a swallow. "Could you have done something?"

"Yes," she said. "And left myself too weak for what's still to come."

Regret edged her words. So did steely resolve. Ryn just felt numb. He pushed himself up. "Let's get this done."

The door had three locks. That meant three keys. The archbishop likely held the first, the captain of his guard the second, and his chief steward the third.

"Now's the time to show me how you got into the reliquary in Dragon's Claw," Ryn said.

Kara ran her hands over the door. "That was Horgrim's doing, with Blood Thorn."

"Blood Thorn?"

"His sword," she said. "Picking a lock is no bother, even one made of witch iron."

The benefits of a blade that could change shape. "This door isn't," Ryn said.

"Which means I just might be able to tease it open." She pressed her brow to the door and stroked the first keyhole as she might a cat curled up for a scratch. The tumblers shifted with stubborn reluctance and the bolt slid back. The second bolt followed, then the third.

Ryn put his hand to the handle. "Stand clear." He kept behind the door and gave it a hard pull. It opened easily on well-oiled hinges.

Are you alone?

Yes.

Ryn knelt and did a quick peek just to be sure an itchy trigger finger didn't lie in wait. None did.

He spared hardly a glance to the assorted treasures within. All that mattered was the chest—a simple strong box, sitting on a shelf where it wouldn't warrant special attention. A heavy padlock secured it. Kara had it open in a blink. He passed her the crossbow and opened the lid.

Mordyth Ral lay within, nestled in a bed of blue velvet.

Ryn's fingers were poised over that woven hilt before he could think to stop himself. But he remembered how the Sword had almost driven him to kill Horgrim, probably would have, if the palatars hadn't taken him down.

"I'm a danger to you," he said.

"I know the bias of that sword," Kara said.

Ryn dumped Mordyth Ral onto the floor with a clatter, tore the velvet lining from the chest, and pulled the manacles from his belt. He teased one manacle around the blade below the guard, making sure not to touch the Sword itself.

You think such a trifle will contain me?

Ryn picked up the Sword by the manacle's loop. Kara took a step back, but his will, his senses, remained his own. He wrapped the chain around the blade till there just enough slack left to close the other manacle around the hilt above the guard. He locked it closed, with the velvet wadded to wedge it in place so it wouldn't slip off. The lower loop couldn't slide past the fat swell of the leaf-shaped blade. A loose and sloppy restraint, but it would just have to do. "What now?" he asked.

Kara hefted the crossbow. "Back to the dungeon."

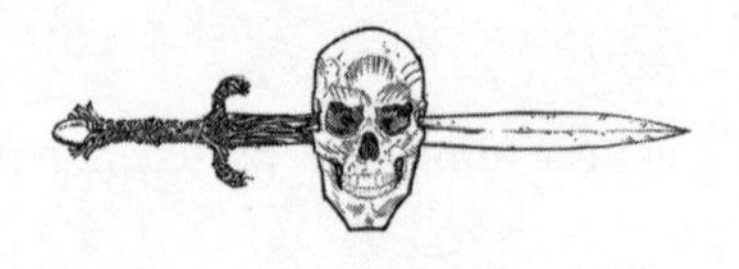

TWENTY-SIX

yn discovered that Kara had left the other guards and the initiate-valet slumbering in the bath. She'd even laid low the two in the outer hall and dragged them into the foyer out of sight.

It looked like a clear run down that hallway with the vaulted ceiling and stained-glass windows.

Halfway down, a door opened. Then a bell rang. Not the measured tones that dictated life under the Clerisy's heel, but the shrill clang of an alarm.

Ryn cursed and quickened his pace. He drew the arming sword he'd borrowed and stomped the first slippered foot that crossed the door's threshold. His elbow took the owner in the face.

The fellow dropped without a sound. He wore the vestments of an archbishop.

Captain Tovald stood beyond. He fell back and ripped his sword from its scabbard, gaze fixed on Mordyth Ral in Ryn's left hand. "What have you done, Lieutenant?" He carried a pistol, too, but obviously hadn't seen any reason to have it primed and loaded.

Ryn had frozen at the sight of his former commander. His shoulder throbbed with a sudden ache. But this wasn't the jail cell—this time, he had the upper hand. "I've ruined His Lordship's plans for a delightful day."

"Do you really think you can just walk out of here?"

The crossbow brushed Ryn's ear as it came to bear over his shoulder. "We don't plan to," Kara said.

Tovald scowled. "And you are?"

"A herald of Our Goddess, of course, who brought truth to Aegias through Her angelic host," she said.

"A witch and now a heretic—I never made you for such an easy mark, Lieutenant," Tovald said.

Ryn refused the bait. "Drop your sword, turn around, and kneel with hands behind your back."

Tovald threw his weapon down with a clang and complied with stiff-backed reluctance. "You are being played, son—by the Sword, the witch, and this woman, too, no doubt. Only a bad end can come of it. How many innocents will you feed to that cursed blade along the way?"

"Far fewer than Bucardas would," Ryn said. He had to believe that. Mordyth Ral couldn't be left to fall under the Clerisy's control.

Ever.

The burden of that, the sheer outlandish enormity of it, left him light-headed and off-balance. He leaned back against Kara to steady himself.

We will do nothing more than Need demands, Heir of Aegias.

"The savior of us all—is that it?" Tovald snorted. "Vanity and conceit *do* blind you. What shameless and self-deluded arrogance. You're not fit to—"

The absolute certainty, not the scorn, with which those words were spoken grounded Ryn—Tovald's belief that his former second had proven himself a prideful fool, the self-destructive villain who had to be stopped. Ryn snarled and smashed the pommel of the arming sword across Tovald's skull to shut him up. The captain slumped out. Blood welled.

Kara knelt and probed under his jaw for a pulse. A tightness in her shoulders eased. "You didn't have to strike him so hard."

The alarm continued to ring. Ryn desperately wanted to beat senseless whomever had their hand on the rope. "What good will it do us to be cornered in the jail?"

"We won't be," Kara said.

He stared down at Tovald, at the captain's hand, ruined in service to the Clerisy. Another palatar forced to compromise his oath to

Aegias and the Order for the sake of a church that saw him as nothing but a loyal hound. But Tovald's divided allegiance didn't make him wrong about how Mordyth Ral might damn Ryn's soul. Did a desperate sort of arrogance drive him? Had it always driven him, sprouted from the same flaw of character that had drawn the Sword to him in the first place?

If Tovald was right, it wasn't the cost to himself that haunted Ryn, but the cost to everyone else.

He startled when Kara's hand covered his own—warm in that odd way, like Josalind's. "Did Aegias not say a man should aspire to become the best of himself and no other?" she said. "Let the Virtues be your guide, Ryn." Her fingers touched his chest. "And your truest heart. Fraia asks no more of us. That is your greatest defense to deny the Sword from gaining mastery over you."

Ryn swallowed past the stone lodged in his throat and didn't trust himself to answer.

She tugged his arm. "Now, come along."

They encountered no further resistance—who would expect a fugitive to flee *back* to his cell? But Ryn knew it wouldn't be long before someone decided the dungeon warranted a check. The tongueless jailer's gap-toothed smile greeted them through the grate of the door. Ryn spotted a chink in the planking and considered ramming his sword through into the morbid little fiend's guts.

"Hold the shot," Kara said. "Timson is a friend."

Ryn considered a punch in the face fair payback for the man's morbid mockery. "I suppose the joke was on me, then."

Timson laughed, though it sounded more like choking, and unlocked the door. Ryn followed Kara past the jailer. Then he saw his cell, just as he'd left it, the table still stocked with that array of cruel metal. The skewer Tovald had stabbed him with still lay out of place, crusted with his blood. His pulse took off at such a lopsided gallop, his knees buckled.

Kara touched his arm. "Are you well?"

"I'm fine." He wasn't, of course, but he didn't care to say more. Never again would he allow himself to be so helpless, so vulnerable.

Timson opened Horgrim's cell.

Kara gasped. “Grace Above, old lion, they took you for pelts.”

“Just get me out of here,” came the weary reply.

Crusting blood oozed from scores of scabby wounds. Even Horgrim’s ears had been lopped. Infection from his own filth would take him before a noose could. Ryn released the ratchet lever so Horgrim could lower his arms. At least the poor bastard still had all his fingers and toes.

Ryn took the key that Timson offered and unlocked Horgrim’s manacles. “I’ve seen worse.”

Horgrim managed a chuckle. “As they say, trials of the flesh purify the spirit.”

“They’re fools to think we can be broken this way.” Kara pressed a hand to his broad chest.

A soft radiance grew from her fingers and seeped into him. Ryn stood there, amazed to see such extensive injuries begin to fade away. His wonder turned to horror as the same wounds blossomed on Kara’s flesh. Blotches of blood soaked through her linen habit. She scowled with the agony, teeth clenched, knees shaking, but didn’t stop. A tortured moan tore out of her. Even her earlobes turned mangled and bloody as Horgrim’s were restored. Still, she didn’t relent.

Horgrim yanked her hand away from his chest. “Enough.” His wounds had faded by more than half. He drew Kara down on to his lap and cradled her against his chest. The rub of her habit against those wounds must have burned like acid. She cried out and whimpered.

He pressed his lips to her shaven scalp. Tears gathered—spring had come to melt the ice from his eyes. “My pain I can bear, My Herald,” he said. “But not yours, never yours.”

Ryn did look away at that point, feeling like some boorish intruder. Timson, too, had retreated to the hallway. But Ryn did peek from the corner of his eye for what came next. As with Josalind back on the beach, Kara’s wounds slowly faded.

When they were gone, she took a fulsome breath and ran her fingers through Horgrim’s chest hair in a familiar way. “Don’t ever scare me like that again.”

A heavy sigh drained out of him. He planted a kiss on her forehead. "It's not like I go out of my way to try."

"Liar. Now, we should probably find you something to wear."

That mischievous twinkle took light in Horgrim's eye. "I don't know—maybe those atavists who seek penance bare-arsed are onto something."

Ryn cleared his throat. "How about we leave the frolicking till later?"

They both looked up at him as if they'd forgotten he was there—not with embarrassment so much as vague annoyance that he'd interrupted the moment. Kara labored to her feet, obviously wrung out, habit blotched with fresh blood. Horgrim rose after her and stretched, but the tenderness of his remaining wounds left him grimacing.

"Have you found the spot?" Kara asked Timson.

The jailer motioned them to follow and took off toward the testing chamber.

Someone rattled the latch of the jail's door. "Timson, you laggard, open up," a man called.

The door had a double-barreled lock—someone on the other side was bound to have a key and wouldn't wait to use it if Timson didn't answer. "Where are we going?" Ryn asked.

Timson led them down a side passage to a dead end.

"Right here," Kara said.

Ryn tapped Mordyth Ral against the stone. "Another walk-through-a-wall trick like you did at Dragon's Claw?"

"Not quite—there's only solid earth on the other side." She knelt to examine the floor. "But under here, there's a sewer vault."

Ryn suspected he was about to wish, again, that his nose remained too swollen to smell. "I don't suppose it's only ankle deep?"

"Afraid not," she said.

Timson grinned and mimed gagging. Ryn couldn't fathom the man's bizarre sense of humor. "I don't see a grate."

Kara knelt down and rubbed her hands over the floor's flagstones like she meant to brush them clean. The stone softened and rippled with a watery cast.

The door to the jail crashed open.

Horgrim clenched his fists. "Kara."

She gave a curt nod. "Go, Timson."

The little man jumped through Kara's portal, feetfirst.

Ryn braced himself and followed. As before, he had the feeling of melting into sand, the gritty rub of each grain as it slid between skin, meat, and bone. His feet splashed water. The fluid stone swallowed his chest, then his head.

His arm caught.

Maybe it was Mordyth Ral, the witch-iron manacles that bound it, or both. But the hand that held the Sword stuck as though the stone around it had turned solid again. Ryn flailed and yanked to no avail, head trapped in stone, fighting a rising panic. His chest spasmed with the need to draw air. He forced his head back and saw the painful concentration on Kara's face as she fought to hold the portal open.

Horgrim's bare foot came down with a stomp that bruised Ryn's fingers.

That served to drive the Sword through. Ryn splashed into the sewer, eyes and mouth shut tight as he scrambled to find his footing and keep his head clear. The filth reached to his groin. He spat to clear his lips and breathed through his mouth to avoid the worst of the stench. It didn't help much. A stew of fermenting shite and sour piss, crowned with the gassy fume of rotting guts. He hoped a slaughterhouse accounted for the latter and not something more gruesome.

A big body splashed down and almost bowled him over. Another followed. The bluish gleam faded as Kara's portal closed, leaving them in utter darkness. Then a soft yellow light blossomed—a golden flicker that sputtered on Kara's palm. She looked ready to faint from the effort. Hollow knocks echoed through the stone as the palatars beat in vain upon the jail's now solid floor.

Ryn's eyes burned from the reek, but he didn't dare rub at them with filthy hands. "We need to get out of the city." The Clerisy had already tracked him once with contagious magic. Now it had an ample stock of Horgrim's blood to track him with, too.

"Made arrangements," Kara said. She sagged against him. "Spare a perch for a tired hen?"

Ryn caught her weight and looked to Horgrim before taking further liberty. The big man didn't look much better, standing there still looking half skinned. He gave a weary nod.

Ryn ducked under Kara's arm to haul her along. "You can kiss me later."

They trekked through that river of filth for an eternity, until Ryn felt certain that raw shite coated his lungs and his skin would forever wear the stench like a brand. He didn't fathom the odd tingle in his left hand at first, too weary, too nauseous, too focused on just keeping his footing on slick stone while helping Kara along.

Her touch is foul.

The ridiculously fussy comment almost made Ryn laugh, given the circumstances, but he realized Mordyth Ral didn't care about a sewer. He still found the prospect of conversing with the murderous thing repulsive, but he needed answers. Principles weren't worth spit if ignorance got him killed.

How were you made? In the *Aegian Codex*, the Clerisy told of how Vulheris in his hubris had tricked the Earthborn for the knowledge to forge Mordyth Ral some two thousand five hundred years ago, believing he could control such a thing and destroy the Great Deceiver. It painted him as the supreme villain, the Gods Bane. But of course, the *Codex* didn't acknowledge the existence of the Goddess Fraia or give any detail of the Sword's crafting.

I was forged by the will of the Invader Goddess.

That wasn't quite what he'd asked. *To kill the Great Deceiver.*

Yes.

Vulheris forged you at Fraia's behest.

With the aid of the Earthborn.

The *aid* of the Earthborn. Vulheris hadn't tricked them after all—they had helped, ostensibly as either allies or worshippers of Fraia. The contradiction hardly surprised Ryn, given the Clerisy's biases. *You attacked the Four instead—why?*

They bore the taint of their parentage.

I don't understand—how is it that Fraia and the Great Deceiver are 'foreign'? Kara had first made the reference back at the inn before the fiends had arrived.

They have no place in this world.

Ryn wondered how much more abuse his battered nose could endure in this hell shaft before it simply rotted off. *They come from somewhere else?*

Yes.

Ryn struggled to understand. *Do you mean from somewhere else in the heavens?* Astronomers and philosophers speculated about the existence of other worlds. The idea had always intrigued Ryn, even if he found debating it pointless, given that the theory could never be tested.

Some things are unknown to me.

Which made sense—why share your secrets with a weapon that might want to kill you? Fraia had been so desperate to rid the world of the Great Deceiver, she'd risked creating a weapon that could turn on her. It had compelled Vulheris to slay her children, the Four, but not her or the Great Deceiver. Had it not been powerful enough?

It is men who are weak. My strength has no boundary.

Ryn's breath caught with sudden understanding. His vision of that cave—a man in ancient armor, working magic on some snowy white being. Vulheris and Fraia.

Vulheris thwarted me. He would not kill the Invader Goddess and instead wrought a prison of Her children's blood.

Thwarted you? How? Ryn dredged up every detail he could recall from his vision of the cave, but nothing stood out that might explain how Vulheris had managed such a thing or made such a prison, either.

Nor did Mordyth Ral offer any answers. Ryn gave the Sword a frustrated shake. Maybe it wouldn't lie, but it could withhold details easily enough. If the Sword had a weakness, of course it wouldn't share it with him. Kara had said Ryn's truest heart and devotion to the Virtues were the keys to denying the Sword control of him. Had that been what Aegias had meant when he'd said, *Find your anchor?*

Ryn had his doubts. Hells, he still doubted that he should even trust that vision of the Prince Messiah.

The assault on his smell and taste only deepened and took on new character. Ryn had to squint his eyes shut to endure it, before he went mad with the need to rub them. Kara might have more answers, he just had to be careful. The Sevrendine would no doubt have grave concerns about the strength of the Sword's hold on him if they learned of how it spoke to him. He would, in their shoes.

"The *Codex* speaks of how Vulheris struck down but failed to slay the Great Deceiver," he said. "Why didn't he finish the job then?"

"It's hard to say," Horgrim said, sloshing along behind them.

"The Sevrendine must have some theory."

"The life the Sword consumed for the power to force Vulheris to kill the Four, and then to just cripple the Great Deceiver, laid waste to most of a continent," Kara said. "With Fraia imprisoned, maybe her angelic host wouldn't risk any further destruction."

"Because the Sword would have needed more fuel to finish the Deceiver," Ryn said.

"Yes."

Why didn't you finish the task? Ryn asked the Sword.

The one you call the Deceiver escaped me. The angels convinced Vulheris not to pursue out of their fear I would be lost to the enemy. Humanity is not alone in lacking resolve.

Fraia's angels had feared the loss of the Sword more than further loss of mortal lives. It left Ryn wondering where the line was that *they* wouldn't cross. "Well, what did the angels do, then?" Even if this was pure conjecture on the Sevrendine's part, the answers fascinated him, all the same.

"They urged Vulheris to give up the Sword and hide it," Kara said.

"How could they convince Vulheris of anything if the Sword had such control of him?" Ryn asked. "Does it see angels as abominations, too, because they aren't of this world, either?"

"We don't know, and yes, it does," Horgrim said.

Care to explain?

The Sword remained silent, which left Ryn certain that the answer struck too near those secrets it preferred to keep. But he'd learned that the Sevrendine knew nothing of how Vulheris may have "thwarted" it. "How could Vulheris have hidden the Sword without being separated from it?" he asked.

"He couldn't, which would mean he entombed himself with it," Horgrim said. "Or maybe his heart just gave out by that point. Or the burden of it all finally drove him to suicide."

Ryn felt his cheeks warm with the suspicion that the warden was making a deliberate attempt to dig under his skin. He refused to take the bait. "Then Xang came along."

"To be his crippled father's legs and strong right arm," Horgrim said. "To inspire fear and fervor as a godly general on the battlefield."

"Hundreds of women died trying to carry the Great Deceiver's seed before that abomination was born," Kara said with obvious disgust. "His priests worked at it for centuries before succeeding. Most of their failures were stillborn, thankfully."

Ryn left it at that. With Fraia still imprisoned, her angels had obviously thought it worth the risk to use the Sword to stop Xang seven hundred years ago, with the expectation it could be achieved without the scale of destruction Vulheris had wrought before. But Aegias hadn't been able to bear the Sword's price for putting a final end to the dreaded sorcerer. Conscience and Virtue had compelled Aegias to show mercy for the innocents who would have died to sate the Sword's hunger. Fraia's angels in the end helped him bind the Sword to the skull instead, but had they agreed with his choice?

Learn from Aegias's cowardice—half measures cost more in the end.

A glimmer of light at last heralded the end of the tunnel. The sewer dumped them outside the breakwater, near the tanneries that accounted for that new signature of stink. A skiff waited with four men on the oars and another at the tiller. Horgrim's nakedness and their loathsome state earned some crude jests.

Their rescuers had come prepared with strong lye soap and changes of clothes. They cleaned up as best they could in the frigid waters of the Iceberg Sea. Ryn expected squads of palatars to announce their presence at any moment with a volley of muskets.

"Drovers are having trouble with their herds on the road today," Kara said when she noted Ryn's attention on the bluffs above.

Had she failed to consider any detail? Ryn kept Mordyth Ral sunk at his feet out of sight until he could bundle it up quick in a woolen blanket. He took stock of every pair of eyes that asked a question of that bundle as he climbed aboard and got settled.

His teeth chattered as the crew got them underway, gut wracked by a torturous mix of hunger cramps and nausea. Not even his bones had anything left to fight the cold, but he didn't dare let down his guard. These men were smugglers, likely pirates, too, judging by the blades and pistols and baubles they wore. A wrapped sword still looked like a sword. He just didn't want them to spot how different, and potentially valuable, this one was.

About two miles on, his suspicions were confirmed. They made for a sixty-foot sloop that sat at anchor—the kind of stealthy ship favored by criminals for its speed and shallow draft.

Kara sat beside him. He leaned close and whispered in her ear. "You trust this lot?"

"So long as they believe I'm paying more than what the Clerisy's going to be offering for our heads," she said.

One of the smugglers looked at Ryn as he leaned into his oar. An old scar pulled his lip into a permanent sneer. "You're looking a mite bleached, son," he said.

"Ghostly, even, like a dead man walking," added his bench mate.

Ryn forced himself upright and treated them both to a lazy smile. When the wolves circled, deny them even a drop of fear. "I'm just not sure that bucket of yours can get us where we need to go."

"Don't you worry your pretty little head," Sneer Lip said. "The *Sea Hare* will get you to the Deceiver's Infernal Court and back."

Ryn rested his hand on the bundled Mordyth Ral. "Good, it just might have to."

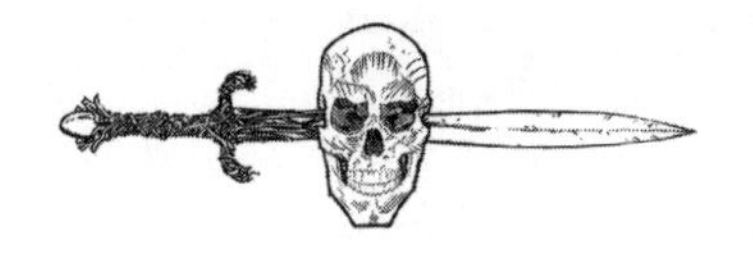

THE CHILD AND THE FORTUNE-TELLER

How Aegias unmasked the old religions

As I said last time, pet, Xang's victory simply could not be allowed.

But what to do? The Four Kingdoms had invaded the Teishlian Empire and left the Teishlians so desperate, their Emperor had given over his rule to Xang in all but name. Through the darkest sorcery, Xang had turned the tide of that war against the Kingdoms. But his victory would have meant the downfall of both sides.

By this time, seven centuries ago, Fraia's prison had begun to weaken. Her angels could hear her once again, even if they couldn't reach her. Fraia took the risk of having them guide Prince Aegias to Mordyth Ral, so that he might use it to stop Xang.

She saw the kind of man Aegias could become—one who might reject the arrogance and entitlement of his royal birthright and embrace the Nine Virtues. The sort of leader humble enough to take counsel and comfort from the wisdom of others. All these things would give him defense against the Sword as it fought to break his will and twist his mind.

Lastly, she had her angels tell him the truth about the Four Kingdoms' religions.

I see it so clear in the leaves. After his hard victory at Basker Gorge, Aegias gathered his armies on the slope of a hill. He took to a large flat rock at its bottom and faced the sun so that it glittered from his armor as if he were an angel ablaze. Then he told of how Xang was the mortal-born son of the Great Devil, weaned by his father's priests in the Keshauk Dominion. A liar who'd seduced the Teishlians and corrupted their beliefs.

A deception, he added, much the same as the one foisted upon their own ancestors. The Four Gods were in fact gone. Their "servants" who responded to the prayers and sacrifices of the Kingdoms' priests weren't angels or Earthborn, but demons in disguise.

Now this, of course, roused cries of "heresy" and "blasphemy" from the priests standing there, all dignified and resplendent in their finery. Aegias called on Cresimon, the most senior priest and a follower of Sturvia's own god, Kyvros the Elder. He challenged Cresimon to summon the most powerful minion of the fire god at his disposal.

Cresimon summoned what appeared to be a chandral, an Earthborn of searing crystal that towered thrice the height of a man.

Aegias confronted this entity with Mordyth Ral in hand and commanded it by its True Name. The facade was stripped away to reveal a terrifying demon. Under the threat of the Sword, the demon bore witness to Aegias's words and admitted its true master.

When the demon had confessed all, Aegias wiped it from Existence with a single blow.

This, of course, consumed those poor priests with dismay and outrage. Some renounced their beliefs, others took their own lives. A handful denied this truth. They condemned Aegias as a sorcerer in service to the Great Devil intent on leading them astray. They tried to kill him, but nothing they mustered could stand against the Sword.

Aegias decreed the practices of the old religions outlawed and delivered his Injunction against prayer on pain of death, fearing it would only summon demons wearing a mask of virtue. He offered instead the Nine Virtues. Forevermore, the Great Devil would be known as the Great Deceiver. Men who had lived their lives in fear of the Kingdoms' priests and their bloody rituals rallied to his words.

It happened just like that—the leaves don't lie. Is it any wonder why the man is a legend? If only the Clerisy hadn't been founded by such a squint-eyed pack of jackals eager to abuse his legacy for their own ends.

But on that fateful day, before those assembled thousands, Aegias never spoke of Fraia. That truth he gave only to those he trusted most. The demon he had vanquished gave him proof to discredit the old religions. But Fraia remained imprisoned, and those old myths and fears I told you about before of a Dark Goddess still ran deep.

Yes, pet, you're right, an angel could have appeared and spoken on Fraia's behalf. Aegias did expect one to do that very thing. So, he waited, before his assembled armies, for this angel to appear, but they never came. Why? The Great Deceiver's demons were not about to allow it. Always, the ranks of angels have been outnumbered by their demon brethren. I will tell you sometime of this angel, and the fate that befell them.

But can you imagine, having set such a stage, having such expectation that an angel would stand and speak with you, only to be left in the lurch? Poor Aegias. Rather than risk his words ringing hollow, he held his tongue, biding a better time to reveal Fraia. It never came before his death. That was his mistake, I think—Aegias should have revealed all that day, even without that angel at his side.

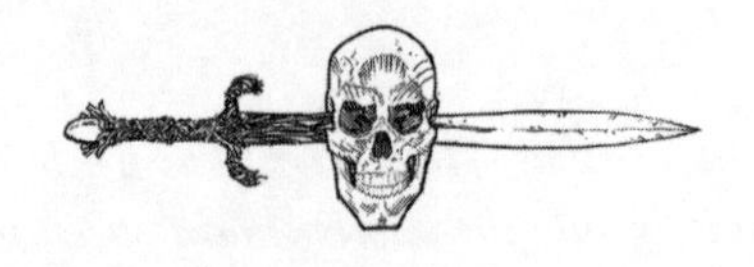

TWENTY-SEVEN

Once they'd tucked up alongside the *Sea Hare*, Ryn took to the rope ladder first, with Mordyth Ral still wrapped in its blanket and tucked under his arm. He heaved up and over the gunwale with as much vinegar as he could muster. The effort left him stifling a groan. He couldn't let these wolves smell blood.

A barrel-chested fellow as bald as a melon and with a drooping mustache waited for him on the sloop's deck. On the man's wide belt, Ryn noted a cutlass and a wheel-lock pistol, of all things, heavy with gaudy gold filigree. The antique was likely too unreliable to be more than a status symbol. A more modern and functional doglock lay nestled beside it.

"Captain," Ryn said with a nod. "Permission to come aboard?"

The captain tapped his brow. "Granted—you're the one called Ruscroft?"

Ryn's hand drifted to his arming sword. "I am."

The captain took off his spectacles and cleaned them with a scrap of cloth. "Quite the fuss you've raised with the Clerisy. They've got you painted to be spitting firebolts."

Ryn noted the crew on deck—six, plus the five in the skiff. "Is that going to be a problem?"

The captain settled his spectacles back in place. "Not so long as you keep your trouble off my ship and Mistress Aldebart's coin remains as good as her word."

"That won't be a problem, Captain Fesk," Kara said, as she accepted a crewman's hand aboard. "Has our guest been quiet?"

"Plenty quiet—since I gagged her."

"'Gagged'?" Ryn's sword was half clear of the scabbard before he had sense enough to think twice. He looked square at Fesk and ignored the grumbles from the crew. "Where is she?"

"If you're going to draw on me, laddie, you'd best wait until you've got the spunk to go the distance," Fesk said. "You're barely standing and don't think I can't see it." He jerked his thumb toward the sole cabin in the stern. "Your girl is in there, with all her crazies."

Ryn slammed his sword home and made for the door. It wasn't locked. He flung it open and ducked his head in.

Josalind sat on a narrow bed, gagged with rope and rag. Witch-iron manacles bound her wrists, with the chain nailed to the headboard. She had slack enough to sit up and lie down and not much else. A bruise ripened on her cheek. Ryn vowed to repay the dog responsible. Her brow knotted as she yanked at the manacles and mumbled something with desperate urgency.

A sharp edge pressed under Ryn's jaw.

"Now, this is how it's going to be," Horgrim said in his ear with deadly intent.

Gods be damned. He'd just made the emperor of all mistakes by turning his back on the bastard. The sudden betrayal roused less surprise than it did disbelief. "What are you doing?"

"Put the Sword down," Horgrim said.

Ryn rammed Mordyth Ral back into the big man's groin, or tried to. Horgrim must have had his hip turned. The pommel hit clenched muscle. Horgrim barely flinched.

The blade nicked the skin under Ryn's jaw. "I won't ask again."

He ignored the pain. "If you wanted me dead, I already would be."

"Said the hog to the farmer." The blade bit deeper. "It's all about timing, isn't it?"

A well of blood tickled Ryn's neck. Josalind mumbled frantically and shook her head. He let the Sword fall. "I didn't take you for a backstabbing coward."

Horgrim pulled Ryn's arming sword from its scabbard. "I know you have the key."

Ryn fished the key for the manacles from his belt and tossed it over his shoulder. "Anything else?"

"I'll let you know," Horgrim said. "Have a seat next to your herald."

Lacking a better option, Ryn did as he was told. The Sevrendine had gotten the drop on him with only a belt knife. "Too bad you lost that witch blade of yours—Blood Thorn, is it?"

Horgrim grimaced as if the name alone were a state secret. "It will be along." He nudged Mordyth Ral over to the far corner with his foot.

Kara crowded in after him. "Timson, please make certain we've some privacy," she said over her shoulder before drawing the door shut. She took the measure of the cramped cabin. "Well, now, aren't we as cozy as a basket of kittens."

Josalind answered with a glare and a shrill growl.

"Grace Above, Ryn, do take that thing off the poor girl," Kara said. She claimed the stool that sat before the captain's desk. Horgrim squatted in the corner, unfazed by the roll of the ship. Outside, Fesk bellowed orders as the crew hoisted canvas to make sail.

"Turd-licking gutter swipes," Josalind spat as the gag came off.

"Are you all right?" Ryn asked.

She rattled her chains. "The gods are lost to me, this *woman* keeps the skull, demons are lurking around and . . ." Her nose wrinkled. "Spit and spray, what a stink. Have you all been rolling in shite?"

Ryn didn't miss how Horgrim's posture tensed and his lips peeled back in that feral way at the mention of demons. The man's reaction ripened his own fears at the prospect of being hunted by one after the personal account Tovald had given. He looked to Kara. "What does she mean?"

"I can smell them," Kara said. "Nosing about in their natural form, but not in numbers that suggest they know their prize is here. Josalind's binding on the skull appears to be working."

"It won't for much longer. I'll have to freshen it by sundown," Josalind said.

Kara regarded her with forced patience. "Which brings us to this sorry state. She must redo her binding about every three days. When I last let her near it, she called on those martichora and almost made off."

"How did you stop her?" Horgrim asked.

"A right cross."

Horgrim chuckled. "That's my stone-fisted lady—and the martichora?"

"They decided to veer off after I gave their feathers a singe," Kara said.

Ryn looked at Josalind with wounded disbelief. "You were just going to leave me?"

She seemed genuinely affronted by the suggestion. "No—I just wanted to get the skull away from *her* to gain some leverage by putting it in Astrig and Oma's care." Her expression softened. "I would never abandon you."

"Of course not," Horgrim said. "You need the Sword and the fool who wields it for this demented scheme of yours."

Josalind scowled at him. "It's not mine. It's theirs."

"The Four intended all along for me to take the Sword, didn't they?" Ryn found himself gripped by the eager need to throttle something.

Josalind developed a sudden interest in her toes, face lost under that wild tangle of curls. "Mordyth Ral already called to you—they could hear it." She squared her shoulders and faced him with tearstained cheeks. "Only the Sword can kill the Great Deceiver. They need a hand to wield it and they got one."

We were meant to be.

"That's the real reason why you broke the seal, isn't it?" Horgrim said to her, lip curled with disapproval. "To play the lad into this position."

"No, it wasn't," Josalind said. "I didn't understand this then."

The thought that Horgrim's accusation might be true left Ryn's heart aching. He took some solace in the apparent sincerity of Josalind's quick denial before a swell of outrage crowded to the fore.

First Tovald and now this Sevrendine—both so quick to condemn Ryn as some mindless string-puppet. To the Hells with them both.

He fixed Horgrim with a steely glare. "I chose to take up the Sword, knowing full well the consequences. No one forced me to do it. If I hadn't, you'd be dead and Xang would likely be breathing by now." The fact that he'd almost killed Horgrim not long after was beside the point.

Horgrim's lips moved, but no words came out. Then he looked away. The self-righteous bastard for once had nothing to say.

Ryn looked to Kara. "Where are we going?"

"Home, to Sevrenia."

Josalind tossed her head back. "No. The skull must never go east."

"Here we are again," Horgrim said. "I fear to ask, but where do you intend to take it?"

"Somewhere else."

"Where?" Kara asked.

Josalind held her tongue.

Gold fire flickered in Kara's eyes. *"Where?"*

"I'll tell you," Ryn said.

Josalind kicked his ankle. "Don't you dare."

Ryn weighed his options even as Horgrim's lips peeled back at the delay. Lice and boils take him. Ryn owed him nothing. But sharing some information might build goodwill that he could use to his advantage.

Josalind squeezed Ryn's hand, pleading now. "Don't, please—they don't need to know."

"Gostemere," he said.

Josalind pulled her hand away. She muttered something he couldn't hear and likely wouldn't have wanted to.

"Gostemere is lost," Kara said. "Our Goddess has never revealed its location to us."

"But the Four have to me," Josalind said.

"And what exactly have they told you about it?" Horgrim asked.

Josalind bit her lip and said nothing.

The woman put the stubbornness of mules to shame. Ryn kicked *her* ankle. "This isn't helping."

"Nothing so far that makes sense," Josalind said, no less churlish than before. Ryn suspected that wasn't entirely true.

Horgrim rolled his eyes. "Grace Above." He heaved himself up as tall as the ceiling would allow. "This is how it's going to be: Kara will mind the skull, no one will touch the Sword, and we will *all* be taking the way east."

"What if I'm not of a mind to play along?" Josalind said.

Kara pulled a canvas sack from under the captain's desk. "If the skull is heard by Xang's followers, sweetie, we all lose. You know that. I don't think it's in your fiber to take so callous of a gamble."

She scooped the skull out of the sack and sat it on the floor at Josalind's feet. Ryn couldn't help but shiver as its phantom chill swept the cabin in a storm of tormented shadows.

"Now, are you really so eager to engulf us all in fire and blood?" Kara asked.

In the end, Josalind wasn't. She freshened the seal upon the skull and let Horgrim clap her back in the manacles with only a few choice curses of complaint. Kara stood ready with a blast of her fire all the while, though Ryn doubted she could've mustered much after her prior exertions.

Later, after he'd caught a few bells of desperately needed sleep between bowls of watery gruel, Ryn sat with Josalind in the captain's cabin. He felt almost civilized again but decided to give it another day before daring the crew's stock of beans and salt pork.

They didn't say much. Maybe because too much needed saying.

"What do you know about Fraia—about how Vulheris imprisoned her?" he asked at last.

Josalind shrugged. "Not much. The bits the Four show me from that time don't add up."

Damn. No answers as to how Vulheris had managed it and thwarted Mordyth Ral. "But was she still, in the time of Aegias?"

"Her bonds had weakened, but She didn't break free until Sevren's time," Josalind said.

Sevren—founder of the Sevrendine faith. That had been several hundred years ago, though Ryn knew little beyond that, thanks to the Clerisy's censors.

"That's when she chose Sevren to be her first herald of our age and to right the lies told by the Clerisy," she added.

Ryn tapped the manacles. "Is this so bad?"

"Bad? I'm a bloody prisoner."

"But you wouldn't have to be—if you wore bracers of witch iron, you'd never have to hear the Four again. You'd be free. I saw how quick you were to suffer again when these came off."

"They swarmed like angry bees, screaming and roaring." Her head sagged against his shoulder. "They want the skull in Gostemere and don't care what it takes to get it there, even if it means killing anyone who gets in the way."

"You mean Kara and Horgrim."

"Yes."

"Could you?"

Josalind shrugged. "I don't know. Kara is so strong."

"Would you?"

She said nothing for a spell. "If the Four push me far enough, I think I might do anything."

Ryn didn't care for the hopeless way she said that. His attention drifted to the corner where the Sword had been. Horgrim had taken it, along with the skull. Both were no doubt tucked in some hidden cubby Captain Fesk used for smuggling his best goods. "Then don't let them." He took her hands in earnest. "For Aegias's sake, Josalind, why be their slave if you don't have to?"

She sniffed and looked him square. "Because I know what's at stake. It haunts my dreams, as sure as Sablewood does yours, whether they're in my head or not." She hugged herself as much as the manacles would allow. "The horrible things the Four have shown me about Xang—I live it all again like I'm there when I touch Xang's skull. So much misery and death because the Deceiver's priests still have the authority of his power. Xang's return will just make it worse."

"You see his mind?"

She nodded. "I think the priesthood is trying to restore his father—to make the Great Deceiver whole again. The Old Devil is still broken from the wounds Vulheris dealt him twenty-five hundred years ago."

"I know," Ryn said.

"That's what this is all about for Xang—conquest to grow his father's flock," she said. "As if all the pain and suffering the priesthood inflicts has the power to heal the Deceiver. But they already rule millions and it's not been enough. It's never been enough. That's why they finally decided to create Xang." She shuddered from a sudden phantom chill. "He's willing to bathe the world in blood, if he thinks there's half a chance it will make a difference."

Ryn caught on his fingertip a tear that had come to hang from her jaw. "And you're certain it will be disastrous if the Sevrendine take Xang's skull east."

"*The Four* are—the Sevrendine won't be able to keep it safe."

"But what's in Gostemere?"

"It's where Vulheris imprisoned Fraia. And it's where the Earthborn wait."

Ryn's eyes widened. Just when he thought the point had long passed where he could ever be surprised again. "The Earthborn—you expect me to believe the Elder Races still exist?"

"Don't look at me like that. I'm just the messenger. *The Four* say the Earthborn wait."

"'Wait'?" The Sword had just admitted to him in the sewer that the Earthborn had helped Vulheris forge it by Fraia's will. To hear now that the Earthborn still lived, that they still had a part in all this, left him burning with so many questions that the prospect of being trapped on this ship heading in the wrong direction left his fists clenched. "Wait for what?"

"The skull, the Sword, I don't know." She gave the manacles a shake. "I might, if these were off long enough. But I . . ."

"But what?"

Her shoulders slumped and she looked away. "I am sorry for all this. I never wanted that thing to be your burden."

"I know." And he did, despite his earlier suspicions. As much as he couldn't trust where her desires ended and the Four's began, that much he didn't doubt.

"It's all my fault—I should have been stronger." She spoke with such frustrated anger and shame, she began to shake. "Damn their sour souls. I shouldn't have let them—"

"No." He clamped one hand on her shoulder and cupped her chin with the other.

She tried to twist away. "Don't."

He held her chin firm until she gave in and he could look deep into those haunted eyes. "You, Josalind Aumbrae, are the single strongest person I have ever met."

She tried to protest again, but he wouldn't hear it.

"No, listen to me," he said, charged with sudden emotion. "At Dragon's Claw, when the Sword first spoke to me and I thought I was going mad, do you know what kept me sane? You—thinking of all you've suffered for so long." He shook his head. "I still don't know how you've endured it all without becoming a bitter and broken wreck."

She closed her eyes and nodded emphatically before managing a wry smile. "Sometimes I *am* bitter and broken, or hadn't you noticed?"

"Never." He gave her knee a squeeze then rose and went to the door.

"What are you going to do?" she asked.

"It seems all of our answers are waiting in one place," Ryn said. "I'm going to get you to Gostemere, and then we will see what the Earthborn have to say."

The *Sea Hare* skimmed across frothy waves beneath a thick mantle of stars.

Most of the crew clumped around the brazier amidships, savoring the warmth and playing trumps. A simmering pot of spiced port dressed the briny air with cloves. Kara and Timson sat in the thick of the card game, both with impressive piles of coins in their bowls. Maybe that was how Kara planned to cover their passage—give these pirates back their own money.

Ryn snagged two rations of port and made for the bow. Barred from the Sword, he apparently posed so little threat he'd been allowed to roam the ship. The illusion of freedom didn't fool him—with the crew in Kara's purse, he doubted he could spit without it being noted. If not for the fact that killing him would simply free the Sword to call to another, he expected he would already be dead.

Horgrim had taken roost in the bow. He sported a new straw hat with a broad brim to replace the ratty one he'd lost in Tanasgeld. A piece of wood lay in his hand and a pile of shavings gathered on his lap. His carving tool proved to be a white shard that curled out from the cuff of his sleeve—his shape-shifting witch blade.

Ryn eased down onto his rump with his back to the gunwale. "I see that thing found its way back."

The shard retreated out of sight. "I said it would." Horgrim took the offered cup and gave the contents a wary sniff. "They don't have *any* stout onboard?"

"Not that Fesk is willing to share," Ryn said.

Horgrim's half-finished carving had the obvious shape of a bust. Ryn decided to take a gamble. "Do you carve Kara often?"

That twinkle took light in Horgrim's eye—he knew full well that Ryn probed for a chink in his armor. "I'm not sure who it will be yet."

Ryn put his cup to his lips but didn't take more than a taste. His gut wasn't up for it yet, nor did he care to soften his wits. The sparring had just begun. Two opponents conducting themselves with the false civility of rival royal courtiers. Ryn didn't doubt that Horgrim understood the nature of this game as surely as he did. He would have been quite content to beat the man senseless for that prick in the neck earlier in the day, but that wouldn't accomplish much. "I've got a notion about that sword of yours, if you're willing to hear it."

That twinkle deepened, matched by a smile that bore a trace of mockery. "Go ahead." Horgrim still hadn't drunk.

"The shamanists of the Teishlian Empire claim their power is a form of earth-magic," Ryn said. "They call on 'nature spirits' that draw their power directly from the life force of the earth—what they call the animas. I'm betting that's what Blood Thorn there is—a thing grown from the 'animas.'" As Mordyth Ral obviously must have been, at least in part.

"The Clerisy says there's no such thing as earth-magic," Horgrim said. "It's just sorcery, by another name."

"The Clerisy says all sorts of things that aren't worth green pennies," Ryn said. "I have a list that grows longer by the day."

Horgrim saluted him with his cup. His expression bore no sign of mockery now. In fact, it had turned solemn in a way that could have been mistaken for respect. "It's no easy thing, for a man to change his beliefs and reject the truths he's been weaned on."

"'Truths'?" Ryn snorted. "One man's truth is another man's heresy."

Horgrim laughed aloud. "Indeed! That is the only truth in which we can all trust." He finally took a drink, or perhaps only pretended to. "All a man can do is act in accord with his conscience for the greatest good." His smile faded. "I sense there are things that weigh on yours."

Ryn had no intention of venturing down that road. "You still haven't answered my question."

"Humph." Horgrim took another sip.

Ryn just stared at him. A collective groan rose from mid-deck. Kara crowed as she took another hand.

Horgrim's brow wrinkled. "You are not going to let this go, are you?"

"Considering I don't care for cards, not likely," Ryn said. "Besides, you owe me."

"And just how do you figure that?"

"You intend to cart us off to this promised land of yours without telling us anything about it?"

Horgrim conceded the point with a grudging nod. "Fair enough." He put his cup aside. "When our people went east to fight the Keshauk, we brought Sevren's remains with us. After the Clerisy's withdrawal, our most honored dead were laid to rest with him. A seedling was planted above his crypt. By Fraia's will, this Blessed Oak grew mighty within a fortnight. Its seed fell among our fallen heroes and sprouted a grove."

That white material began to grow from his sleeve. "I went to the grove as a lad of nineteen. Our Honored Dead have foresight. They speak sometimes, of things past, of things to come, of what fate might await. I kept vigil without food or sleep for five days. At the end of it, I had no glimpse of my future, no answers to my questions, but a voice led me to the crypt of Sanjaryn—a great warden. It told me to press my hand to his oak."

His eyes glistened in the starlight with such frank emotion Ryn found it hard to bear.

"The oak opened its heart and gave me this." That monstrous sword took shape in Horgrim's hand. "Its edge will remain true so long as I do. I have forsworn family, possessions, and status. I am a warden of Our Goddess, with no purpose but to protect our home. When I die, this sword and I will be put to rest together. A new oak will grow from our crypt and bear another sword for the one found worthy." He drew a mighty breath and let it slide out slow. "Earth-magic that draws on the animas? Yes, you could call it that."

Ryn risked a real swallow this time. "Does Blood Thorn speak to you?"

"It has no will in that respect, no voice," Horgrim said. "It's a symbol of Fraia's faith in me."

"It's also a rather big stick," Ryn said.

"It was—before that girl unleashed Mordyth Ral." Horgrim cupped the silken blade in his palm and ran his hand down its length. "Unlike this cryptwood, the Sword is an end unto itself. Better, perhaps, to free yourself than be its puppet."

Ryn's eyes narrowed. "Death is the only freedom."

"That's right."

"Kill me and claim Mordyth Ral—is that it?"

"You know the Sword considers me abomination." The "crypt-wood" softened and slithered back up Horgrim's sleeve, out of sight. He stood, drew his dagger, and tossed it on the deck between Ryn's feet. "This is the kind of thing a man must decide, and do, for himself."

Kara drifted over despite the calls for another hand from the men she'd just impoverished. "What's afoot, old lion?"

Horgrim's attention never left Ryn. "We're just having an honest discussion about the nature of honor, My Herald."

"'Honor'?" Ryn heaved himself up from the deck. "This isn't about honor. It's about taking responsibility. Aegias didn't—" He cut himself short. His vision was for certain not the Sevrendine's damned business, whether he could trust it or not.

Horgrim leaned toward him. "Didn't what?"

"All I know is the line I'm not willing to cross," Ryn said. "I won't see the Sword used for genocide or ambition."

"Is that so," Horgrim said. "But here I am, alive only because a palatar clubbed you—or can you tell me different?"

Ryn grimaced.

"Are you so naively arrogant as to believe you can somehow master that thing?"

Arrogant. Again, Horgrim pinched the nerve that Tovald had. Ryn bristled with indignation, but it faded quick as he remembered that feeling of helplessness as Mordyth Ral sank toward Horgrim's chest, his burning need for the Sword's company in that jail cell. "No, I'm not," he said, in a dejected whisper.

"Which leaves us with what you are ready to do," Horgrim said.

Find your anchor.

"'Do'?" Ryn balled his fists and stepped up toe to toe. "I can't do much of anything. You have the Sword, you have Josalind, and you have the skull. So, what in Hells is it that you want from me?"

"Yes, old lion, what are you rooting after?" Kara asked.

"Just a better measure of this lad's character." Horgrim stooped to retrieve his dagger.

Ryn scoffed at the idea with a snort. "Why do you care, if you're just going to imprison me?"

"When I'm forcing a man into a corner, I like to know the kind of man he is and what he's likely to do," Horgrim said.

"Oh, well, then *please* do enlighten me."

"I don't doubt you're a man of conscience, maybe even integrity, as rare as that is," Horgrim said. "A palatar true to the Virtues who has had the sense to wake up and reject the Clerisy." He picked up his cup and drained it. "I do respect that. I do. But I just can't trust it to be enough—not with what we know about how hard the Sword works to break a man."

Ryn regretted not having gone for the dagger when he'd had the chance. It wouldn't have done much good, considering his odds against these two and the crew. Still, he'd rather the satisfaction of going down the hard way than swallowing this like some meek little mouse.

"You will be treated with respect," Horgrim said. "You and Josalind both. This I swear by Our Goddess. But so long as you're bound to the Sword, you simply cannot be given your freedom."

Ryn's temper came to a sudden, explosive boil. He hit the self-righteous bastard with all he had.

It should have felt good, crashing his knuckles into that bearded jaw, but Horgrim stole all joy out of it. The warden saw it coming and just took it. An explosion of pain lanced up Ryn's arm to the shoulder. Maybe if he'd gone down, Ryn would have still found it gratifying, but Horgrim just rocked on his heels and took half a step back.

He wiped his bloodied lip on the back of his hand. "Are you good now?"

Kara hissed in exasperation. "Men."

Ryn flexed his aching hand. He probably wouldn't be able to squeeze a fist come morning. "To the Hells with you and your Goddess," he said, before taking his leave.

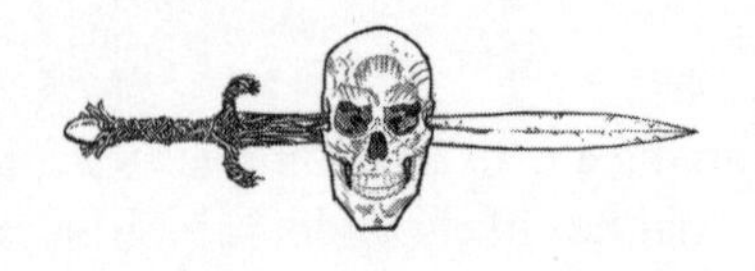

TWENTY-EIGHT

he problem was twofold—Horgrim would fully expect Ryn to make some attempt at escape and Kara knew he could sense the Sword's location. The odds of success by any measure were piss-poor.

Ryn welcomed the distraction that came of working their escape. He needed to occupy his mind with something other than the burden of the Sword. If not for Josalind's absolute certainty that letting the Sevrendine take the skull east would be disastrous, he might have welcomed a future as Horgrim's "honored guest." At least then he wouldn't have had to fear becoming a genocidal monster.

He had to trust that Gostemere and the Earthborn held a better answer. First, he needed Josalind free of witch iron. She could call on the martichora to pluck them from the sea once they jumped overboard. But he lacked a decent set of lock picks, not to mention the skill to use them.

He had an idea about that, a brutal one.

"It's going to hurt," he told Josalind the following morning.

"I'm used to hurting," she said. "It won't be for long."

"It will seem forever."

She looked at him cross. "Are you trying to discourage me?"

He shut up after that.

Discovering where Horgrim had squirreled away the Sword and the skull posed little challenge—Ryn just reached out with his thoughts. The fleeting images from Mordyth Ral appeared to indicate the aft hold. A hatch led down to it but lay in plain sight before the captain's cabin.

Ryn spent much of the day snoozing on deck and easing his way through bowls of beans and salt pork. Points of land passed on the southern horizon. Several times, he saw a pair of winged figures astern that he was quite certain were not birds. Horgrim kept his distance, but his attention clung harder than a barnacle. Whenever Kara crossed Ryn's path, she treated him to a cheerful smile that made her eyes dance. A wasted effort, if she meant to charm him.

Dusk came. A front moved in and swallowed the stars. Ryn hoped those clouds didn't mean a storm brewed—his plan already set a new standard for stupid, given the sea's lethal chill. Captain Fesk kept at full sail in a bid to outrun it, with an extra man aloft on lookout. Bergs weren't common this time of year but running hard at night still posed a risk. That left Ryn toying with the thought that going down with all hands might be for the best. Sword and skull lost to the Deep Dark. The risk of another Devastation averted.

Mordyth Ral dashed the idea. **Xang would be heard. The skull would be found. Demons do not fear the Deep.**

Once the crew had settled for their evening game of trumps, Ryn took two rations of port and headed into the cabin.

Josalind perched on the edge of the bed, almost crackling with anxious tension. "Is it time?"

"Not yet."

They talked about small things to pass the time and distract from the hard task ahead. Ryn told a couple of rude jokes that men in the barracks would share and left Josalind helpless with snorts of laughter. And then she told him a sailor's joke even more outrageous. Ryn had never found it so freeing to just laugh. It broke his chest free of iron bands that had been squeezing him for what felt like an age. Their hands touched, then clasped—as they had during those nights aboard another ship bound for Dragon's Claw, when misery had shared company.

Their laughter died in the same breath, like they'd both thought it at the same time.

Josalind raised a hand to wipe at her eyes. Thanks to the manacles, the effort dragged at her hand that held Ryn's, but she didn't let go. He didn't want her to.

He rubbed his thumb across her knuckles, noting how much colder her skin felt with witch iron blocking the Four. "It will be time soon."

The brave smile she mustered came in such somber contrast to her belly-aching laughter of before that his heart ached. He wanted to feel her lips again on his own—a true and honest kiss this time, not one meant to heal. Her brow furrowed ever so slightly as her head tilted. His pulse raced as her mouth parted.

As maddening as it was, he found himself pressing the back of her hand to his lips instead. Considering the injury he meant to inflict on her, it just seemed perverse to do more.

"Be back soon," he said.

Her shoulders sagged and she pressed her brow to his. Those curls tickled his face. "I won't be going anywhere."

He finished his last swallow of port and went for more.

Horgrim had planted himself right outside the cabin door, sitting on the edge of the aft hold's hatch.

Ryn breezed past and made sure his liquored breath caught the warden full in the face. "Grown tired of playing with that big stick of yours?"

Horgrim's chuckle implied that he knew exactly what his captives intended and that they didn't stand a chance. Ryn dismissed it as empty bluster.

Timson, along with a few of the crew, took note of Ryn's coming and gave knowing winks, no doubt certain a seduction was underway with only one sure end. Horgrim held the same position when Ryn turned back, but had no doubt poked his head into the cabin to satisfy himself that Josalind remained duly confined.

Ryn looked back at him from the open doorway. "Would you care to watch?"

The sailor on the ship's wheel snickered. Horgrim rolled his eyes and knocked the door shut with a quick thrust of his foot.

Inside the cabin, Ryn handed Josalind her cup. She drained it in a swallow, then grabbed the other from his hand and drained it just as quickly. "Let's get on with it."

Ryn greased up his fingers from the oil lamp and worked the warm lard around her raw wrists. The manacles fit too snug to be wiggled off. "What was it you said about big wrists and small hands when you escaped the pyre in Dragon's Claw?"

"I fibbed," she said. "The Four had a part in it."

He took her left hand, wrapped his fingers around the base of her thumb, and gripped the manacle with his other. She looked to the porthole. He felt how she trembled, but she left her hand limp and didn't tense up.

"Take a deep breath and let it out slow," he said as he steeled himself to break her hand.

It wasn't much different than wringing a chicken's neck—a hard jerk with a quick twist. Ryn clung to that thought, but it didn't make it any easier. Under normal circumstances, this could cripple Josalind for life.

A wet *pop* came from her wrist as things gave. A strangled gasp caught in her throat. He'd done far worse in his time, but not like this, not to *her*. It made his gut squirm. He worked the manacle off as quick as he could. Trying to be gentle would only be cruel. She bit her lip till it bled, tears streaming, fighting the need to scream.

And then it was done.

He went for the other. It wouldn't do either of them any good to wait. She couldn't help but flinch away, but that jostled her broken hand. Her whimper made his throat ache.

"Near there," he said.

She kept her attention fixed on the porthole and let him get to it. Her breathing turned so shallow and rapid, she'd soon black out. He worked quick, expecting Horgrim to stick his nose in at any moment.

The second manacle came off. The Grace of the Four returned and set her eyes ablaze. Her lips twisted with agony and ecstasy as her hands knit themselves.

After the rapture had passed, she cupped his jaw. Not in a casual gesture, but more like she meant to grant some blessing of forgiveness. Her touch made his flesh tingle.

He pulled her hand away and squeezed it. "The martichora—are they close?"

"Yes."

"The Sword's in the hold below us—the skull, too, I figure."

Josalind winced and rubbed at her temple. "It is."

She knelt on the floor and spread her hands outward across the decking as if parting drapes. The wood flexed and warped with moody groans. Nails squeaked as they pulled from the timbers. The sounds set Ryn's teeth on edge. The door had a bolt, but the sound of throwing it, even carefully, was even more likely to draw attention.

"Quick, now," she said.

Her eye-shaped breach stretched barely wide enough to fit him. He dropped into darkness and turned his ankle on what by touch turned out to be a coil of rope.

Gods be damned—of all the fool things.

The cabin door banged open. Horgrim roared for Kara.

Josalind landed behind Ryn. The decking snapped back to form so quickly that it cracked.

"What about the hatch?" Ryn blinked to see, but they might as well have been sealed in a crypt.

"Tighter than a spooked clam," she said with a note of smugness. A flickering light broke the gloom as a flame with no heat grew on her palm.

Horgrim cursed from above. Something thwacked into the hatch cover and split the wood. An ax, likely. Ryn took that for a good sign—Kara wasn't rushing to use magic in front of the crew. Still, time didn't run in their favor.

He spotted Mordyth Ral. Josalind found the sack bearing Xang's skull, resting in a chest a prudent distance from it. Favoring his ankle, Ryn ducked around the rudder's linkage to the stern bulkhead. He knocked the wood. "Might you spare another hole?"

Josalind soon had the bulkhead planking warped open, just above the waterline. Icy spray showered them. Ryn wedged the bound Sword into his belt and tried not to think about the cold. Unlike Kara's portals, he didn't have to worry about getting stuck because of Mordyth Ral and witch iron. The planking held its new shape without any further effort from Josalind. He heaved himself up and through as the hatch cover splintered behind them.

The cold crushed him.

He'd broken through the river ice back home more than once. Sea water bit much worse. It numbed his skin almost immediately, but a dull ache blossomed in his joints. His lungs refused to draw a decent breath. The harder he tried, the worse it got. He sputtered on salty gulps of liquid frost before his limbs got moving in the right rhythm to tread. Aching joints screamed louder with the effort. Up a wave and down, over and over. No sense of direction, no spare wind to call for Josalind. He wore only trousers, shirt, and buckled shoes from the ship's stores, but they weighed as much as a mail shirt. Already he'd lost feeling in his hands and feet.

Calls and cries from the ship faded into the distance. Or maybe his ice-bitten ears no longer had the capacity to hear them. The Sword and its manacles dragged at his waist. Damn the thing. Better to let it go. Give it to the Deep Dark. He pawed at it, but that left him choking on sea water. He came up gasping. His brain no longer worked right. He still had the sense to notice, but not the will to care.

Time to close his eyes and just sleep.

Weakling, rouse yourself.

Something hooked his arms and bore him up.

"I have you, man-child," Oma said.

The rhythmic jolt of her wings threatened to dislocate his shoulders, but the pain helped to muster his wits. A thousand needles stung his flesh—searing cold or blazing hot, he couldn't tell. His teeth chattered so much, he thought they might shake loose.

Thunder cracked and lit the sky with an orange flash. It came again and again.

No, not thunder, cannon fire.

Gods damn that Horgrim—did he mean to bring them down with the *Sea Hare*'s swivel guns? He must have known the sea couldn't hide the Sword and the skull for long from the Deceiver's demons—just as Mordyth Ral had said. Unless Kara had the means to fish them up.

Ryn glanced around, cramped muscles crying in protest. Glints of starlight dusted the waves far below. Two more cannon fired.

What in Hells?

The shots didn't come from below but from the left—up in the sky.

In the smoky flare of the muzzle flashes, Ryn glimpsed the dark silhouette of a ship's hull. And it *flew*—just like the fabled City Above down in Vysus. But that lump of rock had been born aloft by demons bound to serve the city's Sorcerer Brotherhood.

Xang's worshippers have come for him.

Ryn might have been awestruck if he weren't turning into a shard of burning ice. *F-f-f-rom where?* Kara had said that the Kun-Xang sect—the branch of the Keshauk priesthood tasked with resurrecting Xang—had agents searching for Xang's other bones and likely controlled the Brotherhood of Sorcerers down in Vysus. But while the sorcerers of Vysus might have had a floating mountain, Ryn had never heard tell of flying ships that could navigate the skies.

The leash of the Vysusian Brotherhood is held in the East.

Then that skyship—

Comes from the Dominion.

For Ryn's entire life, the Keshauk had been more myth than real—bogeymen to scare children found only in musty old texts. To think they were *here*, now, hunting *them* was too surreal to be believed.

The skyship fired again. The flash outlined six figures, maybe more—winged creatures bearing on them. Ryn couldn't tell the distance to judge their size, but their shapes were wrong for birds. A vague dread made him yearn for solid ground and a reliable blade.

"F-f-f-fly faster," he said. "We're being chased." He couldn't spot Astrig and Josalind.

A spear of light hurtled from the sea below, struck the skyship, and returned to its point of origin. That had to be Kara or Horgrim, mustering some power of their Goddess. Ryn couldn't see the sloop—a mist had risen out of nowhere. Kara had used that trick before.

He just couldn't figure out how the sect had chased them down—Josalind had been certain she'd kept Xang well muzzled.

Unless . . .

Horgrim had spilled enough blood in that dungeon for a hundred spells to track him by contagion—as Tovald had tracked Ryn with that compass. Demons in their natural incorporeal form could slip in and out of just about anywhere. Or another fiend could have been posing as a member of the clergy with access to any part of the Tanasgeld cathedral. It really had been only a matter of time before the sect tracked down the Sevrendine, whether its minions could sniff out Xang's skull or not.

That spear of light struck again and the cannon fell silent. Moonlight painted the skyship's silhouette. Three tall arches appeared to rise from its decks instead of masts or sails. The depth of its hull suggested at least three decks below—a massive vessel, with a forecastle and sterncastle in the manner of a conventional caravel. The skyship's bow pitched down, cannon still quiet. The Sevrendine must have done damage enough to cripple it.

Ryn caught the outlines of their pursuers against the sky. Man-shaped, with bat wings. And they were gaining.

Grenlich.

With wings?

Their Keshauk masters breed them to many forms.

Ryn remembered what Ogagoth the tar-vrul had said as he'd died that night at Dragon's Claw. *Our lost brothers, rulers of the sky—fear them.*

"Trouble's gaining," he said to Oma.

"Not far," she said. "An island."

The skyship steadily receded as Oma carried them on for what must have been several more miles. Ryn had given up on trying to spot the *Sea Hare*. Without warning, she arched her wings for a dive. "Prepare yourself."

"For what?" He still dangled like a trout hooked from a river, unable to do much of anything. His arms had gone numb from her grip. Or maybe they'd just frozen solid. Swirls of grit bit at his eyes, and he forced them shut.

Then she let him fall.

Before he could think to scream, he landed hard on his rump. Mordyth Ral's hilt jabbed under his ribs. They'd reached a pebble beach. He heaved himself up, sure he'd never be warm again. Muscles stiffer than harness leather offered a chorus of complaints.

Something big dropped from the sky before him.

Ryn's heart thumped so hard it threatened to burst from his chest. He staggered back and pulled Mordyth Ral from his belt, though he couldn't do much with it, tangled up in the manacles.

A grenlich confronted him—bigger than any he'd ever seen. The ugly bastard had a bat-like face and stood close to seven feet tall.

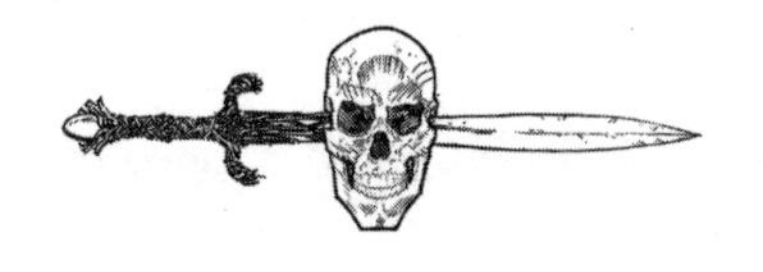

TWENTY-NINE

The grenlich hefted a heavy mace.

He carried a firearm, too, holstered at his hip. The odd contraption had the length of a carbine with a pistol's stock and multiple large-bore barrels. No grenlich Ryn had ever known had mastery of black powder. The brute also wore across his naked chest a bandolier stuffed with metal canisters, each a little larger than a shot glass.

Lean sinew and dark hide stretched so tight over the grenlich's bones, he looked more like a starved corpse than something living, but the hungry glare of those yellow eyes left little doubt. The skunky smell of grenlich musk made Ryn eager to cave his skull. The grenlich sniffed the air with obvious disdain, as if he found the stench of humans equally intolerable.

Ryn did the only thing he could, considering he had little chance of winning a fair fight—trick the brute into dropping his guard. Mordyth Ral hit the ground at the grenlich's feet. Behind Ryn, big bodies crashed through the trees with spitting snarls and hoarse roars. A firearm discharged with a rolling echo. Shrieks and screams followed. The grenlich paid no mind to any of it. He didn't even look down at Mordyth Ral.

Ryn wasn't about to get a chance at a cheap shot so easily. He stumbled back and cowered under his arms—the image of harmless cowardice—and let his knees shake for added effect. Given how he'd lost feeling in his feet, his knees were inclined to shake anyway.

The grenlich hefted his mace and stepped over the Sword, grinning to show his pointed teeth.

"That's right, you big, ugly . . ."

The mace swung, straight for Ryn's head.

The grenlich was damned fast and no doubt stronger than an ox but too quick to take advantage of an easy kill. Ryn ducked under the swing of that ropy arm, knocked the blow wide with his forearm, and thrust his other hand under the grenlich's kilt.

No different than wringing a chicken's neck—a hard jerk and quick twist.

The grenlich howled and slammed a fist into Ryn's back. His knees crumbled, but Ryn didn't let go. He used the leverage to twist around onto his rump and slammed the inside of the grenlich's knee with his heel.

That blow would have left a normal man ruined and writhing in pain. The grenlich's knee bowed out at a nasty angle but didn't break. A horned fist caught Ryn square in the jaw and sprawled him out. His wits swam in a starry haze. The mace came whistling for his skull. Then it went wide and thudded into the pebbles beside his ear.

Ryn blinked to see. Oma had buried her stinger into the grenlich's skull. He dangled a foot from the ground and twitched as her tail pulsed and flooded his brain with poison. Serrated teeth sank into his shoulder. Oma ripped off his arm in a spray of dark gore. Ryn looked on in disgust as she spat it out.

"They taste no better than they smell." Oma ripped the bandolier from grenlich's shoulder and flung it out to sea.

Ryn thrust out his hand. "Wait!"

And then that weird firearm followed. "Foul and evil craft," she said, as she tossed the body aside.

Maybe so, but he still needed a weapon and he'd wanted to examine this one's design. Those canisters in the bandolier must have been some kind of reload. Ryn caught her mane and dragged himself up. A wave of dizziness made the stars in his eyes do a merry dance. Oma cradled him with her wing.

A grenlich's enraged roar echoed from inland over the lap of the waves on the beach.

Gods be damned. Ryn scooped up Mordyth Ral and forced his lead feet into a run over the slick stones, muscles cramping from the cold shakes that gripped him. He needed to get warm or he wouldn't see another sun rise. Oma loped along beside him.

They left the beach and pushed into scrub and cedar. A clear path had been trampled through. Smoke swirled from burning underbrush. They passed the bodies of three grenlich, rent by claw and stinger or skewered by martichora arrows. Two more lay charred to the bone, still smoking. The sweet and oily stink made Ryn gag.

They found Astrig just as she snapped the neck of the last grenlich and cast the body aside. Josalind huddled against a tree nearby, the skull in its sack at her feet. Ryn went to her. "Are you all right?"

"I burned them up, like fish too long in the skillet." Her dull stare fixed on some distant place. "They sizzled, too, while they screamed. Nothing deserves to go like that."

He thought of her shackled to that stake in Dragon's Claw and had nothing to offer. She didn't wield the torch now, she'd become one.

"Never know what's going to come when I ask for their help, when they force it on me." She hugged herself tighter. "Can't control them, or myself."

He reached for her shoulder, but she shrank away. "It's no bother, Ryn. I'll be right as rain, soon enough."

But she wouldn't be. He knew too well how these sorts of things never went away. They just balled up inside, knots twisting on knots until something was sure to snap.

With Oma's help, Ryn had soon gathered enough deadfall for a cheery blaze. The martichora stomped out the brushfires before the breeze could whip them into something worrisome. While they worked, Ryn gave Oma the abridged version of how he'd become bound to Mordyth Ral and the consequences of it.

He tried to be as brief and factual as possible, but Oma must have sensed the dread that gnawed at him as he spoke, for she pinned him against a tree, rested those big, clawed hands on his shoulders, and pressed her brow to his. After the sewer, her rancid breath no longer seemed so foul.

"Whatever may come, Ryn Ruscroft, you will face it not alone." She gave him a suggestive, sidelong look. "I, too, know what it is to share a vow of brotherhood."

Ryn remembered saying those same words on another lee shore, the day the martichora had rescued them from Dragon's Claw. He couldn't help but smile at her earnestness and feel lighter for it.

Afterward, around the fire, Ryn told what he knew of the Kun-Xang sect and the skyship's origin.

Josalind acknowledged it all with a knowing nod. "I'd relish the chance to get aboard for a look-see at how she works."

Ryn looked at her askance. "Be wary of what you wish for." He rose to stretch the sea's stiffness from his limbs that not even a roaring fire could dispel. "But we—"

Oma cut him short with a hiss. "We are not alone."

"'But we' what?" Horgrim asked.

Josalind cursed so fiercely it would have made a sailor blush, snatched up the skull, and scuttled back toward the shadows. Ryn tensed and turned slow.

Horgrim stood in the middle of the trail that led back to the beach, dappled by the moonlight spilling through the trees. Blood Thorn, the sword, hung easy in his hand with a milky gleam. Kara wasn't in sight. She likely snuck around to flank them.

Ryn eyed Mordyth Ral, lying there on the ground, bound up by the witch-iron manacles into a clumsy club of a weapon. "You caught up rather quick."

"The wind turned sudden in our favor." Horgrim's attention strayed to the Sword. His feral smile bore not a drop of humor. "Are you going to make a play for that?"

In a blink, Oma had her heavy recurve bow in hand and an arrow nocked and drawn. Golden venom glistened from the arrow's head. "He doesn't have to," she said. Astrig followed suit.

Ryn pressed Oma's arm down. "No need for that." *Not yet, at least.* "It's you that skyship is tracking," he said to Horgrim. "Thanks to that bucket of blood you left in Tanasgeld."

"Is that so." Horgrim took a casual step into the clearing.

"You being here is likely to bring its cannon down on us," Josalind said.

The warden took another step. "I wouldn't worry—its crew is going to be awhile just keeping that tub in the air."

"From what Kara's told me, I doubt that skyship is the only thing Xang's followers have hunting us." Ryn wondered where in Hells Kara lurked. "If it had the means to track you by contagion, so will the rest."

That did give Horgrim pause. He looked upon the dead grenlich with a calculating eye, lips peeled back into a lopsided snarl. "There's nothing for it, then—*Kara*, you know what to do."

Horgrim raised Blood Thorn parallel to the ground before him. The cryptwood blade stretched and lengthened, then the tip snapped back with the flex of a bullwhip to pierce him through the heart.

Ryn stared in utter disbelief as the warden's eyes rolled back and his knees gave out. A gush of blood soaked his shirt and waistcoat before he hit the ground.

"What madness is this?" Astrig said.

Kara barreled out of the woods from the right, skirts raised to keep from tripping. She crashed to her knees and cradled Horgrim's head in her palms. "You crazy old boar."

And then she started to count.

Ryn exchanged a puzzled look with Oma as she lowered her bow. The Sevrendine must have meant to defeat the tracking spell with death, as old Sagren the Fourth-Born had written in his treatise on sympathetic magic. But for how long did Horgrim have to be dead? How long could he be and still come back?

Ryn came up to Kara. "You've done this before?"

She reached ten without paying him any mind before pressing her hand to Horgrim's wound. Just like in the cathedral's jail, a radiance grew from her touch and seeped into him, but brighter this time, and sharper.

Her features crimped with pain. She wilted and hugged her other arm to her chest. Then her power began to fade. Horgrim appeared no less dead. Ryn couldn't tell through the mess of blood if the wound had healed or not.

Kara slammed the ground with her fist. "No, I can't lose you, not like this." She tried again. This time, her healing touch barely flickered before it faded.

And then Ryn understood. She'd already exhausted herself playing with the weather to escape the skyship. He knelt and probed Horgrim's wrist for a pulse but found none.

"Help me," Kara said, her voice small and brittle.

Ryn grimaced. "He's gone, there's nothing—"

"Not you." Kara looked past him. "I don't have the strength—*please*."

Josalind's eyes flashed silver from the shadows. "Why should I?"

Ryn understood how desperately she needed to reach Gostemere but still, Josalind's blunt callousness took him by surprise. With Horgrim dead, they only had to contend with Kara. A considerable shift in the balance of power. Ryn should have welcomed this. Leave Horgrim dead and take Kara down while she remained too weak to muster any righteous fury.

Yes. Seize the moment.

Why, then, did it feel so wrong? This was their chance, *his chance*, to avoid ending up a Sevrendine prisoner. But he'd known Horgrim long enough to consider him a decent man—a faithful follower of the Virtues, if the Sevrendine's claims could be taken at face value, doing what he honestly thought served a greater good.

Ryn had killed enough good men already. The Sword's eagerness to see Horgrim die only made the prospect that much more revolting.

"Help her, Josalind," he said.

NO.

The word blasted Ryn's skull as if firecrackers had gone off in his ears. He cursed and clutched his scalp, barely able to see straight. How could the Sword be doing this? It must be mustering everything it had, all the power drawn in Tanasgeld, to fight him through witch iron.

"Do it," he gasped.

Kara wiped at her eyes. "Please." One word, but it carried the weight of a world.

"Blessed child," Astrig said. "This will scar you—have you not scars enough?"

Josalind dragged herself from the shadows. She sank to her knees at Horgrim's side and took Kara's hand.

Ryn's hand burned to slap them apart, fueled by a furious intent not his own. He clenched a fist and slammed the ground, dug at his scalp till he felt the ooze of blood.

Oma's big hand clamped his shoulder. "Steady, man-child."

"Thank you," Kara said.

"I haven't done anything yet," Josalind said. "They might not let me."

No. More a plea now than a command, weak and distant. Ryn sagged back onto his rump with a weary sigh.

Kara and Josalind pressed their palms to Horgrim's chest, bathing him in a multihued radiance. A moment passed, then another. Josalind's breath turned hard and rapid. Sweat glistened on Kara's dark skin. They both cried out as blood seeped from their breasts and Horgrim's injury became their own.

Just when Ryn thought they'd both faint with nothing to show for it, Horgrim's broad chest heaved with a sudden breath. The warden coughed and tried to roll over. Blood Thorn jumped to his ready hand.

Kara slumped to the ground, gasping. Ryn couldn't tell if she wept from pain or relief. Likely both. "Easy, old lion," she said. "You need to rest still."

Josalind turned away and nursed her own wound, as if embarrassed to look Horgrim, or any of them, in the eye. "It's a patch job, the best we could do."

"She . . . helped?" Horgrim said in a raspy whisper.

Ryn rose to his feet. "You'd still be dead if she hadn't."

"My thanks," Horgrim said.

Josalind shrugged. "Thank the Four. Don't give them reason to regret it."

Horgrim took Kara's hand and pressed it to his lips. "Can you forgive me, My Herald?"

"You did what was needed." She wiped at her eyes. "But I almost lost you this time."

Horgrim labored to his feet using Blood Thorn as a crutch and looked to Ryn. "Well, *swordling*, where do we stand now?"

Ryn bristled at the nickname. "*We* are leaving. You and Kara can stand around here as it pleases you."

Despite his condition, Horgrim had Blood Thorn's tip under Ryn's jaw lightning quick. "I don't think so."

Oma hissed and edged around the warden's flank. Astrig took the other. Ryn batted the white blade aside as he took a quick step back. "Spare me the bluster—you're in no state."

"We will let you take the skull to Gostemere," Kara said.

Horgrim's face flushed scarlet. "What!"

"Grace Above, calm yourself before you fall into fits," Kara said.

"But—"

"Because Our Goddess asks it of us."

Horgrim's legs failed. The impact of his rump with the dirt left him wheezing and nursing his chest. "When?"

"Just now." Kara crawled over and drew his head onto her lap. "When my need was greatest, I heard, 'Follow them and bear witness.'"

Ryn frowned. "No offense, but that sounds just as obscure as the ramblings Josalind gets from the Four."

Josalind came to his side. "What do you mean, 'bear witness'?" she asked, with obvious suspicion.

"Our Goddess does not command us or force us to express our devotion with mindless obedience and sacrifice." Kara toyed with Horgrim's hair. "That is the way of the Deceiver. Fraia would have us let you take the skull and the Sword to Gostemere, see what there is to find, and then act as we see fit."

"Without giving you any idea of what she wants done." Ryn found that unbelievable, but then, he had no practical experience with living gods.

Horgrim cleared his throat. "If we can't be trusted to choose wisely, to ignore our own wants and balance our conscience with a greater good, then we are not fit to serve our people. This is, after all, our world, not Fraia's."

Kara nodded. "Fraia's faith in us is just as important as ours in her—our power flows from this."

"This doesn't sound like worship—it sounds like a partnership," Josalind said, no less suspicious.

"We are partners," Kara said. "Trying to bring justice and mercy to a world made harsh by small-minded men and a cruel god." She treated Josalind to a smile. "I would have thought that might appeal to you."

Josalind had nothing to say to that. She just stood there, rubbing at her temple like she meant to wear a hole for the Four to spill out.

Ryn threw up his hands. "Fair enough." He had no idea how much of this was honest truth or pure gibberish. It didn't much matter at present. Fraia did exist and did exert real power over the world, though far too little as far as he was concerned, considering the Clerisy's hold on the Kingdoms. He could only judge her benevolence by his measure of Kara and Horgrim. Despite their disagreements, the Sevrendine appeared to be true devotees of the Virtues—he could work with that.

He looked to Mordyth Ral, bound by the witch-iron manacles. "I expect you do still intend to hold the key?" he asked Horgrim.

"I'm considering the merits of just swallowing it," the warden said.

Ryn couldn't deny that might be for the best, given how the Sword had just fought him. He noted the absence of the tongueless jailer. "What happened to Timson?"

"He joined Fesk's crew," Horgrim said. "He deemed that less risky."

"A wise man," Ryn said.

"Captain Fesk couldn't part ways with us fast enough," Horgrim said with a glimmer of a smile. "He left us the skiff and set course back to Tanasgeld. For some reason, he didn't even care about payment anymore."

Kara granted Oma a respectful nod. "Will you give us passage, ancient one?"

Oma bowed in return. "We have no quarrel with the Mother Goddess's flock, blessed child, if you speak faithfully of truce."

"A key," Josalind said to no one in particular.

Everyone just looked at her.

She raked back her tangle of curls. "What?"

"You just said 'a key,'" Ryn said.

"Did I?" She looked genuinely puzzled, then nodded like she repeated the obvious. "Yes, we need a key." She rubbed at her temple again. "They've been screaming about it for ages."

"What manner of key?" Horgrim asked.

"I don't know what it looks like," Josalind said. "But Gostemere isn't a place you can just finger on a map. It's hidden with misdirection magic to keep it safe. You can't find it without the key."

"Kara, are you ready to trust in this?" Horgrim asked. He waved his hand in Josalind's direction. "No offense, girl. I don't doubt it's the Four that speak to you, but death hasn't been kind to their sanity or clarity."

Josalind's eyes narrowed. "I don't say things till I'm sure about them, and now I finally know where the key rests."

"And where is that?" Kara asked.

"The Clerisy has it," Josalind said. "Deep in the belly of the beast. In Viglias."

Viglias—the City of Thrones, capital of Sturvia and seat of the Clerisy's power. Ryn almost laughed at the absurdity. She might as well have said the damned key rested in the Great Deceiver's back pocket.

Horgrim shared the sentiment. "Of course, where else would it be?" He whacked Blood Thorn on the ground so hard that Josalind flinched. "Do you have any idea what pains we take to operate, *in secret*, under the Clerisy's nose? How many brothers and sisters have suffered and died under the Inquisitarem's tender mercies to guard us all?" His scowl widened to include Kara. "And now we've proclaimed ourselves to the High Lord Inquisitar himself."

Kara fixed him with a stern look. "Would you rather I left you in that hole?"

"You might have . . ." Horgrim suffered a coughing fit and hugged his chest until it passed. "Exercised a bit more discretion."

"I'm tired of skulking," Kara said. "The day is coming when we must confront the Clerisy head-on if we ever hope to free the Kingdoms of its yoke."

Horgrim grimaced. "You're talking bloody revolution."

"Yes, and a horrible thing it would be," Kara said. "But you know it won't be done any other way." She drew herself up as much as her exhausted state would allow. "I will live to see the day when the Clerisy falls and the Kingdoms rejoin the fight against the Keshauk."

"Now is hardly the time to start it." Horgrim slapped his knee. "And yet here we are, ready to prod the bear in the arse, in its own den, when it already spoils for trouble."

Ryn intervened before the battle could escalate. "The Clerisy is hunting us all regardless, and its own back stoop is the last place it will think to look." He turned to Josalind. "The belly of the beast—you mean the reliquary that lies beneath the Great Cathedral."

"That's the one," she said.

"Do you know it?" Kara asked.

"I've been to Viglias, while on pilgrimage as a palatar errant after earning my lanyards," Ryn said. "We toured the cathedral."

"Only plebes who rank top of their cohort are granted errancy with such privilege," Horgrim said.

"That's right." Ryn barely remembered that eager young trooper. Now here he was, a fugitive and apostate, contemplating how to sneak into the greatest city in all the Kingdoms to steal some relic.

Quintan would have howled at the irony.

"How do we get in?" Kara asked.

Ryn considered the question. They would need the Sevrendine's help, if they had a network in Viglias to compare with the one in Tanasgeld. "How deep are your pockets?" he asked.

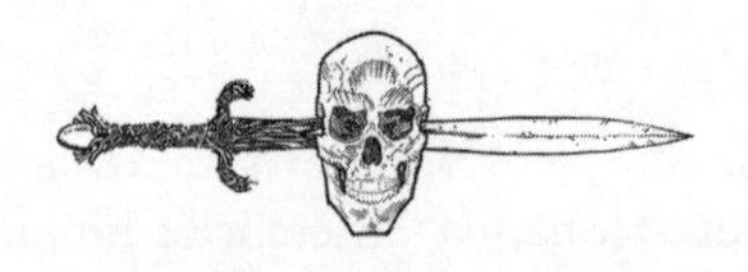

THIRTY

The small island presented too obvious a target should the skyship return to search.

They buried the grenlich bodies and scuttled the skiff to hide evidence of their presence. Oma and Astrig then ferried them in turns to the mainland without further delay.

Ryn, Josalind, and the Sevrendine were left to spend four days living rough while the martichora went to summon more of their kin. Oma made vague reference to the "northern reaches" of her people's territory but declined to offer anything more specific. "Legends should keep mysterious," she'd said with that unnerving smile. Ryn assumed she must have meant the mountains between Morlandia and Jendalia.

"You're doing a lot for us," he told her, as she and Astrig prepared to leave. "I can't thank—"

A long index finger tapped him under the chin. Oma's calluses rasped against his stubble . . . and the point of a dark claw poked his throat knob. That prompted him to gulp and stop talking, even if she didn't intend to threaten.

"We do this not for your sake alone, man-child, but ours, as well," Oma said. "For too long our kind have hidden from the world, lamenting the evil that seeps from the East and doing little of consequence to stem it." She gave her sister a nod. "We would change that, Astrig and I, and give our people purpose again, a reason to *be*. But first, we must learn of the world and bring this knowing back to our prides."

Ryn took her wrist and gently eased that claw from his throat. "Why I am I left with the impression that you're a pair of malcontents?"

Astrig gave a snort and flicked fish scales from her teeth.

"It is true that we are often a grievous thorn in the paw of those who claim lordship," Oma said with somber gravity. Then she smiled so broad her face threatened to split, a display Ryn found both dazzling and terrifying. "It gives *us* purpose."

"And it is also true that the hopeless poke at our soft spots," Astrig added. "You poor ground-bound creatures would be lost without us."

Kara spent most of her time waiting on the martichora's return sleeping to regain her strength. Horgrim refused to let her heal him further, though he suffered from a cough and a wheeze and still bore angry scars from his torture.

A fishing village lay farther down the coast, but they kept clear of it. The people there likely didn't see strangers much. Ryn didn't want to stir them up with some fanciful tale of pirates and shipwrecks. And Horgrim warned there was no telling where Xang's followers could have ears, even here.

"I've seen sorcerers of the Keshauk priesthood bind demons to the shape of horseflies, dragons, even your dear old mum," he told Ryn, as they cleaned sculpin they had caught in a tidal pool. "In their natural form, demons can make themselves invisible and pluck thoughts from your head."

Ryn had read as much, most recently in Tovald's books, though he'd come to doubt the veracity of anything approved by the Clerisy's censors. "What about that skyship—is that some kind of sorcery?"

"Sorcery and alchemy together," Horgrim said. "The Keshauk are clever that way."

Ryn regretted again not having had the chance to inspect one of those multibarreled carbines. There had been a second one, but

Astrig had cast that one away, too. "They arm their grenlich with firearms."

Horgrim nodded. "Hellcasts. Only the elite get them. They fire explosive and poison shells."

"But how did the grenlich even come to be?" Ryn asked. "The Clerisy speaks of some hellish origin, but it's not specific."

"You know how those fiends we fought in Tanasgeld are birthed—a willing human, bound body and soul to a lesser demon through ritual?"

"Yes."

"Well, the first grenlich were the offspring of fiends who mated."

Ryn looked for evidence of that mocking humor but found none. *Gods' Grace.*

"For a thousand years, maybe more, the Keshauk priesthood have bred them like cattle." Horgrim flung the fish guts from his fingers. "Grenlich are slaves—cruel and savage, but they also have their own code, their own sense of honor." He gave Ryn a sideways look. "You might even say they have something in common with your palatar brothers, trapped by their oath to serve and obey the Clerisy."

Ryn scoffed. "I wouldn't stretch it that far." Still, to think that the grenlich clans of northern Morlandia had somehow broken free of that bondage untold centuries ago . . . He couldn't help but respect that.

Josalind didn't say much through that first day. It might simply have been the stress and exhaustion from recent events, but Ryn suspected more. She spent bell after bell sitting on a wave-beaten boulder, staring out to sea. Her busy fingers wove and braided the few hardy species of wildflower that bloomed this late in the season. Bracelets encircled her arms and a crown of autumn crocuses sat askew on her head. But unlike that morning on another beach a couple of weeks before, she had no desire to deliver any more botany lessons from *Tathemay's Menagerie of Plants.*

"I'm right as rain," she said when Ryn asked, in a brittle way he would expect of someone swallowed by grief.

He skipped a rock across the surf. "Really."

"Don't dig at me." The delicate braid work in her hands tore and she tossed it aside with a curse. "Just leave me be. Please, Ryn."

So he did.

They roasted the fish that night on flat rocks once the fire had burned down to coals. Horgrim expressed his longing for a decent stout to wash it down. Halfway through dinner, he poked Kara in the ribs with his elbow. "Have you ever seen a catfish?"

"No," Kara said with utter seriousness. "How could it possibly hold the pole?"

Horgrim laughed loud from the belly.

A grin had broken out on Kara's face. "I miss those fish roasts on Autumn's Deeping."

"Aye." Horgrim reached for another portion. "I was thinking the very thing."

Ryn gave them both a bemused look before glancing at Josalind. She just rolled her eyes and said nothing at the juvenile joke. "What is Autumn's Deeping?" he asked.

"A festival in Sevrenia after the harvest moon," Horgrim said. "To give thanks for our bounty." His eyes twinkled in the firelight. "Young lovers often disappear into the fields to, ah, make offerings that ensure a bountiful crop the next year."

"Is that so." Ryn dug his fingers into the sand to clean them. Mordyth Ral rode across his back in a makeshift sling made from rope and canvas he'd found on the skiff. The Sword had been quiet since the debate over Horgrim's life, but he still endured the hot pressure of it even now, poking, prodding, testing. It left him with little appetite and the need for a distraction. "Who rules Sevrenia? Is there a king?"

"No—and no lords of the manor, either," Horgrim said. "We live by the Virtues in the spirit in which they were intended. Every man is equal to another."

"And every woman," Kara added.

Horgrim doffed his straw hat, stood up, and bowed with a flourish worthy of a royal courtier. "The rest of us poor souls could never hope to stand equal to you, My Herald."

Kara swatted his leg and looked to Ryn. "Every man, woman, and child, every one of us, takes responsibility for themselves as well as their neighbor. No one is left to go hungry. No one is left without a bed. We take care of our own."

"And for that *protection*, there is no fealty, no one has lordship over another," Ryn said with a measure of disbelief. The old manorial system had died out across the Four Kingdoms in recent generations and each now functioned as a constitutional monarchy. No king could create new taxes, or impose tariffs or duties on trade, without the consent of his parliament. But still, power rested with those who had title, even before wealth.

"We work together for the common good," Horgrim said as he took his seat again. "Of course, there are people with rank and title to ensure just governance, but these are positions that are earned on merit, often determined through a public election. There is no inheritance of title and privilege from birth."

"And how does your church figure into this?" Ryn asked.

"The elder heralds provide counsel in affairs of government and defense when needed," Kara said. "But they are only advisors."

"Really." Ryn found that even harder to believe, given the Clerisy's hold on the Kingdoms. He looked again to Josalind. She paid no attention and continued to nibble at her fish like a mouse rationing the last of its crumbs.

"That doesn't mean faith isn't the center of our lives," Horgrim said. "Twice a week, in every town and village, people gather to worship—but not with all that ridiculous pomp of the Clerisy. Kara wouldn't stand up at a pulpit with the *Codex* and rant on about the Hells that await if you break the Virtues. We gather to talk."

"Talk," Ryn said.

"About how the Virtues should apply to everyday life, about our fears and concerns, even our sins," Kara said. "Everyone is free to stand up and confess whatever festers in their heart."

Ryn frowned at her. "Confession is held in public—for everyone to see and hear."

Horgrim fixed him with a wolfish smile. "Not quite what you're used to, eh?"

After dinner, Ryn felt the need for a walk. Mordyth Ral still poked and prodded. The farther he ranged from camp, the less alone he felt. A narrow, rocky spit thrust out into the sea's darkness. He braved the slippery stones to reach its end, eager to lose himself in the restless wash of the surf, the cleansing bite of the icy spray on his cheeks.

If not you, another.

Had that truly been Aegias, or only a trick of the Sword? If the former, could he reach the Prince Messiah again? Ryn had no idea how to go about praying. Maybe if he reached out his thoughts as he would to Mordyth Ral, picturing the Aegias of his vision . . .

He stood on those rocks, yearning and straining until the sea spray soaked him and his head ached. The effort netted nothing.

Maybe Aegias didn't hear him. Maybe Mordyth Ral wouldn't let him. Ryn might have prayed to the Goddess Fraia, but that felt far too awkward. Besides, if Mordyth Ral did block his prayers to Aegias, it most certainly would to her. Could either tell him anything of value, in any case?

Mine is the only truth that matters.

Those words thundered so loud and unexpected that he gasped. They drowned out the sigh and roar of the sea, pummeled him with such unassailable certainty the world shrank to just him, the Sword, and the endless dark that stretched before them. Mordyth Ral had already consumed all else and only this dark eternity remained. Two miserable and wretched things forever trapped in the Void.

The thought brought on a fit of the shakes—the same panic that had clawed at him that night in the Bone Yard when he'd fully realized the consequences of breaking with the Clerisy. How trivial that seemed now, compared to the burden of the Sword.

He crashed to his knees, gashing them on the stones, and barely noticed. The Sword's weight bore on him like a millstone. He wrapped himself in a tight hug, but that only deepened the shakes' violence.

"Ryn."

He tried to breathe but couldn't. The sea spray turned from ice to molten lead.

"Ryn?"

He lived it all over again, the fear and confusion of Tanasgeld's thousands, felt their lives slipping away to feed the Sword, slipping through *him*. How could he ever risk using the Sword against a true threat? What if circumstance left him with no choice?

A pair of hands gave him a rough shake. "Spit and spray, Ryn, what's wrong?"

Josalind crouched beside him. Hands too warm to be right cupped his face. She drew his head to her breast. The feel of her soothed his soul. Her heart's rhythm, steady and strong, provided an anchor to calm the rampant beat of his own.

"I'm afraid of what I might do," he said.

"You'd be a monster if you weren't."

He'd be a monster regardless, a creature to inspire stories for tormenting children. Far worse than any bedtime spook tale about the grimgaust. "I'm a danger to you, to everyone." Tovald's words came back to haunt him—his vanity and conceit could only lead to a disastrous end.

She stroked his hair. "No. We won't let it come to that. I won't."

Ryn caught the brittleness in her tone, that hardness, too. He drew back to see her face by the starlight. "And just how do you expect to do that?"

"Like you said—all our answers wait in Gostemere," she said. "The Earthborn have some plan, they must."

He frowned at the pain with which she spoke. "You say that like you already know it."

She mustered a disarming smile and scoffed at the idea. "How could I? The gods rant nonsense at me most times."

Ryn didn't buy it for a moment. "Really."

The smile faded. "We have to have faith."

And then she kissed him.

Not a healing kiss—one deep and earnest and almost desperate. The tip of her tongue teased Ryn's lips, only for an instant, but long enough to rouse a fire he'd not felt in far too long. He drew her into a tight embrace, charged with a need he couldn't deny, and savored the inviting warmth of her mouth. Her hand cupped the back of his head, fingertips raising a giddy shiver as they stroked his neck.

At last, she drew away and rested her forehead against his. "Let us have one night where none of it matters," she said. "None of it."

He wove his fingers into that mad tangle of hair. "Not even the Four?"

She rose and pulled him up after her. "Help me drown them out, at least for a little while."

He let her lead him from the rocks. Not far off, stunted cedar sheltered a patch of sand from the damp wind that rolled out of the north.

"One night," she said.

He didn't argue. Maybe he was just a means to an end. It didn't matter. A wise man knew when to shut up and go with the moment. Surely his oath to the Virtue of Chastity could abide the occasional bending. For a precious time all too brief, lost in the whole of her, Ryn forgot his own misery and found peace.

Afterward, left lazy by the lingering glow of it all, Ryn lay with Josalind's head resting on his chest, staring up at the navy sky. He'd left Mordyth Ral under a bush as far away as he dared. Their lovemaking, his distance from the Sword, or both had driven that lurking presence from his head. The brief respite proved enough to change his view of himself and the Sword.

He'd told Horgrim aboard the *Sea Hare* that he wouldn't see Mordyth Ral used for genocide or ambition. Bucardas and his kind could never be allowed near it. Until now, Ryn had thought only of the brutal responsibility that cast upon him, alongside the risk that the Sword would prevail and make a monster of him.

But he had to think in a different way.

His life, his fate, had been bound to the single most powerful weapon that had ever existed. A thing of legend and nightmare. But also a symbol of power and meaning. A burden, certainly, but also an opportunity.

He wanted his brother palatars freed of the Clerisy's yoke, free to protect the innocent and fight injustice as they were meant to. He wanted to atone for his failings in Sablewood. The Sword claimed to have somehow used these desires against him to weave its trap. He would damned well return the favor.

Even daring to think that he could bend the Sword to his will in any practical way smacked of the arrogance and conceit of which Tovald and Horgrim had accused him. He knew that. The way these thoughts left his heart fluttering like a frantic moth left little doubt.

Still, he had to try. He had to find a way that wouldn't damn him. No matter what it took, no matter the cost. Twenty-five hundred years ago, Vulheris had found some way to muzzle Mordyth Ral. He forced it to accept the compromise of imprisoning Fraia rather than slaying her, and channeled the Sword's power to craft that prison. If Vulheris could do that, then it had to be possible for Ryn to turn Mordyth Ral to a purpose of his choosing, too.

Of course, the whole affair had apparently driven Vulheris mad. But given the choice between risking madness to tame the Sword or letting it twist him into a monster, Ryn would gladly choose madness.

Not one of these thoughts did he share with Josalind. They were too personal, to unripe and under-baked. Or maybe speaking them aloud would only prove them to be as absurd as he feared. Aegias, after all, didn't appear to have ever managed to tame the Sword as Vulheris had.

Horgrim remained awake to notice their return to camp sometime later. He said nothing, just gave the fire a final poke with a stick before spooning up to Kara, ostensibly to keep her warm, and closed his eyes.

Curse you all to Hell.

Ryn woke from the dream with a start, then slumped back and stared up at a morning sky of moody gray. Not even Tanasgeld could outmatch Sablewood. Nor did he want it to. He owed it to the dead. Besides, that singular guilt kept him focused, grounded. He needed that now, more than ever. As he'd told Tovald, guilt gave a man courage to do what was right and avoid repeating past mistakes.

He had to believe that for there to be any chance of achieving his ends.

Mordyth Ral rested by his side. He felt it again, poking and prodding, and wondered how deeply it could read his thoughts. Could he withhold anything from it? Did it even now wait with patient smugness, confident that the decision he'd reached the night before only proved him to be a self-deluded fool it could easily control?

Voices murmured nearby. The fire had already been stoked to fresh life. Ryn stretched toward it, eager for the heat. Horgrim and Kara knelt by the stream where they'd made camp. The warden scrubbed at the blood in his shirt. Kara had stripped to the waist for a quick sponge bath.

Ryn found the teasing glimpse of her ample breasts as alluring as most any red-blooded man would, but what struck him most was the comfortable familiarity of the scene. He'd only expect such disregard for modesty between a couple long married. On the other hand, these two were comrades in arms, sharing a hard road in service of their faith. Maybe heralds and wardens practiced abstinence and conditioned themselves against physical attraction.

But as Horgrim rose to return to the fire, his gaze lingered on Kara's curves. A slew of emotions stormed across his face—desire for certain, but regret, too, maybe even guilt.

Later that morning, the men headed inland to scrounge for firewood. Josalind had only begun to stir. Ryn expected her to play it bland and act like nothing had happened between them. She'd wanted one night, and he would cherish the memory. Only time would tell if either could truly leave it at that.

As if this lee shore weren't bleak enough, the sodden sky's misty underbelly promised rain before noon. They passed a weathered outcropping of stone. Horgrim drew his belt knife and tapped at various points with the pommel. He grunted at the rather dull-sounding results. "Poor granite for building, that."

It wasn't the first time the warden had passed the time by inspecting the quality of the local stone. "Tell me something, Horgrim."

He sheathed his knife and carried on. "What?"

"You and Kara, you've known each other for some time, haven't you?"

"Decades," Horgrim said.

"Are you . . . a couple?" Ryn asked.

"Grace Above, what would give you that idea?"

"I've known married couples who acted less the part than you two," Ryn said.

"We're friends, nothing more."

"All right." Ryn didn't believe a word but didn't press the issue.

Horgrim said nothing for a spell, then blurted out, as though Ryn had hounded him, "You have yet to fully understand what it means to be a warden, or a herald. Our lives are devoted to one thing—Sevrenia's survival. It hardly leaves time for such commitments."

"I suppose that makes sense . . . if wardens and heralds take vows of celibacy like clerics in the—"

"We don't, but we're dedicated to something greater than ourselves. Our own wants are second to that."

Ryn grunted. "I've known many men in their thirties who've never been with a woman because of their commitments to duty and service."

"I'm not . . ." Horgrim quickened his pace, despite how it made him wheeze with his half-healed chest.

"'Not' what?" After the way Horgrim had hounded him on the *Sea Hare*, Ryn felt owed a turn as the interrogator, especially now that he seemed to have found a soft spot.

"I'm sixty."

Ryn snorted at the absurdity. "How is that possible?"

"Fraia's Grace grants some advantages," Horgrim said. "So long as it can reach us."

"But if you're sixty, then Kara must be—"

"Sixty-three."

"Oh." Older even than Ryn's gran, if the tough bird still lived, but Kara didn't appear old enough to be his mum. The thought roused bittersweet memories of his family. Strangers now, thanks to his father's damned stubborn ambition.

"Now, I'd rather this entire conversation—"

"I'll not breathe a word to another living soul," Ryn said. He couldn't wait to tell Josalind. "But not once, with any woman?"

Horgrim grabbed up a branch as thick as his wrist and snapped it in half across his knee. "Heavens redeem me. You're not going to let this go, are you?"

"Not unless you're going to tell me that your tastes run in a more . . . *coltish* direction." Ryn had no qualms about men finding comfort with men, even if the prospect held no appeal to him personally.

Horgrim stopped cold and turned to look him in the eye. No twinkle this time, just icy hardness. "I've no wish to find myself with children—does that suffice?"

"Because of your vows as a warden—it would be hard to be a proper father to them," Ryn said.

"There's that."

"And?"

Horgrim turned sharp on his heel. "And the rest isn't something I care to discuss."

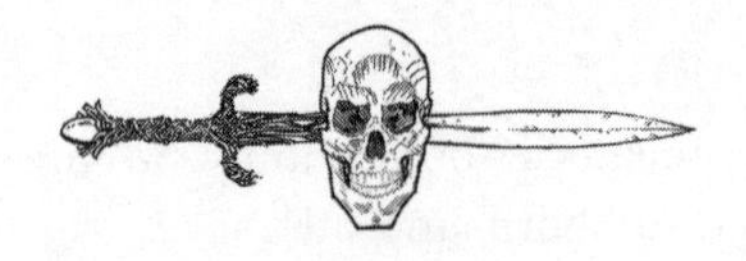

THIRTY-ONE

Oma and Astrig returned with two of their kin two days later. The group left for Viglias after dusk. It took a wind-torn night and day to reach the City of Thrones, with only brief stops to answer nature.

Ryn would have been quite content to never climb higher than a barn loft after that, but they all shared the same urgency. That sky-ship still prowled the skies and those who coveted Xang's skull likely had the means for another tracking spell.

The threat of the Clerisy nagged Ryn even more. Tovald's compass might still have a bearing on him. He said as much while they surveyed Viglias at dawn, from the edge of the king's hunting preserve where the martichora had deposited them under cover of darkness. Over rooftops of dark slate and red tile, Ryn could just make out the forest of masts that marked Viglias's busy harbor. "We might be days ahead of anyone sailing from Tanasgeld. But—"

"A messenger pigeon can fly here as fast as a martichora and carry enough blood for another tracking spell," Kara finished.

"Let's not be tardy with the key-finding, then," Josalind said.

Viglias looked just as Ryn remembered as they watched the sunrise, sprawling far beyond its original wall under the bulk of the cathedral and its great belfry. Four gilded spires crowned the belfry and caught the dawn with golden fire. To the east, where the shore of the Austacian Sea rose up into cliffs, sprawled Thrush's Keep, with battlements of salmon pink and gray granite. A dozen thick hexagonal towers rose from the palace complex within, each capped by a conical roof of copper sheathing weathered green. Farther east, the Royal Observatory with its dome of white marble commanded the highest point on the cliffs, next to the gorge of the Beris River. The City of Thrones housed a third of a million souls, making it the largest in the Kingdoms.

"Some of the finest stonework in all the Kingdoms rests in Viglias," Horgrim said as they entered the city.

He spoke with the enthusiasm of a man who believed no pursuit outshone the noble study of masonry. Ryn cared only for the number of guards at the city gate and how much scrutiny they gave passersby. Thankfully, it proved to be cursory at best, given the volumes of traffic.

Their refuge in Viglias turned out to be an antiquities shop with a large apartment above—the home of a bickering old couple named Jufena and Tojan Rikarden. Both were devoted Sevrendine who maintained the facade by attending the Clerisy's services like clockwork and giving to its coffers. Despite their squabbles and complaints, it was obvious that they shared a love and affection as worn and comfortable as a favorite pair of shoes. Ryn could scarcely imagine being that old, that settled, that content.

They spent several days plotting strategy and assembling the necessary props from the Sevrendine's Viglian network. Ryn kept his growth of beard to mask his features and the scar from Quintan, trimmed to current fashion. Jufena helped Josalind stew her hair in various toxic mixtures to bleach it blonde and straighten the curls.

Josalind didn't say a word about that night on the beach. Ryn didn't expect her to and couldn't bring himself to be the first. Still, it stung a bit that she didn't acknowledge it at all. Not a touch or a look that in any way even hinted at what had passed between them. Such indifference could prompt a fellow to doubt his manhood. Had he left her disappointed?

Better to just bury it and focus on the task at hand.

The shop featured a rooftop garden under a flowering pergola, tended by Jufena's careful hand. When Josalind had first discovered it, she squealed with delight and spent the afternoon pestering the poor woman with questions about a dozen species of flower that had never made it into *Tathemay's Menagerie of Plants*. Bracelet- and crown-weaving followed.

On the morning of their third day in Viglias, Ryn perched on the edge of the roof where he could feel the sun on his face and the breeze blunted the garden's heady stew of scents. The thorns of the ettel flowers that climbed the pergola made for a decent tea, but the aroma of those blooms could choke a man. Across other gardens and roofs peaked and gabled, the Great Cathedral stabbed the heavens with the spires of its belfry. Even here, blocks away, that hulking pile of flying buttresses and stained glass, of columns and crescent arches, eyed him with patient hunger.

The thought roused Mordyth Ral, until he hissed from the maddening rasp of its poking and prodding. The Sword still refused his every attempt to tease out further details of its history. It lay across his knees, still bound by witch iron and now housed in a better-fitting leather sleeve, biding its chance.

You have a weakness and I will find it, he thought.

He startled a bit when he heard a soft step behind him.

Kara came to his side and rested her hands on the low stone rail on which he sat. "What do you think we'll find in Gostemere with the Earthborn?" he asked.

She shrugged. "I don't know—that's why we should have a look."

She said nothing more, which Ryn found vaguely irritating. "Well, what do you hope to find?"

"Answers."

"To find those, we have to know what questions to ask," Ryn said.

"Indeed." She fixed him with those probing gray eyes. "Have you yours?"

He suspected she meant to test him, as Horgrim had that night on the *Sea Hare*, which only added to his irritation. "Why do I get the impression you already have them figured out for me?"

"I wouldn't presume such a thing." She turned and rested her behind against the rail. "But I will say that nothing involving that Sword happens by chance."

Ryn huffed and rolled his eyes. "The only word worse than 'destiny' is 'fate.'"

"True. Fate implies a soul has no free will, that her choices are predetermined." Kara shook her head. "I don't believe that."

"Then what do you believe?"

"Some people are *destined* to make choices that will affect us all." Kara rested her hand on his, where it lay atop Mordyth Ral in its sleeve. "Not because it's been preordained, but because they have it within them to do what no one else will."

He swallowed and looked away, unable to bear that gaze any longer. "Did Aegias make the right choice or the wrong one, when he bound Xang's skull instead of letting the Sword consume enough life to destroy it?"

"Even if he had, the Great Deceiver would still be with us, his priesthood would still rule millions." Kara squeezed his hand. "Fools find it easy to judge right and wrong after the fact."

Ryn couldn't muster a response, rendered as awkward and uncomfortable by the sudden softness in her tone, the empathy, as he was by the soul-scouring dig of her eyes.

"That war, the Sword, the choice Aegias faced—it changed him, scarred him, drove his desire to be a better man and reject the role of conqueror his people expected of him," Kara said. "He wouldn't sacrifice tens of thousands of more lives—*Teishlian* lives—to end Xang forever because he'd already seen the Teishlians suffer enough, from his own countrymen as well as Xang."

But still, the Clerisy had pursued its own vision of tyranny in Aegias's name. How would he, Ryn Ruscroft—the son, not of a king, but a common-born landowner who aspired to a noble title—be remembered? How would the choices he made be spun into a new cycle of myths and lies to serve other men's ambitions?

"What I mean to say is that our beginnings have no bearing on who we might become," Kara said.

Ryn looked her square, noting those exotic features she hadn't bothered to hide today. "And where did you begin?"

She fondled that round object under her collar. "Some of us who live under the shadow of the Keshauk priesthood do escape, but that's a story for another time."

Fair enough. "You seem to have accepted my part in all this." He tapped the Sword again. "And with this."

A devilish smile teased her lips. "Have I? I don't recall saying so." She let that hang for a painful spell. "The old lion and I both fear the idea of Mordyth Ral in *any* hand, sweetie. Neither of us will just stand by and trust in *destiny* if we think the greater good is in peril."

Ryn didn't so much as blink, oddly reassured by the veiled threat. It gave him hope that someone might stop him, before circumstance and the Sword could drive him across a line the world would regret. "I would expect no less."

On their fourth day in Viglias, Ryn and Josalind hustled through thick crowds toward the grand entrance of the Great Cathedral. Brazen interlopers beating a path to the bear's den . . . with a palatar escort.

Summer had lingered late, even for this region of Sturvia. There had been word of droughts and crop failures across the realm, plagues of locusts, too. Biting flies buzzed around, drawn by the stink of unwashed bodies tight together, as a long line of penitents crept into the cathedral. The old and the young, the crippled and the sick, come from all corners of the Kingdoms, eager for a glimpse of the divine.

Dozens of palatars in crisp white half capes ensured a suitable decorum was observed. Ryn had never felt so naked without a sword or pistol at his hip—the ceremonial dagger he wore made a poor substitute. The sight of these men, fulfilling their duty, left him dwelling on what he'd forfeited. Not the promises of the Clerisy about earning salvation in Paradise. Not even the securities of room, board, and a pension at the end. The loss of *brotherhood*, the camaraderie of the Order and the men with whom he served, rankled as his one regret.

Kara lived for the day when the Clerisy fell and the Sevrendine faith would be accepted in the Kingdoms. Ryn found himself yearning for that, too, because on that day, his brother palatars would be free.

Three inquisitars in crimson robes kept a watchful eye on the peddlers who worked the crowd. Scraps of cloth, bits of rusted metal, and splinters of wood were touted as everything from the burial shrouds of martyrs and the swords of Aegias's paladins, to the cradle in which the infant Aegias had slept. Ryn had little doubt that most of it had been scavenged from the trash pits on Viglias's outskirts. The Clerisy tolerated such petty fraud, provided the appropriate bribes were paid. He found the practice just as offensive now as he had those years ago as a palatar errant.

But he and Josalind didn't have to tolerate panhandling, or rub shoulders with the vulgar masses. As a lord and his lady, they could pay for the privilege of private access. He wore a green frock coat and waistcoat with red cravat, along with knee breeches and striped stockings that were all the rage among the fashion-minded. Josalind had chosen a burgundy satin bodice with matching petticoats. Her poofy paned sleeves were as ridiculous as his stockings, but he couldn't deny the full package flattered her, or she it.

"Is it always so busy, Corporal?" he asked their escort.

"Most often, M'Lord."

"I find the sight of such penitents good for the soul, husband," Josalind said. "Land, title, possessions—none of it matters much when it comes time to stick you in the ground. Does the *Codex* not say that when Judgment comes, we must all face it as babes new to the world?"

Ryn gritted his teeth—they'd agreed that he should do most of the talking. Josalind had done a fair job of softening her Fisherfolk brogue, but a keen ear could still catch it. As in Tanasgeld, the freedom of being able to just walk the streets, to explore and see what the world had to offer, to enjoy the simple freedoms that had so long been denied her, had left Josalind almost giddy with excitement. He couldn't fault her for it, but neither could they afford a careless slip that might give them away.

"My dear wife's knowledge of her Scripture rivals that of the Arch-Preceptar himself," he said with a note of apology.

"A man who has a pious wife is blessed," the corporal said.

Ryn thumped him on the shoulder. "So they say. May you be so lucky to find out for yourself."

The corporal just nodded and kept his attention on their destination, likely eager to discharge his duty before finding himself any deeper in a discussion about the virtues of marriage.

A cordon of palatars kept one side of the cathedral's stairs clear and they soon found themselves inside. Even now, Ryn couldn't help but feel that he invited divine judgment by stepping onto the polished green marble. Something in the vein of a thunderbolt, maybe.

In keeping with the Clerisy's standard practice, the cathedral was divided into four naves that formed an *X*, each dedicated to one of the Four. They had entered, as was customary, through the west. The naves met at a large open area—the transept. High above it, a vaulted ceiling rested upon a six-sided clerestory with tall windows of stained glass. The corporal left them by the transept's dais. On it stood the pulpit and hanging above that, a Tetraptych of stained glass three times the size of the one Josalind had obliterated in Dragon's Claw. The stream of penitents filed around the rope barrier on the far side of the dais to gawk at the relics on display and pay homage at the crypts of the Nine.

If only their request had earned the attention of a deacon or cleric. Instead, Ryn soon found himself face-to-face with a palatar officer—noble-born, no less, wearing the polished brass gorget of the Aegian Order.

"Captain Ornalt Setrys, Baron Absentia of Darbren Fields, at your service," the officer said with a stiff bow.

Ryn had known too many of the Aegian Order to be pampered brats, puffed up by the sense of entitlement that came with their birthrights, but this fellow presented as a no-nonsense career soldier. Officers of the Aegian Order who held their family's title were rare—most Aegians were third or fourth sons. That Setrys had inherited and still chose to serve the Order spoke favorably to his character.

"Baron Manfryn Arteos, Lord of Anselbock," Ryn said, bowing in return.

The captain's hawkish gaze lingered upon the silver pin on the breast of Ryn's waistcoat. "I do believe your family holds title near the eastern reaches of the Moor Lands."

Ryn made no attempt to hide his surprise—it wouldn't have been out of character for the real Lord Anselbock. He'd picked the backwater barony expressly for its obscurity and the fact that he happened to have some knowledge of it. "I must say I am impressed, M'Lord Captain."

"I do pride myself on my knowledge of heraldry, even that of Morlandia," Setrys said. His rigid expression didn't soften. "I trust the crop is good this year for that currant wine of yours?"

Ryn's bowel clutched a bit. Did the captain only intend to make polite conversation, or did he have cause to test his guests? He responded with a demure smile. "I'm afraid we've seen too much rain, and it's gooseberry, actually."

Setrys grunted. His attention veered to Josalind. "M'Lady."

She curtsied as well as any princess. "M'Lord Captain."

He looked back to Ryn. "Your first time in Viglias?"

Josalind latched on to the captain's arm. "It's been just wonderful. I never imagined, I mean, I tried to imagine, but there was no doing it fair justice."

Setrys endured her gushing with a thin smile. "The city does leave an impression. So, you've come for a tour, have you?"

"If it's not too much trouble," Ryn said.

"None at all. You have shown the depth of your devotion," Setrys said. If he had an opinion about the fact that their devotion had been expressed with gold coin, he had the courtesy not to show it. "If you will come this way."

He extracted himself from Josalind's grip and led them to the south nave.

Ryn much preferred to see her this way than in the clutch of whatever mood had possessed her in recent days. Still, a single misstep could arouse dangerous suspicion. He put his lips to her ear as they followed. "Don't overplay it, *dear wife*."

"It feels good, being someone else." She stopped cold. "What is that?"

Josalind meant a statue—a martichora that reared up on his hindquarters, claws spread, tail poised, mouth stretched into a terrible grimace. The old thing stood no taller than her, cast in bronze, dark and pitted with age. It hadn't been polished up like the other statuary and icons on display.

Setrys stopped. "That is a martichora, M'Lady."

She sidestepped around the statue and dragged Ryn after her, like she feared it might bite. "From where?"

"Oradar, capital of Lost Pandaris," Setrys said. "As you are no doubt aware, House Imperial took the martichora for its crest." He motioned them on toward an alcove.

The first fiery pain chose that moment to stab Ryn in the gut, no different than what he'd felt in Tanasgeld when parted from the Sword.

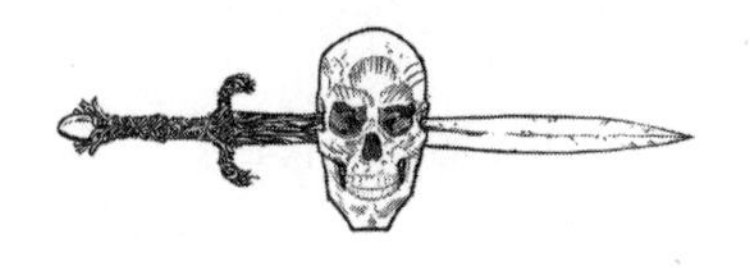

THIRTY-TWO

Ryn couldn't help but groan as his innards wrestled in a bucket of coals.

"Are you well, M'Lord?" Captain Setrys asked.

"I discovered the wonders of the coffee bean yesterday," Ryn said, forcing another smile. "I'm afraid it does not agree with me."

"Surely our black nectar finds its way even to your corner of Morlandia?"

"I never could abide the smell to try it," Ryn said. "But then we visited a coffeehouse, and she says, 'How can you come to Viglias and not even try it?' Barely slept a wink last night, I'm afraid."

"I said try it, not drain the pot, dear husband," Josalind said.

Setrys pulled the ring from his belt and selected a large brass key to unlock a rather unassuming door. A guardroom lay beyond. Six palatars were on station. Ryn's gut began to churn in earnest. Horgrim had Mordyth Ral on the cathedral grounds somewhere. At least, that had been the plan, but they'd obviously strayed too far apart.

It had better be a short tour.

The captain led them down a circular stairwell. Oil lamps lit the way. No additional guards waited below, just a short hall and another door that called for another key. But it was the second door farther down, which Ryn remembered from his previous visit as a fresh corporal, that drew his attention.

"Does the Clerisy keep other treasures there?" he asked.

"That leads to the catacombs," Setrys said.

Josalind shivered. "Are they haunted?"

"That depends on who you ask, M'Lady." The captain opened the door to the reliquary and motioned them through first. "Please."

The reliquary's vaulted ceilings rivaled a duke's banquet hall. Rows of racks and shelves stuffed with all manner of things stood wall-to-wall: Bones of martyrs, even their vital organs, pickled or shriveled. Antiquated armor and weapons that had belonged to Aegias and his paladins. Things worn, things used, things associated with some miracle or other that looked no more holy than the scraps hawked by the hustlers outside.

Some of the relics might have inspired awe, but the flaming spikes that skewered Ryn left him in a poor state to appreciate them. He could barely keep walking and nodding as Setrys droned on.

Near the end, they reached an item that finally caught Josalind's attention with more than passing interest. She dug her nails into Ryn's arm. He jerked away, in too tender a mood to be poked without warning.

"My pardon, M'Lord Captain, but what is this here?" she asked.

It was a stone.

Not an ordinary one. A lopsided egg, a bit larger than Ryn's fist. Bluish quartz, with swirls of silver.

"Why, that is called the Heart of Sovaris, M'Lady," Setrys said.

Sovaris—patron goddess of Morlandia. Who rattled around in Josalind's head with her brothers. The loudest of the Four, she often complained.

Josalind did a fair job of hiding her fascination, but Ryn could tell she itched to pick it up. "Truly," she said.

"What are the odds, M'Lady, you would be drawn to a relic so dear to your own heritage," Setrys said.

His gaze fixed on her with such predatory intent, Ryn's hand instinctively drifted to his dagger.

"But it isn't really her heart—is it?" Josalind asked.

"It is said that Aegias sailed with favorable winds whenever he carried it. Even the brine drakes of the south seas would let his ships pass unharmed." Setrys shrugged. "Regardless of the truth in that, it has no match, so it is a rare and precious thing by any measure."

Ryn groaned and sagged against a table.

Setrys afforded him that same thin smile. "It would seem M'Lord Anselbock has suffered enough for one day. You are of course welcome to return, should the chance arise."

Ryn intended to, that very night, provided the ghosts in the catacombs had no objection.

They found Horgrim in the cathedral glebe, lounging under a cherry tree, slurping down a bowl of soup and a pint of cider.

The Charitable Virgins freely served all comers from under canvas awnings. Ryn might have gone for a pint himself, but first he had to close the distance with that damned sword. The spikes in his gut had already faded, but that didn't matter. He had to touch Mordyth Ral, feel the weight of it, no different than an addict in need of his next fix of poppy tears.

The compulsion left him feeling fouled.

A bench lay on the opposite side of the tree. Two atavists, naked and smeared in ashes, already occupied it. Their sort believed Paradise could only be attained by giving up all trappings of civilization. If only his redemption could come so easily. Instead, he had the Sword to mortify his soul until the grave. The atavists got up and left to make way for so fine a lord and lady. Ryn sank down on the bench, rested elbows on knees, and focused on the rhythm of his breathing.

Josalind touched his arm. "Are you all right?"

He gave a half-hearted chuckle. "That's a poor question for either of us to ask the other." His hands clenched and unclenched with the need to grab the Sword. It lay bundled in what appeared to be a bedroll stuffed with a poor traveler's necessities. Horgrim played the part of a humble pilgrim. The half dozen medallions sewn on his tunic documented the shrines he'd visited.

"Where in Hells were you?" Ryn asked.

"Here, for the past bell or more," Horgrim said quietly from his side of the tree.

That meant Ryn couldn't stray more than a hundred yards or so from the Sword for long without suffering for it.

"Did you find it?" Horgrim asked.

"Yes."

"The catacombs?"

"Yes." Ryn touched Josalind's knee. "What was with you and that statue?"

"I could feel it watching me, like it *knew*," she said with a shiver.

"What statue?" Horgrim asked.

Ryn described the bronze martichora.

"Sounds like a sentinel," Horgrim said. "Something that can smell sorcery, the Grace of Fraia and the Four, too, no doubt. Josalind got its attention, but not enough to trigger an alarm. If she were to manifest any power, on the other hand . . ."

Damn. "Then we'll have to do this the hard way," Ryn said.

Horgrim climbed to his feet and savored a stretch. He'd finally allowed Kara to finish the job of healing him before he ended up a mass of scars. "Then let's get to it. We've skulked around for long enough."

Everyone agreed Kara and Josalind should remain at the safehouse to guard the skull since neither could risk mustering any divine intervention with the sentinel present in the Cathedral. Josalind still kept Xang muzzled with a seal of her blood, but Ryn didn't care to take chances. Nor did the Sevrendine want to risk exposing their local network by involving anyone else in the actual heist, should things go south.

That left just Ryn and Horgrim.

When they entered the sewers that night, Ryn carried Mordyth Ral, slung across his shoulders in its leather sleeve, still bound by witch iron. He wouldn't tease the snake a second time by leaving it out of reach. At his hip rode a longsword of plain steel. It felt good to rest his hand on the pommel. Contrary to city ordinance, he also carried a pistol, primed and loaded. The least of his crimes, should they be caught.

Viglians prided themselves on the City of Throness's superiority. The pinnacle of culture, science, and art in the Four Kingdoms, heir to the glories of Lost Pandaris. So far as Ryn could tell, their shite stank the same as anyone else's, they just did a better job of disposal.

Which made the trip through these sewers much more pleasant than their escape from Tanasgeld. The arched vaults were high enough that even Horgrim only had to stoop a bit as he led the way with a lantern. Side ledges kept them from having to wade through the filth.

Horgrim nudged a big fat rat out of his way. The local vermin weren't intimidated in the least by two-legged intruders. "Can I give you a bit of advice?"

Ryn snorted. "Since when do you bother to ask permission?"

The warden stopped and turned. "I see the way you look at Josalind."

Ryn swallowed, painfully aware of the hot flush rising in his cheeks. His attention drifted to the rat trying to push past his boot.

"We don't know what we might find in Gostemere." Horgrim's hand came to rest on Ryn's shoulder. "We don't know what the Four intend . . . for her."

Ryn forced himself to look into those ice-blue eyes. "No, we don't. Should that make a difference?" He would stand by her, protect her, no matter what they found. And damn any god, alive or dead, who came between them.

"She is your herald, as much as Kara is mine," Horgrim said with somber gravity. "We defend them, we honor them, but we must limit how much we let ourselves love them. Given the things we face, it just . . . complicates things too much."

If he suspected what had transpired with Josalind back on that beach, he had the tact not to mention it. Ryn cleared his throat. "Is that what you tell yourself whenever you look at Kara?"

Horgrim turned away and continued. "I tell myself what I must."

They found the breach in the sewer wall not long after—the work of smugglers, trying to dodge the tax collectors on the docks.

A secret gleaned from Sevrendine faithful within the city's public service, with knowledge of shadowy dealings between crime lords and bureaucrats on the take.

Loose bricks had been restacked to pass casual inspection. Horgrim pushed the pile over with no concern for the clatter and ducked through. Ryn followed him into a cramped passage the smugglers had dug. Around a sharp bend, he found himself nose to nasal cavities with a wall of skulls.

The catacombs were in fact old quarry tunnels. Centuries of urban growth and outbreaks of plague had forced the dead to be relocated here from the city's overflowing cemeteries. Bones from countless thousands had been stacked and mortared into whimsical shapes and patterns. It was artful and impressive for certain, but Ryn still found it ghoulish. The arrangements of bones gave way to ossuaries, sarcophagi, and gargoyles meant to guard the dead's rest. If the place were haunted, it had to be damned crowded.

Before long, they found themselves at a door.

Horgrim pressed his ear to the wood and waited for a spell. "It sounds quiet."

He sat the lantern down and pressed his knuckles to the lock plate. Blood Thorn's cryptwood matter wormed from his cuff and into the keyhole. Ryn drew his sword as the tumblers gave. For all they knew, even this discreet exercise might trigger some alarm. Horgrim pulled the door open, a shard of cryptwood, dagger-like, in his palm.

The hallway beyond lay empty and dark.

Ryn took up the lantern and shouldered past him. "This way."

The reliquary's door proved no harder to open than the first, but the hinges gave a squeal when Horgrim nudged it open. Ryn grimaced and glanced up. He didn't doubt the guard room above remained fully manned.

No boots came pounding down the stairs.

The reliquary held darker than pitch, too big and crowded with the Clerisy's treasures for the meager light of one lantern. But the Heart of Sovaris rested only twenty feet from the door. Ryn sheathed his sword and went straight to it while Horgrim kept watch. He looked at it, nestled on a small cushion of white silk. The heart flickered with some inner fire, kin to the godly radiance he'd seen burn in Josalind's eyes.

Or maybe it was only a trick of the light.

He reached out to Mordyth Ral. *Is it really Sovaris's heart?*

Josalind had said so, but he valued a second opinion, all the same. The Sword kept silent.

Ryn covered the heart with his hand. Cool and hard, no different than any other stone. He slipped it into the pouch on his belt and left. Horgrim drew the reliquary's door shut and locked it again. The catacombs' door still hung open before them. Ryn saw only darkness beyond.

The darkness came alive with a stamp of boots that made his neck tingle.

Leather and steel scraped and scuffed as bodies jostled for position in tight quarters. The lantern painted four grim faces—palatars, each wielding a pair of pistols. Ryn lurched back with a curse and went for his own pistol.

Horgrim charged with a bellow, ruining Ryn's clear shot. Four pistols fired. The collective roar left Ryn's ears ringing and clouded the passage with sulfurous smoke. Cryptwood lashed out in a blur. Deflected pistol balls shattered against the walls with shrill whines. Ryn ducked out of reflex as shrapnel stung his cheek. One ball slipped past Blood Thorn and tore into Horgrim's shoulder. He staggered to keep his footing and plowed into the palatars before they could bring their other pistols to bear.

More palatars stormed down the stairs.

Ryn flung the lantern in that direction and threw himself after Horgrim. The warden had already knocked two of the palatars senseless and worked on finishing the third. Ryn clubbed the fourth with his pistol's butt before the fellow could shoot Horgrim in the back.

Other pistols fired behind them.

They both dropped. Ryn fired blind and tried to knock the door shut. A trooper's leg barred the way. He shoved it aside and got the door closed just in time to catch several more shots. If not for Blood

Thorn's soft light, they would have been as blind as mole rats. "The lock."

Cryptwood stretched past his ear. After the door was secure, Ryn took a dagger from one of the palatars, rammed it into the keyhole, and hammered it home with the butt of his pistol.

A hand jiggled the latch.

Ryn took up two of the palatars' still-loaded pistols. He didn't care to kill good men for doing their duty, but he wouldn't go quietly, either.

A key jiggled in the lock. The tumblers didn't budge. The dagger wiggled a bit but stayed put.

"That actually worked." Horgrim sounded impressed, though the pain clipped his words short.

"Of course it did." Ryn would never admit that he'd doubted it himself.

A voice called from the other side. "Ryn Ruscroft."

Damn. Captain Setrys.

"Traitor—you will never escape the judgment of the Clerisy or the Order," Setrys said.

A volley of pistols fired at the lock, but the old iron refused to yield. A ram would follow soon enough. Ryn patted the belt pouch to make sure the Heart of Sovaris still rested there. Horgrim slouched against the wall, a shade paler than his sword.

"Let me see." Ryn hooked the pistols on his belt and ran his hand behind Horgrim's shoulder. He found no exit wound.

"It cleaved the shoulder blade," Horgrim said. "Can't move the arm much. Just pack a wad to stop the bleeding."

Ryn worked quickly to tear strips from the warden's shirt to plug the wound and bind the makeshift dressing into place. His instincts screamed for them to flee, but already Horgrim bled too much to let this go. The poking made the warden's eyes roll back and tore a moan out of him. He shook it off and stumbled down the passage the moment Ryn had the knot tightened.

"Enough coddling," he said. "Are you coming?"

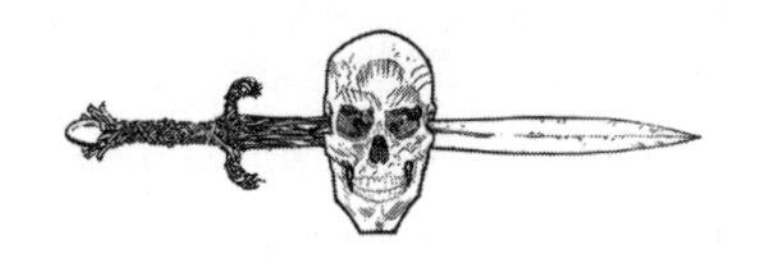

THIRTY-THREE

The boom of a ram soon rolled through the catacombs. Setrys's men had probably conscripted statuary from the cathedral proper. That door wouldn't hold for long.

"Is there any place in all the Kingdoms now where you dare show your face?" Horgrim asked.

Ryn knew how the fox must feel, run ragged by a pack of hounds. "If they have the means here in Viglias to track me or you, they would have had us at the house." Setrys must have linked the pegs *after* they'd left him that afternoon, from whatever word had been sent from up north. Nothing else made sense.

"So he set his trap and waited," Horgrim said. "Let us in to see what it is that we want, *then* blocked our escape."

The thought roused a sudden fear—had the real Heart of Sovaris been switched? Ryn's hand instinctively went to the pouch at his hip. But no, this stone looked no different than the one he'd seen earlier in the day. It wasn't the kind of thing for which a decoy could easily be found. "Setrys hadn't counted on you and your big stick."

Horgrim stopped cold and looked to the floor. "Are you certain of that?"

"You think we're still in the trap." Of course, it only made sense—Setrys wanted to get them clear of the cathedral and its cherished relics for fear of what might happen if he backed Mordyth Ral and Sevrendine into a corner. Those four palatars hadn't been expected to stop them, only give the illusion that they'd made a clean escape to lower their guard.

"Your captain must know about this smuggler's run and means to catch us between here and the sewers," Horgrim said.

Ryn smashed his fist against the wall in a sudden fit of anger. "Bloody Hells!"

"Look here." Horgrim lowered Blood Thorn's glowing blade to show a mess of boot tracks in the dirt. They ended at what looked to be a solid wall. "Sloppy work by our smugglers, leaving a tell like that." He sized up the wall and tapped at various spots.

The ram no longer boomed—Setrys and his men had entered the catacombs. Ryn felt around for some kind of release, surprised that smugglers would have the means to engineer such a hidden door down here.

They didn't.

A section of ceiling swallowed all light and gave nothing back. He probed it with his sword. A crooked hole, big enough to hoist sacks and small chests through.

Blood Thorn retreated up Horgrim's sleeve. "Give me a boost."

Ryn sheathed his sword, cradled Horgrim's boot, and heaved him up with a grunt. The warden had the weight of a draft horse.

"Got something," Horgrim said. "Higher." He stepped up onto Ryn's shoulders. "Stand taller."

"This is as tall as I get," Ryn hissed, bracing Horgrim's ankles.

Somewhere above, something heavy slid aside with a gritty rasp. "I do have only the one good arm now."

Horgrim planted a boot on Ryn's head. The outhouse stink from the sewer proved hard to ignore. And then Ryn heard trouble coming down the passage, from the direction of the sewers. He hated being right.

"Now, Horgrim."

Ryn's clenched teeth ached to the roots as the warden's full weight bore down through his spine, sure to leave him an inch shorter. And then the pressure lifted away. Something slapped his head and draped over his shoulder. A rope.

Lantern light spilled down the passage.

Ryn jumped to catch the rope high and shimmied up as quick as he could. The hole broke through about four feet of solid stone.

Horgrim hauled him sideways onto a level floor. Ryn fished the rope up and froze.

A stream of palatars passed below. A dozen or more.

Ryn didn't dare breathe, certain one would glance up and spot them, caught in the lantern light. But no one did before they were gone.

Too damned close.

Blood Thorn's light waxed just enough for them to see. Horgrim sagged against the wall, puffing hard. Blood soaked his whole side now.

"How did you manage it?" Ryn asked.

Horgrim tapped the cryptwood blade, then pointed at a nearby post that supported the floor above. "Hoisted me up once it found something to wrap around."

Ryn slid an empty crate back over the hole, then ducked under Horgrim's good arm to get him moving. They'd trespassed on a cellar stocked with crates and barrels. He doubted smugglers would be hospitable toward strangers who'd just crept in through the back door, on the run from the Clerisy, no less. But they were in luck—the cellar had its own stairs to outside.

They found themselves in an alley. They couldn't stay on the streets. Setrys would soon realize they'd slipped his snare and rouse every palatar in the city for a block-to-block search. Ryn guided Horgrim to the street. Storefronts and shuttered stalls—a market ward. The city had many and Ryn had visited only one since their arrival. They'd already known that the route through sewer and catacomb would take them close to the safe house's neighborhood, but nothing looked familiar.

Boots sounded from up the street.

They ducked back into the shadows as men of the Night Watch passed, wearing hardened black leather, armed with short swords, cudgels, and small-caliber pistols. A ball in your companion's shoulder was a hard thing to explain, especially when you carried pistols and stank of sewer. Viglias took a hard stance on crime. The Night Watch had a reputation for cracking skulls without worrying about questions.

Once the watchmen had gone, Ryn left the palatar pistols behind and hustled Horgrim across the street and down another alley. The story Ryn had told Setrys about his unfortunate visit to the coffeehouse had been mostly true. If he could find that street, he could get his bearings, assuming they were anywhere near it.

The third street over, he found it. The Sevrendine safe house lay only a few blocks away.

The sign over the front door read "Tojan Rikarden—Relics & Rare Antiquities." The old grump had never housed such rare artifacts under his roof as he did now.

Ryn guided Horgrim past without pause, expecting a watchman's whistle to blow at any moment. Moths skirted death in the glow of streetlamps and cast frantic shadows against dark windows. Several doors down, they ducked into a narrow alley and circled around to Tojan and Jufena's back door. Ryn gave a quiet knock.

Kara opened it. She summed up Horgrim's sorry state in a glance without a drop of dismay. "Get him in here."

"I've a need for a deep tankard and a cheery fire," Horgrim said. He pushed away from Ryn and made for the chair by the kitchen hearth.

"You need to learn to duck, old lion," Kara said.

"There were four of them," Ryn said.

Tojan stumped into the kitchen. His bed robe sagged open to display an expanse of white chest hair. "That looks nasty. Jufena," he called over his shoulder, "fetch that jug from the cold well."

"Fetch it yourself, you old goat," her husky voice responded from upstairs. "Both those boys made it?" she added a moment later.

"Mostly." Tojan looked to Ryn. "Did you get it?"

Ryn patted his belt pouch.

"Let's have a look now."

"Never mind that," Kara said.

She peeled Ryn's makeshift dressing from Horgrim's shoulder. Fresh blood poured from the wound. She drove her finger into it without mercy. Horgrim roared and thumped his fist upon his knee. Her finger came out with the fragments of the ball clinging in a clump. She flung them into the hearth, then took on his pain to heal the wound, not completely, but enough to stop the bleeding.

Tojan touched his brow at the sight. "Blessed be." He eyed the crimson puddle that had collected on the tile beneath Horgrim's chair. "Jufena, there's a mess in the kitchen."

"Then clean it up."

Instead, Tojan fished a pair of wire spectacles from his pocket and perched them on his spotted nose before looking to Ryn. "Well? Come on, then."

"The fire needs stoking and I don't see that stout on the table," Horgrim said.

"We'll all have a look soon enough," Ryn said. "Where's Josalind?"

He found her in the common room.

Tojan and Jufena's home and shop, like many in the city's more affluent neighborhoods, bore a Teishlian influence that had migrated up the Pilgrim Road from Vysus. Marble tile covered the floor and heavy cove moldings edged the ceiling, with plastered walls between. Frescoes of pastoral scenes adorned the walls, but Ryn could barely see them past shelves crowded with old books, scrolls, and assorted curiosities. Instead of chairs, floor pillows woven with floral designs surrounded an oval table of tropical ebony. A round pool lay in the middle of the room, fed by a marble fountain in the shape of three seahorses.

Josalind sat on a floor pillow, bare toes in the pool, lost in some distant place. Xang's skull sat in its sack beside her.

Ryn crouched and held out the heart. "Here it is."

She gave a start like he'd surprised her, but she must have seen him come in. Her attention fixed on the relic. A sad *coo* sounded low in her throat. She scooped the heart up in both hands and pressed it to her brow, eyes shut tight. Tears leaked through and glistened on her cheeks.

He put his hand on her knee. "What's wrong?"

She dropped the heart on her lap and wiped at her eyes. "Nothing, everything is happening just as it should."

These weren't happy tears. "And that troubles you."

She squeezed his hand but looked away. "What would've happened, do you think, if we'd met a different way—just a man, just a woman? No gods, no Clerisy, no fate or destiny."

A jagged ache sawed his throat, sparked by a sense of impending loss with no clear cause. He thought of the lives he might have had, of what might have been.

"I don't know," he said. "I would've liked to."

"Me too," she said, almost too faint to hear.

He could think of nothing else to say, nothing he was ready to, at least. He wanted to tell her . . . *something*—about how he felt about her, if only he could find the words to do it. "The Clerisy is onto us. We have to leave the city," he said instead. "Can you reach Oma? Ask her to bring her kin to the King's Gardens in half a bell."

Josalind rose quick to her feet, the Heart of Sovaris pressed to her own. "Let's get ourselves to Gostemere."

The wind kicked up with a fury before they'd made it one city block.

It bit the eye with swirls of dust. Canvas awnings over door and window snapped and tore. Streetlamps snuffed out as licks of wind wormed through the cracks of their glass shutters. Ryn couldn't spot a single star or glimmer of moonlight. He kept Josalind's hand tight in his own as they hunched over and followed the Sevrendine at a trot. She had Xang's skull slung over her shoulder by the drawstrings of its sack. Ryn had put the Heart of Sovaris back in his belt pouch. Mordyth Ral still rode across his back in its leather sleeve. They all carried haversacks with foodstuffs and other necessities. Josalind and Kara had given up skirts for the practicality of trousers.

"Can martichora fly in this?" he asked.

"You expect me to know?" Josalind said while under attack by her whipping hair.

Even Horgrim had to lean to keep from being blown sideways as the wind gusted harder. The sky split with a crack so violent it gave them all a start and blanked their eyes with a flash sharper than the midday sun.

Rain came next, in stinging sheets.

"I hate soggy shoes," Kara said.

Even the Night Watch appeared to have been driven to shelter. Ryn doubted the Clerisy would be so quick to give up the hunt, whether it had a tracking spell or not.

A shutter whizzed over their heads and crashed into a window. Roof tiles shattered on the cobblestones. Then the street opened onto the blackness of the King's Gardens. They took the broadest path to keep from being flattened by breaking branches. Blood Thorn came alive in Horgrim's hand with a steady light. Fruit trees, flowering shrubs, and hedges, pruned and cultured to perfection by royal gardeners, were lashed and beaten without mercy.

Flying debris had left them all bruised and scratched by the time they reached the koi pond. Oma and her kin huddled on the lee side of a stone shed.

"We'll not be flying out in this, man-child," she said to Ryn, eyes narrowed to slits.

The rain had eased, but the thunder and lightning came harder, faster. They had no choice but to wait it out. Ryn did what just about anyone would do, trapped by a storm. He looked up to watch the show.

But he saw only the Keshauk skyship, bearing down on them with gunports open.

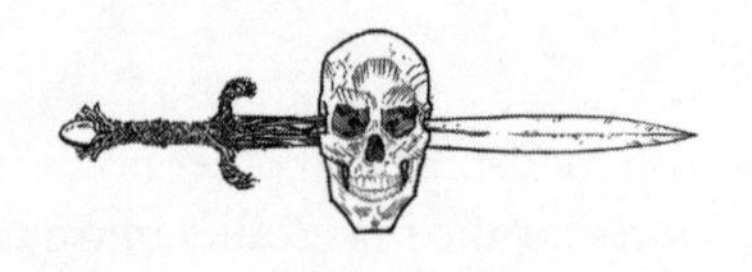

THIRTY-FOUR

Ryn jerked back and drew steel. A fool's gesture, but he couldn't help it.

The skyship didn't loom as close as he'd thought at first glance, but the size of it—seventy yards long at least. Larger than any royal flagship. Details emerged in flashes of lightning. Great triangular sails fanned out like wings from port and starboard. Instead of masts, three dark arches rose from its broad decks. Large sleigh runners ran on either side of the flat keel. The hull had been painted a steel blue to blend with a twilight sky. Its bow jutted out in a thick double beak—one point curving up, the other down. A pair of red serpent eyes as large as carriage wheels had been painted alongside.

The skyship boasted two lower gun decks, more than eighty cannon in total—firepower enough to ravage Viglias. But it hadn't come for the city. Ryn had no doubt its masters meant to claim Xang's skull. It moved with deadly majesty as the crew worked to bring the bow around. He couldn't fathom how it didn't keel over in the winds with sails torn off. Whatever alchemy made it fly, sorcery surely kept it in one piece. Dozens of figures lined up along the top decks, including winged grenlich.

Horgrim stood tall and flung Blood Thorn toward the skyship. The cryptwood missile shot in a blaze of heavenly light toward one of those arches rising from the decks. They must have had something to do with keeping the skyship aloft. But an invisible barrier knocked Blood Thorn aside just short of its target. After the damage the warden had done up north, the crew had come prepared. Blood Thorn returned to Horgrim's waiting hand, a falcon to its keeper. He flung it again.

The skyship's cannon fired.

Ryn ducked reflexively. They didn't have a chance. The skyship's gunners had a clear target, their prey lined up against the shed. Josalind had described before how Aegias's paladins couldn't destroy any of Xang's bones through the mundane means available to them. The skyship's masters didn't have to worry about damaging their prize with a barrage. Nor did Ryn expect that Mordyth Ral would be any easier to destroy than Xang's skull.

A transparent wall of shimmering gold flung up out of the earth a foot from Ryn's toes, just in time for the cannonballs to strike it. That shimmer dimpled like taut fabric poked by a giant's fingers. Ryn watched in stunned shock as a cannonball strained to reach his nose. Time itself held its breath. His flesh erupted with a maddening tingle from ears to toes as that wall of gold brushed against him. Then it sprang back to form and flung the spent cannonballs away. They splashed into the pond.

Ryn staggered back and gasped for breath. He should have been dead, head snipped clean off and splattered against the shed's stone. Kara had saved him, saved them all. She stepped past him. Fraia's fury burned in her eyes. The shimmering wall poured from her fingers in a sparkling cascade.

Horgrim still hammered away with Blood Thorn, trying to breach whatever force protected the skyship. It kept coming, sinking to earth like any seafaring vessel easing into port. Another volley of cannon fired. Ryn flinched as the balls struck Kara's wall and bounced away. A sword had never felt so useless in his hand.

That probing pressure flared between his ears. **How goes the battle, Heir of Aegias? Will you spurn me still?**

Josalind's nails dug into his arm. "They come with the storm. There's nowhere to run—*nowhere to run*."

The words spilled out, frantic, mindless. Her eyes strained to leap from their sockets, simmering with that rainbow shine, just as they had in the Dragon's Claw chapel. And then Ryn understood—silver was the color when she drew on the gods' power, but the rainbow meant they had possession of her, body and soul. He feared the weight of them might crack her sanity beyond mending. "I can see it, Josalind."

Oma gave him a prod with her wing. "She does not mean that flying ship, man-child."

Josalind thrust her arm out behind them.

Ryn spun around, sword raised. He saw nothing but tattered trees in the flashes of lightning. No watchmen, no palatars, no demons or grenlich.

Then he spotted the funnel that clawed the earth.

The tornado churned barely half a mile away with a funnel just as wide. The bloated monster ate the sky and bore down on them. Ryn just stared, trapped by the dumbfounded need to catch another glimpse in the next flash of lightning. Between the cracks of thunder and cannon came the drone of its gathering roar, lashing the earth till it trembled beneath his feet.

Josalind grabbed his sleeve and tried to drag him around the shed. He slapped Kara's shoulder and pointed before following, desperate to find any kind of shelter.

They found the shed's door. The earth shook harder as the tornado came. A broken timber shot out of the darkness past Ryn's head and shattered against the shed's sturdy wall. They crowded in, tripping over tools, buckets, and barrows. The martichora tossed out all they could to make room.

Ryn could scarcely imagine the terror that would be sweeping the city, thousands of voices, crying for salvation that wouldn't come.

They will die anyway, Heir of Aegias. Let me feed. You have need of me.

His hand itched for Mordyth Ral so much it burned. He wouldn't. How could he, in any case? The witch-iron manacles still bound the Sword and Horgrim had the key. He hunkered down with Josalind between Oma and Astrig.

Josalind rocked back and forth, knees drawn to trap the skull against her chest. "They're not going to get you, old salt. Not tonight, not ever."

Horgrim and Kara piled in.

The warden shut the door and dropped the latch. It didn't do much to deaden the tornado's roar.

"The skyship?" Ryn asked.

"That tub is limping off while it can," Horgrim said. "I finally cracked one of its arches." He looked up at the timber ceiling. "If we make it through this, we'll be fine."

Kara took a deep breath to muster herself and called up that shimmering wall again. This time, it settled over them as a dome-shaped shield.

But Josalind still rocked. Her rainbow eyes burned brighter. "No, no, *NO*. The roasting spit's fallen into the fire. Nowhere to run."

Horgrim cursed in some tongue Ryn didn't know. "Demons—I can smell the stink."

The wind roared even louder. The shed shook as if a company of heavy cavalry charged past. Ryn expected it to ease as the tornado moved off, but the fury only grew. He eyed Kara's shield. "Is that going to protect us?"

"It's all we have," Horgrim said.

Ryn didn't find that reassuring. He leaned close to Josalind. "Can you hear me, Jos?" he asked, not sure if he spoke to her or someone else. "Kara's going to need your help."

"No. Keep it safe, keep it safe."

The doors hammered and rattled, then tore clean off, leaving only a gaping maw of raging darkness. Roof tiles went next, flicked away as easily as bits of straw. Tornadoes didn't stay in place like this.

Ryn grabbed Josalind's wrist, expecting to get scorched for the presumption, but well past the point where he might care. "If she fails, the skull *won't* be."

The rafters followed the roof tiles with squeals of protest. If not for Kara's shield, the tornado would have gulped them down right there.

But the tornado only served as a shroud for something worse. Ryn felt the chill first, like a door had opened on the kind of winter's night that shattered iron and froze piss in the pot. A charnel stench followed—currents of meaty decay that seeped through Kara's shield and made him choke. He looked up into the tornado's heart and saw a swirling mass of smoke and shadow, edged with a sickly green light—another twister that couldn't be natural, tucked inside the tornado. It perched directly above, targeting the shed and everyone within.

What fresh Hell is this? Ryn meant to ask aloud but his mouth refused to move. His knees quavered and his jaw clenched vise-tight. Frost blossomed on his sword and his breath billowed in clouds. The hellish twister had no eyes. Even so, Ryn could feel its glare, the draw of a hateful hunger that leeched his strength. Around them, the tornado continued to roar, but here in its heart, all held still.

He dragged his eyes away and finally found his voice. "What is that?"

Horgrim matched the twister's glare with a gritty snarl. "Demons—a legion of them."

Sorcerers, perverting Nature to mask this unholy creation. A cry burst from the twister's heart. Not one voice, but many. The hideous chorus drove icy spikes through Ryn's brain. His heart stuttered and burned his throat sour.

He thought of Tovald and how the captain's encounter with a greater demon had left such a mark on him. These couldn't be greater demons—by all accounts, those were rare and too powerful for most sorcerers to manage. But they were demons, all the same. How much deeper would those spikes have dug, how much closer to failure would his heart have slipped, without the shield of Kara's faith?

Horgrim flung Blood Thorn through Kara's shield, but found nothing to strike, or maybe too much. The cryptwood returned to his hand without giving the twister any bother—a stick against a swarm of mad bees.

Something shot out of the twister's heart.

A stunning boom shook the air, then another, and another. A timber, a statue, even a fine carriage still hitched to mangled horseflesh, shattered against Kara's shield. The demons had her under siege with the city's ruin. She stood with arms outspread and palms up, as though sustaining that shield were a matter of muscle as much as will and faith.

But the demons had ample stock. A whole city block must have come, one piece at a time. Horgrim roared his defiance and threw Blood Thorn again and again, but it gained them nothing. Kara's shield dimpled with each blow and took longer to spring back to form. Blood began to ooze from her ears and nose.

Oily tendrils—the essence of demons in their natural form—shot down and beat themselves against Kara's shield. She cried out and fell to her knees. A tendril slipped through, then two more, then a score. Horgrim chopped through them. Where Blood Thorn struck, the hellish matter shriveled and vanished.

But more came as Kara weakened.

A cluster of tendrils slammed Horgrim square in the belly and flung him out the door into the storm. Others lunged at Josalind.

Ryn tried to strike them down, but plain steel bounced from those smoky, wispy things with a clang.

Fool—will you heed me now?

Even if he dared use the Sword, the manacles' key had just been lost with Horgrim. A tendril lashed Ryn's face. The cold burned as fiercely as a branding iron. He howled and hacked with all he had. Tendrils mustered so thick he could see little else. Rainbow blasts split the darkness as the Four's fury spewed from Josalind.

Then they were gone.

Everything vanished—the demon twister, the tornado, even the storm that had been their chariot. The clouds parted and the rosy hues of the greater moon flooded over them.

Ryn didn't see Xang's skull.

He gasped in horror at the sight of Josalind. Her arms were seared and blistered no different than if she'd plunged them into a fire. She sprang up and screamed her rage at the sky, screamed until her voice broke into a raw cough. Then she collapsed into a sobbing mess.

Ryn knelt beside her. "Josalind?"

"Gostemere, Gostemere, got to get to Gostemere, only chance now." She clung to the name as if it were the only thread left to stitch her nerves back together. Astrig cooed and nuzzled her cheek.

Ryn touched her shoulder. "Jos—talk to me. Where's the skull?"

"They took it." She looked to him with vacant, bloodshot eyes, saddled by dark bags. "They took it and there won't be no more Josalind now. Her time's done."

Her utter despair thrust a jagged knife through his heart. He wanted to ask what she meant but couldn't find the will. His thoughts clung to that night on the beach, that brief moment of peace, wrapped tight in each other's affection.

He couldn't lose her, not now.

Kara crawled over. Pale, haggard, she looked every inch her sixty-three years. "What do you mean, girl?"

Josalind sat back on her heels and wiped her eyes. "Things happen and there's no going back." She no longer sounded like she skirted the edge of madness, just seemed worn out. Already her burns had begun to fade. She wrapped an arm around Astrig's neck and hauled herself up. "We can't be lazing about."

"She speaks true, man-child." Oma sniffed the air and looked to her kin. "See that our flanks are clear."

Ryn suspected Josalind kept something from them, some fresh piece of the puzzle that the Four had finally revealed. Maybe the last piece. Kara thought so, too, judging by the narrowed look in her eye. But Oma was right—they couldn't afford to linger.

A sound rose and carried on the air from all around, mournful and haunting. Cries for help, cries of pain and grief and loss. A grim day would soon dawn in Viglias. Worse ones would follow as disease and desperation took hold.

Horgrim staggered through the door, bruised and bloodied from crown to foot. "It's been taken, then?"

Kara hung her head. "Yes."

The sight of Kara, a woman of such strength and divine favor, dejected and shamed by failure, struck Ryn with despair where even the loss of the skull and Josalind's frayed sanity hadn't. He steeled himself against it. They weren't done—they couldn't be. If they were, that left but one option.

You deny the inevitable, Heir of Aegias.

Horgrim eased himself down and patted Kara's knee. "There was nothing more you could have done, dearest, no single herald has ever withstood such a herd."

She toyed with that object under her collar. "What will that matter when Xang is born again?"

A sudden splashing sounded from the pond. "Come, Warden, we've caught a plaything." The call came from Ashavinx, the male martichora who carried Horgrim.

Ryn and Oma followed after Horgrim. Rubble and wreckage from the demons' attack had piled against the shed. The other martichora had gathered on the pond's edge, wings arced, scorpion tails twitching, no different than cats toying with a mouse.

Oma's big hand thumped the earth. "Away and be still, dear hearts."

"It smells of flowers and oddness," said Irsta, the martichora who bore Kara.

It was a man—a pudgy fellow of middle age with a shaven head and a sprig of chestnut beard. His swarthy olive complexion marked him as a Carinzian with mixed Teishlian ancestry—that likely meant he hailed from Vysus. He sprawled out on the ground, dull eyed and moaning. A bruise already ripened above one ear. Robes of fine yellow silk, cut in a strange style and embroidered with foreign symbols, covered him. And he did smell of flowers—jasmine, to be exact. An odd choice for a man, Ryn thought, even one who favored scents.

"Stand clear of him." Horgrim pointed with Blood Thorn. "See that diamond symbol? That's—"

"The Tetracle Shield—sigil of the Sorcerer Brotherhood of Vysus," Ryn said. "But that skyship was Keshauk."

"It is," Horgrim said. "But I doubt that demon twister was the work of Keshauk sorcerers. It's not their style. I'll hazard the brethren in Vysus mustered that twister while the skyship held back in reserve. We just got caught between their hammer and anvil."

Gods be damned. Ryn eyed the pudgy little man with fresh suspicion. Captain Tovald's *The Forbidden Mysteries of the Vysusian Brotherhood* had dramatized how demons bound to service answered a sorcerer's every beck and call. "We need him to talk, but if he wakes, he'll bring all Hells down on us."

"That's right," Horgrim said. "We'll have to take precautions."

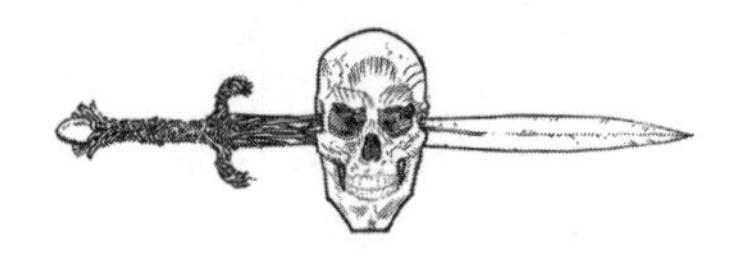

THIRTY-FIVE

They left Viglias without further delay and headed southeast. It took only about two bells to reach the Stormcrest Hills, even with Astrig bearing the weight of both Josalind and their captive sorcerer. Kara had mustered enough strength to ensure the fellow didn't wake while dangling in the martichora's grip, but the effort finished her. Irsta had to hoist the herald onto her back. Horgrim used rope from the shed to lash Kara in place for good measure.

They touched down in a small vale walled by jagged ridges, far from any sign of civilization. The sun had risen by then, making for a crisp morning that burst with far too much cheery birdsong to be appropriate, Ryn thought, given how the night had passed.

Kara slipped Horgrim's knots, slid off Irsta's back, and slumped to the ground. "Burn too bright and you might burn to nothing," she said in response to Ryn's concerned look.

He gestured at Josalind, who had wandered to some gnarly wild apple trees to pick some breakfast, lost in a world all her own. "What about her?" He expected she would start picking and weaving flowers next and found himself hoping she would, complete with a botany lesson. That would be predictable, expected, a sign that she was still herself.

Kara shook her head. "Watch her."

"I intend to." Ryn savored the idea of a few apples, too, followed by a long nap, but too many questions begged for answers.

Horgrim had their hapless prisoner propped against a stony outcrop. Ryn rubbed his hand over the weathered rose granite. "Fine stone?"

"Indeed."

Ryn eyed their perfumed prisoner. "What do you have in mind?"

Horgrim fished something from his belt. "Time to let the Gods Bane free, swordling."

He held up the key for the manacles that bound Mordyth Ral.

Ryn stared at it. His palm burned with that nagging itch. Scrubbing it against his trouser leg didn't help. "Are you mad?"

"You said it yourself—we can't have this demon herder waking without a muzzle," Horgrim said. "That witch iron is all we have."

"The last time I had the Sword in hand, I almost killed you."

"I'm not asking you to wield it."

Ryn dug his nails into his palms and took a step back.

"We need answers, Ryn." Horgrim stepped toward him. "Kara might be able to pull his thoughts—it's a herald's gift. But this a *sorcerer*. His mind is well trained. If she starts digging around, exhausted as she is, he's likely to wake and reach out to his demons before she can stop him."

"That's right," Kara said, though with obvious reluctance.

Ryn couldn't deny their logic. "Gods be damned." He unslung the leather sleeve from his shoulder and shook the Sword out to grab it by the blade. Even now, he didn't care to risk taking it by the hilt, though he had no idea if it made a measurable difference.

Horgrim gingerly wrapped his fingers around the first manacle and unlocked it, then the other. The witch iron slid off with a rasp and hit the ground.

Mordyth Ral hummed in Ryn's hand. The veins that rose from the blade's strange metal pulsed with life.

You cannot deny me, Heir of Aegias.

The Sword swelled Ryn's senses. He tasted the apple Josalind crunched into twenty yards away, heard the last squeal of a chipmunk taken by a hawk, almost swooned on the sorcerer's jasmine perfume.

"You will *not* act without my consent," Ryn said to the Sword.

Our purpose must be served.

That metallic, probing pressure swelled Ryn's brain, cinder hot. Horgrim retreated a step. Cryptwood wormed from his sleeve.

It took all the vinegar Ryn could muster to force his fingers open, to let the Sword fall. Mordyth Ral struck the stony ground with the blunt authority of a sledgehammer. The impact rattled his teeth. Kicking it farther away did little to dampen the coals that packed his skull. He snatched up the manacles, clutched the witch iron to his brow, and savored the coolness of the metal. Inch by inch, the fire faded. As intense as this struggle had been, denying the Sword here had been far easier than in Tanasgeld—holding it by the blade instead of the hilt did make a difference.

Ryn handed the manacles to Horgrim. "Nothing to be worried about." The fire still smoldered, though at a level he could tolerate . . . at least for a while.

Horgrim cocked an eyebrow but said nothing. He clapped the manacles around the sorcerer's wrists and stowed the key.

Ryn recalled Kara's failed effort to read the High Lord Inquisitar's thoughts through witch iron. If they wanted answers, they'd have to dig them out the hard way.

Horgrim struck the sorcerer with such a slap, his pudgy body flung sideways.

He bolted awake and thrashed with sudden confusion. "What . . . where . . ."

Horgrim grabbed a handful of collar and slammed the fellow up against the outcrop. "What's your name, friend?"

The sorcerer's mood turned in a blink from startled bewilderment to seething anger. Then he saw Oma, sitting nearby on her haunches. She treated him to a broad smile that displayed rows of serrated teeth. He gulped and looked back to Horgrim. "I am Olparc, a Prime of the Savant Council of Vysus."

"Indeed," the warden said. "We are honored by such an esteemed presence. I am Horgrim, and this is Ryn. That fine lady over there is Oma. She hasn't had breakfast yet."

"I know who you are," Olparc said. "I'll have you flayed for this humiliation." He shook his fist with outrage, then realized what it was that bound him.

Horgrim let the reality of it sink in. "You'll be doing no flaying today. But if you answer some questions, I *might* make sure you're dead before Oma starts eating."

She growled and licked her lips.

Olparc spat in Horgrim's face. "Go choke on horse dung, along with your whore goddess."

Oma bounded forward, bowled Ryn and Horgrim aside, and had her nose pressed to Olparc's in a blink. He yelped and tried to twist away, but her big hands had his shoulders pinned. Pointed claws dug into the stone with a cringeworthy shriek.

"Ill manners will avail you not, tender morsel." She licked his cheek. "I could start now with your toes."

Olparc shuddered, head turned aside, eyes clenched shut. The tang of fresh urine caught the air—the gritty earth under his feet grew damp. Ryn couldn't blame him. Oma's manner had even his flesh crawling. He didn't doubt she meant every word.

Horgrim took a seat on a convenient rock. "Now, Your Primeship, why don't you start with how you came to be in that fishpond?"

"I was flung overboard," Olparc said. "By one of your strikes."

"Why were you on board at all?" Ryn asked. "You're from Vysus."

"I am the liaison for our chapter, with our Keshauk peers."

Horgrim scratched under his chin. "Hmmm . . . And what happens now that you and your peers have Xang's skull? Have you the rest of him, too?"

"Thanks to centuries of effort by our chapter in Vysus, yes," Olparc said with obvious pride.

Ryn thought he'd kept stone-faced despite the shocking reveal, but the way Olparc smirked proved he hadn't.

"Does that dismay you, Gods Bane?" the sorcerer said. "You pathetic fool." His attention widened. "All of you, fools damned by your own actions. Kun-Xang will carve you each Himself."

Horgrim just stared at him, as hard as the granite Oma had the sorcerer splayed against. "When will Xang's resurrection take place?"

Oma gave Olparc a lick. "Be candid, tender morsel."

The sorcerer cringed away, jaw clenched, and said nothing.

Josalind drifted over, still munching an apple, heedless of the juice that ran down her chin. "Secrets are such slippery things to keep." She spoke in the tone of a confession, distant from the matter at hand, but her attention fixed squarely on Olparc.

"So many choices," Oma said. She roused a yelp and a bead of blood when she nipped the lobe of Olparc's ear. "Mayhap I start with this treat."

Ryn slapped his hands together. "Out with it."

Josalind sat down next to Horgrim. "This ought to help—the Four tell me Xang will be wearing skin come noon, if not sooner."

"Then his skull *can* be used to bring his spirit forth in a willing host," Kara said.

Gods be damned. Ryn had forgotten that she'd warned of that possibility during their escape from Tanasgeld.

Oma kissed the sorcerer's bald pate. "Is this true, tender morsel?"

"Stop calling me that, vile beast."

Oma snipped his earlobe clean off with a quick snap of her teeth. Olparc screamed. Ryn couldn't deny how her surgical precision impressed.

"Shhh," Oma said. "It cannot be so bad as all that. But it will be."

"I'll see you all eaten alive by—"

This time, she took his whole ear. The audible crunch of cartilage made Ryn flinch with disgust. Olparc's howls echoed from one end of the vale to the other. Oma lapped up the blood that ran with a throaty purr. Horgrim remained stone-faced, while Josalind bit into her apple like she hadn't noticed. Maybe it all seemed to be a dream to her, with the gods twisting her reality.

Ryn ignored how this sickened him and stepped in to give Olparc a quick slap. "Get ahold of yourself and answer the question, before she takes anything else."

"Yes, yes—Xang will take a host," Olparc said.

"Meaning what?" Ryn asked. "What power will he have?"

"Enough to take his rightful place and command the obedience of us all," Olparc said.

Ryn leaned close to Olparc's remaining ear. "Then Xang will be resurrected? When? Where?"

"I know not."

Oma smacked her lips.

"You need to do better, Olparc," Ryn said.

"*I don't know*—how could I?"

"You're a learned and clever fellow," Ryn said. "Make a presumption."

"The master of my chapter—he won't have it done back in the Dominion where our peers are supreme in their power and could claim our triumph as their own," Olparc said. "He will demand respect be demonstrated for our efforts by having the ritual take place on some neutral ground, so we might meet as equals."

Politics, it seemed, transcended borders and beliefs. Neutral ground between Vysus and Keshauk territory had to mean some remote place in the Kingdoms. Ryn slapped his palm against the stone above Olparc's head. "When?"

"As soon as possible."

"Why?"

"To restore his full strength." Olparc looked to Mordyth Ral, lying there in the dirt. "Because the Gods Bane is free."

So, the threat of the Sword would only hasten Xang's full return. Ryn felt, again, the weight bearing down on him, of responsibility, of inevitability. "How soon could that be?"

"Not sooner than four or five days," Olparc said.

"Why so long?" Horgrim asked.

"This is a delicate matter. Careful preparation must be made."

Ryn patted Oma's shoulder for her to back off and afforded the sorcerer a nod. "Thank you."

Olparc sagged to the ground in a miserable heap.

Ryn turned to Horgrim and Josalind, feeling weary to the point of collapse for reasons that had nothing to do with lack of sleep. "Anything else?"

She shook her head and looked anywhere but at the sorcerer. The warden rose. "Nothing comes to mind," he said.

Olparc snagged Ryn's trouser leg. "Please, what's going to happen to me? Don't let her eat me."

Horgrim eyed Olparc as any man would filth stuck on his boot. "Did you know, Ryn, that every ritual a sorcerer uses to summon and bind a demon requires the blood of an innocent? They must spill it by their own hand. Not just a dram or two, but pint's worth—victims seldom survive the letting."

He kicked Olparc's hand from Ryn's leg. "This scrap of demon's dung was likely a mass murderer by his twentieth year."

Olparc whimpered and clawed the dirt. "Please."

Horgrim squatted beside him. "Would you repent if given the choice, forsake the Deceiver and all he grants you to embrace Our Goddess Fraia?"

His turn to mercy took Ryn by surprise.

"Yes, yes, whatever you ask," Olparc said.

An edge of cryptwood shot out of Horgrim's sleeve and sliced the sorcerer's throat. "If only I believed you."

Blood soaked the thirsty ground quick. Olparc gagged and gurgled his last breath, then went limp as his eyes glazed over.

Ryn forced himself to watch. He'd known plenty of men who took pleasure in the kill, or felt nothing at all, which somehow seemed worse. He wasn't either sort. But they couldn't afford to let Olparc go, and they couldn't risk keeping him a prisoner. It was simple, brutal necessity. Horgrim may have done the deed, but Ryn could at least share the burden by bearing witness.

Horgrim gave Oma a hard look. "Don't touch him—go find a sheep."

She grimaced in disappointment but retreated without a word.

Josalind still sat on the rock, fists clenched on her lap, eyes fixed on some distant point. She couldn't have seen anything past Horgrim's bulk, but she would have heard plenty.

Ryn put his hand on her shoulder. "It's over now."

"It's just starting." She reached up and gave his hand a squeeze. "And there's no stopping it."

Ryn looked to Horgrim. "You've said Xang exists to be his father's legs and iron fist—to be his godly general. So what really will happen if he's reborn?"

The warden sighed and rubbed at his chin. "You have to understand the Dominion isn't a single, unified whole. The Keshauk have a score of vassal states that they rely on for supplies and troops. And these vassals chafe under that authority without a strong figurehead, ruled as they are by tyrants with their own ambitions. They often quarrel among themselves. The Keshauk priesthood has its demons of course, and its legions of grenlich, to keep its vassals in line, but the vassals have their sorcerers, too."

"Xang would change all that," Kara said. "The Keshauk's god made flesh on earth would end the discord and inspire manic devotion."

"The Dominion would then drive against us as never before with a combined force of hundreds of thousands," Horgrim said. "And if Sevrenia falls, the Kingdoms will be next."

Kara staggered over on shaky legs and sat down beside Josalind. "The skull has your mark on it—you can track where it is."

"For now," Josalind said.

"Where?" Horgrim asked.

She pointed southwest. "That way, hundreds of leagues."

"Vysus," Ryn said.

Horgrim laughed. "Of course, where else? We won't have a beggar's chance of getting near it."

"But think about it." Ryn eyed Olparc's corpse. "If the sect intends to meet on some neutral ground here in the Kingdoms, it won't want to draw attention to itself with large delegations."

"There's a cartload of 'maybe' in all that—I don't care for how 'maybe' smells," Horgrim said. "And we'll still be sorely outnumbered."

"It's the best chance we've got," Ryn said.

"But we'll lose the means to track the skull by *midday today* with this ritual to bring Xang's spirit forth in a host," Kara said. "That will break Josalind's binding."

Ryn dared reach his thoughts out to the Sword and grunted in pain as the fire flared up. *Can you track the skull?* Perhaps they could steal it back while en route before the resurrection took place.

The sorcerers take steps to confuse my senses.

Ryn cursed aloud. "The Sword can't help us."

"We don't have to track the skull," Kara said. "We only need to know when and where this meeting will take place."

"Last I knew, My Herald, divining the future wasn't among your gifts," Horgrim said.

Kara's eyes narrowed as her attention strayed to Josalind. "No, but the Four—"

Josalind whacked her own knee. "*I know*—stop badgering me."

She leapt up, yanked open the pouch on Ryn's belt, plucked out the Heart of Sovaris, and bolted for Astrig.

Ryn lunged after her and snagged a sleeve. "Josalind, what—"

A silver thunderbolt drowned his senses and left his ears humming. He found himself arse in the dirt, gasping for air. Josalind's blast had broadsided Kara and Horgrim, too.

In two shakes, Astrig had Josalind aloft. "Are you coming?" she called as they sped off to the east.

"Grace Above, we should have kept that moonstruck lass trussed up," Horgrim said.

Kara struggled toward Irsta. "That moonstruck lass might have the answer we need, if we can dig it out of her."

"How so?" Ryn asked.

"She speaks with dead gods, does she not?" Kara said. "And the dead have foresight."

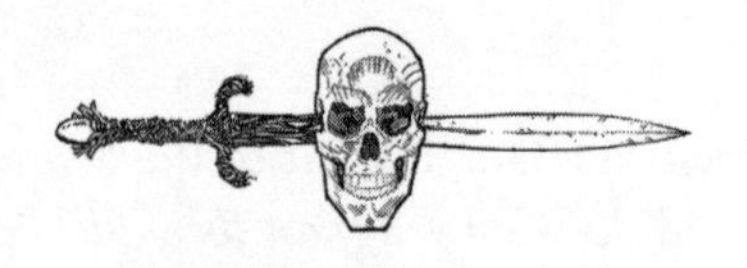

THIRTY-SIX

Segas Tovald kissed the High Lord Inquisitar's new ruby ring and wondered which fanatic in waiting might soon be wearing it.

Anton Bucardas had fallen ill with the blood fever from the wound Ruscroft had dealt him. He should never have left Tanasgeld. The surgeons had said so. But here they were, at anchor in Tesla's harbor, only a few days shy of Viglias.

Tovald still waited for a decent explanation as to why he had been reassigned to Bucardas's retinue. He had his suspicions, none of them good, but he knew better than to press the issue. Palatars didn't achieve command rank by demanding answers from their betters. But bad news often came swift—lack of such implied his fate remained undecided. He might still have a chance to redeem himself.

"Do I look as bad as all that, Captain?" Bucardas asked.

Tovald forced a brief smile to brighten his expression and rubbed at the stumps of his missing fingers. He held the damp turn in the weather responsible for their ache today. "No worse than I did, Your Lordship." A lie, but a kind one. He didn't remember being such a shade of gray when he had fought the fever. Ice had more warmth than the man's hand.

"And yet, here you are, hale and hot-fired by your apostate officer's treachery."

Bucardas shifted higher on his pillows. The effort left him gasping. A book that had been lost in the folds of his blanket slid free. Tovald caught it before it could fall to the floor. A fragile old thing of a size to fit in a large pocket, with a cover of brown leather, cracked with age. It stank of a musty cellar.

"Give it here," Bucardas said with sudden sharpness.

Tovald frowned and handed it over.

"A recent discovery from the Clerisy's early years," Bucardas said in a milder, almost apologetic, tone. "A heretic's journal that questions doctrine." He tucked it away again in a fold of his blanket, then clasped his hands together. "You've read the reports from Viglias?"

Every pigeon in the City of Thrones must have been dispatched to all points with the news, though Tovald still found it hard to believe: Ruscroft's brazen theft at the Great Cathedral, the ruinous storm that had killed thousands, accounts of a great skyship. "I did."

"Only a fool would think these things unrelated," Bucardas said. "A great evil has risen in the Four Kingdoms. Ryn Ruscroft, his witch, and these heretics are its messengers. I fear for every soul, for the very fabric of order that binds us together. Most of all, I fear the Sword, left in such hands."

"He did say things to me in Tanasgeld," Tovald said.

"Truly? Do tell."

Tovald picked his words with caution. "He thinks himself the Sword's steward, to prevent its misuse."

"Does he?" Bucardas's tone turned curt. "Ah, to be fueled by such youthful presumption."

"I call it vain arrogance," Tovald said.

"Naive idealism, to be sure. But labels hardly matter. He has proven himself a dire threat—that is enough." Those fatherly eyes never lost their warmth, yet something dangerous took light in them all the same. "Were these flaws of character not obvious to you?"

Tovald's fingers ached with a fury now. "He practiced mortification of the flesh at Dragon's Claw. Deeds weighed on him. I knew his file, of course, but I didn't push him. Men leave their past behind when they come to the Claw."

"Not all." Bucardas toyed with the flame pendant of gold and Jendal scrimshaw about his neck. "No doubt you wonder why I've brought you along, Captain."

"The thought has crossed."

"I need you to hunt him."

Tovald stifled an incredulous laugh. "No offense, Your Lordship, but he's taken to beasts that fly, at twice a full gallop, from what I saw." The sight of those martichora launching into the sky had left him every bit as shocked as that skeleton dragon stomping around. "And now we can't even rely on contagion to track him."

"Mordyth Ral on his person may confound your compass, Captain, but the Clerisy is custodian of many relics from Lost Pandaris."

Tovald hardly considered the device that Aelin had pushed on him to be his. "Is that so."

"You don't approve, Captain?"

"I don't presume to judge, Your Lordship."

"But you do—speak."

Tovald grimaced and again spoke carefully. "It does seem necessity forces all manner of compromise, given the Dark Arts the Pandarens practiced, Your Lordship."

"But have you not already used the compass, on the just belief that the needs of a greater good outweigh a lesser evil?"

"I did," Tovald said with a tight nod. The burning hypocrisy still left him tempted to tear the lanyards from his shoulders and throw them in the man's face. But he had found himself with a surplus of time to think since leaving the Claw. He wouldn't surrender his commission if it remained his to surrender, not yet at least.

"I would think less of any man in your position who didn't question the morality of using such objects." Bucardas's expression hardened. "But it is *my* place, *my* burden, to decide how and when any ethical line should be blurred."

Tovald swallowed the rebuke with a dip of his head. "Yes, Your Lordship."

"It must have been difficult for you in Vysus, serving a man with Archbishop Besk's appetites, given the shadow it might cast on your own *inclinations*."

Tovald couldn't help the way his eyes widened, stunned to discover His Lordship knew. Why had he even brought it up? If Bucardas meant to intimidate him, the sanctimonious swine could go choke on his tongue. No one would ever shame Tovald for who he was. His fists clenched despite his best efforts to restrain himself, blood boiling with sudden outrage. "I am no pervert. I don't—"

Bucardas raised a soothing hand. "You misunderstand, dear man. Your nature is of no concern to me."

"Then do me the courtesy of speaking plain, Your Lordship." He could muster nothing more civil.

"What I must know, Captain, is if the man who so loyally served in Vysus despite Besk's shortcomings is the man I should trust with this task."

Tovald regained his composure and looked him in the eye. "Is loyal service not answer enough?"

"You also made an admirable sacrifice in Vysus for the sake of a father driven by grief to murder." Bucardas rubbed idly at his ring. "On the other hand, Besk did die under your watch."

Tovald dared rest his hand on the bed's headboard and leaned close. "May I now speak plain, Your Lordship?"

"Please do."

"This is *my* mess to clean up. Ruscroft was an officer under *my* command. Maintaining the sanctity of that abbey was *my* burden." He made no effort to hide his regret and shame. "If I leave Mordyth Ral loose in the world, I will wear every death that follows."

But more than that, what did it say about his choices, his sacrifices, the denial of his own true self, all for the sake of his oath to serve and obey, if he let Ruscroft walk free? He had meant what he'd said to the arrogant pup in Tanasgeld—Ryn's apostasy was a slap in the face to every palatar who had ever sworn to serve. An act of selfish cowardice that couldn't be allowed to escape justice.

Bucardas drank every word Tovald had spoken with a growing smile. "You confess your guilt, your failure of duty, your honest need to atone."

Tovald drew back. "I suppose I do, Your Lordship." He didn't consider himself an idealistic man by any stretch. The world was cruel and unjust, and he could do little to ever change that. But he was still a palatar, one who considered the Virtues to be more than just words. A man who didn't hold to something, who didn't rule himself with some kind of code that curbed his darker half, ranked among the basest of animals.

"Very good, Captain," Bucardas said. "You just deferred a public hanging in Viglias."

The revelation came as little surprise. Of course, this had been a trial from the moment he stepped through the door. The ax had been hanging over his head since Ruscroft and his witch fled the Claw.

"You now have the rank of marshal," Bucardas said. "I will have papers drawn that will grant you jurisdiction and the right of requisition throughout the Clerisy's domain. Once we reach Viglias, you will have access to the resources and the men you need."

Tovald couldn't decide if he should consider himself lucky or damned. He felt belittled either way, which smothered the relief he should have felt. "And what of the threat from the Sword?"

"Writings from Aegias's time tell of how his paladins wore witch iron as a shield from its hunger."

"Truly." No works sanctioned by the Clerisy that Tovald had ever read made any such mention.

Bucardas arched an eyebrow and offered his hand. "Is that all, Marshal? I need my rest."

Tovald kissed the ring and turned to the door. Bucardas had said *deferred*. Those gallows still waited, should he fail. Maybe even if he succeeded, given his knowledge of how His Lordship chose to blur the line.

Tovald eased the door shut behind him and headed up to the ship's main deck. A breath of fresh air would do him good. Dealing with Ruscroft was one thing, putting that Sword into the hands of the Kingdoms' chief fanatic quite another. After Vysus, after the shame of covering for that child-buggering excuse of an archbishop, he had sworn to never again betray his conscience for the Clerisy.

And yet, here he was, Bucardas's personal hound. He found himself craving a drink—malt whiskey. That smoky sweetness swamping his tongue, the burn of it flooding through him, warm and soothing. It had become an old friend since Vysus, the one confidant with which he could dare be honest.

No, damn the Four. He lost enough nights, years, even, in a drunken stupor. And what had any of it done to ease his guilt, to make amends to those children in Vysus?

In that jail cell, Tovald had told Ruscroft that the Clerisy served a purpose greater than any evils that circumstance and convenience might force it to commit. If he didn't hold to that, keep faith with it, what did he have? Still, that didn't mean a man like Bucardas should be obeyed without question and left unchecked. He had to have enemies in the Clerisy who would gladly use knowledge of how he chose to "blur the line" against him, whether on honest moral grounds, or only for political gain. Something to consider and investigate, should the need arise to save his own neck or prevent the Sword's misuse.

There were, of course, more direct methods. The best thing for the decent folk of the Kingdoms might be a pillow over His Lordship's face in the dead of night, if that fever didn't claim him first. Tovald had toyed with such thoughts in Vysus but had done nothing. Too often he had done his duty by doing nothing. But if it came to it, if Mordyth Ral lay in Bucardas's grasp, he would have to do something.

That wouldn't be a betrayal of the Clerisy, but an act to preserve and redeem it.

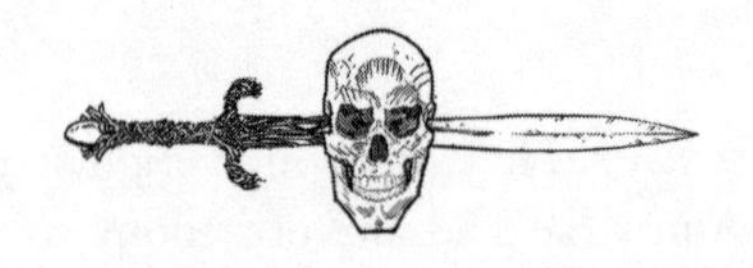

THE CHILD AND THE FORTUNE-TELLER

Fraia's return and the rise of the Sevrendine

So, my little angel, you've to come to ask me about the Sevrendine and Fraia's return.

I've told you before about the legends of a Dark Goddess that were seeded in the West by Keshauk agents. All with the intent to poison Fraia's chances of rebuilding her flock should she ever return.

These old myths endured and Aegias, as I have said, missed his chance to set the record straight.

So, there we were after his death some centuries ago. Clerics of every stripe across the Kingdoms faced with a crisis of faith. After Aegias's revelations about the Four and the Kingdoms' old religions, they feared that any "divine power" could too easily be the work of the Great Deceiver. Aegias's paladins spoke of a goddess, Fraia, but without Aegias to stand by them, this was received with mistrust. Those holy men who would guide the Reformation that gave us the Clerisy instead adopted Aegias's Injunction against prayer or supplication of any kind. They outlawed as heresy any claim that Aegias had served a goddess.

Instead, they decided, the angels who had appeared to Aegias must have been orphaned servants of the Four, come in a rare time of need to guide him to the Sword and prevent Xang's conquest of the West. And while angels are, of course, divine beings of no particular gender, it is understood that one or more often appeared to Aegias in a feminine form.

Mortals, my pet, be they men or women, can convince themselves of most anything if they wish it hard enough and find the truth too sour.

Centuries later, when a rural Jendalian bishop named Sevren rose up and claimed to be Fraia's herald, the Clerisy easily dismissed it as just another misguided heresy with sorcery at its core. It wasn't the first time that a "goddess cult" had risen.

But this one persisted and grew, despite the Inquisitarem's cruelest efforts to stamp it out. True Faith, at last, could no longer be denied, for by this time, some three centuries ago, Fraia had finally escaped the prison wrought by Vulheris with the Sword twenty-five hundred years before.

And then a thirst for new lands and new riches led the Kingdoms to ignore those old stories of a dark empire in the East. Settlers attempted to colonize the Steppe Plateau out there beyond the Impalas Mountains. They violated the western marches of the Keshauk Dominion, rousing the West's ancient enemy. Though the Clerisy came armed with witch iron and demon-enchanted relics of Lost Pandaris, the Kingdoms faced a foe they couldn't quell.

So began the Keshauk Aggression. With it, the time had come for the Sevrendine to be forged into one people and fulfill their purpose, Fraia's purpose, and counter the Great Deceiver for the sake of us all.

By this time, the Sevrendine were led by the Herald Armos of Carsis. An angel of Fraia bade him go to Viglias and surrender himself for an audience before the Clerisy's Council of Prelates.

Despite being beaten and tortured by the Inquisitarem, forced to parade naked through the streets in witch-iron shackles, Armos carried himself with a measure of pride and purpose that neither scourge nor brand could strip from him. He stood before those preceptars and made a bold offer—the Sevrendine in all their number would depart the Kingdoms and go east to fight the Keshauk.

After much debate, the Council decided to accept his offer. If the Sevrendine could not be stamped out, those squint-eyed jackals must have thought, why not give them leave to depart the Kingdoms altogether? Let them go and commit mass suicide in some mad gesture of heretical zeal.

And so, the Sevrendine left the Kingdoms in a great Exodus. Tens of thousands of them—far more than the Clerisy had ever dared imagine there could be. They streamed through Penance Pass and came upon the killing fields of that Aggression, to fight a war not of their making with the blessing of a church eager to abandon them to their deaths.

The Kingdoms then gave up that war, blocked the mountain pass, and forbade any Sevrendine from ever returning on pain of death.

But the Sevrendine have survived and prospered—don't you doubt it. They alone are standing between us and utter doom.

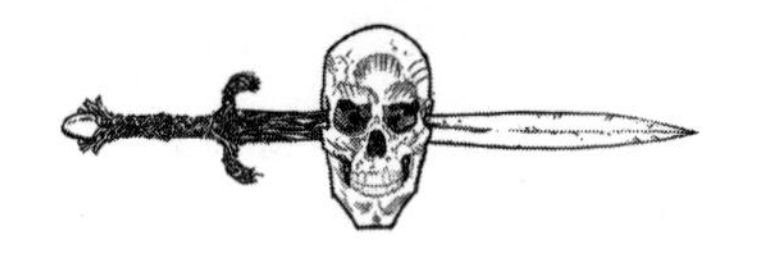

THIRTY-SEVEN

Ryn urged Oma on, but the martichora couldn't close the distance, given Josalind's lead and how easy she was for Astrig to carry.

Josalind led them south and east toward the farthest reaches of the Impalas Mountains. Those icy peaks marked the boundary between the Kingdoms and all that the Clerisy shunned and feared—the Sevrendine, the Keshauk, and other things likely to be more myth than fact. But her course took them too far south of those lands. Only the Boiling Sea and a chain of volcanic islands called the Crescent of Fire lay east of the mountains at this latitude. Legend held these were the breeding grounds of the brine draken—territorial sea dragons that made sailing southern waters a fool's venture.

The weather turned fickle as they climbed up into the mountains. Swirls of soupy mist arose from nowhere, only to be swept aside by fierce gusts that tossed Oma about. Ryn's shoulders and thighs came to burn from his desperate clench to hang on. He imagined falling, wind screaming and tearing at him, bones snapping as he crashed through the trees, before what was left splattered the ground like an overripe melon.

Aegias, spare me and I'll never take wing again.

The weather settled after what seemed an eternity. Ryn had lost sight of anything but snow, ice, and weathered stone. The thin air left him wheezing and shivering—they'd fled Viglias dressed for fall and flown into winter. Astrig and Josalind banked and veered between the peaks and ridges with a lead of almost a mile.

"Where in all Five Hells does she go?" he asked at large.

"You have asked this three times now, man-child," Oma said with a wheeze of her own. "It grows tiresome."

He glanced back. Kara and Irsta trailed by about fifty yards. The herald slumped over at risk of falling off. Horgrim and Ashavinx had fallen even farther behind.

"Would you look at that," Oma said.

The mountains opened upon the head of a broad, fertile valley that met the sea.

Meltwaters from alpine glaciers gathered in a small lake below them, then took a dizzying plunge. Josalind and Astrig dove past the waterfall's head and kept to a straight course. The falls fed a river that snaked down the valley. Parcels of cropland and pasture climbed into the foothills on either side of the river in a patchwork quilt of greens and yellows. Large herds that may have been sheep dotted the pastures white. Mounds of mine tailings and plumes of dark smoke up in the hills gave evidence of industry.

For a dozen miles or more the valley sprawled, before it ended at towering sea cliffs so sheer and straight they could have been cut with the same blow of a giant's ax. The river drained over the cliffs' edge in another great waterfall. Ryn looked out to sea—cone-shaped peaks stained the distant horizon with sooty smears. That could only be the legendary Crescent of Fire.

He didn't notice the city until they'd wheeled around to follow Josalind and Astrig back up the valley.

A great city of terraces, a score at least, rose in steep tiers alongside the mountain waterfall: building facades crowned by triangular pediments and supported by columns with bulbous capitals, dozens of ramps and walkways with colonnades that curved from one terrace to another, massive statues with folded arms. At the city's highest point, four great obelisks stabbed the sky like the spires of a cathedral that honored the Four. Ryn doubted that was a coincidence.

Gostemere. It had to be. He couldn't imagine that men had built this place, any more than the mice in the eaves had built his family's manor house. Its monumental scale dwarfed even Viglias, despite the fact that the other city sprawled to cover more acreage.

An eagle's cry caught Ryn's attention. Their arrival had attracted an escort—creatures with the hindquarters of a lion, and the wings, heads, and talons of an eagle. Two *V* formations had settled on Josalind's flanks, a dozen creatures in each.

Gods be damned. Griffins. What else lost to legend still dwelt in Gostemere?

The griffins were only half the size of the martichora, but they had numbers on their side. Ryn could only hope they wouldn't turn hostile. A wall girded the city's lowest level, its single gatehouse a mighty fortress in itself, built square and blocky—even its four towers were square and flat topped. This alone had been built from quarried stone. The rest of Gostemere appeared to have been hewn direct from the mountain itself. The stone's natural patterns left the city awash in an organic mosaic of grays and pale reds.

Josalind and Astrig descended toward the gatehouse. A gong sounded. The city's wall came alive with a swarm of activity.

Ryn cursed and clutched Oma's mane, expecting a hail of arrows, grapeshot, or gods only knew what else to bring them down. "She'll kill us all."

"Have faith, man-child," she said.

The gates opened. Dozens of figures marched out between two rows of tall statues that flanked the approach to the city. Ryn blinked tears from wind-burned eyes and squinted for a clearer look at what manner of death they raced toward.

The people of Gostemere weren't people.

He saw creatures that had two arms and two legs, but the proportions were wrong. They stood too tall and slender to be human, with skin of blue or green and flowing hair to match. A few even had wings that glittered. These could only be sprites of the waters and sylphids of the skies, if the legends about the Earthborn held true. Others singed the earth on which they walked with squat bodies that appeared molded from cooling lava—salamandars.

Josalind and Astrig landed in their midst. Oma followed. Palms slick, heart pounding, Ryn ached to reach for Mordyth Ral. He forced himself instead to draw the longsword of plain steel that rode at his hip.

The ground thumped and shook. Oma reared back with a hiss.

A giant twice as tall as Horgrim bore down on them. Ryn had dismissed it as just another statue, to all appearances shaped from tan sandstone, clad in a simple toga. A hide grown thick and stiff enough to compare with Sturvian plate armor covered even its head, as if it wore a helm with cheek guards. Beady glints of yellow glared through narrow eye slits.

A dolusk? Ryn thought with childlike wonder, just before a bucket-sized fist swatted him from Oma's back. Wind gone, ribs shrieking, he hit the ground hard.

A swirling void swallowed his senses and hungered for more. Ryn let it have him without complaint.

Curse you all to Hell!

Ryn woke from the Sablewood dream in a hazy muddle, nose stuffed with an earthy, acrid stink. Finding himself in a strange place—a big and sparsely furnished room—didn't help.

The city of terraces . . . The Earthborn . . . The dolusk.

Panic took hold. Not fear so much as a warrior's instinct for survival. He tried to sit up, but aching ribs chastised him for it with excruciating detail. In the absence of an obvious threat, he eased back on his elbows and focused on slow breaths to ease the pain.

The room's simple functionality reminded him of his quarters at Dragon's Claw. As he had suspected, the city had been hewn direct from the mountain, every surface polished till it gleamed in those swirled shades of gray and soft red. A wooden desk and a chair were fashioned from square slabs and straight slats without decorative details. Plain shutters and woolen drapes dressed the deep-silled window. Grass mats covered the floor. A curtain of colorful beads hung in lieu of a door.

An odd flatness hung over the place, as if Ryn had been trapped in a painting or in that blink of time between one breath and the next. Maybe his aching head accounted for it.

"Good morn to you." The voice spoke in Common Islari and bore the hoarse smoothness of wet sand cascading down a chute.

Ryn snapped his head around. *It* sat on a stool in the corner behind his bed, a thing that resembled a sculptor's half-finished effort to mold a man from clay. The right parts were there, but in proportions too broad to be natural. It had no nose to speak of and only a slit for a mouth. Ears sprouted like two great mushrooms and gleaming rubies served as its eyes.

The creature just looked at him, lumpy hands folded on its lap. A garment similar to a Teishlian toga draped over one thick shoulder and reached its knees. As with everything else in the room, the toga had a plain and simple cut.

Ryn noticed that he too wore a toga. His clothing and gear lay, neat and tidy, on a low bench beside the creature. Mordyth Ral's leather sleeve rested on the bench, too, and so did his longsword, both well out of reach. "Where am I?"

"Gostemere, of course," the creature said. "You are a guest in my home."

"And just *who* are you?" The question Ryn most wanted to ask was *what*, but that might give offense. He wouldn't risk that till he had a better sense of his circumstance . . . and a weapon in hand.

That slit mouth twitched with something akin to a smile, to suggest the creature had heard what Ryn hadn't said. "I am Karxist."

"You're a gorbling." Earthborn masters of stone and ore said to have once served the god Koglar.

"For some time now."

Ryn still found it hard to fathom, despite the evidence that sat there, calm and sedate.

"Do you suspect wily deception by your own orbs?" Karxist asked.

"'A wise man knows not all he sees is truth,'" Ryn said. A line from the *Codex*. He'd never found a more fitting occasion for it than now.

The gorbling laughed, if a clatter of pebbles could be considered a laugh. "I am no demon come to deceive, if that is what tasks you. Prick me—I will bleed."

Ryn had a better test. He reached out to Mordyth Ral. *Is this true?*

He is a gorbling. He will bleed . . . and die, too.

Ryn tried not to stare at Karxist's strangeness in a rude way. "How long have I been here?"

"A day full—your nut took a fair crack."

The dull throb between Ryn's ears didn't dispute it. "Where are my companions?"

"I believe they break their night's fast," Karxist said. "Would you join them?"

"I would." He eased his legs over the side of the bed. "Are you lord of Gostemere?"

"My role is earned," Karxist said. "Consider me akin to a first minister in the parliaments of your Kingdoms."

"How do you know the common tongue?"

"I know much from the World Beyond." Karxist tapped one of those mushroom ears. "I keep earth-rooted and hear what the Four see fit to share."

"The Four."

"They speak to me."

What did that mean for Josalind? Something good, surely. For the first time in her life, she'd have others who might truly understand her burden.

Ryn tried to rise, but his ribs wouldn't have it. Karxist came to his side. Ryn forced himself not to flinch from the pain when the gorbling took him under the armpits.

"A cracked breastbone and three cracked ribs," Karxist said.

"An odd way to treat a guest."

"You must forgive Grist for striking you, he holds much regret. He meant only to protect Our Lady Savior when he saw you draw steel."

Ryn realized that earthy stink came from himself. He touched his chest, swaddled in bandages.

"Grist brewed the salve himself, from rare herbs and fungi," Karxist said.

Ryn figured his body would heal faster just to escape the stink. Maybe that was the point. He gathered what bits of memory he could of that stone giant. "Grist is a dolusk."

"Yes."

Karxist's claylike hands hoisted Ryn to his feet with no effort. The gorbling barely came to his shoulder, but Ryn suspected power few men could match rested in that thick frame. How much brute force could a dolusk muster, then? Grist had likely pulled his punch. Ryn took a few careful steps and probed the bandages. "'Our Lady Savior'—I suppose that would be Josalind?"

"Why, of course," Karxist said.

"So, a gorbling prophecy, then?" A dozen other questions fought to be asked, threatened to burst out in a tirade. Ryn held them back. He knew too little about the lay of this strange land, about its people and what threat they might pose, to risk being too aggressive . . . yet.

"Prophecies are for fables," Karxist said. "There is only a plan, long in the making."

Ryn found Josalind and the Sevrendine seated around a table, under the branches of a tree unlike any he'd ever seen.

The tree reigned over a courtyard terrace with the gnarly girth of an ancient oak. Its trunk and branches resembled a sprouting of stone rather than wood, given their smooth textures and gray tones. Narrow leaves hung in clumps like a willow's, silver-white and spotted crimson. Ryn's sense of oddness about this place, of a collective breath caught for eternity, hadn't changed. In fact, it deepened at the sight of this tree. A grand old thing, burdened by the roll of centuries, weeping in despair for all it had seen. The thought came unbidden, as if it didn't belong to him, but Mordyth Ral remained silent.

He tried to give the tree a wide berth to reach the empty chair by Josalind but couldn't escape its shadow. Those great branches stretched across the whole of the terrace and over the low wall that served as a railing. The drop to the valley floor beyond must have been a hundred and fifty yards.

Josalind smiled at the sight of him, but it struck him as wan and bittersweet. That stirred even more unease than the tree did. Karxist hadn't explained what he meant by *Our Lady Savior.* Ryn didn't want to hear the answer from the gorbling, in any case.

"Are you all right?" he asked.

She busied herself with buttering a biscuit. "Right as rain."

Ryn eased into the chair with teeth clamped and breath caught to keep from groaning. He carried Mordyth Ral in its sleeve and laid it across his lap. Karxist hadn't said a word when he'd gone for it, even offered a hand to help him pick it up. The gorbling took the chair across from him.

Horgrim grinned around a mouthful of what must have been oat porridge and strawberry preserve, judging by the heavenly smells. "You're doing well for a man who crossed a walking battering ram, swordling."

Ryn gave the jest the sneer it deserved and went for a teapot, but it lay out of reach. Kara rose to pour him a mug and fixed Horgrim with a withering stare.

"Don't be like *this* old boar and too prideful to ask for help when you have need," she said.

Ryn noted how her hand trembled ever so slightly while she poured. She still looked worn out, aged, after Viglias. He glanced between her and Josalind. "I don't expect either of you to suffer on my account, but why do I need help at all when I have two heralds who can heal?"

"Neither Fraia nor the Deceiver has any power here," Karxist said. He gestured at the branches overhead. "The Tree of Sorrows does not permit it."

Tree of Sorrows. Ryn looked to the nearest leaves with their ruddy spots. Their sad droop left him expecting a drizzle of blood. "And why is that?"

"This tree wards the whole valley from any power that isn't born of this earth," Kara said.

"What about the Four?" Ryn asked. "Aren't Fraia and the Great Deceiver their parents?"

"They are half of this world and half of another," Karxist said. "But the Tree does not condemn them for this as Mordyth Ral does."

Still, that left one obvious question. Ryn looked to Josalind and wondered why she hadn't bestowed another healing kiss.

She fixed her attention on her bowl. "I told you before they don't always come if I call."

Her obvious shame at the admission left Ryn eager to be alone with her, where he could hold her tight without this damned audience. He settled for squeezing her knee under the table.

"Our people know that Fraia and the Deceiver are not native to this world," Horgrim said. "But that is all. You seem to know more."

"Would it surprise you to learn, Noble Warden, that ours is but one of many worlds in the heavens?" Karxist waved at the blue sky above. "Multitudes of them. The stars are suns like our own, unimaginably distant."

"There are those who say so." Horgrim shrugged. "They're outnumbered by the skeptics who think they're fools."

He gave no indication as to which camp he favored. Ryn recalled his conversation with Mordyth Ral in the sewers of Tanasgeld that had alluded to this very thing.

"Beings like Fraia and the Deceiver—they have the means to bridge these vast distances and travel from world to world," Karxist said.

The gritty sound of stone rubbing stone drew Ryn's eye up to another terrace, this one walled by a lattice grown over with flowing vines. "We've got an audience."

The tips of Karxist's ears curled. "Your pardons begged for my fellow ministers. They are shy . . . and cautious."

Given that strangers likely hadn't come to Gostemere in centuries, Ryn could appreciate that. "If the Great Deceiver has no power here, then this place is a trap."

"That is not its principle purpose, but yes," Karxist said.

Josalind placed her hand over Ryn's. "That's what the Four want, what they've wanted all along. For the Deceiver to be lured here, held here, until he can be slain with Mordyth Ral."

"Our Lady Josalind speaks with a hammer's clarity," Karxist said. "Here, he will be weak. Here, he will be mortal. Mordyth Ral can slay him without the great cost of life that we saw before."

"When Vulheris tried to kill him the first time," Ryn said.

"Yes," Karxist said. "This is what was intended then, but the power and the will of the Sword proved too great for Vulheris, and, well, all of us here know the rest—he attacked the Four and when he faced the Deceiver those millennia ago, he did so outside of this place."

"Hold up," Horgrim said. "Why does this place even exist? What do you mean, trapping the Deceiver isn't its 'principle purpose'?"

Karxist treated him to a nod that bordered on a bow. "Wise questions all, Noble Warden." He spread his hands flat on the table. "When the Great Deceiver came to this world—"

"Pardon, but when was that exactly?" Kara asked.

"Some four thousand years ago," Karxist said. "He came to consume our world and Fraia pursued to stop him, but they both found that this world already had its own . . . *proto*-gods, if you will."

Ryn exchanged a look with Kara and Horgrim. They looked just as surprised as he. Josalind, however, kept her attention on her bowl of porridge, stirring the contents round and round in endless circles.

"The Deceiver killed them, didn't he?" Kara said.

Karxist nodded. "They stood in his way."

A sudden suspicion gripped Ryn. "There were four of these 'proto-gods,' weren't there? Each tied to one of the natural elements—earth, air, fire, and water."

"I see the understanding in your eyes," Karxist said. "Yes, the proto-gods existed in symbiosis with all life in this world—their deaths guaranteed utter extinction. The Deceiver would have been content to gorge while he could and move on to another world, for that is his compulsion, but Fraia would not allow it. She battled him to an impasse to keep him here and snatched what she needed of his seed."

Snatched his seed? The bizarre image that this conjured didn't suit mixed company and would have prompted Ryn to chuckle under different circumstances. "And so, we had the Four."

Karxist spread his arms wide in acknowledgment. "Sovaris, bound to water; Mygalor, bound to air; Koglar, bound to earth; and Kyvros, bound to fire. Each created from the last sparks that remained of the proto-gods and the combined life force of their parents—the Goddess Fraia and the Deceiver. The Four are vital to the continuation of life on this world."

Ryn frowned. "But they're dead—just ghosts now."

That slit-mouth twitched. "Are they? And yet, their power and influence delivered you here."

The gorbling's coy manner only served to grate on Ryn's nerves. His eyes narrowed. "Don't—"

Horgrim interrupted with a sharp thrust of his spoon. "I have questions about that myself, but first, this place and that tree—your yarn still hasn't explained their part in this."

Karxist looked up at the Tree of Sorrows. "We sit here on the very spot where the proto-gods perished. This Tree sprouted from their remains. Its sorrow is the sorrow of the world when it suffered their loss."

He reached out and cupped a cluster of those spotted leaves in his palm. "In its own way, the Tree is as powerful a thing as Mordyth Ral. The Veil it casts over this whole valley is a defense of a sort, to protect the sanctity of the proto-gods' resting place. Whether the effect of this on Fraia and the Deceiver is by accident or design . . ." He shrugged. "We cannot say."

Ryn had so many other questions—about the origins of the Earthborn themselves, and of mankind. The lover of old books and history deep within him yearned for the time and the freedom to just linger in this place, to *learn*. If only they had the time to spare. "You said the Deceiver came here to consume our world—how do you mean?"

"The lifeforce of all living things—the spark of the animas that we each carry within us," Karxist said. "It proved such a rich milk for the Deceiver, even with the Goddess Fraia's power and that of the Four combined, she could not achieve a lasting victory. So—"

"She sought to create a weapon capable of doing the job," Horgrim said. "She gave Vulheris the knowledge to forge Mordyth Ral."

Karxist fixed him with those ruby eyes, his expression unfathomable. "She gave him the power . . . but *we* gave him the knowledge."

"Gods be damned," Ryn breathed.

"Indeed they were," Karxist said. "To our everlasting shame and horror, we helped to create Mordyth Ral and unleash it upon the world." His ears thrust forward. "We live on now with only one purpose—to see done what Vulheris failed to do two thousand five hundred years ago."

He folded his hands on the table and regarded Ryn for a long moment before continuing. "In this place, Palatar, with the Sword in your hand, the Deceiver will die, the world will rejoice for it, and we will find some small measure of atonement."

Ryn just looked at him, not caring how he gawped. What the gorbling said made sense—easy, convenient sense. This mad idea of slaying the Deceiver with Mordyth Ral wasn't so mad after all. Everything had been reduced to simple tactics and strategy, to achieve victory with fewer casualties and less collateral damage—like Aegias's battles, which Ryn had studied as a boy.

But the devil's hand always lay in the details. His expression hardened as he looked from Josalind to Karxist. "What else?"

She kept her attention fixed on her now cold and gluey breakfast. "The skull would have been the key—it could have been used to work a kind of spell that would have compelled the Deceiver to come here, just like—"

"The ritual that Bucardas wanted to work on me, to lure you," Ryn finished. The law of contagion used to draw a witch to her thrall, only in this case, the catalyst was the blood, the essence, whatever it was that Xang shared with his father.

Karxist's ruby eyes gave nothing, but the way his mushroom ears wilted said plenty. "Without the skull, we have no means now to bait the Great Deceiver and lure him here, save one. Our Lady—"

Josalind slapped the table. "Please, don't say more."

Ryn's heart knotted with a breathless fear. He didn't know what Karxist meant to say, but it frightened him all the same. Did the Sevrendine already know? Likely not, considering how Horgrim had frozen, spoon clenched in a ham-fisted grip halfway to his mouth, or the manner in which Kara's piercing gaze had grown even sharper. "Tell me."

Josalind hung her head as though the truth would be too much to bear, for either of them. Then she squared her shoulders and faced him with chin high. "It's got to be, Ryn. Always was. I just didn't understand, not until a few days ago." She put on that feeble smile again and cradled his jaw in her palm, as if she felt the need to comfort him and had the strength for it. But he could tell she was the one shattered inside.

"The Four must be reborn," she said. "Through me."

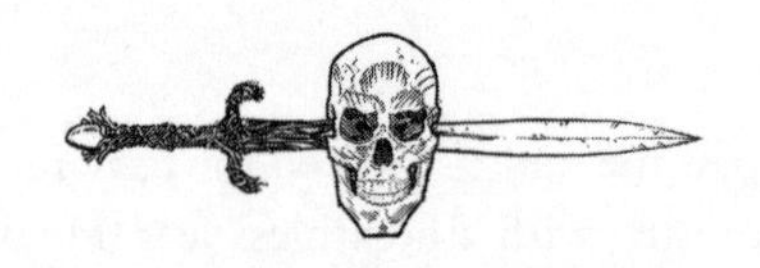

THIRTY-EIGHT

The gods, born again, through Josalind.

Ryn's chair crashed over as he heaved to his feet. The roar in his ears smothered the cry of his cracked ribs. He slammed Mordyth Ral upon the table hard enough for the settings to jump. "What does she mean, *gorbling*?"

Karxist just looked at him, hands still folded on the table. He hadn't even flinched. "Our Lady Josalind was born to this, Gods Bane."

"Don't call me that." Ryn rapped his knuckles on Mordyth Ral. "*That* is the name of this thing; it's not who I am."

"As a warrior, would you deny that a weapon is one with the hand that wields it?" Karxist asked. "For the man who carries Mordyth Ral, this is doubly true."

Ryn thought of the blade with which he'd killed Quintan, the blade he'd seen melted for horseshoes. But the fault rested with him alone, not some lifeless piece of steel.

Kara drummed the table with her nails fiercely enough to leave marks. "Be so kind as to answer the question he asks, First Minister."

Karxist tapped his brow in respect. "I intend to, Herald. The Heart of Sovaris guided you to us, drawn to its kin that rest here. That alone is the reason you could find Gostemere through the Veil cast by the Tree of Sorrows."

"What kin?" Ryn asked.

"Why, the hearts of the other gods, of course," Karxist said. "They rest here in Gostemere, waiting for Our Lady Josalind. The enduring essence of the Four will combine and be birthed anew with her through a glorious union."

Ryn just stared at him.

Josalind spread her hand over his. "That's why it was always so hard to hear them clear. They only reached me at all because Sovaris was outside Gostemere."

"But even then, with this Veil of yours, how did Josalind hear them at all?" Horgrim asked.

"As I said, the Four were created, in part, from the remaining sparks of the proto-gods," Karxist said. "This binds them to the animas—the Tree and its Veil are, of course, extensions of the animas. So, where Fraia or the Deceiver would be completely powerless and cut off here from the outside world, the Four are not. Sovaris's brothers can still be heard through the Veil, and despite what Mordyth Ral did to them, they can still act in some measure, as you have seen."

A convulsive shudder rolled through Ryn and roused sharp throbs of pain from his chest. He clenched his fists to stifle it before his knees gave out. "How do they survive at all?"

"I have provided that answer already, Sword-Bearer," Karxist said.

Ryn forced himself to think rationally. "If the Four were utterly destroyed, we would be right back where we started when the Deceiver killed the proto-gods—the world facing extinction."

"It would be inevitable," Karxist said. "Vulheris didn't force the Sword to spare the Four—Mordyth Ral knew it had no choice but to spare them. Yet it still felt compelled to deny them freedom and a full life because of its bias toward their parents. So, it reduced them to a state where they could endure to serve their essential purpose—balancing the elemental forces of Nature—and no more than that. The Four are not truly 'dead' in a mortal sense. They never were."

Ryn reached out to Mordyth Ral. *Is this true?*

They remain a necessary evil to maintain Nature's Balance.

"What about Fraia?" Ryn asked. "Nothing barred the Sword from utterly ending her."

"That *was* Vulheris's choice," Karxist said. "You must understand that, when it . . . *reduced* the gods, Mordyth Ral did so by leeching their life force—you have experienced the Sword empowering itself, correct?"

Ryn remembered the horror of Tanasgeld. "Yes."

"The Four attempted to kill Vulheris and spare themselves," Karxist said. "In that battle, their blood, such as it is, was spilled. Through some vagary of fate, Vulheris ingested some. Such a substance would have killed most men, but he had the constitution to survive. The Four's blood gave him a new strength—to resist the Sword and even direct its power in unexpected ways."

"But he still went after Our Goddess after crippling the Deceiver," Kara said.

"Yes, driven half mad by the struggle raging within him, but in the fateful moment when it mattered most, Vulheris found the will to force the Sword to accept a compromise—to imprison Fraia here rather than slay her," Karxist said.

So, Ryn did have a way to force Mordyth Ral's obedience—more than that, to direct its power beyond its base purpose. He could use the Sword to serve a greater good. All he had to do was drink the toxic blood of a god . . . and survive.

Of course, why not?

The ridiculous idea left him trapped between the urge to laugh and the urge to weep, which stripped any appetite to hear more. He smothered the despair that threatened to swamp him with a snarl. Josalind mattered, his fate didn't—not while she faced this nightmare.

"Why now?" he demanded. "Why her?"

Karxist went to the Tree and ran his hands over its gnarled trunk with obvious affection. "These old roots still run deep, but not with the vigor they once did. The Veil weakens. This is how Fraia managed to escape three centuries ago. We must act, and soon, while the Veil still has the power to trap the Deceiver. When the Four sensed the decay of Aegias's seal upon the skull, they knew the time had come. They found a vessel, a girl child to become Our Lady."

Ryn rapped the table with his knuckles. *"But why her?"*

Karxist shrugged. "I doubt even they can say."

The gorbling's patient serenity made Ryn's outrage burn that much hotter. "And what becomes of her, once the gods are reborn?"

Josalind squeezed his hand. "I won't be me, Ryn, not anymore."

"This is a turn most unfortunate, man-child," Oma said several bells later, from her perch on the wall before the Tree of Sorrows.

"Unfortunate?" Ryn's hands flexed, in sore need of smashing something. He'd stormed away from the table that morning before the urge to test a gorbling's capacity to bleed got the better of him. Since then, he'd avoided everyone, knotted and stretched in too many directions to bear company, least of all Josalind's, given how she seemed so gods-damned resigned to all this. He'd only ventured here again because his dark mood left him oddly drawn to the Tree, gripped by a vague sense that it might have something useful to offer, but it kept silent. Then Oma had found him.

"The gods have used and abused her all her life. But that's still not enough, not until they've taken all she is, all that's her." Ryn didn't trust this sense of urgency for the Four's rebirth through Josalind. The argument that the Earthborn needed some means to lure the Deceiver before the Veil grew too weak to trap him rang false. Even if Josalind had brought Xang's skull to Gostemere, the Four would still crave their union with her for the simple reason that they hungered to walk the earth again in some form, in *any* form. The more he thought on it, the surer he became.

Oma's tail twitched in distress. "I mean not to belittle her sacrifice, man-child, or the pain it brings you."

Ryn forced his hands flat on the wall. A sultry haze kept him from spotting the pristine sparkle of the Boiling Sea. He saw only ugly stains on the horizon, the fume belched by the Crescent of Fire, spreading like a cancerous rot across the sky. "I know you don't, I just . . . This can't be how it's meant to end."

"You must see this as a glorious new beginning, Ryn Ruscroft," Karxist said from behind him. "We all must."

Ryn snarled. "Josalind will die—what glory is there in that?"

"As one with the Four, she will live on, part of something far greater and more enduring than a mortal life."

Ryn turned sharply on his heel. He couldn't tell what lay in those inhuman eyes—patient sympathy or heartless curiosity. It didn't matter. He knew a fanatic when he saw one, no different than the High Lord Inquisitar. "Who she is won't exist anymore. She'll be dead, by any measure that matters."

Karxist's slit of a mouth pressed into a tight line. "I know your pain, Ryn Ruscroft. But we must all think of the common good. Josalind does. She understands what must happen here. She accepts it."

"Of course she does," Ryn snapped. "Those four ghouls have her so beaten down and turned inside out, she's lost all hope of having a choice."

"Circumstances leave us no options," Karxist said. "Lest you propose to unleash Mordyth Ral outside this sanctuary and lay the world to ruin."

Oma's claws shrieked on the stone as she shifted her weight. "He does speak with a true point, man-child."

Ryn answered her with a fresh scowl.

"You think me callous," Karxist said. "But there is something I would have you see."

Karxist led Ryn down stairs and through galleries and halls with arched ceilings—all as breathless as a tomb, despite the presence of the Earthborn. Every corner stuffed with the pregnant expectation of *something* momentous and imminent. Ryn wondered if the Tree of Sorrows had always cast such a mood over Gostemere or if that had only come with Josalind.

He saw little symmetry in the architecture and even fewer square corners. The Earthborn favored organic curves and fluid lines. Abstract sculptures that twisted into fantastic shapes resided in alcoves and nooks, to all appearances drawn direct from the mountain stone. Such unique craftsmanship must have had Horgrim beside himself.

They reached another terraced courtyard. Flowering vines grew thick across stone arbors and pergolas. A few dozen gorblings had assembled there. All appeared to be adults. Those nearest afforded Karxist solemn bows.

Every pair of gemlike eyes fixed on Ryn—ruby, emerald, amethyst, and more. Not at all a comfortable feeling. He bowed after their example but hung back behind Karxist.

"When the Four lived, our kind numbered in the thousands," Karxist said. "Few by the measure of mankind, but we live long. You might consider us immortal, but we are not." He swept out his arm to include all those gathered. "Here is all that remains of my race. All that we were, all that we are." He pressed hands to brow, bowed to his people, and spoke in a language both grinding and sibilant.

The entire group returned the gesture and spoke as one, repeating the same words, so far as Ryn could tell.

"We say, 'Through hammer, stone, and song, we endure till none live to remember.'" Karxist looked to him. "So it is for all Earthborn who linger here, Ryn Ruscroft. The Great Devastation, when Vulheris reduced the Four, crippled the Deceiver, and entrapped Fraia marked the beginning of our end. Those who survived grew barren. We are the orphans who remain."

He displayed no more emotion than he had when speaking about Josalind's fate. Ryn just looked at him, then at the gorblings before them. "You think the Four's rebirth will somehow save you."

Karxist shrugged. "This cannot be known. We are not by nature given to vain hope. But the Great Deceiver is an affliction that must end. Nothing else matters to us now."

"What about *Xang's* resurrection?" Ryn asked. "You've given no weight to the fact he could live again in just days."

"Xang will be nothing against the Four reborn."

"And where is Fraia in all this?"

"When the Deceiver had his full might, Fraia and the Four together could not outmatch him," Karxist said. "Even crippled, he remains too strong for Fraia to challenge directly alone. The Mother Goddess needs an ally able to help her flush him out and either lure or drag him here. She needs the Four reborn as One."

The fanatical little mudball had an answer for every damned question and counter. "Show me this place where Fraia was imprisoned."

Ryn recognized Fraia's prison from his vision the moment Karxist led him through the great brass doors. Kara and Horgrim had already come. The warden carried Blood Thorn in the form of a staff, crowned by those crimson thorns.

The cavern could hold hundreds, lit by a pale aqua light given off by radiant fungi that crept up the walls. Three pedestals stood in the midst of it to form an equilateral triangle. Each bore a crystalline stone—one red, one green, one white. The colors of Sovaris's brothers. The colors of the Clerisy.

Ryn circled the pedestals in a bemused daze, overwhelmed by the weight of history, by the weight of the thing strapped across his back. The prison's trappings were unbelievably mundane—a simple cot, a wicker hanging chair, bundled manuscripts on a shelf. The creature comforts of a goddess with millennia to idle away.

"The Tree of Sorrows stripped Fraia of her power, and Vulheris used the hearts of her own sons to keep her here," Karxist said.

Kara stood before the nearest heart, hands hovering close without touching. Where the Heart of Sovaris resembled blue quartz with swirls of silver, this one was red and gold. The Heart of Kyvros—Elder of the Four, Lord of Fire, Forge, and Hearth. Patron of Sturvia.

Tears sparkled in Kara's eyes and ran unabashed down her cheeks. "To think, she existed here for so long—so real, so mortal." Her words rode a wave of breathless wonder. She caught Ryn looking at her and mustered a smile. "I only ever hear her in dreams. But I've never truly *seen* her. I'd like to, someday."

Ryn again considered telling her about his vision, but still held his tongue.

"Nothing living could pass between the hearts," Karxist said. "It was beyond the craft of any Earthborn to break that seal, till it failed through the course of time."

Horgrim cracked his staff upon the floor. "If you'd chopped down that damned tree, Fraia or her angels would have had the means."

"She would not allow it," Karxist said.

Horgrim turned a sour eye on the gorbling. Cryptwood twitched in sympathy with his mood. "Do you really expect us to believe Our Goddess denied her own freedom?"

Ryn's attention fixed on Blood Thorn's movement. *The Tree of Sorrows doesn't strip cryptwood of its power.*

"She would not deny the world a chance at destroying the Great Deceiver without mass death," Karxist said. "Consider, Noble Warden, the consequences—without the Tree, this place would have lost its power to strip the Deceiver of his."

"But how did Vulheris imprison her?" Ryn asked.

"As I told you at breakfast, ingesting the Four's blood gave Vulheris a strength and power that allowed him to deny the Sword," Karxist said. "When he realized the benefit, he drank more, though it eroded his sanity to do so. This gave him the will to force Mordyth Ral to direct its energies in new and unexpected ways."

Ryn remembered from his vision a vat of some golden substance into which Vulheris had dipped his hand—not to anoint himself, but to drink. "But why use only three of the hearts?"

"Vulheris saw how grievously our kind had suffered from the Devastation he had wrought when the Sword had control of him," Karxist said. "And he knew, too, of our heartfelt desire to atone for our part in the events that led to it. Many of our kind still lived in the world at large, among mankind. As word spread of our complicity in Mordyth Ral's forging, humans turned against us."

Karxist rested his palm on a heart of purest white and shimmering diamond. Mygalor—Lord of Air, Wind, and Storm. Patron of Jendalia. "Through his madness, Vulheris still found the will to leave one heart free, to serve as the key for all our kin to find their way to safety here in Gostemere. Only the Four could ever see through the Veil. Without Sovaris's heart, even those who know where Gostemere lies find themselves misdirected and unable to reach it." His ears drooped. "The time came all too soon when Sovaris's heart did not return, for no more Earthborn remained alive in the World Beyond. So few had survived."

Ryn eyed the hearts in turn. "I've seen the Four's power manifest through Josalind, how fickle and unpredictable it is." He turned and faced Karxist square. "I still can't believe that having them 'reborn' through her is going to create some entity as powerful as you say."

"We can't know what Josalind might become, when Four are One, but Our Goddess might." Kara turned from Kyvros's heart to address them all. "This may be what Fraia wants, why she had us come to bear witness. Whether with Xang's skull or through Josalind's rebirth with the Four, Fraia would see the Deceiver destroyed. She has trusted us to see this done, by whatever means."

Ryn and Horgrim gawped at each other, then at her. She ignored them both.

Karxist bowed low. "Fraia's faith in you is well placed, Wise Herald."

Kara dipped her head in return. "We do what we can, with what Grace sees fit to provide, First Minister. I presume the rebirth involves a ritual?"

"At dawn, tomorrow," Karxist said. "Preparations are underway."

"With some manner of bloodletting?"

Karxist's ears turned back, reminding Ryn of nothing less than a rabbit on its guard. "The hearts will be brought together, then Our Lady Josalind must, by her own hand, spill her blood and anoint them."

Ryn's gut sank. "What else?"

Karxist bowed his head. "Please understand, Sword-Bearer, these are but crude details of something truly glorious."

A hot flash of dread left Ryn storming toward him. "Out with it."

"Our Lady Josalind's own heart must be removed at the opportune moment," Karxist said.

Kara caught Ryn's arm before a fist could fly. Her weight came to bear so heavily against him, the screaming protest from his chest smothered all else. He planted his heels and clenched his jaw against the pain.

"Blessed be us all who are fortunate enough to bear witness," Kara said.

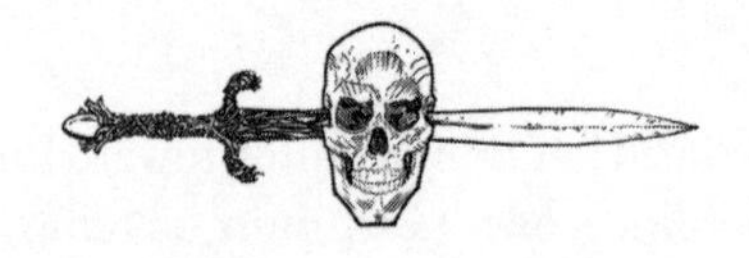

THIRTY-NINE

Grace Above, don't tell me you believed that cartload of demon's dung," Horgrim said, once they had left the cavern and reached a corner beyond range of those mushroom ears.

Kara grimaced and wiped her chin. "There's no need to spit, old lion." She sagged against the wall, looking even more tired and haggard than before.

Ryn remembered her shaky hand, pouring tea. "This place . . . it wears on you, doesn't it?"

Horgrim steadied her. "Like I said before, what Our Goddess grants lasts only so long as Her Grace can reach us."

The knots in Ryn's shoulders conspired to make his chest ache all the more. "That deranged mudball means to cut out her heart."

"He does believe it's for the good of us all," Kara said.

Ryn looked sideways at her. "You don't trust him."

"I don't know him," she said. "As for the Four, I suspect it's selfish need that motivates them most of all."

Ryn nodded. "All they care about is being able to walk the earth again—I'm sure of it. They want to see this done before Josalind can have second thoughts, before we can move to stop it."

"Indeed," Kara said. "And we don't know what manner of being will come of this rebirth, given their state of mind. It's too much of a risk."

When she said nothing more, Ryn gave her a hard look. "Is that all? I thought you might say you don't hold with sacrificing an innocent, either."

Horgrim growled. "Tread lightly, swordling."

"It certainly never was my first choice," Kara said.

"What was?" Ryn asked.

She chewed her lip. "To learn how Our Goddess was trapped here in the hope it would give us a weapon against Xang other than the Sword."

"Well, we haven't quite found that, have we?" Ryn said, making no effort to mask his sarcasm. "You've 'borne witness' as Fraia asked of you. What now?"

Kara looked to Horgrim. Something unspoken passed between them before her attention returned to Ryn. "We need you to talk some sense into Josalind."

"'Talk'?" Ryn scoffed. "We need a sound plan beyond that."

Ryn found Josalind on a terrace that overlooked the waterfall. Astrig kept her company. So did Grist, the dolusk whom Ryn had to thank for the aches in his chest.

Those beady yellow eyes regarded him through the slits of Grist's naturally armored face. "Salve make better, Sword-Bearer?"

That gravel voice mangled the common tongue bloody. Coupled with his size, it gave the impression that Grist was a dull wit. Ryn suspected that dismissing the dolusk as some stupid hulk would be a mistake. "It does, my thanks." He'd just about gotten used to the salve's acrid smell. "Could we have some privacy, please?"

Grist didn't budge. "I keep safe."

Until you cut her heart out. "I've been doing that for months," Ryn said.

The dolusk's weight shifted from one foot to the other. "Not be far." He lumbered off. The top of his head just cleared the archway.

Astrig indulged in a long cat stretch. "Shall I go as well, man-child?"

Ryn wandered to the edge of the terrace. In lieu of a proper rail, it had only a raised lip, ankle high. He looked over. Oma waited within sight two levels below—as planned. Better if Astrig remained. "That's not necessary, but a little privacy would be appreciated."

After she had retreated to the far side of the terrace, Ryn sat down on the bench beside Josalind. The late afternoon sun painted the mists from the falls' thunderous cascade with rainbow halos. He'd never seen such a wonder, but she only had eyes for the Heart of Sovaris, cradled in her palms. The stone, the specter within, had already claimed her.

"I can hear her now," she said. "So much better than before."

Ryn considered throwing the damned thing into the mists. He stuck his hands under his thighs to keep them out of trouble. "What does she say?"

"Time runs out. This has to happen, before Xang has a chance to gather strength."

"This isn't right, Josalind."

"Spit, spunk, and arse boils—what has *that* to do with anything? When has it ever?" She rubbed her brow with the back of her hand. "It's needed, Ryn. That's what matters."

He took her hand and squeezed it. The Heart of Sovaris slipped from her grasp and hit the terrace with a crack. She gasped and made a lunge for it, but he held her back. Her sharp elbow caught his ribs. "Let go of me."

Ryn gasped from sharp bursts of pain but didn't let go. He couldn't. "Leave it and just listen to me—you don't have to do this. We can find some other way." His voice cracked as he fought to draw a decent breath. "Please, Josalind. There is something off about this. I don't trust Karxist or the Four. Neither does Kara."

"Since when do you trust her? Those Sevrendine have been the prickle in our pudding from the start."

"I trust them more than anyone in Gostemere, that's for damned sure," Ryn said. "This is happening too quick."

"I've been bearing straight for this my whole life. It's taken too long already."

"But you will die, Josalind. In every way that matters."

"Some part of me won't. But if I'm wrong, it still won't be for naught. There's a reason for it, a good one."

His throat burned with a sudden ache. "Not good enough."

"I've lived with nothing but misery and doubt my whole life—you can't understand what it's like to be a child feared by your own family." She brushed her fingers along his jaw. "I need that pain gone, Ryn. That won't happen till I'm something else."

"No." He pulled her hand away. "When we met, you were bitter, alone, certain no one and nothing could help."

"It doesn't—"

"But you weren't the sort to just give up—you were strong."

"You're not wrong, Ryn." She looked to her feet. "But things were different—"

He gave her hand a yank. "The only thing different is now you know the reason for it all."

She closed her eyes tight to smother the tears. "Yes, and I know what needs doing."

"You think I don't know what it's like to be broken inside?" He'd begun to shout and didn't care how it echoed. "That doesn't mean you give up. So long as you keep fighting, there's always a chance."

"You don't understand—"

"No, I don't. What are you not telling me?"

"Nothing."

"Don't lie to me."

"I'm not."

Ryn winced as his ribs flared up and stole his anger away. He cleared his throat, mindful of how Astrig eyed them from a distance, and lowered his voice so she wouldn't hear what he said next. "I can't lose you. I—"

Josalind pressed her fingers to his lips before he could utter that fateful word. "*Don't.* Please don't. We had one bonny night. That is all."

Ryn ignored the ache her denial provoked. He rose, faced Sovaris's heart where it lay near Josalind's feet, and slipped Mordyth Ral from his shoulder.

"What do you intend, man-child?" Astrig called.

"To get an honest answer out of Sovaris. I expect she can still feel pain," Ryn said.

The color fled Josalind's face. "You can't."

"I will." He took Mordyth Ral by the hilt and shook it free of its leather sleeve. The witch-iron manacles still muzzled the Sword, but if he dug the blade's tip into the heart, maybe it would be no different than poking mortal flesh with a glowing poker.

An interesting hypothesis.

"I'm trying to save you from using that thing, you damned fool." Josalind surged to her feet, fists balled, eyes blazing through the tears. "You want *truth*? Here it is—I'd rather see the end of me than let that thing make a monster of you." She hugged her arms to her chest. "Don't you see? I can't let you leave here to go after Xang."

Ryn just looked at her, too overcome for words.

"I just can't, no matter the cost," she said, her voice small.

"You love me." She might not have been willing to say it, but Ryn was sure she did.

A shudder heaved through her. "Just let me go—for your own sake."

He let the Sword sink until its tip scraped the terrace stone, overcome by a forlorn anger that gnawed him hollow.

Flesh is weak.

"No." He stepped close and touched her cheek. "Don't you put a burden like that on me. We will find another way. But we have to leave this place, together—*now*."

She stepped away. "I won't risk it."

They didn't have time for further debate. Ryn cast the Sword down on the bench and pulled the thorn from under his cuff. He closed on her with a quick step, and pricked the back of her hand.

She yanked back with a gasp. "What have you—" Her eyes rolled back. Ryn caught her as she slumped. A single tear's worth—Oma had said that should be enough martichora venom to knock Josalind out without doing any permanent harm.

Astrig charged over, her claws screeching on the stone. "What possesses you?"

"The one thing sure to make idiots of even wise men." Ryn eased Josalind down on the terrace, grimacing as his ribs complained. She had begun to convulse, but not violently so. He looked the martichora in the eye. "I intend to fly her out of here. Is that agreeable?"

Astrig's broad mouth stretched into a toothy grin. "They forbid us to eat the sheep—what nonsense is that?" She arched her wings and reared back. "Let us be gone."

Ryn rushed to the terrace's edge and waved Oma up. "Kara and Horgrim are—"

Astrig shrieked.

A weighted and barbed net that must have been flung from a terrace above had her tangled up. Ryn's hand went for a longsword that wasn't there. All he had was Mordyth Ral—he hadn't wanted to risk suspicion by strapping on all his gear. Astrig tried to free herself, but the metal barbs cut her flesh. She whined and gnashed her teeth with helpless fury. Ryn took up the Sword to try to cut her loose.

"I told you, I keep my ears earth-rooted."

Ryn growled at the sound of that calm and measured voice.

Karxist stepped out onto the terrace. "Nothing happens in Gostemere without my knowledge."

Grist followed with several more of his kind. One dolusk carried another net, two others carried catchpoles. Grist's bucket-fists hefted a staff of blackened iron that must have been ten feet long. His beady eyes burned angry. "You lie."

The sweep of Oma's wings buffeted him from behind. "Sister mine—what wickedness is this?"

Astrig clacked her claws on the stone. "Your deception was better wrought in the dark, Oma."

"Step away from Our Lady Josalind and give up Mordyth Ral," Karxist said.

Grist spun the staff hand over hand with practiced ease. His kin spread out in a half circle.

Ryn backed away—toward the Heart of Sovaris. "What do you mean to do, Karxist—kill me so you can claim the Sword?"

"I will suffer no life to be taken in Gostemere but the Great Deceiver's."

Ryn fixed him with a cold look. "I will." He booted the Heart of Sovaris over the terrace's edge. *"Oma."*

The martichora dove after it. The attention of Karxist and the dolusks followed. Ryn took Mordyth Ral by the hilt in both hands. *How keen is your edge?*

The Sword thrummed. **I shatter diamond.**

Ryn brought the blade down on the stone bench. The stone cracked and the manacle splintered with a shrill ring. He shook the other manacle off over the pommel and wedged the length of chain into his belt—a bit of insurance he loathed to leave behind.

"Do you think Mordyth Ral will so easily obey you?" Karxist asked. "Have you learned nothing?"

Ryn barely heard him over the sudden roar in his head. A searing flare threatened to burn away all reason. *Weaken the Earthborn, but no more.*

I am not yours to command, Heir of Aegias.

It's the only way we're going to get out of here—you cut down the Four, surely you don't want to see them restored?

I will suffer it, if it is the most expedient means by which to end the Great Deceiver. He is the greater evil. Once he and Fraia are gone, we will again deny the Four their freedoms.

Grist crept around his flank, as well as a giant could creep. Ryn backed toward the edge of the terrace. That staff would make bloody mush of him with one blow.

You are not the only hope we have.

Hope is meaningless. There is only the sum and measure of opposing forces. I alone tip the Balance.

Karxist walked toward Ryn, hands folded across his belly. "The Sword opposes you."

"The Sword won't tolerate your reborn god for long. It will work to put the Four back in their box."

A slight smile twitched that slit-mouth. "That's to be expected. Measures will be taken."

Ryn hissed in frustration at the mudball's serene certainty and edged toward Astrig. She clawed and gnawed at the barbed netting, smeared in blood from nose to tail. He had no leverage at all with which to compel the Sword—no threat, no promise, no flaw of character to exploit. With the dolusks closing in, he had no choice but the hard way. His odds weren't worth green pennies.

"Surrender, Sword-Bearer," Karxist said. "There is no point to this."

A big shadow glided over the terrace.

Horgrim dropped from the sky and landed in a crouch within easy reach of Grist's staff. That mass of iron swung quick, as if Grist had expected him, but Horgrim moved faster yet. He tumbled away with an acrobat's grace and came up behind the dolusk with the net. Blood Thorn caught the setting sun with the shimmer of rustled silk as it cut an arc. The dolusk went down with a roar, hamstrung behind the knees.

Ryn used the distraction to slice through the net and free Astrig. She caught his shirt and yanked him aside.

The loop of a catchpole brushed his head as he stumbled around for balance. Fiery shards lanced his chest and left him gasping. "Take Josalind—go."

A dolusk loomed over him, blotting out the sky. Ryn ducked under those massive arms. The end of the catchpole snapped around to club him. Mordyth Ral sheared it in half with ease.

No.

Ryn's skull exploded with such hot agony, it smothered all else. He fell to his knees.

Kill the spawn of the Invader Goddess.

He felt that swirling warmth as Mordyth Ral began to feed—but not nearly with the dire appetite that it had in Tanasgeld after starving for centuries. Instead of gulps, it sipped, siphoning just a trickle of energy from life across the valley that few would notice. As the Sword had claimed in Tanasgeld, it took only what it needed for the task at hand, dispersing its hunger as broadly as possible to avoid needless death. Against a god, that need ramped with such depth and urgency that mass death couldn't be avoided. But the effort to kill a warden—that equated to swatting a fly.

Ryn tried and failed to drop the Sword, his fingers stiffer than hooks of iron hammered to form. *I won't.* What he wanted didn't matter. His body flung itself up—a string puppet, empty of will.

Astrig still hadn't taken Josalind away. She attacked the dolusk who'd tried to snare Ryn, tearing at that armored hide with stinger and claw. Her wings misted the air with crimson from scores of minor cuts as they beat madly for balance. The Sword swelled Ryn's senses so that he smelled nothing but blood, even tasted it, rich and warm from the vein, from Astrig, the dolusks, and Horgrim from where he'd taken a scratch.

We will have him.

Horgrim had Grist on the defensive—not even the dolusk's slab of iron measured up to Blood Thorn. Pieces of it littered the terrace. But Horgrim couldn't slip past Grist's guard without risking his own neck—the other dolusk with a catchpole threatened his flank. The poor bugger that Horgrim had hamstrung dragged himself away on his elbows. The slick of green blood he trailed smeared Ryn's tongue with sulfur.

Ryn walked toward them, a prisoner in his own body, barely able to think past the clash of anvils between his ears. He fought to recognize that figure who wielded a white sword as Horgrim instead of a *thing* that was too foul and twisted to live. His arms raised Mordyth Ral high.

The corner of his mind still his own noted how Karxist just stood there, watching, that cursed non-smile fixed on his mud-ball face. Ryn *did* want to kill someone—ram Mordyth Ral through the little bastard's guts to see what color came out. Instead, he would kill a good man. Just like that night in Sablewood, when he'd killed Quintan, his friend, for committing the sin of conscience.

When he'd let a village be slaughtered.

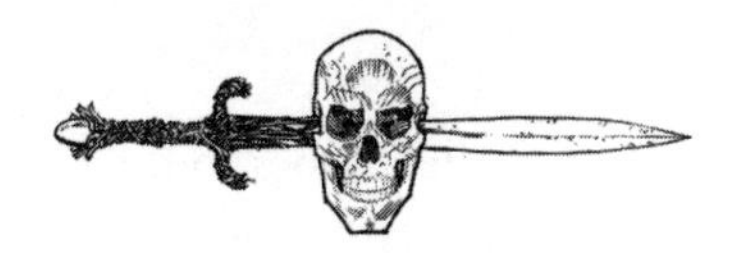

FORTY

rist's staff lost more iron to Blood Thorn. The thing called Horgrim ducked away from the other dolusk's catchpole but slipped on a trail of gore. It caught its footing before Grist could land a quick jab.

Ryn stepped over Josalind, intent on his prey.

Let all abomination be cleansed.

His foot froze on the next step, skull throbbing so hard his eyes ached. *No.*

Defiance is the path to pain.

It's the path to freedom. It had been all along. Quintan must have known it that night in Sablewood, but Ryn had been too cowered by duty and his oath to the Clerisy to understand. Punching Her Ladyship for maligning Quintan's memory, challenging Aelin and Tovald at the Claw, turning apostate to flee with Josalind—had they all been steps to this moment, where everything hinged on denying this cursed piece of metal?

Find your anchor. So Aegias's spirit had said . . . while standing over Sara and Tamantha's bodies.

For the first time since Sablewood, Ryn didn't hide from those memories. All the guilt, all the grief, all the doubt he had suffered since that night pierced his soul with fresh cruelty and he embraced it.

I can free you of this misery. Did that soulless voice tremble with a speck of desperation?

Ryn lingered on every detail he could recall. The smell of ruptured bowels, the lard-like texture of Sara's frostbitten flesh, the gurgle Quintan made as he died.

The pain lost its grip. Ryn again saw Horgrim as the man he was.

He swung Mordyth Ral at Karxist's head, aiming to knock him senseless with the flat of the blade. As much as he might have relished the idea, he wouldn't kill an unarmed man, no matter the color in his veins.

Karxist blocked the blow with his bare arm. His opposite fist struck Ryn's bandaged chest, thankfully with less power than he knew the gorbling capable. Still, Ryn staggered back, choking on his own breath, lungs knotted with spasms. Cracked ribs screamed like they'd been doused with molten lead, leaving him certain one or more had broken completely.

"You show me mercy but would doom thousands to the Sword." Karxist stalked him with a measured step. "All for something that was never yours. She is ours and she will curse you for this."

Ryn threw all he had into a desperate attack before he blacked out from the pain and the lack of air. He feinted high from the right. Karxist dodged away, straight into a left hook. The blow hardly fazed him and sprained Ryn's knuckles. He followed up with Mordyth Ral's pommel square to Karxist's temple. That was enough to knock the little bastard out cold.

Seized lungs broke free with a wheezy rasp. Ryn sorely wanted to suck air by the bucket, but his ribs could bear only timid sips. He pulled the half manacle from his belt, slid it over Mordyth Ral's hilt till it wedged against the cross guard, wrapped the loose end of chain around the grip, and held the whole sloppy assembly together with both hands. He may have managed to break the Sword's hold for now, but only an idiot would dare carry the thing around bare-handed.

Astrig's dolusk lay twitching and frothing at the mouth, taken down at last by her venom.

"He will live, but would rather not for a while," she said.

Horgrim had managed to leave the last dolusk with a catchpole nursing a belly wound. Shallow wounds scored Grist's armored hide. His big iron staff had been hacked to a cudgel. He flung the last of it straight at Horgrim's head. The warden ducked and lunged for Grist's groin. He stopped short when Blood Thorn had dimpled that big toga far enough to grab the dolusk's attention. Grist froze and growled something in his own tongue.

Metal scuffed on stone.

A dozen heads poked over the edge of the terrace above. Gorbling and dolusk and salamandar, the later wreathed by wisps of smoke. Weapons glimmered dull in the fading daylight. The distance was too great for a man to jump, but these weren't men.

Ryn pointed Mordyth Ral at Karxist's throat in the hope the threat to their leader would cower them. "Keep your distance—it's over." Considering how long the Earthborn had lived here, fading away in isolation, he didn't expect much in the way of bold action.

They didn't retreat, but they didn't attack, either. Ryn looked to Astrig. "Take Josalind—and where in Hells is the help?" Oma and Ashavinx carried no passengers to hinder use of their bows, but he didn't see a single martichora arrow sticking out of any Earthborn.

"Keeping those others busy." Astrig scooped up Josalind and took wing. "I will send Oma."

Ryn matched Grist's glare and didn't drop his guard until he heard the flap of leathery wings. He snatched up Mordyth Ral's sleeve and stuffed the Sword into it as Oma caught him under the arms. She hoisted him high overhead and plunked him down on her back. He almost swooned from the squeeze of his chest. Horgrim took to Ashavinx.

Grist flung his bucket-fists overhead. "I come for you, Godbane."

Oma threw herself off the terrace and dove steep before her wings carried them up again. Ryn's stomach complained with a queasy flop. There were some things no sane man could ever get accustomed to.

"Where's the Heart?" he asked.

Oma patted her haversack. "Well tucked."

And then Ryn saw Astrig's "others." The griffins.

Gods be damned.

Kara and Irsta shot past with three on their tail. A shard of lightning tore the air. Two griffins shrieked as their eagle's wings were clipped and they listed in drunken spirals. Blood Thorn returned to

Horgrim's waiting hand. The third griffin broke off pursuit with an angry squawk.

A dozen or more had turned after Astrig as she bore Josalind over the waterfall and into the mountains.

Ryn slung Mordyth Ral's sleeve across his back. "Can you catch up?"

"The odds are poor, man-child," Oma said.

A fireball shot past with a fluttering roar so close, Ryn smelled the scorch of his own hair. "Gods' Grace!" He ducked and looked back but saw no catapult or other engine that might have flung it. Another came flying from the terrace above the one where he'd left Karxist, to all appearances thrown, *by hand*, by one of the figures who stood there. One of the salamandars? The fireball cut a smoking arc for about three hundred yards and fell short of them.

Horgrim and Kara settled onto their flanks. Irsta carried the bundle with Ryn's gear. Astrig continued to pull away from them, but the griffins looked to be gaining on her. The air grew cold and thin as they climbed out of the valley.

Ryn had no idea where the Tree of Sorrows's Veil ended. He could only hope the griffins had the intelligence to know and would care enough to turn back before they flew too far and the Veil's misdirection magic prevented their return home. Icy peaks rose on each side. He shivered and hugged Oma's warmth. Trousers and shirt did little to cut the chill. The miles passed. His skin burned, then went numb. A dull ache settled into his joints. It was trial enough to muster a decent breath, without fits of shivers.

"Beware, man-child."

The griffins had turned back but weren't giving up.

They swarmed in a fury of hooked claws and snapping beaks. Oma veered and swooped. Ryn was no stranger to fighting on horseback but hanging in the sky without stirrup or saddle proved altogether different. He kept thighs and arms tight while Oma ripped through the griffins. Screeches and roars tore the air. Blood sprayed and splashed warm down his side. Oma jerked left with a howl and almost dumped him. Her tail whipped around and stabbed a griffin in the throat. It convulsed and dropped out of sight.

And then they were through. Kara and Horgrim still rode their flanks. He couldn't tell how much of the blood Irsta and Ashavinx wore was their own.

Oma had lost speed and groaned with each flap. Her left wing bore a tear. Ryn looked for Astrig and Josalind. "Where are they?"

One desperate mile passed, then another, before a martichora's trumpet call carried faint on the air.

"There, man-child," Oma said, as she banked.

Astrig had found a mountain vale with warmth and shelter enough to be free of snow, carpeted with patches of green and violet. They joined her along the calm waters of a tarn. Ryn slid off Oma's back and went to Josalind. She lay on a bed of lichen, still out. He knelt and brushed his fingers along her cheek.

"I hear Fisherfolk women enjoy filleting a man's plug-tail if he raises a hand to them," Horgrim said. "Usually as he sleeps."

"I didn't actually hit her." Ryn found himself bottled up with feelings he didn't care to express, embarrassed now by how close he'd come to admitting his love for her.

"No, but consider it fair warning, all the same."

"We can't stay here the night," Ryn said in an effort to change the subject. "There's no fuel for a fire."

Horgrim ground his staff into the earth. "Mordyth Ral almost had you back there, didn't it?"

Ryn looked up at him. "If you're asking if I've almost killed you twice now, the answer is yes."

"And what stopped you this time?"

"Guilt." Ryn rubbed his brow. A headache had begun to nag. "Have we just damned the world?"

"Well, that scheme of Karxist's has plenty of holes in it," Horgrim said. "Flush out the Deceiver?" He snorted. "The Great Devil is spook and shadow, that creeping thing you can only glimpse from the corner of your eye. If not for the power his sorcerer priests still wield in his name, I would think he crawled into a hole and died after Vulheris struck him down."

"But he didn't," Ryn said. No matter how he might move the pieces around in his head, weigh one course against another, it came down to him, Xang, and Mordyth Ral, and the ruin they were doomed to wreak.

Unless the stirrings of an idea gave him a reasonable alternative.

Ryn watched Kara as she worked her way among the martichora to address their wounds. She suffered the pain only to heal the worst of the gashes Ashavinx had taken, and the tears in Irsta's and Oma's wings. Still, he could only marvel at her fortitude. It left him humbled to watch her endure such suffering for another's sake, to push herself so far when Gostemere had given her little chance to recover from Viglias.

He tried to beg off when his turn came, but she wouldn't have it. She freed him of all but a lingering ache and a shortness of breath. He relished having some discomfort, but not for the reasons he might have had back at the Claw with the hair shirt. It reminded him that he was human, still a man distinct from the Sword. He needed that assurance.

The lesser moon had crested the horizon by the time they left the mountains. Ryn put them somewhere near Riverhead and its fabled gold mines at the headwaters of the Beris River. The river's fertile valley was well settled and home to a large abbey with its own garrison. He remembered little else from the geography lessons of his youth, but that was enough.

"Find us a dark spot," he told Oma.

Astrig called out from their right. Her silhouette against the starry sky wove about erratically. A stream of Fisherfolk curses polluted the air.

Gods be damned. Josalind hadn't woken happy. It had been anyone's guess for how long martichora venom would keep her under with the Four involved. The forested hills below looked untamed enough—Ryn saw no light and smelled no fire on the damp air. "Tell her to put down where she can."

Oma trumpeted the message. They followed after as Astrig found a hilltop clearing.

Josalind barely waited for Ryn's feet to touch the ground. He never saw it coming. Her palms caught him square in the chest and knocked him onto his rump. No shock of divine power this time—her own anger gave strength enough.

She loomed over him with balled fists. "You selfish, *windward-greasing hog rider*."

Ryn had picked up enough Fisherfolk slang by now to know he'd just been accused of buggering pigs. He took Horgrim's warning to heart and covered his "plug-tail" in case she decided to follow up with her feet. Then her eyes flashed silver. He remembered those grenlich up north that she had cooked to the bone and cowered away with sudden fear.

But a blast of holy fire didn't scorch him. Josalind hugged herself tight and turned on Astrig. "You promised to serve me."

The martichora bowed her head. "No, blessed child, I vowed to *protect* you."

"We cherish you dearly, but it's not affection alone that compels us," Oma added. "As dire as the need may be, we cared not for the smell of things in Gostemere."

Ryn climbed to his feet. "See? Don't be so eager to martyr yourself, don't be so quick to give up on being who you are." He dared lay his hand on her arm. "I don't need you to do that for me."

Josalind didn't warm to his touch, or even look at him. "Just tell me you have Sovaris's heart."

Oma had returned it to him. He let his hand drop and patted his belt pouch. "We can find our way back . . . *if* we must."

"We have a better use for it than that," Kara said.

"And what would that be?" Ryn asked.

The crisp look in Kara's eyes rivaled the fire in Josalind's. "Our Lady Sovaris is going to tell us where Xang is to be resurrected."

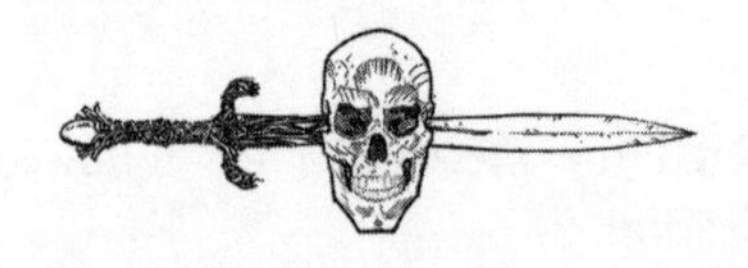

FORTY-ONE

yn edged between Josalind and Kara, his hackles raised by the latter's predatory tone.

Josalind held her ground. "What are you talking about?"

"You know full well." Kara came closer. She had found a stick to serve as a cane and hobbled along with small steps, but crippling exhaustion did little to diminish that stare. "The heart is Sovaris's essence. She is in there and she can speak with us."

"Thc dead have foresight." Horgrim ran his fingers down Blood Thorn's length. "I said before—our Honored Dead back home sometimes speak of things to come."

"I doubt it's any different for a dead god," Kara said. "Their power to know the future might even be greater."

Josalind stepped back behind Ryn. "Pray to Fraia, then—get her to go gaff with your Honored Dead."

"It's needy to ask for what's already before me."

"Like Karxist said, the Four aren't really dead," Ryn said.

"They may be dead enough—we won't know until we ask, will we?" Kara almost stepped on Ryn's toes now, but he didn't budge. She gave him one of those pleasant smiles. "You are in my way."

Ryn's hand strayed to the longsword of plain steel that once again rode at his hip. "Am I?"

Horgrim growled. "Careful."

"Sovaris won't just answer a question you put to her," Josalind said, words clipped with pain. "She's in a choice foul mood right now."

"Does she want to see Xang resurrected?" Kara asked.

"She doesn't want to see Mordyth Ral kill thousands to stop it," Josalind said.

"That's why we must act quickly," Kara said. "Before his followers can complete the ritual."

"That won't matter," Josalind said. "Ryn will still have to use Mordyth Ral. There's no telling how far its hunger will reach. Xang isn't important—his father is. We need to go back to Gostemere. The Four must be reborn." Her words drifted into a ragged sigh. "It's our only chance."

Ryn stepped clear of the women and shrugged Mordyth Ral from his shoulder. "No, it isn't."

Horgrim's lips peeled back. "And just what do you think you're doing?"

"In Gostemere, the Tree of Sorrows didn't muzzle Mordyth Ral or Blood Thorn," Ryn said. "Cryptwood may grow by Fraia's will, but it's still tied more to the earth than it is to Her—just like Mordyth Ral. If it wasn't, it wouldn't have worked within the Veil."

"You're not seriously—" Horgrim began.

"We need to test this," Ryn said. "It's the one chance we have." *The only chance I have.*

Horgrim snorted. "A chance—is that what you call it?"

Kara eyed them both. "Just what are you two going on about?"

"Indulge me for a moment, My Herald," Horgrim said, before fixing Ryn with an icy stare. "Let's recount the record, shall we? In Tanasgeld, you almost sucked the life from an entire city."

Ryn conceded the point with a contrite nod. It didn't matter that those lives had been spared—the horror of what could have happened remained ripe. "The Sword takes what it needs as it needs it."

His honesty earned a nod of respect.

"Has it been quiet since?" Horgrim asked. "Surely, it must wear at you, as the Four do at Josalind."

"I can feel it poking from time to time," Ryn said. That narrowed look in the warden's eye left him unwilling to admit he heard its voice.

"When you wanted me to help Kara save Horgrim's life, it fought you," Josalind said. "You looked like your head might burst."

Of course, she'd cling to anything that argued in favor of returning to Gostemere for his sake. Ryn couldn't help but love her for it, though it left him fuming.

"Despite being muzzled by witch iron," Horgrim said.

"And in Gostemere, it cared only to see you dead—it refused to attack the Earthborn." Ryn looked Horgrim square. "Do you think I don't see how it tests me by degrees? But if Karxist's plan isn't an option, what other choice have we?"

"You told me guilt stayed your hand in Gostemere," Horgrim said. "Do you claim some power over the Sword that Aegias lacked?"

"I'm learning how to take the boar by the tusks, as Aegias did," Ryn said. *Find your anchor*—the Prince Messiah had obviously found his, no doubt in his remorse for the innocent lives he'd taken in war.

"How can you know what Aegias did?" Kara asked. "No works sanctioned by the Clerisy give such detail."

"I . . ." Ryn huffed and rubbed at his brow. *Gods be damned.* He could see no other way to win their trust. "In Tanasgeld, in that moment before I took up the Sword, I had a vision . . . of Aegias."

Both of Horgrim's eyebrows peaked. "Indeed—and you hold this for truth?"

"I wasn't sure. I'm still not." Ryn held Mordyth Ral up by its sleeve. Even now, he found it so easy for the gleam of moonlight from that goose-egg pommel to bewitch him. "What Aegias's spirit told me worked today—that I do know."

He dragged his eyes from Mordyth Ral and looked between the Sevrendine. "Aegias was just a man—a sinner and a sufferer like me, like anyone. But he set a standard for himself and struggled to live by it, and he didn't do it alone. That's how he kept the Sword from breaking him. If the Sword frightens you so much, then help me, as his paladins helped him."

Horgrim looked to Kara, but she just regarded Ryn with that uncomfortable stare.

"I didn't want this," Ryn said with such earnestness, his voice broke and his eyes welled. "I still don't. If I thought the world would be better for it, I'd gladly agree to be locked up in your gilded cage. But it won't be—surely, you can see that? Mordyth Ral is too great a threat. That sorcerer Olparc already told us that fear of the Sword is driving Xang's followers to rush his resurrection. Do you think they won't come for it—that *Xang* won't? The best way to protect it is to use it and take the fight to them."

"How?" Kara asked.

"However we can." Ryn looked to Josalind. "But we can't let fear keep us from using the most powerful weapon we have."

She appeared ready to contradict him, but then she tossed her head and looked away with arms crossed.

Horgrim gave Ryn's shoulder a squeeze. "It's the struggle that makes us better, or at least kills us quick." His icy gaze softened with an empathy and understanding Ryn hadn't seen before. "Cowards only end up with a surplus of time to chew on their regret." He stepped back and thumped Blood Thorn against the earth. "Now, how do you want to do this?"

"You two are as reckless as she is," Kara said, though she hadn't said anything else to dissuade the experiment. She kept her distance, silhouetted by a gold shimmer.

Ryn couldn't fault her for calling upon Fraia's Grace as a defense, futile as it may be if he couldn't contain the Sword. Josalind held to the shadows by the martichora. He looked over his shoulder at Horgrim. "Ready?"

The warden held Blood Thorn high in a two-handed grip, poised to take Ryn's head. "By the Deceiver's black arse, what do you think?" he said. "But don't let that stop you."

Ryn wrapped his hand around the uncomfortable weave of Mordyth Ral's hilt, felt it stir and pulse under his touch, and drew it.

As in Tanasgeld, the Sword's hum deepened into a roar he couldn't hear, a subtle assault sure to melt marrow from bone. That prismatic swirl danced at the edge of sight. Even shrouded by evening's twilight, Ryn could see it. The life Mordyth Ral stole from all around poured through him with a warm tingle. As in Gostemere, it only sipped—from the martichora, from the night creatures that hid around them, from each tree and blade of grass. The reason it felt compelled to feed at all stood not forty feet away—Kara and Josalind, heralds of the Invader Goddess and her spawn.

The Sword latched on to the two women like a magnet to iron with the need to draw more, to snatch their last gasp of life. Ryn felt, too, the abrasive rub of some other being, defiled beyond redemption by her parentage. The rub originated from the pouch on his belt—Sovaris's heart. Mordyth Ral didn't hunger for the goddess as it did the women—the Sword had dealt with Sovaris to its satisfaction long ago—but Ryn's heightened senses still caught the goddess's terror as she recoiled.

He clung to his memories of Sablewood, the smell of shite and blood, the toll of the abbey's bells. Still, he tasted the life leeching from Kara and relished it. Josalind, too—the flavor of her soul recalled that night on the beach. Perverse urges spawned by the Sword's hunger threatened to spoil the memory.

He felt for Horgrim but didn't find him. Only a humming pillar of power he couldn't breach, stark and pristine—Blood Thorn. *He* could still see Horgrim. Mordyth Ral, of course, knew where the warden stood and wanted him no less dead than before, but its hunger couldn't touch him. Blood Thorn shielded him.

Enough.

They task me.

ENOUGH.

He tried to fling the Sword away. His arm refused to move. Josalind's heart beat like a bird desperate to escape its cage, as if he'd carved her chest open to wrap his fingers around it. Kara's Grace—

the revolting discharge of the Invader Goddess—sputtered and died. He savored the heady bouquet of the panic that engulfed her.

The Goddess's dog moved to strike him down—he heard the crackle and pop inside the joints of Horgrim's arm. Ryn's feet acted of their own accord, twisting him aside with unnatural speed. Cryptwood whistled past his ear.

He turned on Horgrim with a roar, fueled by a hateful disgust. This time, he would end it. This time, he would snuff the spark of the warden's soul.

No.

His skull exploded with an inferno of pain.

I am Ryn.

The assertion didn't stop him from attacking with a wild combination that left Horgrim on the defensive.

"Will they eat me?" Little Sara had asked. She nestled against his shoulder to smother her fear of the grenlich and escape the cold as he carried her from the forest, back to her mother in Sablewood.

"No, they won't eat you." But they butchered her, all the same.

"You're gonna keep me safe," Sara had said with a child's simple faith.

But I didn't.

Horgrim parried and counterattacked. Ryn clung to Sara's memory, to the sight of her lying there with her mother, dead in the crimson snow, certain his brain had melted to slag. He did the only thing he could—slow his arm as it moved to block.

Blood Thorn slipped through his softened defense. Its rounded tip thrust through his shoulder and grated bone. He cried out and grabbed that silken blade, cupped it tight between palm and fingers. Stubby thorns sprouted from the cryptwood to impale his hand.

He embraced the pain. *You won't control me.*

Mordyth Ral fell from his nerveless fingers.

The fire in his head blew out. Its absence left his shoulder and hand screaming that much louder. He let go and slumped back as Horgrim pulled free.

The warden balanced on the balls of his feet, ready for more.

Ryn cradled his arm against his stomach. He could still feel Mordyth Ral inside of him, the metallic blaze burning away his control, his sense of self. His stomach turned foul. He found himself hunched over, puking up what little he had to offer, blinded by starbursts as each heave roused fresh torment from his shoulder.

When it passed, he spat and wiped his mouth on the back of his hand. Horgrim helped him find his feet.

"Cryptwood protected you," Ryn said.

"From the Sword's hunger, yes; from your madness, no," Horgrim said.

"I'm gaining on it." Ryn turned after the others. The martichora had suffered only a whisper of the Sword's hunger and already shaken off the effects. But Kara had collapsed against Irsta. Josalind looked even worse, bone-pale and shaking to crumble. He tucked the fingers of his bad arm into his belt and reached for her. "Jos? Are you—"

She slapped his hand away with a hiss. "That hurt us, Ryn. Her pain, my pain—all the same." She clutched and yanked at her hair. "Buried in a box of nettles, scratching to get out, you pour oil and light a fire."

Ryn was certain Mordyth Ral hadn't actually bitten into Sovaris as it had Josalind and Kara, but its touch had no doubt forced the goddess to relive her past trauma.

Kara prompted Irsta to carry her over. Once the martichora had, Kara caught Josalind's hands and fought them down. She likely relied on Josalind's resistance as a brace to keep herself standing. "Then tell us, *My Lady Sovaris*, what we need to know," Kara said. "The Sword still hungers."

Her cold bluntness took Ryn aback. "I don't—"

Horgrim's hand landed on his shoulder. "You started this, swordling, let her finish it."

Ryn bristled. "I really don't care for that name."

The warden leaned close. "This needs doing, Ryn, and the threat of the Sword is the only angle we have."

Ryn couldn't deny it, nor did he have the vinegar to argue, but he refused to back away even as the air thickened with a static charge around the two women, just like it had in the inn back in Tanasgeld.

Josalind tossed her head and tried to twist away. Kara wouldn't let her. "Tell us, My Lady Sovaris."

The goddess's heart throbbed hot and flared with a silver-blue light in Ryn's belt pouch. "What in Hells?" He dumped it out on the ground, where it pulsed with a steady rhythm.

"We seem to have her attention," Horgrim said.

Josalind's eyes blazed to match the stone. Her shoulders pulled back and her head tilted to assume as haughty a posture as Kara's grip would allow. Ryn knew from that carriage, the calculating way she looked at Kara, that the Josalind he had come to cherish had gone. A sneer of disgust curled her lip, as if Kara were a beggar who courted a beating for daring to touch her. The expression was so foreign to Josalind that Ryn found himself taking a step back.

"Why do you task me so?" Sovaris asked.

"Apologies, My Lady, but you know the urgency of our need," Kara said. "Where will Xang be resurrected?"

"And when?" Ryn added.

Josalind rolled her head around to glare at him. "Gods Bane. Why do you deny her, deny us? For love? I loved once. I was theirs and they were mine and the world was ours. And then our cursed mother forged the means of our destruction."

Did she allude to divine incest with her brothers? Ryn didn't much care. What mattered was that Sovaris had known love and heartbreak. "Then you understand why I can't let Josalind martyr herself if there's any other way," he said.

A wail burst from Josalind's throat, thick with such tortured longing, the hairs on Ryn's neck tried to crawl away. "Misery and butchery and madness," she said. "That is what you will bring—Earth-Breaker, Soul-Taker, *Bane of All Things*."

A sudden wrath overcame Ryn, fueled as much by dread as anger. He staggered over to Mordyth Ral and pulled the broken witch-iron manacle from his belt. Blood soaked his side. Light-headedness had started to gain on him.

"Ryn—" Horgrim began.

"I started this, I *will* finish it." Ryn clapped the manacle around the blade below the hilt, and then picked the Sword up by it.

Kara flinched when he leaned in beside her. He brandished the pommel under Josalind's nose. But this wasn't Josalind, and he couldn't afford to let himself think so. "Tell us."

Mad hatred burned in her eyes. "As I suffer, so will she."

"I will see that you suffer more," Ryn said.

The fire in Josalind's eyes burned brighter.

Kara's arm crackled with a static charge against Ryn's. "Don't dare it, sweetie," she said in a strained whisper. "His grip on the Sword is hair thin."

Sovaris scowled, but her fire faded. "I see a place, lost to time, swallowed by swamp and sea . . . Sarenepra."

Ryn had never heard the name. He looked to Kara. She shook her head. "Where is that?" he asked.

"The swamp called Gloomen," Sovaris said.

The edge of that swamp lay maybe a hundred leagues to the west. "Thank you, My Lady," Ryn said. "Can you tell us when?"

"Time means little to me, Gods Bane, but soon—too soon."

Sovaris's fire snuffed out. Josalind gave them a bewildered look before her eyes glazed over and her legs failed.

Kara all but collapsed herself with the effort to ease Josalind down. "It's all right. She's just sapped."

Ryn was glad to hear it, even if nothing felt at all right. Fate meant to herd him toward a showdown with Xang and it refused to be denied.

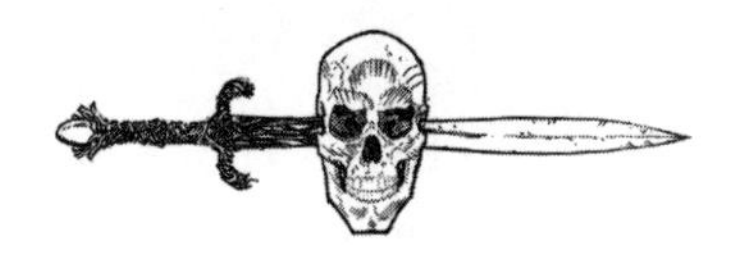

FORTY-TWO

Earth-Breaker, Soul-Taker, Bane of All Things.

Josalind woke with a start, anxious and confused. Anxious because of cloudy memories that might have been bits of a nightmare, but she knew weren't. Confused to find herself outdoors in a setting she didn't recognize. Sunlight came dappled through leafy branches that remained wholly green despite it being mid-autumn. She smelled the smoky damp of a spent fire nearby, and something else—a briny scent from far away. Not the smell of the north seas—this blue had a different flavor, hints of melon.

A big face with eyes the color of robin's eggs crowded her view of the sky. "Are you quite yourself, blessed child?" Astrig asked.

Yourself . . . myself. Josalind rolled the odd concepts around. Had there ever been a time in her life when she had been herself? When Kara bound her with witch iron, maybe, but even then, the Four's presence had lingered. She couldn't forget the horrors they'd shown her, of things past, of things to come.

She expected to feel them now, prowling in the shadows of her thoughts, wolves testing the firelight's edge, but she caught only a whisper of Sovaris. Her nose itched. She reached up to scratch it and felt the weight on her wrist, the bit of chain slap her ribs.

Witch iron.

Half a pair of manacles. No wonder she could barely hear them.

The thought of being bound again, muzzled again, should have stoked her ire. Instead, it left her relieved. She eyed Astrig. "You don't trust me."

Kara's face pushed in. "We chose to be prudent," she said. "What do you remember from last night?"

Hate. Despair. Rage to the brink of madness. And that from Sovaris alone. Josalind rubbed at her temple. "Enough."

Ryn. Not all the anger she'd felt last night had come from Sovaris. He'd drugged her—*poisoned* her. She understood his reasons, right enough, but still . . .

Ryn, bleeding.

She sat up with a start and almost swooned. Her stomach roiled and fuzzy blackness tinged her eyes. "Ryn was hurt."

Kara propped her up. "Easy, girl. He's fine. I only had the muster for half the job, but I sent him off with a proper field-dressing."

Josalind frowned. "Sent him off where?"

"The boys went into town this morning."

Morning. The slant of the sun meant midafternoon, then. "What town?"

"Sturvenwatch," Kara said. "We are on the eastern edge of Gloomen Swamp."

Josalind suffered a rising panic. "But they can't just *go into town.* The Clerisy will have warrants posted in every last ale house and outhouse across the—"

"They are being discreet," Kara said.

The way she said it sounded more like a hope than a fact. Josalind shared the feeling, considering the debacle in Viglias with Captain Setrys.

"We know nothing about this place, Sarenepra," Kara added. "They expect someone in that town might." She gave a shrewd look. "Unless you . . ."

Josalind shook her head. She knew no more than what she'd already told them . . . than *Sovaris* had. She drew her knees to her chest and shivered. The sun held a warmth she craved, but not enough. There could never be enough. She'd thought the Four could throw no more at her, that she knew the worst of them. She'd known nothing, understood nothing, till she had Sovaris all the way inside—like a witch who'd spread legs and soul for the Deceiver.

"Vulheris's prison bound Sovaris's brothers as much as it did Fraia—so long as it endured, even Sovaris could barely hear them." Josalind toyed with the manacle's chain. "She lost herself in loneliness and despair for so long, I can't bear to think of it. But once the prison failed, Sovaris found her brothers again and they shouted to be heard." Saying it aloud left her wondering who might have come before her—other would-be vessels accused and condemned during the Kingdoms' witch hunts of the past.

Kara traced Josalind's cheek. "They've put so much on you, child. It's a wonder you are still sane."

"There've been times I wasn't." Josalind took Kara's hand. "They blame Fraia for what happened to them, to the world, because she had the Sword forged in the first place. Sovaris always doubted the wisdom of it, but her mother wouldn't listen."

Kara drew her close. "Sovaris admitted hatred for Fraia, didn't she?"

Josalind at first stiffened at the woman's presumption, then let herself sink into that motherly embrace, craved it with sudden need. When had her ma last held her like this, with love and affection, without fear? Her throat swelled with a jagged ache. "For thousands of years, the Four have had nothing to feed on but sorrow and hate. Left crippled without arms or legs."

"Does it not make you wonder what dark power might rise from your union with them?"

"You don't think they'll stop with the Deceiver," Josalind said.

Kara shrugged. "Maybe they wouldn't admit to such a thing, not yet at least, not even to themselves. But once their father is dead, how easy would it be to justify the death of their mother?"

The ache in Josalind's throat deepened till she thought she might choke on it. She found herself doubting anything Sovaris had ever told her, including the assertion that allowing the Sevrendine to take the skull and the Sword east would have been disastrous. "I just . . . I just wanted to save Ryn."

"I'm not sure it wouldn't have had the opposite effect," Kara said.

Josalind pushed away to turn and look her in the eye. "What do you mean?"

"He loves you—you must see it." Kara fondled that thing under her collar. "Losing you that way might drive him to a place where the Sword would have him for certain."

He loves you. Josalind couldn't bear to confront that right now. To love openly, to accept it in return . . . the prospect scared her too much. Having the Four rattling around for so long, knowing her every thought, twisting every desire to their ends, had piled the scars too thick. Admitting love would leave her too exposed to heartbreak and loss, given the risks they faced. They had shared a night, one wonderful night. Circumstance didn't allow for more.

She swallowed hard and pointed to Kara's neck. "That's a marriage bracelet, isn't it?"

Kara gave her a smile, a small one, tinged with sadness. "His name was Rijak, a smith." She pulled the object out—a thick bangle of beaten gold. "A bull of a man who could drive even Horgrim's knuckles to the table." She held the bangle up by its chain and watched the sunlight gleam from it, even as it gleamed from her well of tears. "He made this himself: 'If I'm going to bind myself to one woman, might as well forge the chain myself,' he'd jest."

Josalind swallowed hard. "What happened to him?"

"He died," Kara said simply. "That's when I felt Fraia's call to be more than an artisan's wife, to do whatever I could to prevent more widows or orphans."

She tucked the bangle away and looked Josalind square. "So I know something about the cost of love, child, the risk of heartbreak, and how precious it is to have regardless."

"And what about Horgrim?"

Kara drew a deep, shuddering breath. "I would love him if he would let me, but that's not a tale for today."

Josalind looked away to escape the owlish intensity of those eyes. "We have to let Ryn use the Sword, don't we?"

"Yes."

"But what about . . . Surely, there must be other wardens and heralds at large in the Kingdoms. Enough to stop Xang without resorting to the Sword."

"There may be a few," Kara said. "But it would take too long to track them down and bring them."

"But what about Fraia's angels? Didn't they come to Aegias?" *Spit and spray*, there had to be something.

"They did, but like demons, Mordyth Ral is a threat to them, too—they have no defense when the Sword is unleashed." Kara tucked a stray curl behind Josalind's ear. "And you must understand that our border with the Keshauk Dominion is a constant battleground, between human and grenlich, between angel and demon. Always we are outnumbered. Few can be spared for anything else. So, I'm afraid—"

"We're on our own," Josalind finished, dejected by the admission.

"Fraia has put her faith in us. It's our task to stand by that desperately noble and anxiously brave palatar of yours. Do what we can to ease his burden and contain the collateral damage—as Aegias's paladins did for him." Kara raised Josalind's chin till their gazes met. "But there is one thing Ryn has that Aegias never did."

"And what's that?"

"You, sweet."

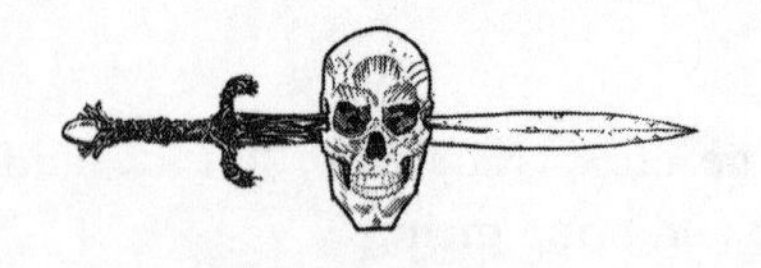

FORTY-THREE

yn and Horgrim agreed on a plan of attack as they walked into Sturvenwatch—keep a low profile and ask a few discreet questions. They cleaned up at a bathhouse and dressed for modest respectability in collars and waistcoats with what they had brought from Viglias and could procure on the spot from a local merchant.

Days behind the Tree of Sorrows's Veil must have confounded any attempt to track them by contagion. But they had no way to know whether such a spell would have been broken or only interrupted. Nor did it take magic to catch a fugitive, just a dispatch sent by pigeon and an astute eye.

They could only trust that no one in such a backwater would be on the lookout for them, regardless of what messages had been received. Slip in, avoid any contact with the Clerisy, slip out—how difficult could it be?

Bells spent nosing around town, however, forced them to one inescapable conclusion—only one man in this gods-forsaken place had the information they needed . . . and he called the local monastery home.

They had to visit the bear in its own den . . . again.

By midafternoon, Ryn found himself looking Aegias in the glassy eye, wondering what the Prince Messiah would have to say if his lips weren't frozen in lead. The monastery had an impressive industry in stained glass, and Ryn and Horgrim had been left to wait in a showroom of sorts. A dozen panels stood on display, a few large enough to be worthy of a lord with the coin to show his devotion on a grand scale.

The Aegias panel portrayed the Prince Messiah life-size, from crown to foot, in modern armor that contrasted with what Ryn remembered from his vision. Aegias's surcoat bore his sigil—the nine-pointed star with the Sword in its center. Slivers of glass could only achieve a certain stylized version of his features, but Ryn easily saw the details of the spirit's face superimpose themselves over the hard image before him.

Horgrim's sour mood left him with little appreciation for craftsmanship. "I can't believe we're turning to the Clerisy for help."

"*Gods be damned*, must you keep saying that?" Ryn's shoulder ached, his chest still complained if he breathed too deep, and he'd slept far too little. Base instinct screamed at him to be anywhere but here. He'd also been forced to bring Mordyth Ral unbound—the risk had been too great to leave Kara without some means to contain the Four when Josalind awoke.

Even now, concealed in its leather sleeve, the Sword poked and prodded, tainting his every thought and feeling with that metallic edge that singed his nerves raw. Horgrim's irritating complaints didn't help.

Snuff the spark from his very soul. The thought came unbidden, but not from the Sword. Smoldering cinders behind his eyes threatened to blow into a raging hellscape.

Behind the panels at the far end of the room, a door opened and closed. The whisper of rustling wool carried loud in the quiet. Ryn shared a glance with Horgrim at the sight of their host—not a seasoned scholar, but a lad in his teens. Ryn greeted him with a polite tug of his forelock. "Brother Abenwulf?"

The lad pressed palms under his chin and bowed low enough for a rather long ponytail to flop from his topknot and over his brow. The rest of his scalp had been shaved clean—the mark of a fully ordained brother. Quite the achievement for such a tender age. Ryn doubted the lad's cheeks required nearly as much service from a razor.

"At your service, good sirs," Brother Abenwulf said.

His fingers bore nicks and scars from working the glass, and gray stains from the lead. Ryn had seen men lost to sickness from the toxic metal. The lad would likely join them by thirty—his best years given for the glory of the faith. So empty and meaningless.

"We have been told you have some knowledge of the ruins to the west." Horgrim wore his skepticism plain.

Brother Abenwulf's cocky smile would have earned him a rebuke from his elders for ignoring the Virtue of Humility. "I've mapped them."

"Indeed," Horgrim said. "It's ten miles into that mire, from what I hear. If the swamp fever doesn't get a man first, one bite from a feathered marsh viper will leave him begging for death."

"Fifteen miles, if the truth be told," Abenwulf said. "Leather waders covered in tar confound the serpents, cheese-cloth netting and pickle juice keeps the mosquitoes at bay."

Even so, the lad had guts. "Townsfolk seem to consider the place cursed," Ryn said.

"You mean the treasure hunters who don't return." Abenwulf shrugged. "They fall prey to their own foolishness, if I may speak so bold. I saw nothing of the Great Deceiver's taint and found nothing much of value." He tucked his hands into the sleeves of his tunic. "Now, may I ask what brings two gentlemen of the north to a place so humble and distant to inquire about such things?"

"Our apologies, good brother," Ryn said with a kind smile. "I am Ruan of Teglion and this is Ragthor of Hapneld." He rolled back his sleeve to show the forged mercenary-guild mark he'd done in Tanasgeld. "We are hireswords of honorable association. Our employer is a man of means who fancies himself a historian—from the comfort of his study. We've come on his behalf."

That caught Abenwulf's attention. "'A man of means'?"

"He's creating a gazetteer that documents the ruins of Lost Pandaris and other fallen realms," Ryn said.

Abenwulf boiled with excitement, made all the more obvious by how earnestly he fought to hide it. "You do understand my work on Sarenepra was done at some considerable risk to myself. I can of course copy my drawings for your master's compendium, with due attribution, of course . . . *and* some agreeable donation in support of our good works."

Brother Abenwulf needed several days to copy his work. The abbot gave him leave to focus on nothing else after seeing the stack of coin Horgrim produced from a purse that had been well stocked in Viglias. A transaction all for the sake of appearances, given that Ryn had studied the drawings for long enough to fix to memory what they needed. The good brother would wear his quills for nothing. They could hardly spare the time to wait, in any case.

Horgrim's generous stipend did little to soften the abbot's persistent sneer. He stepped in front of them as they made to leave his study. "It would be our honor to have you as our guests, good sirs." He reminded Ryn of an age-spotted turkey buzzard.

"That is kind, but not necessary, Father Abbot," Horgrim said.

The abbot's attention fixed on Ryn's shoulder. "That looks like it could use tending—our brother surgeon could brew a poultice. A soul can never be too careful with the fever."

They'd concocted a story about brigands on the road. Ryn didn't care for the feel of the man's beady eyes. "Ragthor here makes a fine nursemaid, but thank you." He made to step past.

The abbot held his ground. "A drink, then," he said. "Cider, fresh from the press. I would be most interested to learn more about your master's research."

Ryn rested his hand on the pommel of his longsword. They appeared to be alone, but trouble could be a call away. "We have another appointment—tomorrow, perhaps."

The old buzzard held his ground for a breath longer, then stepped aside. "Of course, but if Brother Abenwulf were to have questions, where might we find you?"

"We've taken lodging down off the docks, the Mermaid's Folly," Horgrim said.

Before long, he and Ryn were heading out the north end of town at a brisk walk—the opposite direction from the docks.

"I didn't much care for the abbot's eagerness to please," he said.

Ryn eyed every detail of each person and alley they passed. "Keep sharp."

Centuries ago, Sturvenwatch had been a port of some status, with fleets that plied the trade route to the Kingdoms' Protectorates in the Teishlian Empire. But the Protectorates had fallen and the brine draken had grown more aggressive. The town's only industries now were fishing, shrimping, and pearl diving—none of which were particularly prosperous.

They walked a street of once-proud manor houses built of fine stone, now divided into tenements. Laborers, tradesmen, and their families, living in near squalor. The sight of two strange men—one wearing a longsword with practiced ease—didn't go unnoticed. Horgrim carried only a dagger, but his size and chiseled physique made a statement all their own. Mothers herded their children off the street, while the few menfolk who'd already finished their day's work eyed them with guarded suspicion.

"So much for not leaving any memorable impressions," Horgrim said.

Ryn teased the pommel of his sword, growing twitchier by the moment. "I don't like—"

"Lieutenant."

"Sir." The word burst from Ryn's mouth out of sheer reflex, even as his mind reeled to hear *that* voice, here, now. He turned sharp and caught the setting sun full in the face. The silhouette of a man stood not ten steps away, his features lost in the glare.

The men Ryn had taken to be humble residents took up weapons that had been laying out of sight. *Gods be damned.* Palatars, the lot of them. More flooded out of the surrounding alleys. The clicks of pistols and muskets being cocked rang loud.

"Well, isn't this a fine pickle," Horgrim said with deadly calm.

Ryn rubbed his fingers across his palm, hand hovering over his longsword. Could he dare use Mordyth Ral? Would it obey his command to only weaken the palatars enough to abet their escape, or would the threat compel it to mass murder? And what of Horgrim? The Sword's compulsion to see the warden dead hadn't softened a wit. Doors slammed shut as mothers went to ground with their children. They thought wood and stone enough to keep them safe. If only it were.

Would you not give your hand if it meant your life?

Ryn stepped sideways for a clearer look at the man who'd spoken. How could it be? "You're a long way from the Claw, Captain."

"That's *Marshal* now, pup."

The man shifted out of the sun's glare. Tovald. Bloody hell—it *was* him. The realization sparked the ache in Ryn's shoulder to new heights, shoving him back in that cell again, naked and helpless as his blood dripped from the skewer in Tovald's hand.

But something had changed. Barely a fortnight had passed since Tanasgeld and the captain—the *marshal*—looked a decade older since Ryn had knocked him cold. Something recent had left those flinty eyes hollowed and haunted, as if they'd witnessed too much and lived too long with the weight of it.

Tovald rubbed at the stumps of his missing fingers with absent-minded persistence. Ryn had grown so used to the habit, he'd come to hardly notice it in Dragon's Claw. But now he saw how the flesh had been worn raw. Thin scabs tore and bled. Tovald didn't seem to mind.

"What have you done, Marshal?" he asked.

"What I had to," Tovald said.

Ryn smelled the High Lord Inquisitar's hand in this. He should have slit the bastard's throat when he had the chance. For all his bitterness and misguided allegiance, Tovald deserved better than to be twisted by Bucardas's bag of tricks.

"How are you here?" Ryn asked. The answer had to account for his ragged appearance.

"That's not your concern, Lieutenant," Tovald said. "Drop the Sword, slow and easy, and back away."

Ryn took Mordyth Ral's sleeve by its strap and slipped it over his head. He held it out with one hand but didn't drop it. "Why should

I? Last I knew, Bucardas wanted me alive. We both know you won't give the order to fire."

Tovald's gaze hardened into that beastly glare. "I will see you dead right here before I let you leave with that thing. Bucardas be damned."

Ryn took a step toward his former commander, prodded on by a swell of frustrated anger. They hadn't time for this nonsense. "One touch while there's still a breath left in me, just one, and the Sword will have you all." Likely a lie, but a convenient one.

If only you had such resolve.

Ryn raised his voice. "Did you all hear that? I carry Mordyth Ral, the Sword of Aegias."

That raised a collective mutter and a shuffle of feet. These had to be men of the local garrison, accustomed to the boredom of a dull posting.

"Hold your ground." Tovald drew his sword. "By the Four, if Aegias were here, he'd weep to see what a gutless lot you are." He released a slow breath and regarded Ryn with a kinder eye. "Come to your senses, son. You know that thing will only bring you to a bad end. Better a quick, clean death as the man you still are." His attention drifted to Horgrim. "Better that than being warped into some monster by these heretics."

The warden laughed aloud. "You are sadly misinformed, Marshal."

Ryn found himself giving Tovald's plea fair consideration. How easy it would be to die here, surrender the burden of the Sword before circumstance could make a mass murderer of him. He might have agreed to it, if his death wouldn't have been sure to deliver the Sword to Bucardas and allow Xang to rise. "I didn't ask for this, Marshal, but it's come to me and now I'm bound to it—I *am* the Heir of Aegias."

Even now, Ryn found it hard to give credence to such a claim, but it didn't matter what he thought. What mattered was what *they* thought—these palatars with weapons aimed. Life and death decided by how well he could plant a seed of doubt . . . or one of hope. Most men hungered for something solid to believe in, beyond hollow oaths to a false church. They just needed to understand the truth about the Clerisy and Aegias. To muster the courage and sense of self-worth to honor Aegias and the Virtues on their own terms.

But it took only one wretch with an itch in his finger to foul the gears.

A pistol fired. Horgrim stumbled back with a grunt.

"The heretic takes no wound."

"Sorcery."

"Divine Grace."

Tovald cursed. "He wears armor, you fools." But even he sounded unsure. No armor light enough to hide under a shirt and waistcoat could stop a ball at such a range. Unless it was cryptwood, of course.

A big shadow swept over the street. Men shouted and screamed, pointing overhead.

"A dragon!"

"Aegias save us."

"The Great Deceiver's Beast has come for us."

Palatars stumbled and tripped over one another in their sudden haste to duck for cover or flee. Firearms discharged at random.

Ryn looked up and staggered back in surprise. A dragon indeed. A true monster armored with scales and plates of black diamond. Bat-like wings spanned forty yards or more, with translucent membranes that had the flex of leather, but flashed in the sun like sheets of smoked glass. Three curved horns of silver crystal crowned a craggy skull. Spiky growths like halberd blades marched down its spine. They ended at a spade-shaped tail that could have flattened a horse with one swipe.

And it had a rider, a giant who looked cut from sandstone.

Grist.

The big bastard had said he'd come for Ryn.

FORTY-FOUR

yn could scarcely believe what he saw, despite seeing it, plain as paint. He'd wondered what else might lurk in Gostemere, but some questions he was quite content to never have answered.

Rider and dragon wheeled about and headed northwest.

Josalind.

Ryn slung Mordyth Ral over his shoulder, too distracted to realize he'd left his back turned to Tovald.

The ring of blades, right behind his head.

He jerked aside, drew his longsword, and swung around with guard up. Blood Thorn had shot out of Horgrim's sleeve to catch the blade that would have cleaved Ryn's skull. The marshal's sword wasn't steel, but witch iron. It had bitten into the cryptwood and wedged. Tovald scowled and tried to pull away.

Horgrim caught the marshal with a left hook that sprawled him senseless in the dust.

Muskets fired. A whizzing ball grazed Ryn's ear, and he hissed from the burning sting. Blood Thorn lashed out to bat aside others.

Horgrim bolted off at a run, head down. "Time to go, swordling."

Ryn's feet already moved. More weapons fired. Shouts followed. They needed faster transportation than their own feet. Two blocks down, he caught sight of a wagon down a side street, a buckboard with a two-horse hitch. "This way."

The wagon parked against the dock of a granary, half unloaded. Several laborers, caked with sweat and grain dust, had forgotten about the job at hand. Two of them stared at the sky with wide-eyed astonishment—the look of men too stunned by the unexpected for fear to have yet set in.

"D-d-did you see that?" one asked.

"Was it a dragon?" the second said.

The third fellow obviously hadn't seen what his comrades had and scoffed. "Have you piss sloshing between your ears? There be no such thing."

They paid no mind when Ryn climbed up onto the wagon's seat. He released the brake and prompted the team with a snap of the reins and a curt "trot on." The dragon had left the team skittish. They stomped and lunged forward, lurching the wagon into motion. Horgrim leapt up beside him.

"Hey! Stop."

"*Gaa*," Ryn called, which he hoped would steer the horses right. He hadn't driven a team in years.

The command worked. The third laborer ran up beside and tried to heave himself onto the seat. Ryn knocked him off with a quick boot to the chest. He prompted the team into a canter to outrun the other two-legged pursuit. Shouts followed them. "We could do without the weight."

"Right." Horgrim stepped back into the bed and tossed the sacks. Ryn expected the laborers' first concern would be securing the grain. These weren't their horses, after all.

Three streets and two turns later found them on the road north, heading out of town. Ryn allowed the team as much head as he dared. The buckboard bounced and rattled to rouse the dead, or join them, which threatened to make the horses bolt out of control. Horgrim spotted no pursuit, but it wouldn't take long for the Clerisy to find witnesses who could point its hounds in the right direction.

"Your marshal meant to kill you right there," Horgrim shouted over the din. "I expect he considered it a mercy."

Ryn didn't answer, stuffed with conflicted feelings. He doubted a quick death would please the High Lord Inquisitar, who likely still had designs on his twig and berries.

They had to leave the road for the last stretch. With the harvest done, laborers would be busy with tasks that would keep them out of the back fields. Even so, the dragon could be seen for miles. The monster had come to rest on the edge of the forest that bordered the swamp, right where their camp lay. Ryn couldn't mistake the location—a half-acre patch of oakenleaf stood nearby. The bushes grew taller than Horgrim and wore a spectacular display of red foliage.

The dragon appeared even larger with its four feet on the ground, sitting tall on its haunches as it watched them come. Grist had already vanished. The horses started to flick their ears with fright and drop speed. Ryn snapped the reins to urge them on. A hundred yards short of the dragon, they squealed and planted their hooves in a spray of dirt. The quick stop almost launched Ryn over their heads.

"Time to walk," Horgrim said as he hopped down.

Ryn tied off the reins, dropped from the seat, and led the team around in a half circle before sending them on their way back to town with a slap to the rump. Then he started walking straight for that craggy head. "Make no threatening move," he said.

Horgrim followed, even now, a twinkle in his eye. "You will understand if I do keep behind you."

It took all the grit Ryn could muster to approach that mass of scale, spike, and horn without the comfort of a weapon in hand. Tear-shaped eyes regarded him with scarlet mystery. The flex of those forelimb claws dug up dirt enough to fill a pair of oxcarts. Plain steel wouldn't do him a lick of good. His fingers itched for Mordyth Ral, so fiercely his whole arm tingled from the burn. He bit his tongue to fight it.

The distance shortened to twenty yards, then ten. Ryn circled just beyond range of a quick lunge by that serpentine neck. The dragon snorted. Ryn couldn't help but flinch. It bared its teeth—piles of nasty teeth. A martichora ranked as a barn cat by comparison.

For a moment, Ryn thought the monster might actually let him pass. He came parallel to its bony snout as it tracked him, with head down and chin high.

Then he took one step too far.

The dragon slammed a forelimb down in the dirt inches from Ryn's toes. Its head snaked around. He held fast as that snout came so close he could see nothing but flaring nostrils. If it meant to kill him, he'd already be dead. He didn't dare think anything else.

That death trap of a mouth opened. Pungent air seared his eyes.

"Sword-Bearer," the dragon said.

Ryn stared in astonishment. The words slid out in a hissing slur, but they were words, all the same.

He mustered his composure. "Let me pass."

"No."

Ryn reached for his longsword. "I'm not—"

That big snout bumped Ryn's chest and sent him stumbling back onto his rump. The dragon inhaled, bobbing its neck like a gull with a fish to swallow, then spat some thick greenish fluid.

The dragon's discharge arced through the air, then carved a path five yards wide through the patch of oakenleaf. Branch and leaf reduced to steaming ash in two beats of Ryn's rampant heart. A vitriol stronger than any he'd ever seen.

Horgrim's lips peeled back. Blood Thorn grew in his hand. The dragon hissed. Its tail gave the earth such a thump, Ryn felt the jar through his tailbone.

Tawny fury dropped from the sky onto the dragon's neck, driving its chin into the dirt. Clawed hands latched on to the dragon's crystal horns as a scorpion tail whipped around. The ivory stinger, glistening with venom, stopped only a hair short of an eye.

"Dare it not, great brother," Oma said.

The dragon clenched its eyes and thrust back with a roar. Oma's stinger struck but bounced away without harm. She beat her wings hard to clear off as the dragon turned on her. Blood Thorn cut the air in a bright streak and tore a plate from the dragon's throat. Ryn scrambled to his feet and reached for Mordyth Ral.

"STOP IT."

The command rang so sharp it froze man, dragon, and martichora alike.

It came from Josalind.

She walked out from under the trees. Grist accompanied her.

Horgrim strode toward them. Icy death flashed in his eyes. "Where is Kara?"

She stepped out next. "Here, old lion."

The warden's pace slowed, but Blood Thorn remained ready in his hand. "How goes the day, My Herald?"

Kara crossed her arms and looked to Josalind. "We're as good as kittens with cream, aren't we, sweet?"

Oma landed beside Ryn. Her kin came out of the tree line and circled around to join her. Ryn walked up to Josalind and Grist, mindful of how the dragon tracked his every step.

Grist didn't say a word. He just stood there, towering over her. That salve of his tainted the air, smeared thick to mend the wounds Horgrim had dealt the day before. In his hand lay a new stave of blackened iron, mounted with a stone—red quartz shot through with swirls of gold. The Heart of Kyvros. Of course—how else could he leave Gostemere and be sure of finding his way back?

Ryn stopped a stride short of Josalind. Those sea-green eyes fixed on him, her jaw set, like she steeled herself for an argument she didn't intend to lose.

"I expect you'd be gone by now, if you were inclined to it," Ryn said.

"I might yet."

He stifled a swell of anger and forced a civil tone. "So, what's keeping you?"

Her attention strayed to the pouch on his belt. "You still have Sovaris's heart."

He rested his hand on the pommel of his longsword, half expecting Grist to make a play for the stone, but the dolusk kept still. "Is that all?"

Josalind's gaze faltered. Her bearing lost some of its pride. Ryn's heart swelled to aching with the hope of what she might say. Here he was, mooning like some lovestruck fool who'd surrendered the last gasp of dignity, waiting for a confession he knew would never come. She had made that clear enough in Gostemere. But he couldn't help himself. He stood there, too awkward for words, certain he reeked of a pathetic angst no creature present could miss. It was laughable, considering the gravity of the matter at hand.

"We have to stop Xang's resurrection," she said.

Ryn's eyebrow rose. He glanced at Grist. "The Four are content with that?"

"I'm not giving them a choice." Josalind raised her arm. The broken witch-iron manacle bound her wrist, its stray chain tied up with a cord. "I can still hear them, but not so loud."

"Why the change of heart?" Ryn asked.

She sniffed and wiped at her eyes. "I've come to realize you can't make do without me."

Sparse at best, but it still gave Ryn a swell of hope. He yearned to sweep her up, to feel her lips against his own, to find in her eyes a sign that she wanted him to, but now wasn't the time. Instead, he stepped up to Grist. "What do you say about this, big man?"

The dolusk knelt and cradled the staff in the crook of his arm. "I serve Our Lady."

"You came to take her back and claim Sovaris's heart," Ryn said.

"Take her not against will."

"I doubt Karxist will care for that," Ryn said.

Those yellow eyes narrowed, no mean feat in a face that seemed too rigid for expression. "Karxist not master."

"And?" Ryn prompted.

Grist's attention strayed to Kara. "She tell plan. I help."

Ryn offered his hand. "You will be an ally we can trust in this fight?"

Grist took his hand with a gentle grip. "Yes."

A weight slid off Ryn's shoulders. They needed all the help they could get. He jerked his thumb toward the dragon. "What about that one?"

"Kreevax," Grist said. "His will his own."

The dragon had settled into a crouch, feet gathered like a cat primed to pounce. Ryn came as close as he dared and gave a nervous bow. It only seemed fitting. He'd dreamed as a boy of meeting a dragon. What boy hadn't? He couldn't help but grin.

"Great Kreevax, we would be deeply honored—"

The dragon tossed his head. "Spare yourself. Stiff words pinch my ears."

"All right, then," Ryn said. "Will you help us?"

Kreevax arched his wings and reared back to scrape the sky. "Let us make plans for war, Sword-Bearer."

Horgrim held his hand out to Grist. "I trust we can put aside yesterday's events."

The dolusk accepted the offer of truce, but something still smoldered. "Kinsmate crippled."

Ryn remembered the dolusk that Horgrim had hamstrung.

"I may be able to remedy that, at another time," Kara said.

"Mean much," Grist said with a nod.

"Why do you carry Kyvros's heart on display like that?" Horgrim asked.

Grist swept the head of his staff around in a sharp circle. The heart erupted into a ball of fire. A lick of flame lashed out and ignited what remained of the oakenleaf. "Kyvros anger burn hot."

Josalind rubbed at her temple. "It usually does."

"And he obeys you," Ryn said to Grist, making no effort to hide his skepticism. They needed the wild card of another wrathful dead god about as much as a plague of festering boils.

"Kyvros is practical enough to appreciate which battles need to be fought first," Josalind said. "Or would you rather not have the help?"

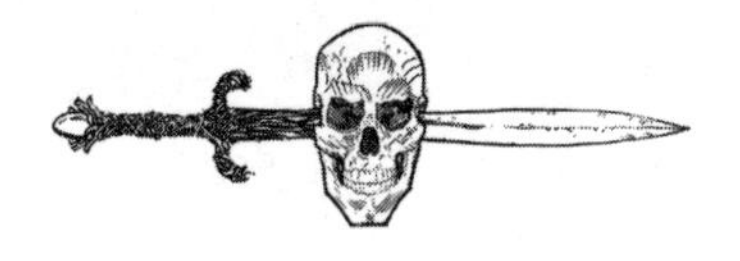

FORTY-FIVE

The martichora found another site for a camp as dusk fell, miles away from the nearest habitation where even Kreevax could crouch back under the trees. They relocated there under cover of darkness.

Once they had settled around their evening fire, Ryn sketched in the dirt what he'd gleaned from Brother Abenwulf's documentation on Sarenepra.

"A headland pushes into the sea," he said. "There's a great tower there, the keep of a fortress. The land around its walls slopes quick into the salt marshes. There was a city once, but the good brother says it's been swallowed up, for the most part."

Oma leaned over his shoulder. Those big eyes of hers rivaled a cat with a spyglass. She'd scouted to within a couple of miles of the ruins with the first glow of false dawn that morning, when it remained dim enough to obscure her shape from sentries. "So it is, man-child, but the fortress still stands, as does its tower."

"And what of our esteemed demon herders?" Horgrim asked.

"Three skyships of the East have come," Oma said. "I saw not the conveyance that bore their peers from your city of Vysus."

"They wouldn't come alone," Josalind said.

"No, blessed child," Oma said. "The walls of the fortress swarm with grenlich. Many have wings."

Horgrim scratched under his chin. "How many?"

"Several hundred, mayhap," Oma said.

The warden snorted. "And we expected this to be a *small* gathering?"

"You know how vast the Dominion is, old lion," Kara said. "This is a token force indeed, considering they have come to witness their messiah's return."

Horgrim pointed to a spot on Ryn's sketch. "The good brother found a discreet way in that should provide cover enough."

"And once you are deep in the serpent's nest, with its coils tight around, what then?" Kara asked.

"We will do what we must, My Herald," Horgrim said.

"If we're too late to prevent Xang's resurrection, I will use Mordyth Ral only to weaken him so cryptwood alone can finish him," Ryn said.

Kara's eyes sparkled in the fire's light. "And you trust the Sword will be distracted enough by grenlich that it won't force you to turn on Horgrim again?"

Ryn forced himself to match her gaze. "If I lose Horgrim, I lose Blood Thorn. That leaves me with nothing to stop Xang but the full might of Mordyth Ral." He drew a ragged breath. "Fear of *that* will be my weapon against the Sword."

Fear, guilt, regret—Aegias also worked to blunt my purpose with these things. What end did it serve? History is a wheel that turns until broken.

Horgrim nodded. "Kara, we—"

"Need a diversion." She forced a smile that failed to reach her eyes and toyed with the object under her collar. "I will bring down heaven's own fury for you, old lion."

"I have no doubt, My Herald," Horgrim said. "I never do."

Ryn soon took to the swamp, eager for solitude, mindful of his footing to avoid crossing paths with a viper.

Dense clumps of swamp willow loomed all around. They filled the night with eerie sighs, a mournful chorus that rolled like waves on a beach. Nothing like them grew anywhere else in the Kingdoms. Mossy strands of foliage thirty feet long or more crowned their gnarled stumps. The strands stood erect, swaying gently in the absence of any breeze, rubbing against one another to produce that haunting chorus. Ryn's botany text when he was a boy had cited trapped lifting gases. But when you were lost among them under the shroud of night, the sensible explanation didn't make them any less spooky.

When he could go no farther without sinking into muck, he closed his eyes and breathed deep of the damp, peaty air. Frogs and toads, crickets and katydids, sang in counterpoint to the willows. The swamp teemed with life, but he could see none of it.

When he'd freed Mordyth Ral of the witch-iron manacles so that Horgrim could bind the sorcerer Olparc, Ryn had learned that it was far less risky to hold the Sword by the blade than by the grip. The grip appeared to be the strongest conduit for the connection between them, the trigger that allowed the Sword to feed. Any contact at all, of course, gave the Sword an avenue to attack his mind, but it did also yield benefits.

Ryn reached over his shoulder and pressed the tip of a single finger to Mordyth Ral's pommel. *Show me.*

As it had in that vale with Olparc, the Sword's senses amplified his own. He gagged on the stench of rotting vegetation, blinded by a sudden glare—the life force of the swamp and all it held, *the animas*, burning with lush brilliance. The sighing of the willows now grated as raw screams. Even the call of the tiniest creature had grown to a numbing roar. He panted hard and clung to the chains of memory that bruised his soul and anchored him to who he was.

The assault faded to a tolerable level. Still, nothing that crawled, slithered, or flew escaped him. Night could hide no secret.

I once left desolation for a thousand leagues that reached even here. But life returned. I take nothing that time cannot renew.

Josalind had come to stand behind him. Ryn had tracked her smell, the rhythm of her breath, even how she walked, from a hundred yards away. He didn't turn, afraid to see her as the Sword would—just another strand in a web too vast to comprehend, an insignificant speck of life. "You should go. Take Astrig and just go. Fly as far and as fast as you can."

"Ryn—"

"I doubt that bit of witch iron will protect you." He took his hand from Mordyth Ral and his senses turned mortal, feeble, once more. He pulled Sovaris's heart from its pouch and turned to her. "Take this. If anyone should lay claim to it, it's you."

Josalind folded her hand over the stone, her head bowed under that tangle of curls, but she didn't accept it. "I was so . . . desperate to find meaning for it all. To have something come of my suffering and know for certain I wasn't mad."

"You're not—"

She pressed her fingers to his lips. "I'll decide what part I play in this war. Not them, not Kara, and not you."

She slid her hand around the back of his neck and drew him in for a kiss. Not a kiss to heal, or even one ripe with desire. Just a kiss, simple and pure. And yet, the feel of her lips, soft and warm, mended something deep inside that the power of gods never could.

When it ended, he rested his forehead against hers and tried to still the tremble in his knees. She trembled, too. "What a pair we make," he said. "Will our lives ever be our own?"

"If we don't let them break us . . . and we won't—*ever*." She touched his cheek. "Let's promise each other that."

"With my heart and soul." He remembered the night they'd first met on the *Fool's Fortune*, how her eyes had begged for company to share their misery. A sudden fit of dark humor made him chuckle. "Misery is a bond between us that no sword or god can ever break."

She frowned at him, then burst out in laughter. He found himself laughing, too, rueful laughter all around that couldn't escape their pain. Still, it felt good to share a laugh, to have that understanding and know they had each other. He didn't doubt she felt the same, even if she refused to confess to something so risky as love.

When the moment passed, he took her hand and pressed it to his lips. "You should still go, while there's time."

Her fingers traced the line of his jaw. "*I* decide my part, Ryn."

She took Sovaris's heart and left without saying more. He had no idea what he'd just done by giving her that stone or what she might do. All of which meant nothing had really changed.

He found Horgrim not far off, propped in the crook of a willow's trunk. The warden's hands moved as if he tossed a ball between them, but instead of a ball it was a length of cryptwood. It broke the gloom with a gentle glow, snaking back and forth from shoulder to shoulder in a helix around his arms.

"Are you ready for this?" Ryn asked.

"We make do with what we have, and trust in that to be enough," Horgrim said. "There is no room for doubt."

"I suppose you'll tell me that's the Sevrendine way," Ryn said.

"Indeed." The cryptwood hardened into the blade. "And if it comes to it, if this gambit of ours goes wrong, do what you must to put Xang down. No hesitation, no concern for the consequences. Just see it done."

Ryn frowned. "I thought you were against using the Sword."

"Before we were chin deep in the shite pit," Horgrim said. "I'm not saying give Mordyth Ral rein to destroy the last spark of Xang's miserable soul, just don't let him live to leave this place."

"Let the Sword kill thousands, if need be, but not tens of thousands." Ryn slammed his fist against the tree. "Gods be damned."

"It's for the sake of *millions*, Ryn," Horgrim said with grave earnest. He took a sharp breath and drummed his fingers upon Blood Thorn's blade. "Up north, I wouldn't tell you why I don't want to father children."

Ryn gave a nod. "It's not my business."

"My father was a stonecutter by trade who earned an officer's commission in the militia."

The warden's obvious need to unburden himself roused as much unease as it did curiosity. It spoke to his fear. Ryn had enough of his own. "So, you didn't see much of him."

Horgrim's eyes welled with sudden emotion. "No, not after he gave his allegiance to the Keshauk, and betrayed the men and women under his command to slaughter."

Ryn grimaced. "Why?"

"I don't know." Horgrim looked off into the dark. "I stopped caring to know when I realized no answer, no truth of his, could ever be of any worth to me. What matters is what I could have done, what I should have, when I suspected him before anyone else. Instead, I did nothing and good people died. Kara's husband, for one."

"Her husband?" *Gods' Grace.*

"That thing she wears but keeps hidden—it's her wedding bangle," Horgrim said.

"Does she know?"

Horgrim gave a curt nod. "She forgave me long ago, but I'll never forgive myself. To do so would dishonor his memory."

Ryn found that sentiment painfully familiar.

Horgrim pressed his brow to that great white blade. "I went to the Grove of the Blessed Oak to see how I might atone. I vowed then to father no child who would bear the disgrace."

The man wouldn't admit his love for Kara out of shame. "You can't hold yourself responsible for your father's actions," Ryn said.

"I can for my own." A feral gleam returned to those icy eyes. "My duty, my responsibility, was to the security of our people. That is where yours lies now—making the hard choice for the greater good."

Ryn hardly needed the reminder. "I don't—"

"I wronged you back on the *Sea Hare*, when I said being a man of conscience, even integrity, couldn't be enough." Horgrim gripped his shoulder. "What other sort of man could possibly be trusted to wield that thing? I have faith in you, Ryn Ruscroft."

The warden's frankness overwhelmed Ryn with something he'd not felt since Quintan had been alive—a true bond of friendship, even affection. He sorely needed that right now, burdened by all he'd done in the Clerisy's name, by the far-worse horrors he might still do as the Sword-Bearer. The lives lost and the legions still to be taken.

Sablewood had damned him. He could only hope it would be enough to save him, too.

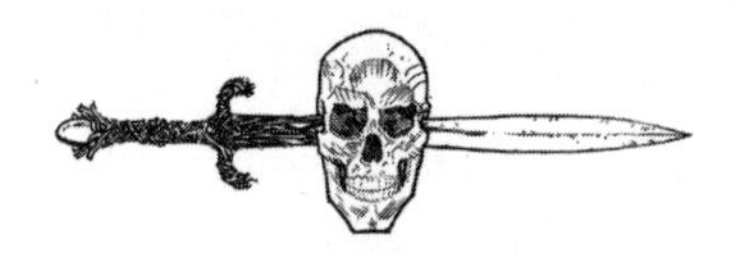

FORTY-SIX

Oma and Ashavinx sped low over the swaying crowns of the swamp willows.

A bank of cloud had swallowed the stars. The odd ghost light given up by the swamp's slow decay flickered below. An orange glow blossomed on the horizon—the watch fires of Sarenepra's new residents.

About two miles short of the ruins, the martichora touched down on an abandoned roadbed. Between skyships, winged grenlich, and whatever tricks sorcerers might have, they'd deemed it too risky to drop in on their target from the sky.

Ryn waited till he had two feet firm on the ground before putting his hand to Mordyth Ral. It didn't rest in the leather sleeve anymore, but rode his hip naked, slipped under his belt opposite the longsword. Horgrim kept a prudent distance with Blood Thorn in hand. Ryn steeled himself for the assault and rested his palm on the Sword's pommel.

His senses swelled with something different than before—a craving that drew him toward the stew of Abomination that plagued Sarenepra. He forced his attention away, back to that *thing* he knew to be Horgrim, which the Sword still saw as a stain to be cleansed. His palms grew slick, heart pounding to crack a rib. This thing had to die. The earth cried for it.

Ryn took a step and gripped the pommel.

Oma's claws pinched his shoulder. "Anchor yourself, man-child."

He found himself again and peeled his fingers away with a shaky breath. "No need for worry."

Horgrim hadn't moved an inch but had the look of a man mustering the nerve to shove his hand into a forge fire. "I never thought there was." Blood Thorn changed to a staff. "Let's go."

Gloomen Swamp didn't care for trespassers.

It tripped them with roots that lurked just beneath fetid waters. Shallow pools hid silty pits neck deep. Cloying webs stretched between mossy branches and caught them in the face. Their eight-legged masters were the size of rats and all fang. Above it all, the swamp willows blotted out the sky and performed their melancholy dance with that eerie chorus of raspy sighs. Even if the clouds parted, barely a glimmer of starlight would reach them.

No fool with half a wit would dare the place in the dark.

But Ryn missed nothing. With palm resting on Mordyth Ral's pommel, he sensed every pitfall, saw and heard every creature as it fled before him, despite how the willows screamed to drown them out. Mordyth Ral, Bane of All Things, had woken. Biting insects came in swarms, but not a single one touched his flesh. Even the snakes so feared by the locals gave way.

Horgrim stumbled blind behind, not risking even Blood Thorn's soft light. He had no choice but to trust in Ryn's guidance to avoid twisting an ankle or bashing a shin. But he still found reason to mutter a curse now and again.

Tovald must have wondered why his former lieutenant had such an interest in Sarenepra. Palatars attempting to reach the ruins on foot faced fifteen miles of this soggy hell. It made more sense from Tovald's perspective to come up the coast, where any conventional ship would be easy prey for Xang's worshippers. For all Ryn knew, Tovald had already attempted it and even now fed the fishes with his corpse. But how had Tovald caught up with them in the first place? Horgrim and Kara hadn't been able to shed any light on it.

Muck had found its way up to their ears by the time they reached the outer ruins. Ryn doubted a bloodhound could have smelled the man beneath the slime, even with its nose planted in their rumps. He wanted to bolt ahead, heedless of the risk, eager to lay waste and rid the earth of Abomination. Mordyth Ral craved its once and final end.

The walls of the fortress came into view, crumbling in places, eaten away by brine in others, but still surprisingly whole and strong after so long. Sentries made their rounds. Even at hundreds of yards, Ryn could spot them all, tell one breed of grenlich from another, which were armed with ranged weapons and which weren't. But the closer he looked, the more his gut churned sick. The Sword's need swelled into a glowing crucible that threatened to hollow his skull.

He went for Brother Abenwulf's arcade—a street roofed by vaults and arches supported by hexagonal columns, all carved from pinkish pale granite. Mosses and vines draped the structure, giving ample cover from eyes on the walls.

Swamp water, turned brackish by the sea, reached Ryn's chest. They waded along slow to keep the water quiet, but he fought the Sword's compulsion to charge ahead at every step. When the arcade started to slope uphill, he stopped and peeked past the moss. Fifty yards ahead loomed the fortress, and beyond its wall of dark granite, the crown of the tower. Little else reached so high in all the Kingdoms. A hundred and sixty yards from its base, Brother Abenwulf had said. It, too, still stood tall against the ravages of time. Ryn found that unnatural, but now wasn't the time to ponder the mystery.

A gatehouse lay at the end of the arcade, sure to be guarded, but the good brother had found a sally port a bit south, with a passage that cut through the bedrock into the fortress's cellars. They just had to wade through open water without being spotted. *And* trust it was a back door that hadn't been discovered.

Ryn could bear it no longer and peeled his hand from Mordyth Ral. The fire in his skull faded. So did the cramp between his shoulders, which he hadn't noticed before. But the loss left him feeling blind and useless. Once his eyes had adjusted, he led the way, sunk deep enough for the water's fishy smell to tickle his nostrils, drifting from one clump of mangrove shrub to the other, testing each step as he went.

Halfway, Horgrim stumbled and splashed.

Ryn didn't dare look to see why. He just froze, head so low he could barely draw breath without snorting water. Horgrim held just as still. Ryn expected the stamp of feet on the wall above, the fluttering roar of a torch, cast down to break the gloom.

He heard neither.

Still, he waited a spell before forging on. Hordes of mosquitos continued to drone and whine around him. They brushed his eyes and nose, less discouraged without his hand on the Sword. He resisted the urge to swat them away.

At the last clump of mangrove, he waited for Horgrim to tuck up close behind him. The sally port stood ajar just ten yards away—a door of ancient bronze crusted green with verdigris. Only a foot of it stood above the water, half hidden by drooping moss. They'd caught a different phase of the tide than Brother Abenwulf—he'd found the door only half flooded.

Ryn motioned for Horgrim to go first, attention fixed on the top of the wall. It rose so near and tall, he wouldn't spot anyone unless they poked their head over.

Horgrim made the door without trouble, peered inside, then motioned Ryn on. He put his back to the frame and tried to ease the door open just enough to squeeze his big shoulders through. Rotted bronze crumbled in his hands and hit the water with gentle plops too faint to carry far. Beyond the door, they barely had headroom. The oily water bore a ripe stink Ryn hoped didn't originate with the bodily functions of grenlich.

They didn't get far before the roof sloped and water kissed stone.

"Isn't this a pickle," Horgrim whispered. "How long can you hold your breath?"

Even without touching Mordyth Ral, Ryn couldn't bear the warden so close without the Sword's urges threatening to get the better of him. "Let's find out," he spat in an angry growl.

Cryptwood crawled out of Horgrim's sleeve, giving off the barest glow. It narrowed to the width of a pinky and wormed its way under the stone before them. On it went, until Horgrim held the last inch pinched between thumb and forefinger.

Ryn rapped his shoulder. "Well?"

"There's a space of air, but I can't say how big it is."

"How far?"

"Twenty-some yards."

That distance on one breath wasn't bad in clear water, but being trapped under stone with two swords dragging along put a whole different flavor on it.

Horgrim pumped his lungs with a few quick breaths. "See you at the end." Then he dove under.

Ryn lost his only light as the warden took the cryptwood with him. The press of darkness drove him to follow. He took the distance with a steady, hard stroke. Lack of sight swallowed any sense of progress and left his lungs feeling more starved than they were. The gritty rasp of his scabbard's chape dragging on the floor made him imagine that some ghoul clawed after him.

A dim glow broke the murk. His hand caught a trouser leg.

He came up slow to avoid cracking his skull on the ceiling, but found he had a foot to spare. The water reached only chest high now. Broad steps spiraled up before them.

"You'd best keep behind me," Ryn said.

Horgrim motioned him past with a flourish. "I certainly don't intend to get in your way."

They'd come up directly beneath the tower. There would be another door, halfway up, a fallback should invaders breach the sally port. Ryn dared tap Mordyth Ral's senses again as he took the stairs. Stale skunk tinged with moldering compost stuffed his nose—grenlich musk. Brother Abenwulf had mentioned murder holes in the walls and ceiling. Ryn kept tight to the wall as the landing came in sight.

The door clung to its hinges, a rusted mess, while the murder holes held only darkness.

Ryn quickened his step. The final door stood neglected, too.

Where?

The inner ward. His return is nigh.

The Sword's urgency gave his feet wings. Ryn bolted down an empty hallway and burst into the tower's great hall.

The hall took up most of the first floor—circular, about twenty-five yards across. Fresh torches burned along the walls, blinding his sharpened sight with the sudden glare. He blinked to clear his eyes, heart racing with the sudden threat of things all around.

Grenlich warriors packed the hall.

Some were squat and bowlegged, with the features of a ram, if a ram had scales. Others stood tall and sinuous—cats crossed with snakes. They glared at the intruders with raw malice, armed with cleaver, mace, and halberd. Ryn spied those multibarreled hellcasts, too—five at least.

Unleash me.

Ryn ignored the Sword despite the itch of his hand to obey as a guttural command rang out. The grenlich stepped aside. A female grenlich, built like a ram, stood in their midst. Arcane glyphs tattooed her hide, and charms pierced her horns. She held a quartz staff that must have weighed sixty pounds. A vauka'rau—a matriarch of her clan.

Her cloven hoof came down with a sharp crack. Pale goat eyes narrowed, nostrils flaring. She spoke to Horgrim in broken Islari Common, which of course was the language of the Sevrendine. "You business here not. Leave now, one chance."

"A fair offer," Horgrim said.

His arm shot back and flung Blood Thorn like a spear.

The missile caught the vauka'rau square in the chest and blew out her back in a spray of blood and shattered bone.

The grenlich warriors surged forward with a collective roar as Blood Thorn returned to Horgrim's hand.

Ryn's hand ripped Mordyth Ral from his belt with a will all its own.

At last.

Ryn brandished Mordyth Ral high in a two-handed grip. His feet carried him past Horgrim with such lightning poise, he felt that he floated. He did these things without any sense of his own will. There was only the Sword, its purpose, its hunger. It hummed so fierce his flesh burned without flame, but he couldn't let go. The agony of it gave a welcome anchor. Pain reminded him of who he was. Pain might keep him sane.

He clutched the hilt in both hands and savored the burn.

The Sword fed. Those hellcasts discharged with a cannon's roar. Hot metal shrieked past Ryn's ear, but no shell could find him as he ducked aside with unnatural speed. Detonations sounded behind him as the shells exploded against the far wall. A few, then a few more, then every grenlich in the hall reeled back in sudden terror. Ryn just stood there as the Sword leeched the life from them, his every thought focused on keeping that hunger confined within the fortress.

Horgrim leapt past him to tear into the grenlich's ranks. Blood, hot and dark, sprayed thick and struck Ryn's face. It splattered upon Mordyth Ral's blade, where it steamed and bubbled. The strange metal drank it up.

Despite his efforts, Ryn felt the Sword reach beyond the hall, to find the pulse of all that lived for miles around. But Josalind waited somewhere out there. So did Kara, Oma, and the rest. Even if the Sword only meant to siphon a fraction of their life force, they could ill afford to be weakened at all, given the battle they faced in the skies above. Ryn tried to let go and couldn't. Pain didn't anchor him, it trapped.

Damn you—not so far.

I thirst, and there is need.

Ryn turned to the only recourse he had: Sara and her mother in Sablewood. The smell of death on that bitter winter's night. The hateful toll of the abbey's bells.

The pressure in his mind eased. The fire in his hands faded to a tolerable level as the Sword reined itself in.

Dead grenlich littered the floor. But a score or more shook off Mordyth Ral's bite and eyed them with renewed hatred.

Ryn fell in beside Horgrim. Gore splattered them both. The warden paid no mind to the flesh wounds he'd taken. This was the warrior's way, the honest way, taking life in a clean fight, blade to blade. This Ryn could bear without feeling that his soul had been stained for eternity.

Even so, the advantage was his. Mordyth Ral sang with music only he could hear, clear and pure as a harp in the hands of a master. It grew louder with each life it took, overwhelming the clang of weapons and the cries of the dying. Ryn surrendered to it. He battled with a speed and grace not even Horgrim could match. Through it all, he clung to the memory of Sablewood's dead, giving purpose to their deaths.

Corpses piled before them, but still the grenlich came, until only five were left, then three, then none. They fought to the last as though death were a blessing.

The Sword blistered Ryn's mind with fresh insistence. **Half measures assure his escape.**

The inner ward, where Xang's priests worked his resurrection, lay just beyond the tarnished brass doors at the far end of the hall. Ryn could smell the Abomination rising, fetid corruption coming to a boil. Nothing else stood in their way. He didn't hesitate.

The Gods Bane—Earth-Breaker, Soul-Taker, Bane of All Things—knew his purpose.

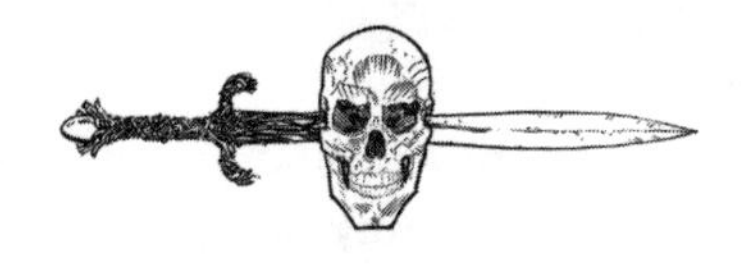

FORTY-SEVEN

yn should have waited in the hall. That had been the plan—give time for Kara and Grist to draw away the sect's forces. But he couldn't. Sword and man—moths drawn to Xang's dark flame, bound to burn together if they couldn't snuff it out.

He flung open the great brass doors that led outside to the fortress's inner ward with strength beyond his own. Corroded hinges squealed in protest. He stepped out onto the landing that overlooked Xang's resurrection, two stories below. The first booms of skyship cannon rattled the air. Dawn had just cracked in the east and the cloud had gone. Ryn found the calm, blue sky unsettling. The grim spectacle that confronted him called for a raging thunderstorm. So did the blast furnace behind his eyes that seared every thought.

The ward formed a square a hundred feet to a side, paved with cobblestones and bordered by forty-foot walls of weathered dark granite. Grenlich crowded the walls' ramparts alongside various humans—a mix of peoples from across the Keshauk's vast Dominion. Sorcerer priests and dignitaries worthy enough to witness their messiah's return.

Xang's ritual had already begun. Ryn's heightened senses noted the dark energies gathering—abominable, deviant, terrifying. He felt something from Mordyth Ral, something akin to fear, something they shared. The Sword's perceptions enabled him to take the full measure of what faced them in a glance and note details he wouldn't have otherwise known.

The cobblestones in the middle of the ward had been swept clean for a tetracle—the construct for any ritual of sorcery. The boundary of the tetracle took the shape of a slanted square, formed with shards of mirrored glass. A robed acolyte stood at each corner, each of them holding a proxy for the four elements essential to any ritual. The diamond, symbolic of Earth, was worthy of a throne—clear and flawless and almost the size of Ryn's fist. For Water, a demon had torn living coral from the ocean's depths. A perfect sphere of blown glass contained the element of Air—no doubt captured fresh and pure upon the Great Glacier in the far north. For Fire, sulfur crystals burned in a small brazier that hung from an acolyte's hand. The smoke's acrid bite stung Ryn's nose.

Inside this boundary lay the outer sanctus—a circle with arcane sigils, all drawn with the blood of an innocent—fresh blood. The smell of that reached him, too. Somehow Ryn knew the blood had come from a virgin child, drained of her last drop, and it sickened him. Within this lay the square inner sanctus. Only its makeup varied with the type of ritual. A resurrection called for grave dirt from the victim of a wrongful death, consecrated with a pregnant woman's birth fluids, taken early.

The inner sanctus held a pile of bones, crowned by Xang's skull. Even now, the part of Ryn that remained free of the Sword, the part that remembered being terrified as a boy by spook stories about Xang, cringed at the sight.

A young man in gray robes lay with the bones—Xang's temporary vessel. Seven flawless youths knelt, naked, around them. They chanted together in the guttural language of the Dark Art with arms raised, heads thrown back.

The master of the ritual, a gaunt old crow with a thick mane of white hair, walked barefoot around them upon the sticky gore of the outer sanctus. He hunched beneath a heavy black cloak as if the slightest chill would end him, but his step held firm. A slower chant rolled from his thin lips in a deep timbre that served as a counterpoint to the youths' harmony.

The attack came without warning. Demons in their natural form boiled from the crevices of the tower stone. They swallowed Ryn with a frosty shroud of glimmering shadow and oily smoke.

Mordyth Ral burned his hand and sliced the darkness. The Sword didn't consume the demons' essence as it did other living things. Wherever its eternal edge found a demon, the creature just ceased to be. These hellspawn that could stop a man's heart with a glare were less than gnats to the Sword. Ryn didn't know if they'd simply been banished back to the Hells, the rituals that bound them to the mortal world broken, or if the Sword had utterly erased them.

The survivors peeled away in sudden terror.

Ryn stepped to the edge of the landing. He felt that *thing* lurking behind him, that servant of the Invader Goddess, and it grated on him. His hand itched to cut it down. He kept his feet planted and refused to move.

Horgrim. His name is Horgrim.

Grenlich stormed down from the ramparts and made for the stairs up to him. Dignitaries muttered and pointed. The master of the ritual looked straight at Ryn. His step didn't falter. He chanted louder, in challenge.

Ryn pointed Mordyth Ral at him. *Take them.* He stayed on that landing as the Sword began to feed, desperate to keep its hunger confined to the fortress, reining it with chains of self-loathing and regret, unwilling to risk even the distraction of walking down the stairs.

That prismatic swirl danced on the edge of sight. The greatest sorcerers in the world cowered as the Sword began to leech their souls. Grenlich staggered and fell. Demons braved the Sword's hunger to swoop down and spirit their masters away while they could.

But the ritual continued. The youths around Xang's bones kept chanting. As he rounded the curve of the outer sanctus again, the master treated Ryn to a wolfish smile. His eyes burned with true belief and triumphant expectation.

Stolen lives tingled warm as they slipped through Ryn and into the Sword, riddled with terror, hate, even bits of memory. *The Gods Bane is cursed to live the deaths of all he consumed*, the *Codex* had warned. No man could bear such a torrent, not without losing his sanity, his will to live. Ryn's foot hovered over the landing's edge. The hard stone below would make a quick end, if he pitched headfirst.

Mordyth Ral had laid low every creature outside of the tetracle. Each death bore its own rare bouquet and seared itself into Ryn's soul. But still, the ritual continued. Still, the master walked without concern.

Why? Ryn could muster nothing else, trapped between the urge to die and the effort it took to keep the Sword's hunger focused.

A tetracle is a construct bound to the earth. It is a barrier I cannot cross.

You knew.

Did I not urge you to make haste?

Ryn couldn't fathom if the Sword's failure to volunteer such crucial details stemmed from petulant aggression or if it simply lacked the capacity to understand what a man might deem important. His blood would have boiled with frustration, if the tide of despair and confusion from the Sword's victims hadn't sapped his strength, even for outrage. That brief flirtation with suicide had been stalled by leaden feet that now refused to move.

Horgrim circled around him and took the stairs. The warden said nothing and avoided eye contact, no doubt fearing either might be enough to provoke an attack.

A reddish cloud seeped from the body of the young man in gray. Ryn could only watch as it bore Xang's bones into the air and spun them in a wild wind devil. The seven youths cried out with a mad mix of agony and exultation. They kept chanting even as their faces turned gaunt and mottled. Their bodies withered. Flesh sagged on their bones as muscle atrophied and joints decayed. Their hair turned white and fell out in clumps. In mere moments, they aged decades—cattle, doomed to nourish their messiah's rebirth, and they welcomed it.

Horgrim charged across the ward to the nearest corner of the tetracle's boundary square and the female acolyte who stood there. She held that flawless, fist-sized diamond that served as the symbol of Earth.

Blood Thorn swung in a two-handed grip, certain to shear the acolyte from shoulder to navel. But that silken blade struck some invisible barrier with a crack like thunder. The recoil flung Horgrim back off his feet. He flew several yards through the air, twisting as he went, and managed to hit the cobbles tucked into a roll to absorb the impact. Still, he tumbled with bruising violence before Blood Thorn could dig into the cobbles to stop him.

The youths stopped chanting, throats now too shriveled to breathe. Spent husks, sucked dry. Even the body of the man in gray had bloated with decay. Xang's bones reassembled themselves. The reddish cloud congealed into muscles, organs, skin.

By the time Horgrim had his feet back under him, a giant of a man with skin of ruddy copper stood in the tetracle's midst. Half a head taller than the warden, and broader in the shoulder, with a barrel chest and a powerful frame so thick with corded muscle that Horgrim's chiseled build seemed puny by comparison. Barely an ounce of fat tarnished that perfect body, nor did a single hair, not even an eyebrow. Veins rose starkly under Xang's skin, pulsing with the divine power that coursed through him.

Ryn found that heavy jaw, those square cheekbones, and that strong brow familiar, even if he'd never before seen them clad in flesh. Xang's eyes, once pits of bottomless dark, burned with molten gold. The demigod regarded Ryn with proud confidence, indifferent to his nudity, as though he'd already gained mastery of the world and now waited for the Gods Bane to concede defeat.

The master of the ritual kept walking, kept chanting. Ryn realized he had to—the moment he stopped, the ritual would end and the tetracle would no longer offer any protection.

A martichora's trumpet call rang clear from the far side of the tower, followed by a dragon's roar. A volley of cannon gave reply.

No one else in the ward outside of the tetracle still lived, besides Horgrim. Those who hadn't fled fast enough lay dead. Mordyth Ral's fire had dimmed for lack of anything else nearby to consume. It cared only for Xang now, but so long as the demigod stood protected by the tetracle and beyond its reach, the Sword didn't feel compelled to sate its hunger further.

Ryn knew that could change at any moment. He slid the Sword under his belt but had to use his other hand to pry his swollen fingers from that gnarled grip. Xang's molten glare threatened to scorch him in a whole different way than the Sword. Even at a distance, the understanding of Xang's nature, his parentage, made Ryn's knees wobble. He'd never felt so insignificant. Facing Sovaris's enraged spirit had been nothing compared to this. He clenched his jaw and forced his jellied legs to carry him down the stairs.

"Have you come to treat with me, Gods Bane?" Xang spoke Islari Common with a surprisingly melodic tenor, an odd fit with such a brutish face. A voice skilled at masking ruthlessness with virtue, at spinning lies into fatal truths.

Ryn wasn't about to show how he quavered inside. His ribs stung, his shoulder, too. Blood from fresh wounds plastered his shirt. He came to Horgrim's side. "Step free of the tetracle and we will."

Xang smiled, an awful thing. "I think not."

"Of course not." Horgrim said. "You are scared, *godling*, and it's all you can do to stand there without pissing yourself."

The master kept walking, kept chanting, but his voice had grown rather hoarse.

"That old vulture isn't likely to hold up much longer," Horgrim said.

"You are Sevrendine." Xang crossed his arms. "My apostles speak of your strength and devotion to the Whore Goddess. Your resistance to my father's Dominion is admirable, if fruitless."

Blood Thorn twitched in Horgrim's hand, betraying the deadly intent that lurked beneath his light manner. "Do you hope to win a reprieve through flattery?"

"I hope for nothing," Xang said. "I expect everything."

"Man-child, beware!"

Oma's warning came from high above. Ryn caught the outline of a skyship, painted dark against the brightening sky, just as it fired. He expected there would have been some hesitation before the decision to fire on their own god. Flame and smoke belched from at least a dozen gunports.

He threw himself down and covered his head. The courtyard bucked and heaved as the balls struck. Debris tore into him. Shockwaves flung him sideways. He tried to get up, but his back screamed in agony and his left arm had no feeling. Wits floundering in a dizzy haze, he first thought the limb had been blown off. It wasn't, but shrapnel had torn it to the bone. How had he come to lie in a red lake?

No lake, his blood. He bled out.

Ryn.

He fumbled for Mordyth Ral's hilt, wedged in his liver. A strange energy coursed up his good arm and through his body in a swarm of pricks and nettles. It dug into his wounds with a maddening tickle, then faded away. His left arm still looked like a rabid wolf had been at it, but most of the bleeding had stopped and some feeling had returned.

Rouse yourself.

You healed me? He crawled to his feet and shook his head to clear the fog. *Is that the best you can do?*

It is not in my nature to give.

The skyship still held position to fire again. Martichora wheeled and dove, pursued by bat-winged grenlich. Kara's gold fire lanced the sky. Dragon acid splattered the skyship's hull.

Ryn staggered straight into the flying brick that was Xang's fist.

Such a blow should have left him senseless with a shattered jaw, even dead with a broken neck, but Mordyth Ral wouldn't have it. The Sword's power coursed through his veins, giving iron hardness to bone and muscle.

Still, his head snapped back, and he flew off his feet. Mordyth Ral made no effort to shield him further as he hit the flagstones hard. He clutched the Sword's hilt as he skidded on his back and let it feed.

Xang bolted for the stairs leading up to the tower's entrance. The master of the ritual and his acolytes had vanished, no doubt spirited off by demons, but they didn't matter. The Sword's need hoisted Ryn to his feet as if by strings. Its renewed hunger reached past the fortress, into the swamp and the sky above. Xang's step didn't falter. He charged up the stairs four at a time and vanished through the brass doors.

Nothing shielded Xang from the Sword's bite. Ryn could feel it, digging into him. But Xang was no man, nor even entirely of the earth. Mordyth Ral would lay land and sea to waste for miles around before the demigod would weaken enough even to stumble.

The destruction wrought by the Sword would surely shred Ryn's sanity.

Mordyth Ral's hunger reached the crews of the skyships. Not just them, but Oma and Irsta, Kara and Grist, even mighty Kreevax. A dragon offered a rich feast like no other.

NO. Xang alone.

That pressure flared in his skull. **I take what I must.**

He fought back with all he had. *Take nothing not born of the Deceiver.*

The Sword's focus shifted. Ryn felt the swell of horror and panic grip the skyships' crews.

Horgrim picked himself up. Blood Thorn must have shielded him from the worst of the blasts. Still, he'd caught enough shrapnel to look as if he'd crawled from an abattoir's gutter.

Ryn sized him up. "Still with me?"

"It looks worse than it is," Horgrim said, though he favored his right leg. "Let's put that bald ape back where he belongs."

They took the stairs into the tower. Horgrim trailed behind, using Blood Thorn as a crutch to hobble along faster, groaning with the effort.

Ryn's feet hungered to leave the warden behind. His hand ached to kill him and be done with it. Fighting Mordyth Ral at every step had worn Ryn numb, but for the phantom chisels that hammered at his temples. Again, knowledge that could only have seeped into his mind from Mordyth Ral left Ryn certain that the draw of the Sword alone kept Xang from mustering the power to escape Sarenepra.

They edged through the tower's doors back into its great hall. The dank air hung thick with the stench of slain grenlich. Ryn had been too distracted before to notice how the timber above had decayed and a third of the ceiling had collapsed. The walls here had no windows. They bore only the tattered shreds of rotted tapestries and rusted wall sconces where the fresh torches now burned low. Dusty beams of sunlight shone down from what must have been windows on the floor above.

Ryn didn't know what he expected to find. Surely not what greeted them. The air in the midst of the hall rippled and tore, a breach in the fabric of reality that defied nature, a fissure of darkness edged with crackling energies that spat green sparks. It widened with a sweep and a billow of its edges like curtains parting. A big bear of a man in the armor of a palatar stepped through.

Tovald. And he hadn't come alone.

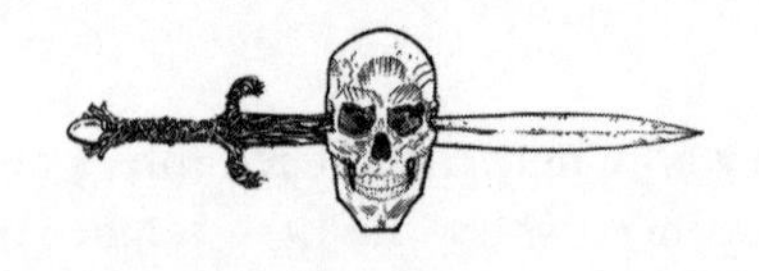

FORTY-EIGHT

yn couldn't believe how much poorer Tovald appeared since Sturvenwatch, aged well beyond his years. Those flinty eyes had sunk even deeper and darker, giving sharp relief to the bone around.

The three men with him fared little better. Darkness lurked beyond the tear through which they'd come, thick with some *presence*. Things of smoke and shadow danced on the edge of sight. Then the tear closed, as if it had never been.

Ryn saw enough to know he'd glimpsed that place before, in the abyssal glare of Xang's skull. A place not meant for the living. Maybe one of the Hells, or the Void between. And these men had walked there, sacrificed some part of themselves, for no other reason than to bring him down.

"Is your oath to the Clerisy worth so much?" Ryn asked.

Tovald's gaze swept the hall. His haggard expression didn't change as he took in the butchered grenlich. "What is this?"

"If you care for your lives, Marshal, leave—*now*." Xang lurked nearby. Ryn could feel him, could taste his darkness through the Sword, more than ever.

Tovald drew his witch-iron sword. "Or you will use Mordyth Ral on us?" His men followed suit and fanned out. They wielded witch iron, too. Each also carried a pistol, primed and cocked, with a second in his belt.

Cryptwood shifted from staff to sword in Horgrim's hand. "Don't compound poor timing with stupidity, you stiff-backed idiot."

Ryn waved him down and looked Tovald square. "It's Xang. He is here, reborn."

Tovald gave a dismissive snort. "You'll have to do better than that, son."

Ryn's throat ached with sudden emotion, nerves worn frail by the rub of the Sword as it yearned to shorten its leash on Xang. "You have betrayed your oath to the Order and to Aegias by using outlawed magic. Don't you see what loyalty to the Clerisy is costing you?" He held out his hand. "Join me. Help me."

A laugh echoed through the hall, full and deep with genuine mirth.

The palatars shifted footing and glanced around. Tovald eye's widened with fear and uncertainty. "Who is that?"

"Take a guess, dear Marshal," Horgrim said.

Ryn still found it almost too surreal to believe. Had chance or fate led him to this moment? Despite all those points between Sablewood and here where he could have turned aside, done something different, here he stood. Who was he to challenge a demigod?

He will bleed and die, like any man.

Xang dropped from the ceiling behind Tovald's men.

Thick fingers hooked under one helm and gave a violent twist. The palatar's neck snapped with a wet pop. He fell limp to the floor, gasping in a vain attempt to scream, legs twitching with spastic jerks. Pistols fired wild. Xang dodged a thrust by another palatar as he caught him by the throat. He hoisted the man into the air single-handed, crushed his windpipe, and wrenched the sword away.

Tovald's last man rushed in, only to be flattened by the flying corpse of his companion. Xang snatched up the sword of the palatar whose neck he'd broken. That man's screams had faded to a breath-starved whimper.

Xang spun the two swords in his hands, golden glare fixed on Tovald. "You are one of these church knights who serve in Aegias's name."

Tovald regarded his men, ashen-faced. The one who still breathed nursed a broken arm. "We honor his memory and stand against the Dark."

"Poorly, I expect." Xang shifted his attention to Ryn. "What shall it be, Gods Bane?"

Ryn's feet already moved. His fingers burned with fresh fury. The Sword swelled his senses and charged his blood with the urge to see this done. But something else ripped through him, so wildly the Sword shook in his hand—something that came from him alone. Hatred. Hatred fueled by what Xang represented.

Ryn let Mordyth Ral have Tovald's men, the living and the dead, desperate for any scrap that would spare Kara and the others. Was it not a worthy sacrifice, a justified act, if it contributed to Xang's defeat? He wanted to blame the Sword for putting such a thought in his head, but that would have been pathetic self-deception.

Only, Mordyth Ral couldn't find the palatars. They must have worn witch-iron mesh—Tovald, too. The marshal seemed content to let this play out, holding back where he had them all in sight. Ryn couldn't read the expression he wore. The surviving palatar did his best to blend in with the grenlich dead.

Ryn prayed the Sword had fed enough to match Xang without needing more. All that mattered was that the demigod be weakened enough for Horgrim to get his chance, for cryptwood to strike the fatal blow before Mordyth Ral's need drove its hunger beyond Ryn's control. The warden already tried to work his way around Xang's flank, but that leg wound hindered him.

Xang didn't rush into battle. He gave ground with quick-footed ease, moving in a circle that forced them both to turn after him. "Always, it comes to this, toe to toe as the world holds its breathe," he said to Ryn. "We are game pieces, you and I."

Horgrim's lips peeled back into a snarl. He flung Blood Thorn.

Mordyth Ral's phantom teeth went for Horgrim—a hound snapping its leash to take a rabbit. Ryn felt it dig in and begin to feed. He tasted Horgrim's fear, the ache for Kara he kept buried deep, the shame he carried for his father.

Xang pivoted on his heel and smashed Blood Thorn aside. Tovald ducked as the cryptwood missile shot past his head.

Ryn tried to drag the Sword's hunger from the warden, but it wouldn't be denied. Horgrim fell to his knees, panting so desperately that spit flew. Blood Thorn alone saved him, shielding him again the moment it returned to his hand.

The distraction almost cost Ryn his head.

Xang rushed him with a right-handed feint meant to hide a left-handed strike. If not for Mordyth Ral, Ryn would never have countered the demigod's speed and power. Their blades beat a sharp rhythm too shrill for common steel before Xang drew back and circled again. The encounter left Ryn's half-healed arm screaming. Despite the Sword's leeching hold on him, Xang displayed no sign of fatigue or exertion, not even a drop of sweat. But those raised veins pulsed harder with the ripple and flex of his heavy muscles.

Do the witch-iron swords in his hands protect him from Mordyth Ral?

They do not.

No—Xang would have to wear, not wield, witch iron for it to protect him. If anything, Ryn suspected holding those swords might in fact weaken the demigod.

And yet, Xang's golden eyes only burned brighter as he smiled.

"Do you consider yourself worthy of the coward's legacy?" he asked.

Ryn snarled. "He killed you, didn't he?"

"Mordyth Ral did, when Aegias at last saw the Sword as his only recourse," Xang said. "The war *he chose* to fight slaughtered more than even the Sword would have to snuff the last of me. I see that cowardice in you."

Horgrim crawled to his feet with a wheeze. "Empty words, from the Lord of Butchers."

"The strong take dominion, the weak give obedience and sacrifice for their security," Xang said. "This is the natural order."

"There's nothing natural about a land of slavery and despair," Horgrim spat.

Ryn realized Horgrim's intent—distract Xang to give him a chance. Given how weakened the warden appeared from his wounds and from Mordyth Ral's bite, Horgrim must have realized he could do little else against such an adversary. But Xang continued to circle, not granting even a whisper of an opening. "Only the faithless despair—that is their failing."

Horgrim fixed Xang with a narrow-eyed glare sharp enough to cut, brow knotted, cheeks puffing with the effort to draw a satisfactory breath. "I will show you faith."

He rushed the demigod with a roar.

Ryn couldn't imagine from where Horgrim found the strength. Everything he had left, focused in one desperate attack. He left crimson footprints from the trickle of blood down his leg.

As Horgrim took Xang head-on, Ryn skirted around to strike from the demigod's left flank. One of those witch-iron swords blocked Blood Thorn and counterstruck even as the other deflected Mordyth Ral.

Ryn found himself fighting to simply hold his ground. Those witch-iron swords spun and flashed with such speed and precision, the demigod's arms seemed to have minds of their own. Xang changed footing only to shift an angle of attack—the bastard didn't even feel the need to give ground and draw his opponents after him. He forced them both on the defensive just by standing there, as rooted as an old oak. The rapid clash and ring of blades beating against each other numbed Ryn's ears.

Still, he heard the wheeze in Horgrim's lungs—it had deepened into something wet and shrill. The warden kept himself in the fight by sheer force of will. He should have had the sense to retreat. Tovald should have had the decency to attack—but there he stood, watching. Ryn would have yelled at the marshal but couldn't spare the effort. Both his arms screamed now, shoulders knotted so much it pinched his chest. Mordyth Ral bolstered him to the extent that it could, but it wasn't enough. He'd lost track of how far its hunger reached now and couldn't risk splitting his attention to give any thought to it.

So intent was he on his own defense, on watching and waiting for that blink of time that refused to come when he might spot an opening, Ryn never saw it coming.

One instant, Horgrim held his ground, the next, a witch-iron blade jutted from his heaving chest.

"NO!" The word burst out of Ryn with a roar.

If Horgrim felt the pain, he didn't show it. His lips peeled into a feral smile as he grabbed that greenish blade and yanked back on failing legs in an effort to pull Xang off balance. Even now, he fought to give Ryn a chance.

It didn't work.

Most men, even trained soldiers, would have pulled back out of reflex rather than risk losing their weapon. Xang let his go without hesitation. Horgrim staggered and fell. Through it all, Ryn found no opening to land a blow of his own. Xang spun away from him with a dancer's grace. Ryn was too exhausted to follow.

Horgrim slumped over on the floor in a growing pool of blood, one hand still clamped on the witch-iron blade, the other around Blood Thorn's hilt. Ryn couldn't see the warden's face to tell if he still lived. His aching chest cramped in a whole new way with a sudden swell of grief. The intensity of it surprised him and threatened to overwhelm him, as though he were watching Quintan die all over again. How had he come to feel so much, so quickly, for this warden—a man who barely a fortnight ago had promised to imprison him for life?

"Commendable, if futile," Xang said.

The mildly amused way in which he said it struck Ryn like a bucket of ice water. It swept away his pain, his grief, even his despair over whether this fight could be won. Only a cold certainty remained.

Ryn drew himself up and pulled his shoulders back to stretch the cramp from his chest. He looked deep into those golden eyes with a heartless smile of his own and stepped forward. "You will not leave this place."

The Sword held silent in his hand—patient, expectant, still with its hold on Xang. Ryn knew that without piercing the demigod's flesh, it could do nothing more, not unless he allowed Mordyth Ral's hunger to reach for scores of leagues beyond this tower. But what more could he do in this fight that he hadn't already? How else could he prevail without Horgrim?

The Sword didn't attempt to compel him. It didn't yank on the leash that he'd woven from memories of Sablewood. It just waited for him to conclude he had no choice but to give it free rein, waited for his inevitable surrender.

Xang towered over him—Ryn stood at eye level with that slab of a chest. Still, he took another step toward the demigod. "The world will forget you, even in legend."

Beyond Xang, Tovald still just stood there, his expression unreadable. Did he wait to fight the victor, expecting they'd be weakened enough to take down?

Xang held his ground and watched Ryn come. "It is time that I took a consort," he said. "Your Josalind intrigues me."

The barb failed to provoke, but Ryn rushed anyway, desperate to end this.

Tovald went for the pistol at his hip.

The marshal carried it primed and cocked, as his men had theirs. As the muzzle came to bear, Ryn wondered which of them Tovald intended to shoot, but he could do nothing to evade. He could only defend against Xang's wild flurry of attacks. Witch iron scored a shallow gash across his chest.

Tovald's feet moved as his finger tightened on the trigger. Ryn's perception of time slowed. From the corner of his eye, he saw the pistol's flint strike the frizzen in a flash of yellow sparks at quarter speed. An eternity later, sooty smoke belched from the muzzle, driving the ball before it.

The ball promised to catch Xang square in the back of the head.

Somehow, the demigod sensed it coming and jerked aside. The ball mangled his ear in a spray of gristle and dark blood. His posture turned defensive, but still, Ryn couldn't find an opening. He pressed his attack, coming in low to get under the reach of those long arms. Xang easily twisted away and managed a weird thrust from an impossible angle. Ryn hissed as witch iron grazed his back.

Tovald's feet had kept moving after he fired, sword held to impale. Xang dodged aside and countered, but his angle was poor—the flat and not the edge of his blade caught Tovald square on the helm as the marshal's sword drove into Xang's torso. Despite the steel shell, Tovald staggered, eyes glazing. Xang ignored the sword sticking out of him and turned on Ryn . . . too late.

Mordyth Ral caught him under the ribs at an angle to split his heart. Ryn drove it to the hilt. Hot blood gushed over his hands.

Xang stumbled but kept his footing. Manic fury blazed in his eyes. He dropped his blades, grabbed Ryn's throat, and dug in his thumbs.

Ryn gagged. His vision sank into a starry haze. Mordyth Ral hummed, gathering itself, turning his hands to flame. The time had come, his plan with Horgrim all for naught. The Sword did as necessity demanded and began to feed on every living thing for miles around. Ryn could contain it no longer. Those nearest would die first. He felt the lives of the skyships' crews sliding through him. Heard the cries of Oma and her kin, as they plummeted from the sky. Tasted the richness of near-immortal souls as the sword took Grist and Kreevax.

The Sword would have them all. Sablewood had faded to a vague feeling, smothered by the urgency of need.

But still, Xang endured.

The Sword's hunger grew, to Sturvenwatch and beyond. Lives began to fail, scarring Ryn's soul forever with their passing. He couldn't tell whose they were, friend or foe. That line had blurred beyond meaning. The Gods Bane alone would leave Sarenepra.

He blinked and struggled to see. Xang loomed over him, features blurred by the truth of his nature. Something foul had oozed from his flesh, a dense black fog that remained tethered to his body, unable to pull more than a few inches away. It yanked like flags on a restless day to break free, raging and roaring at Ryn with a shifting parade of faces, each a bestial grotesque uglier than the last. Xang's flesh smoldered and burned with no flame, reeking with an all-too-mortal stench.

Still, the demigod clung to life.

A silken blade thrust over Ryn's shoulder.

Blood Thorn coiled and tightened around the demigod's neck, a garotte that sheared flesh and bone. Ryn sucked a welcome breath of air as Xang's hands fell away. The cryptwood didn't stop at beheading. It flowed up and over like melted wax to swallow Xang's whole head. He opened his mouth but couldn't find his voice. His eyes turned black, windows into that abyss that had held him for so long, before the cryptwood swallowed them altogether.

Xang's sizzling flesh charred. Muscle tore from bone, knotted and twisting with the fitful angst of worms doused with salt. Organs rotted and shriveled. Then it all just . . . disintegrated. A demigod, reduced to handfuls of ash in two heartbeats. With nothing left to bind them, the bones tumbled in a loose clatter to the floor, along with Tovald's sword. Xang's skull, trapped now in a cryptwood prison, hit the tiles with a crack.

Ryn didn't move, barely able to keep standing. Mordyth Ral lay quiet in his hand. He flung the Sword away with revulsion, disgusted by the fact he even lived. Xang's skull rolled in a lazy loop, resembling some giant egg pushed from its nest. Already the cryptwood blistered with a network of dark spider veins. Xang wouldn't take long to corrupt his new prison from within.

Tovald and the last palatar had vanished. Ryn could only assume by whatever means had brought them. He sensed the person standing behind him and expected, in a wild flash of hope, Horgrim. Then he saw the warden, lying on the floor yards away, not moving, still impaled by witch iron, that pool of blood now impossibly large.

A hand touched his shoulder, the hand that had wielded Blood Thorn. He turned to find Josalind. She looked wasted away, pushed beyond recall, like she'd been left in a hole and deprived of all nourishment until Lady Death waited a breath away.

"I told you I'd decide my part," she said.

Then she fell.

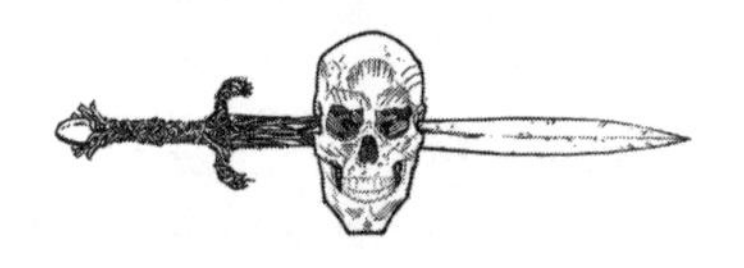

FORTY-NINE

yn left Josalind where she lay. He couldn't rouse her, but her pulse beat steady. She still wore the witch-iron manacle. The bit of metal had barely saved her from Mordyth Ral's hunger.

Horgrim still hadn't moved.

Ryn shuffled over. His battered body teetered a gasp away from shutting down, wrung out more by the Sword's cruel toll than by his physical wounds. He fell to his knees at Horgrim's side and found no breath, no heartbeat. If by some faint chance Horgrim had still clung to life, Josalind had doomed him the moment she took Blood Thorn from his hand—Mordyth Ral would have quickly finished him. But what choice did she have? Ryn couldn't guess how many she'd saved, the lives she'd spared from him, the Gods Bane. He could only wonder why Blood Thorn, bound as it was to Horgrim, had suffered her to wield it at all. Fraia's will must have had some part in that.

The tower doors pushed open. Kara stood there, Grist beside her. Kreevax's craggy head reared behind them both. Oma's cry of anguish sounded from the ward beyond. Ryn realized the sacrifice Astrig must have made, giving her last breath to bring Josalind before Mordyth Ral claimed her. A second martichora joined Oma's lament—Irsta. Ryn didn't hear a third. Ashavinx, the quiet male who'd borne Horgrim, had fallen, too. That any of them still lived at all without the protection of witch iron or cryptwood could only be explained by distance. They had kept theirs, while Josalind and Astrig had dove into the maelstrom of the Sword's hunger.

The ordeal had left the full weight of Kara's years on display. Deep lines radiated from her eyes and her skin hung loose and jowly. She braced herself on the doorframe and took in the sight of Horgrim, lying on the blood-smeared floor. A trembling hand rose to her mouth.

Ryn couldn't muster the will to speak. He just met her gaze and shook his head.

Kara looked past him. Gold fire flashed in her eyes. Her hand clenched into a fist. Had she figured Josalind's role in Horgrim's death and now intended to have her vengeance? Ryn lacked the clarity of thought to reason it out. He struggled to his feet and reached for the longsword that still rode at his hip. Nothing he had left could match her righteous fury. Still, he had to try.

But Grist, too, had taken a sudden hard stance, that great iron staff at the ready. Kyvros's heart erupted into flame.

Kara staggered forward. Sparks danced on her fingertips. "The skull, you fool."

Smoke and shadow spilled from the ceiling in a dense, roiling cloud that sucked all warmth from the hall.

Demons.

They swept Xang's loose bones from the floor and darted away.

Kara's fire shot after them. It struck with a crackle that roused a piercing shriek, but that didn't stop the thieves from vanishing through the far door.

"Grist—the third skyship," she said.

The sect still had some teeth left. Grist barreled out the way he'd come, calling to Kreevax. Ryn went for Mordyth Ral as more demons came for the skull.

But cryptwood encased the skull—demons couldn't abide its touch. They jabbed and pecked at it with grasping tendrils, rolling it across the floor, flinging aside grenlich dead. The blessed wood ate away at their essence with wisps of oily vapor. Kara's fire shot after them, with only a whisper of its former strength.

The demons snatched a grenlich corpse, tore it apart, and tried to pick up the skull using the limbs as a cradle. Kara's fire hit them again, harder this time, but still not enough.

A smaller mass broke off from the cloud and turned on Ryn as he reached for Mordyth Ral. Lashing tendrils split his flesh with bitter cold. The pain left him breathless, but his fingers found that woven hilt. It pulsed with fresh life, eager for the kill.

The Sword's hunger grabbed at the demons and clawed for more. It needed all the life energy at hand to have a chance at stopping them before they escaped. Ryn thought of how deathly Josalind had looked before she fell, how Mordyth Ral had sapped her despite the protection of witch iron. That half a manacle wouldn't save her this time, not this close. Kara had no defense at all. She would die first.

If they lost the skull now, Horgrim and the martichora would have died for nothing. But sacrificing Josalind and Kara bought no guarantees, either. Demons were slippery things, even for Mordyth Ral. Ryn had seen that for himself earlier out in the ward, when these hellish spawn had still been able to spirit away their masters even as the Sword's hunger felled the grenlich around them. Physical contact was the surest and quickest way for Mordyth Ral to end a demon.

Ryn flung the Sword, though he had no idea what threat it posed with no hand to wield it. The blade cartwheeled through the air. It flashed as it passed through the beams of sunlight spilling down through the broken ceiling from the windows above.

Aegias's cowardice does infect you. How many lives will you spend for the sake of one?

Mordyth Ral sliced the cloud of demons and ended all it touched. But its heartless edge failed to find them all before it clattered to the floor. One demon remained to carry the skull in that macabre cradle of torn limbs. It made quick for the hall's far door.

Ryn had no chance of getting to the Sword in time. Kara's near-exhausted fire chased the demon and fell short.

The skull would be taken. The sect would be free to raise Xang again, only this time, it would know what precautions to take. Bitter futility soured Ryn's throat.

A yard away from freedom, the demon found itself tangled in silver fire. It shrieked to shatter glass and squirmed to get free. The net tightened, crushing the demon smaller and smaller. Its cry stabbed the ear with hot spikes.

And then it was gone.

The net carried the skull to Josalind's waiting hand. She hadn't spared the effort to rise past her knees. The unlocked witch-iron manacle lay on the floor beside her. Sovaris's heart pulsed silver-blue in her other hand. She hugged the skull to her chest and looked to Ryn. Those sea-green eyes brimmed with a stew of feelings he couldn't begin to fathom.

Kara tried to bring Horgrim back, of course, to no avail. Even if she'd had the strength, it would have been futile. Josalind said the warden had already passed when she found him.

They didn't linger any longer than it took for Grist to report the last skyship had beaten a hasty retreat with its prize. Kreevax had been too spent to bring it down. Of the other two, one had crashed into the sea while the last had become a ghost ship, adrift with all hands dead. Ryn could only imagine the uproar across the Kingdoms when the winds brought it down.

Kreevax carried Horgrim's body. They flew about sixty leagues to the east. As the day slipped toward dusk, they took their rest in a small meadow that lay along the untamed southern tip of Sturvia's vast Jade Lake. Grayfall Forest—an ancient wood of oak and elm, pine and chestnut—crowded around them. Where the trees up north would have already shed half their leaves, these had just begun to display their autumn colors. Towering ferns and wildflowers spilled into the meadow from the forest floor. A legion of bees droned about, eager to claim one last harvest.

They all needed this place of peace and solace, of quiet and calm. Ryn sat on a rock where he had a clear view of the lake through the dense growths of cattail. He breathed deep of the autumn air. It bore a crisp edge, but still held surprising warmth given the lateness of the season. He savored every bit of it. The lake stretched so far north and west before him that he couldn't see its end. A breeze snaked through the forest's depths. It provoked lazy whispers from the trees and brushed the lake in emerald quicksilver. He took what comfort he could from the chatter of blackbirds nesting in the cattails and the stately repose of herons as they stalked fish in the shallows.

His body craved sleep, but he feared to see what fresh parade of the dead would haunt his dreams. He could still taste their final moments. *Prince Aegias suffered a hundred thousand deaths as the Sword fed*—only now did he truly understand what the *Codex* had meant. Mordyth Ral rode at his hip but his hand gave it wide berth.

He toyed with the witch-iron gauntlet he'd pulled from the corpse of one of Tovald's men. A glove of mail, with a thick leather cuff that could be laced snug. A more practical way to manage the Sword than cumbersome manacles. Still, no amount of witch iron could spare him from its judgment.

You think guilt, remorse, even your affection for her, gives you strength to temper my purpose with mercy. It only makes you weak. *She* knows this.

Of course, the wretched thing would never be content until it had burned every last mote of Xang, his father, and Fraia from existence. It would always work to test him, challenge him, push him to accept genocide as the only recourse to achieve its ends. That made the Sword his adversary, a greater one even than the Clerisy or Xang's followers.

But Ryn hadn't forgotten the vow he'd made on that beach, warmed by Josalind's affections. Somewhere, somehow, whatever the cost to himself, he would find a way to force Mordyth Ral to serve his ends, on his terms. To free the Kingdoms of the Clerisy's lies. To free his brother palatars. Perhaps even to free a distant empire from the blood-soaked tyranny of a vile priesthood.

Vulheris had managed to tame the Sword by drinking the blood of gods and surrendering his sanity in the process. Was that the only way? Did any of that blood even exist after so long?

Ryn could think of only one place where those questions might be answered—Gostemere. He didn't doubt the Earthborn had knowledge of a great many things—if they could be trusted. Grist had proven to be a valuable ally when necessity had demanded a truce. Whether the dolusk would continue to help if it put him at odds with his own people remained to be seen.

Kara tended Horgrim's body nearby. She'd cut off his tattered clothing to scrub the blood away.

"He loved you," Ryn said.

Kara's hand stopped moving and clenched the damp rag. Red water leaked between her knuckles. She kept her head down and face hidden and took so long to answer he didn't expect her to. "I know," she said at last, in a dull voice stripped of emotion. "I thought he might let me love him, if I gave it long enough."

Ryn didn't know what to say to that. "Cryptwood won't hold Xang for long."

"But so long as it does, he can't be heard."

"We have to take the skull to Gostemere," Ryn said. He could think of no other option, short of finding some place so remote he could destroy the skull without sacrificing innocent lives. Even then, what did he risk by giving Mordyth Ral such free rein? He couldn't escape the nagging certainty that the more power he channeled through the Sword, the more it would erode his capacity to resist it—unless he found some other means to tame it, as Vulheris had.

Kara nodded. "I expect the Tree of Sorrows's Veil will keep Xang muzzled so he can't be heard."

"And what if it doesn't?" Josalind asked. "Like Karxist said, the Tree's getting old and starting to fail."

She had Xang's skull tucked under her arm. The witch-iron manacle once again trapped her wrist. Grist loomed over her with Kyvros in hand. Josalind had told them how Sovaris warned her that Horgrim would fail in his task. Kara had confirmed that Fraia must have prompted Blood Thorn to accept Josalind in that crucial moment.

Ryn rose to face Josalind, charged with a confusing mix of emotions that threatened to cloud the matter at hand. "You think we need to work with Karxist—go ahead with the Earthborn's original plan to lure the Deceiver to Gostemere with the skull."

Mordyth Ral hummed at his hip. **There must be a once and final end.**

Ryn ignored it. "Do you really think you can trust Karxist to give up his plan to have the Four reborn through you?" He looked up at Grist. "Can she?"

That rigid face betrayed no emotion. "Be risk."

"Well, that settles that." Ryn stared Josalind in the eye. "I will take the skull to Gostemere and you will *not* go near the place."

He braced himself for a stubborn rebuttal and the argument that would surely follow. But Josalind surprised him by tracing the line of his jaw with her free hand as her expression softened. "I won't run and hide, Ryn. Not from anyone, not anymore. The Four and I need to settle accounts and come to an understanding. I have to face them in Gostemere."

Despite all that had happened since fleeing Dragon's Claw, all their answers still waited in that bizarre refuge. The irony cut deep. Ryn found himself unable to muster any effective counter and settled for pressing Josalind's hand to his lips.

"Then we'll do it together and see what tomorrow brings," he said.

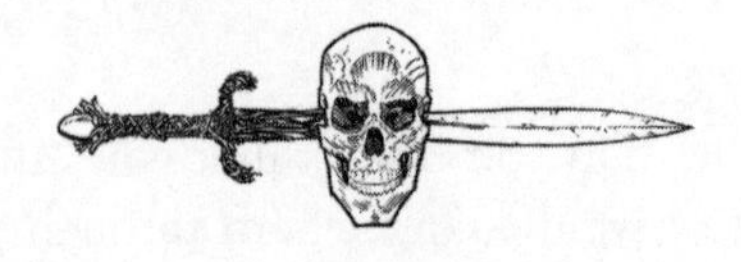

FIFTY

egas Tovald strode past the desk of His Lordship's secretary without sparing the young brother even a nod of courtesy.

"Marshal, wait—"

"Sit and be still." Tovald had cowered mightier men than this pup with that tone, from the drill yard to the battlefield. Though in his present state, those pencil arms could likely take him. The effort to keep shoulders back and step firm demanded all he had left. Bucardas's infernal machine tasked him in a way not even the blood fever had when he lost his fingers.

The brother clammed up and flushed. His rump remained planted in the chair.

Tovald paused at the door to His Lordship's apartments. "How does he fare?"

"The surgeons are amazed by his recovery," the brother said. "Surely the spirit of Aegias watches over him."

Tovald doubted it. He pushed the door open and stepped inside.

The apartments were large, trimmed in marble and mahogany. They befitted Anton Bucardas's role as trusted advisor to both the Arch-Preceptar and Sturvia's King. He alone of all the Clerisy's Council of Prelates kept a residence in the royal palace. But the man behind two thrones did what he could to live a simple life. As he had told Tovald, *trappings and possessions distract a man from his purpose.* No grand furnishings, no lavish works of art, not even statues of Aegias or the Nine, decorated his apartments. The salon where His Lordship received visitors featured a simple desk and a chair with no cushion. A brassbound copy of the *Codex* rested on a lectern before a small Tetraptych.

A comfortable couch lay before the big bay window. Tovald assumed that to be a recent concession in light of Bucardas's injury. His Lordship rested there, looking out. Tovald stopped a few yards short and cleared his throat. A traitorous muscle in his left leg began to tremble. He stiffened his knee to silence it. A book rested on Bucardas's lap—the same old heretic's journal he had been so possessive about back on the ship.

Bucardas beckoned him closer with a wave. "What do you see, Marshal?"

Tovald knew what His Lordship intended. He'd already seen the two bodies that hung from a gibbet over the main gates of Thrush's Keep. Hung where lord and commoner alike would see them—naked, tarred, and bound in chains. Tojan and Jufena Rikarden. Antiquities dealers. Sevrendine sympathizers. Apostates and traitors.

The grim display held a crowd of onlookers, rubbing shoulders with no regard for rank or station. Only the men of Selaran's Axes—the King's own mercenary guard—kept their eyes fixed on their duty as they patrolled the palace grounds, augmented by troops of palatars. From their vantage, Tovald could see several of the cannon emplacements on the walls. Viglias hadn't faced a military threat since the civil war a generation ago. But now crews worked to scour away years of neglect and ready the guns for battle.

He'd seen reports of similar preparations across the Kingdoms, heard the talk about war councils and decrees for martial law, of burnings and hangings by vigilante mobs whipped into a frenzy by what had happened here and in Tanasgeld.

Bucardas stared at those two bodies as if they held the key to it all.

"They died before the Test could even begin," he said. "Just gone, like they willed themselves to death."

"Perhaps they were silenced, Your Lordship," Tovald said.

"Such a thought gives me no comfort, Marshal. They were held by witch iron, secured and guarded, and their bodies bore no evidence of murder."

"And yet, there they hang."

"There they hang, a message to anyone who would challenge doctrine . . . or fail in their duty." Bucardas shifted higher on his pillows and poured himself a cup of tea from the service beside him. "You have returned empty-handed. Have you made such poor use of my gifts? It will be some time before the Mechanism can function again."

The Mechanism. An arcane artifact that should have been destroyed centuries ago. Tovald had violated the laws of nature and reason to walk the Hells' outlands. Using that damned compass to track Ryn had been the start of his fall, no matter how he had rationalized it as an evil necessary to serve a greater good.

But the compass ranked on par with a babe's trinket compared to Bucardas's Mechanism. Even now, with a cheery fire burning in the hearth nearby, Tovald doubted he'd ever be warm again. He'd never felt so violated, so fouled. And yet, he couldn't remember what he had seen, what he had heard, if anything had even touched him while walking in that place. Like a nightmare that left you sweating in the dark with no idea what it had been about. Not being able to remember only made it worse.

"I saw Xang reborn. I saw him slain by Mordyth Ral." Tovald meant to give a proper report, to speak with the reserved professionalism expected of his station. Instead, the words burst out of him with the breathless wonder of some idiot child.

The teacup froze halfway to Bucardas's lips. A soft sound came from his throat. "And were you merely an observer of these things?"

"I joined in the battle to aid in Xang's defeat, Your Lordship," Tovald said.

Those fatherly eyes fixed on him for the first time. "But you did not seize a moment to claim our prize."

"Such a moment did not come, Your Lordship." Tovald couldn't bring himself to speak of the conflict that had warred within him, watching the battle between Xang and Ruscroft. Of how it had stirred something, a feeling that he had become one of the Nine, a paladin, blessed to fight at Aegias's side. Such truths would surely earn him a noose, if one didn't already wait.

"I would know more of this contest and the mark it left on you, Marshal," Bucardas said.

And then I hang? Tovald eyed the pillows and again considered the merits of murder. He kept his expression as bland as possible and dipped his head. "As you wish, Your Lordship."

"It is our curse to live in momentous times," Bucardas said. "We mustn't fear the truth of our hearts if we expect to prevail." His attention returned to the bodies that hung from the gibbet. "I do not do these things because I believe they will earn me Paradise, Marshal. In fact, I am quite certain my hypocrisy has already earned me Eternal Torment. That's why I insist it is my burden to decide how and when any ethical or moral line may be blurred—so that the burden of sin is mine alone."

The frank confession took Tovald by surprise, even if it did little to impress him. Palatars who abided by their oath to serve and obey the Clerisy shared in whatever sins their superiors committed—just as he shared the guilt for Besk's sins in Vysus. It spoke to Bucardas's self-righteous vanity to think he could have it otherwise.

"All that matters is preserving the safety and the sanctity of each soul in the Kingdoms, of the very earth that nurtures us all," Bucardas continued. "For that, we must have the Sword." Smooth fingers stroked the cracked cover of the book on his lap. "I have had a thought for how we might lure Ruscroft. It's time this wayward son found his way home."

-- THE END --

The story will continue in *The Crucible Tree.*

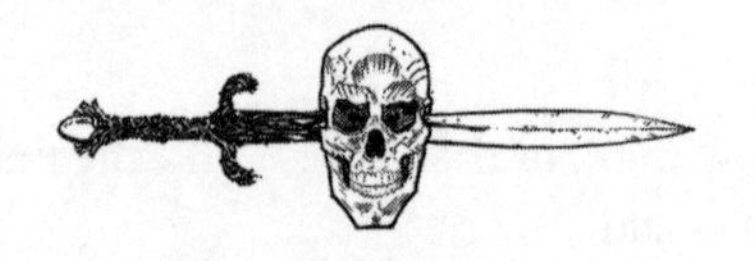

GLOSSARY

Aegian Codex: The principal religious text of the **Holy Clerisy**. Its every word is to be taken as literal truth. To suggest otherwise is blasphemy.

Aegian Order: See **palatars**.

Aegias, Prince Aegias, Prince Messiah: The messianic figure in whose name the **Holy Clerisy** was founded decades after his death some seven hundred years past. He is not worshipped as a god. Instead, the Holy Clerisy preaches adherence to **Aegias's Injunction** and his **Nine Virtues**. During the war known in the **Four Kingdoms** as the Teishlian Aggression (the Kingdoms were in truth the aggressors), Aegias wielded the living sword, **Mordyth Ral**, to slay the evil demigod **Xangtemias** (Xang).

Aegias's Injunction: A cardinal rule attributed to **Aegias** that forbids prayer or any form of supplication meant to ask for the blessing or intervention of the **Four** or of **angels**. The **Holy Clerisy** asserts that the only entities likely to respond are **demons** wearing a mask of virtue.

All-Father: See **Great Deceiver**.

All-Father Priesthood: The ruling sorcerer-priest caste of the **Keshauk**. They rule in the name of the All-Father—the dark god known in the **Four Kingdoms** as the **Great Deceiver**. While their god has not been seen in twenty-five hundred years, the priesthood's power to summon and command the All-Father's **demons** in his name strongly suggests he still lives.

angels: In the beliefs of the **Four Kingdoms** and the **Holy Clerisy**, angels are the principle denizens of Paradise and servants of the **Four** who have largely retreated from the mortal world. In truth, angels are servants of the goddess **Fraia**. Like **demons**, angels in their natural form are incorporeal, but possessed of supernatural abilities that can impact the mortal world. Unlike demons, they cannot be summoned and commanded through any rituals that are known to mortals.

animas: The collective life force of the earth and all living things, *animas* is term that originated among the shamanists of the **Teishlian Empire**. Also associated with the concept of "nature spirits"—primal beings that are not to be confused with **demons**, **angels**, or **Earthborn**.

bell: A common unit of time analogous to one hour. The clock in the Kingdoms divides the day into two twelve-bell halves—midnight to noon, noon to midnight.

brine draken: Territorial sea dragons aggressive and numerous enough to make sailing the seas south of the **Four Kingdoms** inadvisable.

Brotherhood of Sorcerers: The mysterious organization believed to rule **Vysus** in all but name. Its base is the City Above—a mountain raised by **sorcery** that floats in the sky above Vysus. There may or may not be a connection with the sorcerer priests of the **Keshauk Dominion**'s **All-Father Priesthood**. Regardless, their powers stem from the same Unholy Covenant with the **Great Deceiver** (see **demons**).

Carinzia: See **Four Kingdoms**.

Cetuu: A highly intelligent, possibly sentient giant sea creature that is half crab, half squid, and often all trouble for unlucky ships.

demons: In the beliefs of the **Four Kingdoms** and the **Holy Clerisy**, demons are the principle denizens of the **Five Hells** who seek to claim the souls of mortals who forsake the **Nine Virtues** and surrender to sin. Sorcerers, thanks to an Unholy Covenant in which they swear their souls to the **Great Deceiver**, can summon and command demons through complex and macabre rituals. A demon's natural form is incorporeal. It can be summoned in this form, or alternatively, bound to a physical form as dictated by the ritual. Demons vary in their powers and strength between the more common lesser ranks and the rarer greater ranks. If a demon is bound to a physical form, its ability to use its natural powers may be affected.

Dragon's Claw: A remote peninsula in northern Morlandia that is largely under the control of clans of **grenlich**. It is synonymous with Dragon's Claw Abbey. This ancient fortress is a cloister for discarded women and a place of penance for disgraced **palatars**, but it in truth serves another secret purpose. The abbey is under constant threat from the grenlich.

Dread: The name that Ryn Ruscroft gives to the stress disorder he suffers from following the Sablewood Massacre. It manifests as a severe anxiety attack that includes uncontrollable shaking and spontaneous cramping. These attacks are triggered in the morning by the combination of waking from a dream of the Sablewood Massacre and then hearing the bell of any nearby chapel, abbey, monastery, or cathedral.

Earthborn, Elder Races: Races of sentient, humanoid beings that preceded humanity and taught it craft and reason. They are generally considered extinct in the **Four Kingdoms**.

fiend: A hybrid created through a sorcerous ritual that permanently grafts, or fuses, a lesser **demon** to a willing human.

Five Hells: In the beliefs of the **Holy Clerisy**, the Five Hells is the domain of **demons** and their master, the **Great Deceiver**. It is a place of terror, torment, and hellfire that burns cold.

Four: Term common in the **Four Kingdoms** and in the doctrine of the **Holy Clerisy** to refer to the lost gods—the siblings **Sovaris**, **Mygalor**, **Koglar**, and **Kyvros**. According to the Clerisy's doctrine, the Four are dead and wait for the souls of the Virtuous in Paradise. They cannot otherwise influence the world or mortal affairs (see **Aegias's Injunction**). While each is associated in some manner with one of the four elements (earth, air, water, fire) and with one of the **Four Kingdoms**, they are considered a single pantheon honored and revered across all the Kingdoms.

Four Kingdoms: The principle setting of this story. The Kingdoms are relatively insular monarchies with limited contact with other nation-states. Over the past century, they have begun to evolve into constitutional monarchies where the rule of kings is no longer absolute. The dominant sociopolitical force in the Kingdoms is the church known as the **Holy Clerisy**. These Kingdoms are Morlandia, Jendalia, Carinzia, and Sturvia. Morlandian, Jendalian, Carinzian, and Sturvian refer to the individual nation states and their cultural aspects. Morlanden, Jendal, Carin, and Sturven refer to the specific ethnic groups.

Fraia, Mother Goddess, Dark Goddess: The mother of the **Four**. Her existence is denied by the **Holy Clerisy**, but she in fact guided **Aegias** through her **angels**. Fraia is the adversary of the **Great Deceiver**. Her followers today are known as **Sevrendine** and considered heretics in the **Four Kingdoms**.

Gods Bane: See **Mordyth Ral**.

Gostemere: A mythical place that doesn't appear on any modern map, associated through various legends with **Vulheris**, **Mordyth Ral**, and the **Earthborn**.

Great Deceiver: A powerful god who appears to thrive on conquest and bloodshed, but is in truth driven by a purpose that is both loftier and more twisted. He is known by this name and also as the Great Devil in the **Four Kingdoms**. He is considered ruler of the **Five**

Hells and the **demons** that reside there. Among the **Keshauk** of the Distant East, he is worshipped as the All-Father and honored with sacrifices of blood and flesh. Twenty-five hundred years ago, he was crippled in battle against **Vulheris** and the living sword, **Mordyth Ral**, and subsequently disappeared.

grenlich: A sentient, humanoid race of demonic origin, bred in the **Keshauk Dominion** to serve as slave soldiers. Grenlich live in clans ruled by matriarchs and each clan has a physical appearance distinct from the others. Their culture is governed by a harsh warrior code that has little tolerance for weakness, cowardice, or disability. Hundreds of years ago, several clans somehow escaped their Keshauk masters and fled west to claim the wilderness of northern Morlandia as their own, where they live free and often come into conflict with their human neighbors. Most grenlich remain bound to service in the Dominion.

Heart of Sovaris: A relic in the form of a stone that is purported to be the eponymous goddess's heart. It has alleged mystical properties to calm stormy seas, tame creatures of the sea, and lead to what cannot be found.

hellspawn: A general pejorative term for **demons**, **fiends**, and **grenlich** collectively.

Holy Clerisy: The all-powerful church of the **Four Kingdoms**, founded in **Aegias**'s honor. It is ruled by a council of prelates called preceptars, from among whom is chosen an Arch-Preceptar who rules from a throne called the Four-Faced Chair. The Clerisy's single religious text is called the ***Aegian Codex***.

inquisitar: See **Inquisitarem**.

Inquisitarem: The investigative and punitive branch of the **Holy Clerisy** charged with carrying out inquiries related to heresy, **witchcraft**, or **sorcery**. The organization is presided over by the High Lord Inquisitar. This is a preceptar second only to the Clerisy's Arch-Preceptar, but still answerable to, and subject to censure by, his fellow preceptars. Inquisitars are notorious for conducting "the Test."

Islaria: Name of the subcontinent occupied by the **Four Kingdoms** and **Vysus**. The people therein are sometimes collectively referred to as Islari. While various regional dialects are spoken, there is a popular trade language called Islari Common.

Jendalia: See **Four Kingdoms**.

Keshauk: A desert people of the Distant East who rule a vast Dominion of vassal states in the name of the **Great Deceiver**, whom they worship as the All-Father. They are led by a theocracy known as the **All-Father Priesthood**, which relies on its legions of **demons** and **grenlich** to maintain power.

Keshauk Dominion: The vast realm in the Distant East that includes the **Keshauk** homeland as well as the many vassal states over which the Keshauk maintain precarious control.

Koglar: A god of the **Four**. He is considered the patron deity of Carinzia and associated with the earth—both the bounty of the harvest and the riches of the mine.

Kun-Xang: See **Xangtemias** and **All-Father Priesthood**.

Kyvros the Elder: A god of the **Four**, generally regarded as senior among his siblings and considered the patron deity of Sturvia. He is associated with fire in all its incarnations, from the hearth to the forge, from the volcano to the thunderbolt.

Lost Pandaris: See **Pandaris**.

martichora: A sentient race with humanlike upper bodies, the hindquarters of a lion, the wings of a dragon, and the tail of a scorpion. The martichora's past suffering at the hands of humans led them to retreat to remote valleys in the Islarion Mountains beyond reach of most any creature without wings.

Mordyth Ral, Gods Bane, Sword: The living sword forged twenty-five hundred years ago by the human man **Vulheris** to destroy the **Great Deceiver**. The Sword is known to some as *Earth-Breaker, Soul-Taker, Bane of All Things.*

Morlandia: See **Four Kingdoms**.

Mygalor: A god of the **Four**. He is considered the patron deity of Jendalia and associated with the air, the winds, and the storms that bring the seasons of change.

Nine Virtues: The precepts attributed to **Aegias**, which the **Holy Clerisy** purports to champion. Only those who live a virtuous life might ascend to Paradise and join the lost gods, the **Four**, upon death. These Virtues are Humility, Piety, Courage, Diligence, Truth, Moderation, Chastity, Justice, and Brotherhood.

palatars: Martial orders created in honor of **Aegias** and his Peers (or paladins), to uphold and champion the **Nine Virtues**. Two orders exist—the Aegian Order, typically reserved for the nobility, and the Peers Order, for the common-born. Only men can serve in either order. While each order was founded to operate independent of any other authority and requires members to swear an oath to their order alone, both have been for centuries subordinate to the **Holy Clerisy**. After his oath to his order, a palatar must swear a second oath to serve and obey the Clerisy.

Pandaris, Lost Pandaris: An empire that predated the **Four Kingdoms**, ruled by House Imperial under its **martichora** standard. The Pandaren noble houses constantly warred and plotted with one another, wielding sorcery, poisons, betrayal, and intrigue with artful abandon. Pandaris eventually fell victim to its own excesses and internal strife.

Peers Order: See **palatars**.

Prince Messiah: See **Aegias**.

Protectorates: Northern provinces of the **Teishlian Empire** that were for a time under the **Four Kingdoms**' control after the war known in the Kingdoms as the Teishlian Aggression. The Teishlians eventually reclaimed their territory.

Sevrenia: A supposed promised land where the **Sevrendine** might practice their faith, free of persecution.

Sevrendine: Followers of the goddess **Fraia**, so named for their founder, Sevren. Considered a heretical cult by the **Holy Clerisy** and outlawed in the **Four Kingdoms**.

skyship: A warship of the **Keshauk Dominion** that relies on an arcane combination of metascience and alchemy to fly. A typical example of a skyship is seventy yards long with two gun decks.

sorcery: See **demons**.

Sovaris: The single goddess among the **Four**. She is considered the patron deity of Morlandia and associated with the waters of river, sea, and sky.

Sturvia: See **Four Kingdoms**.

Sword: See **Mordyth Ral**.

Tar-vrul: Among the **grenlich**, this term denotes a war chief or captain, and is a respectful form of address for anyone of this station.

Teishlian Empire: The empire south of the **Four Kingdoms** and site of the war called the Teishlian Aggression in which **Aegias** slew the demigod **Xangtemias** seven centuries ago. It trades with the Four Kingdoms through the independent city-state of **Vysus**, along a trade route known as the Pilgrim Road.

Tree of Sorrows: An ancient and magical tree that might guard a certain mythical place from easy discovery and also strip some higher beings of their power.

Viglias, City of Thrones: The capital of Sturvia and arguably the greatest and most important city in the **Four Kingdoms** by virtue of the fact that it is also the seat of the **Holy Clerisy**.

vrul: Native term for a grenlich warrior. Gender-neutral.

Vulheris: The human man who, some twenty-five hundred years ago, forged the living sword **Mordyth Ral** (**Fraia** and the **Earthborn** may have been involved) with the intent to use it to destroy the **Great Deceiver**. Instead, the Sword drove Vulheris mad. He attacked the **Four**, imprisoned Fraia, and only succeeded in crippling the Great Deceiver.

Vysus: The independent city-state that acts as a buffer and trading hub between the **Four Kingdoms** and the **Teishlian Empire**. Ruled in name by an elected civilian government, it is generally believed to be under the control of the mysterious **Brotherhood of Sorcerers**. While the **Holy Clerisy** maintains a presence there, its influence is weak.

witchcraft: A practice banned by the **Holy Clerisy**. It is believed that a witch (female) or warlock (male) invites the **Great Deceiver** or his proxy (namely, a **demon**) into their bodies for a period of time, thereby gaining unnatural powers. The cost, of course, is their immortal soul. This differs from the practice of **sorcery**, in which a sorcerer summons and commands a demon, external to their own body.

witch iron: A metal alloy created in **Pandaris**, the craft to smelt it long forgotten. Witch iron is known for nullifying and providing protection from **witchcraft** and **sorcery**. The **Holy Clerisy** hordes all that can be found, which is most often in the form of weapons, armor, and restraints.

Xang: A common short form of **Xangtemias**.

Xangtemias: A demigod, the mortal-born son of the **Great Deceiver**. He was slain by **Aegias** and the living sword, **Mordyth Ral**, about seven hundred years ago. In the Distant East among the **Keshauk**, he is revered as Kun-Xang, which translates as "Divine Xang."

ACKNOWLEDGMENTS

That you can read these words would never have been possible without the generous support of the more-than three hundred friends, family, and kind strangers who preordered *Bane of All Things* back when it was a crowdfunding project on Inkshares.com. I am eternally grateful to each and every one of them.

I must also express my appreciation for the broader Inkshares community—fellow authors at all stages of their journeys who understand we are in this together and that a rising tide floats all ships. I work to repay the generosity shown to me by so many people by paying it forward.

While Inkshares may employ an unconventional approach in deciding which books to publish, I can fully attest that it adheres to what have always been the best practices of the traditional publishing industry. The goal with every title is to ensure that it becomes the strongest possible version of itself. In working with the Inkshares team, I found validation and encouragement, as well as challenge and pushback, which ultimately made me a better writer.

My deepest thanks to everyone at Inkshares: Adam Gomolin, for saying yes in the first place; Sarah Nivala, for putting me to the test in the best way during the developmental-editing phase and enduring occasional grumpiness; Avalon Radys, for her patient counsel and tireless project management; and Noah Broyles, for his efforts during that key stretch of marketing and promotion to get this book to you.

Kudos are also warranted for Tim Barber, who designed this awesome cover; Kevin Summers for his great interior design and typesetting work; and Pamela McElroy and Delia Davis, for their sharp eyes and insights on the copy edit and the proof, because divinity is in the details.

GRAND PATRONS

Megan Alink
Rosa and Yves Beauchamp
Willie Bloom and Sarah Mifflin-Bloom
Jean-Luc Boissonneault
Hugues Boisvert
Frederic Boulanger
Stephen Brown
Paul Butcher
Howard Campbell
Lee Carey
Tony Chahine
John Clark
Andrew Cox
Tara Cox and Colin Gschwind
Natalie Cox-Valiquette
Catrina and Michael Curran
Andrew Fisher
Debra and Kevin Ford
Steve Georgopoulos
Guy Giorno
Claude Haw
Hala Hawa
Steve Hermanos
Andrea Houghton
Jay Kerr-Wilson
David Lockhart
Aydin Mirzaee
Linda and Francis Moran
Deborah Naczynski
Pierre Paradis
Nick Quain
Eve-Ann and Brian Reid
John Reid
Sheldon Rice
Linda Simpson and Ian Grant
Sanjeev Sinha (TIE Ottawa)
Andrew Slipchenko
Phillip Smith
Jim Stechyson
Don Wilcox
Bryan Yorke

LEO VALIQUETTE

Leo Valiquette (pronounced "valli-ket") grew up in rural Ontario, Canada, but had become a regular tourist of Tatooine, Middle Earth, and that farm in *Charlotte's Web* by the age of eight. He trained to work in museums before taking up the pen as a journalist and business writer. This love for the fantastical and the historical, as well as finding the root of a story, fuel his need to create worlds of his own. He lives with his wife and son under the apple trees by the banks of a lazy old river. *Bane of All Things* is his first published novel.